THE YEAR!

ROBERT ROU...

Copyright © 2006 Robert H Brown

ISBN   10 0-9552453-0-3
ISBN   13 978-0-9552453-0-5

THE YEARS BETWEEN

BY

ROBERT ROCKALL-BROWN

July 1921 - September 1939

The War to end Wars is over
But many young men have not returned
Children remember their fathers' names
Carved in the obelisk on the Village green

They will grow up not knowing a father's love
Not knowing their turn will come
For twenty one years peace will be theirs
As they live through the years between

What bliss it is to be ignorant
Of things that are yet to be
As we grow from child to adult
And live through the years between

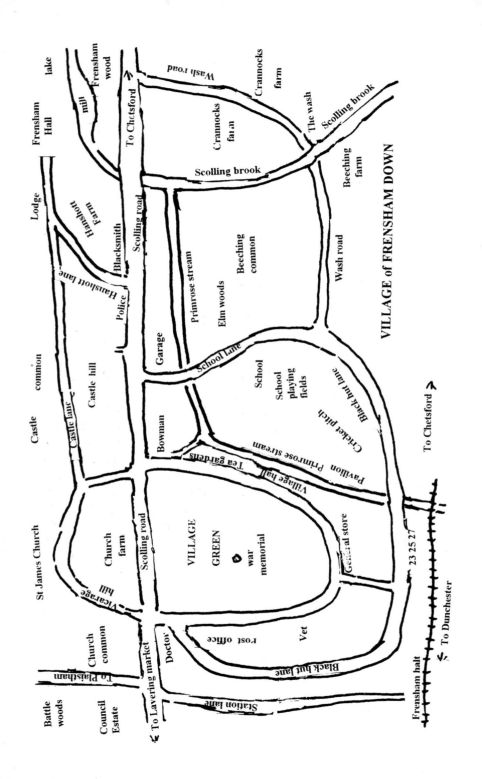

VILLAGE of FRENSHAM DOWN

CHAPTER ONE

1921

It was a fine summer's evening in July and Wilkin Frensham was getting ready to attend the Memorial Dance in the village hall. The occasion was to raise funds to erect an inscribed obelisk in the centre of the village green in memory of those villagers who had given their lives in the Great War. Wilkin was a returned veteran himself, having served first in the RFC and later as a Squadron Leader in the newly formed Royal Air Force. He did not want to go to the dance, but his father, Sir James Frensham, was adamant that he should go. Sir James had made a large donation towards the memorial fund and it seemed fitting that the family should be represented at the dance by his only son. He further aggravated Wilkin by insisting he should wear his RAF uniform.

Wilkin's wife, Victoria, refused to accompany him. She was the second daughter of the Duke of Selchester and, as Lady Victoria Lavington, had been raised in an atmosphere where one did charitable works but never did anything to prejudice one's standing in Society. She was nearly nineteen when she was introduced to the charming RAF officer at a Victory Ball given by her father at Selchester Towers. Wilkin Frensham was ten years her senior, but she was so dazzled by this tall, lean, war hero that her natural haughty reserve deserted her. To the young Victoria he was a knight in shining armour and she could not take her eyes off that handsome moustached face. To Wilkin she was just another young debutante; but the social status, and the not inconsiderable personal fortune she possessed more than outweighed her plain looks when it came to marriage. It was love at first sight for Victoria and she was so nervous that she dropped her dance card. Wilkin picked it up and, without asking her permission, confidently took the tasselled pencil that hung from the card and filled in his own name in every blank space. He returned the card to her and said "I see the next dance is mine Lady Lavington, shall we?"

Unable to speak, Victoria smiled at him and nodded. Taking her in his arms Wilkin swept her away to the tune of a waltz and she felt a glow when she saw the envy on the face of every other young girl in the room as they whirled round the floor. Even the Duchess smiled to signify her approval that her rather plain daughter had, apparently, found a suitable match. She knew all about Wilkin, having carefully vetted every young man before inviting them to the Ball, so when, despite the difference in their ages, he asked permission to 'call on' her daughter she welcomed him. Wilkin's proposal was met with warm approval and, after a short engagement, they were married in July 1919. Their daughter, Julia Margaret, was born in June, 1920.

Married life at Frensham Hall was a far cry from that of the daughter of a Peer of the Realm at Selchester Towers and Victoria, in an attempt to maintain her formal status, insisted she continued to be addressed as "Lady Victoria Lavington"; refusing to answer to plain Mrs Wilkin Frensham. As the years passed and the infatuation of first love faded, Lady Victoria Lavington reflected that her impetuosity had led her into a marriage beneath her station; the latter being an opinion which she had expressed on many an occasion when she was annoyed with her husband.

Lady Victoria accepted that it was her duty to open fetes and to patronise village garden parties; but beyond this she drew a firm line. Hence her haughty reply when Wilkin pointed out that it would be prudent if she accompanied him to the Memorial Dance.

"One simply does not join in the frolics of the peasants! You go if you must, Wilkin, but I have a headache and prefer the peace and quiet at home".

She returned to the book she was reading and Wilkin gave her a resigned look to the back of her head

"That being the case, my dear, I shall go alone!"

As he turned away to pour himself a drink he flung a final barb over his shoulder

"I am sure the villagers will be more comfortable for your absence!"

She was about to offer a bitter retort when the door opened revealing Nanny with her charge, two year old Julia Margaret, whom she had brought to say the customary goodnight to her parents. Lady Victoria's haughty demeanour was not lost on Nanny who paused, uncertain whether she should be a witness to a domestic argument. But, suddenly noticing Nanny and her small daughter, Lady Victoria abruptly changed her tone. Whatever she thought of her husband, she loved her daughter dearly and, in any case, it was not etiquette to continue an argument in front of the servants.

"Come in Nanny!"

She took the child in her arms

"And how is Mama's little angel tonight?"

She kissed her daughter on the cheek and held the child out to Wilkin

"Say Good Night to Daddy".

Julia reached out her tiny arms but her father, unable to conceal his annoyance, merely crossed the room to kiss her perfunctorily on the cheek before turning back to the drinks cabinet. Nanny took back her charge and, hampered by the weight of the child, awkwardly attempted to curtsy

"Goodnight Madam. Goodnight Sir"

She backed out of the room.

Wilkin finished his drink in one gulp and headed for the door

"Well! Goodnight, my dear. Have a pleasant evening"

Lady Victoria was once more buried in her book and she did not look up or answer him. He shrugged his shoulders as he quietly closed the door behind him.

Wilkin Frensham stood, aloof, at the side of the dance floor. The only alcoholic beverage available was draught ale and he longed to get back to the Hall for a Scotch and soda. In anticipation of this situation, he had brought a bottle of whisky with him; but he had left it outside in the car. Although some of the villagers had turned up in the garb of various military units they were hardly distinguishable one from the other. By contrast, Wilkin was very noticeable and he stood out in his RAF officer's uniform; a tall elegant, auburn haired, distinguished man of thirty two. Whether or not he expected it, he got neither attention nor conversation from the other veterans; these being conscious of the long-standing military code that forbade other ranks from mixing socially with commissioned officers. Such code being strictly enforced during the Great War. So he stood there alone, wondering how long duty demanded that he should remain at the Dance. With a bored expression Wilkin looked round the dance floor. There was something familiar about the pretty youngster who stood apart from the other village girls. A farm boy was talking to her but she kept glancing in Wilkin's direction. Strangely, he felt an almost uncontrollable urge to take her in his arms and the feeling surprised

3

him until it suddenly dawned on him who she was. He had experienced that feeling before when he had seen her at the hall. Well, perhaps the evening won't be wasted after all, he thought, and walked towards her.

Madeleine Benhope had been working in the kitchen at Frensham Hall since she left school at thirteen. Recently, as a mark of her 16th birthday, she had been promoted to housemaid. She admired the handsome Young Master at the Hall and had convinced herself she was in love with him. Cook would have taken her to task had she known Maddie dreamed of the Young Master as the hero of the romantic paperbacks she read covertly in her bedroom at night. Whenever Maddie spied him in the garden from her attic window she would sigh and indulge in adolescent dreams of romance. Although the household referred to him as the 'Young' Master he was almost double Maddie's age but, so besotted was she with him, that this did not matter to the girl. Even witnessing his marriage from the organ loft, where she had hidden before the ceremony for fear of not being allowed into the church, had done nothing to dampen her foolish teenage hopes that one day he would notice her and carry her off on a white charger.

As she matured Maddie's natural blonde hair, pretty face and desirability became obvious to all, including Wilkin Frensham. She was constantly pursued with the attentions of boys of her own age from the village but she spurned them all, content with her older, though unattainable, dream lover. On the night of the Memorial Dance several boys had asked her onto the floor. Even Reg Hanshott, who thought dancing was for effeminate men, had, contrary to his convictions, roughly asked her to dance. But she refused them all.

Maddie could not keep her eyes off the handsome RAF officer. She became confused when she realised Wilkin was approaching, but she moved aside from her companion and waited. She felt a blush suffuse her face and she dropped her eyes to the floor. Seeing the polished shoes before her, she slowly looked up. Wilkin stood there looking down at her

"It is Maddie isn't it?"

"Yes Sir!" She didn't know what else to say

"Will you do me the honour of accompanying me in this dance?"

Maddie had never been treated like a lady before and she could

4

only nod her head as he took her in his arms. It had been many years since Wilkin had been so close to such a lovely creature and the desire to clutch her close to him was almost unbearable. He realised she was very young but that made her all the more desirable. Maddie was in heaven and she was conscious of the envy in the eyes of the other village girls as the tall elegant war hero swung her round the floor. Wilkin was enjoying himself for a change and he did not want to leave her when the Dance ended. As he held her close, gliding across the floor to the gentle rhythm of the last waltz, Maddie was in a dream and she hardly heard him say, quietly,

"My car is outside. You needn't walk back. I'll give you a lift".

Maddie felt 'grand' as they swept along the Scolling Road. When they passed Reg Hanshott and Jennie she wanted to call out so that her friends would see how 'grand' she was; but she kept quiet because she knew the Young Master would not like her to draw attention to the fact that he was with her, a mere servant girl. Wilkin said nothing as he negotiated the sharp corner into Hanshott Lane and began to accelerate up the hill. Just before reaching Hanshott Farm house Wilkin stopped the car and got out. He unfastened a five-barred gate at the side of the road and swung it open wide. He climbed back in the car and pulled in through the open gateway. He stopped the car alongside the hedge out of sight of the road. He switched off the engine and the car lights before he clambered out to re-fasten the gate. When he returned to the driving seat he could see the alarm in Maddie's white face and paused as she nervously asked

"Why did you do that, Sir?"

His reply seemed logical to the naive young girl

"I want to talk to you for a while without your friends seeing us as they pass"

Maddie sat there silently. Wilkin broke the silence

"Let us have a drink!"

He reached into the back of the car and hoisted out a wine box. He opened the box and took out two glasses and a bottle of Scotch. He filled the glasses and balanced them on the dashboard while he hoisted the wine box onto the back seat. Maddie took the glass he handed to her, but hesitated, for she had never tasted strong drink before. He cajoled her.

"Go on, drink up! A lovely girl like you should enjoy the good

5

things of life"

Trying to appear sophisticated, she drank deeply and, although she coughed a little at the first swallow, the afterglow made her feel wonderful. She timidly accepted a refill. Wilkin refilled his own glass and they drank together; Wilkin making small talk.

They had just finished the third glass and Maddie was feeling a little giddy when Wilkin lapsed into silence, and raised a conspiratorial finger to his lips. They could hear Jennie talking animatedly to Joe Hanshott as the pair approached the hidden car on the other side of the hedge. When they had passed up the Lane out of earshot Wilkin gently took the now empty glass from Maddie and placed it to join his own on the dashboard. He turned to her and, without more ado, gathered the unresisting Maddie to him. He kissed her; a long lingering kiss such as she had never known before. She was feeling dizzy from the unaccustomed drink and she succumbed without a murmur at first. But, when she realised he had lifted the hem of her dress and his hot hand was caressing her inner thigh, she came to her senses. Her voice, though slightly slurred, was firm.

"No! Sir. Please don't do that"

Undeterred, Wilkin persisted. Maddie struggled and pushed his hand away. She shook the fuzziness from her brain for a moment and her voice was steady and determined.

"No! Leave me alone!"

She tried to squeeze herself as far away from him as she could up against the car door. He looked at her and he saw that, despite the timidity in her voice, there was a resolve in her eyes.

"Please take me home now!"

Maddie had recovered her composure by the time the car stopped on the driveway at the front door of the Hall. It had not occurred to Wilkin to drive round to the back; in any case that might look odd to any of the servants who happened to be awake at that hour. Wilkin reached over and drew Maddie into his arms again. She did not resist; her romantic mind thinking this might be the last time she would be kissed by him. She almost passed out when he kissed her this time and, for a while she lay there savouring the moment. Then she realised he was fondling her breast and she quickly drew back. At first he tried to hold her but, when she struggled determinedly, he released her quickly. She flung open the car door and, unsteadily, made her way to the side of the building. Just before she reached the corner Maddie paused and looked back. Wilkin could not see her face but he could sense her laughing as she gave a quick wave, then disappeared round the corner on her way to the servants' entrance and the solitude of her attic room. Wilkin, frustrated, muttered as he watched her go

"You teasing little minx!"

Wilkin sat alone in the car for a while. Then he climbed out and let himself into the silent house. A light was on in the drawing room but there was nobody there. He sat down with a glass and a bottle of Scotch. It was after two in the morning when he rose, leaving the bottle half empty, and moved unsteadily towards the stairs. Staggering a little he took off his uniform in his dressing room and donned pyjamas. He climbed into bed alongside the sleeping Victoria but, when he attempted to wake her, she pushed him off

"Go away. You are drunk"

She turned away from him and went back to sleep. Wilkin lay there silently for a moment. Then he got up and sat on the side of the bed in the moonlight. He could not get Maddie out of his mind. After a while he rose and, donning his dressing gown, left the room. Lady Victoria was fast asleep so did not see or hear him go.

Still under the influence of the alcoholic spirit Maddie half woke to feel a hand groping her body. She tried to scream but no sound came from of her mouth. It was a hot night and she had been sleeping naked under a thin cotton sheet in her attic room. The weight of the man who now straddled her sixteen year old body was stifling her and she struggled to push him off. The room was moonlit but, try as she would, she could not open her eyes to see her attacker. She could not understand why her eyes would not open. Her mind was befuddled with the alcohol she had consumed and she felt as though she was only partly there as she tried, desperately, to scream again but still no sound came. She heard a slurred voice

"No! No! Leave me alone! Please!"

It sounded vaguely familiar and she realised it was her own. Her arms felt like lead and the beating of her hands against the man's chest was ineffectual as he, silently and effortlessly, held her down. Her mind wouldn't function properly and a feeble attempt to scratch his face only ended in a brief touch of the small moustache

7

that adorned the invisible face. Exhausted, she let her hands fall. No longer beating her little fists against him, she lay still; her bosom heaving painfully. The man was panting from the struggle and she could smell the whisky on his breath

"Keep still you little minx. I'm not going to hurt you!"

He, effortlessly, held her down as she twisted and tried to turn over but to no avail. She tried to scream again but only a low despairing moan issued from her mouth.

For a moment the man lay there, head down as he nustled her neck, whispering

"Maddie! Maddie!", drawing out the name, in a husky voice.

Once more she became aware of the strong smell of whisky on his breath. He could hear the muffled sobs but, now he had come this far, he could not restrain himself and he ignored the desperate eyes which she now opened to stare up at him when he raised his head. She cringed with shame as she felt his eyes on her naked body and once more tried to wriggle away from him. Bur her struggles only served to inflame his lust further. .

"Maddie! Maddie!" again the husky voice, panting this time.

She tried to beat at his back with her feeble strength; but all to no avail. His hands wandered over the soft skin of her young body and she tensed herself. With a supreme effort she raised her knees in an attempt to push him away. But he cruelly forced them down again, spreading them wide with his weight. She could feel him hard against her and she gasped at a sudden sharp pain, as she lapsed into an alcoholic stupor and lay still. When she came to she was alone in the moonlit room. Her mind still befuddled, she pulled the sheet around her and drifted off into a deep sleep.

Maddie was still trembling when she woke to find the sunlight streaming through the window. She could hear the dawn chorus of the birds in the tree below her window. She had kicked the sheet off the bed during the night and, now, she leaned over to reach for it; anxious to cover her nakedness as though she thought this had caused the nightmare and somehow covering herself up would drive the fear away. For a while she lay there, cuddling her knees and huddled in the sheet, staring ahead and trying to collect her thoughts. She was perspiring and her body was still trembling. Attempting to derive some comfort from it she said to herself

"It was only a dream!"

But she was still apprehensive. It had all seemed so real! There was a bitter taste in her mouth and she could still recognise the faint odour of whisky. Maddie had never drunk hard liquor before and swore she never would again if it caused nightmares like that.

After a while she calmed down and clambered off the bed. A washstand with a marble top stood in the corner. On it was a shallow china wash bowl and a large china jug of cold water. She poured water into the bowl and washed away the taste of whisky as best she could. She felt better when she had washed herself down thoroughly and, after drying her body on a course white towel, she sat down on the bed, with the sheet wrapped round her, to think. There were bruises on her arms and thighs but she could not think how they came to be there. It was strange but she could not recollect much of what had happened after the Dance last night. She remembered the Dance itself and the fact that the Young Master had been there. How could she forget the blissful feeling when he asked her to dance? She remembered riding in his car but, after that, it was only a vague collection of images. She remembered being frightened at some stage but could not recall what had frightened her. She could not even remember coming back to her room or undressing and getting into bed. She shook her head, trying to recall the events of last evening; hoping, perhaps, she could account for her nocturnal terror in some measure and the fear that now lurked in her heart. Some more recollections came. She remembered being kissed in the car by the Young Master when he drove her home from the Memorial Dance but, after that, it was all a blur. She was about to get dressed when she realised it was Sunday, her day off. She sank back on the bed, her pretty brow furrowed as she strove to remember.

Maddie jumped at the sound of someone knocking at her bedroom door and a voice called.

"Come on, Maddie. You can't lay there dreaming all day. It's Sunday and you don't want to waste our day off, do you?"

It was her friend, Jennie.

"Just a minute"

Maddie jumped up and began to dress hastily. She was startled to notice a stain on the white bed sheet. Could her dream have been real? Goodness knows what Jennie would say if she saw it. Maddie grabbed the sheet, screwed it into a ball and thrust it under the bed.

9

She was straightening the top sheet and bed cover when Jennie, impatiently, knocked again. Her voice was insistent

"Oh! Come *on*, Maddie. We'll be too late for breakfast"

Jennie was full of the Memorial Dance

"Wasn't it wonderful? I danced with Charlie Baker and Joe Black and...."

She prattled on

"...and there was Reg Hanshott. Where did you get to after the Dance? Before the Dance finished Reg asked to walk me home and when we left you were still dancing with the Young Master. Reg kept asking about you. I think he was jealous that you didn't pay any attention to him"

Maddie shrugged her shoulders

"He's alright but he's too old for me"

"He's no older than your Mr Wilkin. How did you get on with the Young Master? Did he try anything on?"

Maddie blushed as she lied

"Of course not! He's a gentleman! Not like your Reg Hanshott!"

Jennie laughed

"Well! You're right about Reg. He tried it on round the back of the Hall but I soon sent him packing. What sort of girl does he think I am?"

Her indignant protest made Maddie feel embarrassed, but she said nothing. She wondered whether she should tell Jenny about her nightmare but the words would not come. As they finished breakfast Maddy suggested they miss the Sunday morning service and take a picnic basket over the hill past the ruins of Benley castle to Battle Woods. Jenny agreed

"It is a lovely day and it *is* our day off. We don't *have* to go to church if we don't want to"

Cook did not press them to attend the church service

"It is going to be a hot one today and you two young things don't want to spend your time indoors. I always says you can worship God in his own good countryside just as easily as in a stuffy old church. But you had best be off early before the Family is astir"

She packed an old wicker basket with sandwiches, slices from a fresh-baked fruit cake, two bananas and two crisp red apples. In a grease-proof bag she put some deep red tomatoes, lettuce and radishes. Adding serviettes, cutlery, two small enamel mugs and a two-pint bottle of home-made still lemonade, she said

"There! That should keep going until tea-time"

Their heads shaded by wide brimmed straw hats and wearing ankle length summer-print cotton dresses, white cotton stockings and white canvas shoes the girls each clutched a handle on either side of the picnic basket as they set off down the drive. Jenny animatedly made small talk but Maddie was not her usually bubbly self. Jenny looked at her friend and asked

"Are you alright, Maddie?"

"Yes, Jenny! Had a bad night. But the fresh air will brighten me up"

As they left the drive, instead of taking Castle Lane which was the route the Family would take to church, they crossed Hanshott Lane and climbed the stile to the path which led up to the ruins of Benley Castle. The hill was covered with short grass which was fighting for survival in the chalky soil. What little moisture was left from overnight rain and morning dew fed the small hazel bushes and clumps of bramble which dotted the grassy slope. As they picked their way between the bushes, the girls were constantly stopping to gently remove bramble branches which reached out to cling to their dresses. It was still early but, as they approached the castle, they could see figures climbing on the ruins. They were not local villagers and, on the evidence of the bicycles lying on the grass, they were probably day trippers. The girls wanted to be alone so they skirted the castle keeping well away from the visitors. Jenny suggested

"Let us go to Battle Wood. There are plenty of picnic spots in the wood and we are less likely to be disturbed"

"Alright. But we'd better keep well clear of the church"

"The woods are pretty thick and no-one will see us if we keep to the right paths"

They could see the church steeple through gaps in the trees to their left as they walked along in silence. Ferns and white flowered brambles covered the ground on either side and dog roses grew in clusters adding their delicate pink blooms to the multicoloured butterflies that rose as the girls passed by. Although it was only 10.30am they could already feel the warmth of the sun which permeated through gaps in the trees to cast dappled bright patches in the tree shadows across the wide grassy path. The hum of bees broke the silence and Jenny paused for a moment to brush an inquisitive wasp off the lid of the picnic basket. Twenty minutes later they came across a large grassy clearing. The hill sloped away to the south and from the upper end of the clearing they could see over the trees down to the Scolling Road and the village green beyond. They were too far away to hear voices but, through the foliage, they caught occasional glimpses of villagers climbing Vicarage Hill on their way to church. They set down the basket and Jenny heaved a sigh of relief as they both sank to the ground and, straightening their skirts, stretched out on the grass, pulling their hats down to shade their eyes. It was too early to eat but a cool drink from the lemonade bottle revived them after the long walk.

The peel of the church bells and the raucous cries of crows, as they flew from the steeple tower, were the only sounds to break the tranquillity of the woods as the two girls lay there enjoying the freedom from daily chores at the Hall. It was Jenny who broke the silence

"You've been very quiet, Maddie. Is something troubling you? You said you had a bad night. Was it a nightmare?"
Maddie burst into tears and Jenny reached over to comfort her.

"There, there, now. Come on tell your auntie Jenny all about it. It must have been an awful nightmare to affect you like this"

"That's the problem. I'm not so sure, now, that it *was* a nightmare. You remember I told you the young master was a gentleman?"
Jenny nodded

"Well, I was telling a lie. He *did* try it on when he brought me home in his car"

"You mean he forced you in his car. Why, the dirty beast!"

"No! no! not then!. I managed to keep him off me in the car. It was later when he came to my bedroom"
Between sobs, Maddie blurted out how Wilkin had got her drunk in the car so that she didn't know what was happening when he came to her room later. She showed Jenny the bruises on her arms and thighs and told her about the stain on the sheet.

"Now I don't know what to do"
Jenny was both sympathetic and adamant that they should do something

"We can't let him get away with it. You must tell Cook. She will

12

know what's best. But its no use going back now. The family isn't at home for dinner tonight so Cook is taking the opportunity to visit her sister in Lavering Market this afternoon. She won't be back until this evening. So! Why don't we stay here, have our picnic and go down to the Primrose tea rooms in the village after that, before we go back to the Hall?"

"I don't think I could face the young master"

"You won't have to. Not today, at least. As I said, the Family will be out and you'll have a chance to see Cook before they come back"

Cook listened quietly while Maddie told her about her trouble. But she was not satisfied until Jennie told her about the young Master's interest in Maddie at the Dance. Cook was experienced in the ways of the Gentry. Gentlemen often took advantage of their power over young servant girls. Cook had seen this situation many times before and she went to see Mrs Mellish, the housekeeper, who agreed that Lady Sarah should be informed.

There was no doubt in Lady Sarah's mind who was the culprit and she acted accordingly without consulting her son. With experienced tact Lady Sarah talked to Victoria; convincing her that the matter should be hushed up so that no scandal threatened the family. Victoria accepted the situation with the stoic reserve of English upper class women; but, privately, this did not mean she forgave Wilkin his little peccadillo, as it would be regarded by his contemporaries. She resolved he should be made to suffer; so she barred him from her bed. Fortunately for him the strain proved greater for her than for him and, within the year she relented; the ardency of their reunion resulting in the birth, early in 1923, of their son Willis Mark.

So far as Maddie was concerned there was only one thing to be done. The strict code of Victorian etiquette, which still ruled English Society in the early twentieth century, condoned the reprehensible behaviour of the young male aristocracy but preached morality to the masses. The girl must be made to feel she was to blame. This was the way of the world and it was not difficult for Mrs Mellish to convince the naive young girl of her guilt. Lady Sarah endorsed Mrs Mellish's actions.

"The wretched girl must go at once. Send her packing"

Mrs Mellish, though firm with her staff, was not an unkindly

13

woman. She accepted the code of Society but felt sympathy for its victims.

"But, Madam, how is she to explain her dismissal. Suppose she becomes....."

Lady Sarah glared at the Housekeeper as she interrupted

"There is no suppose about it, Mellish. You will see her mother, commiserate with her on the wayward behaviour of her offspring, and convince her that it would not be in her best interests to involve the Family".

She handed over a purse containing a considerable sum in sovereigns.

"This will probably help the girl's mother to agree to your suggestion. I am sure I can rely on you to do the right thing. Remember, in any event, a scandal in the Family must be avoided"

Mrs Mellish bent over and took the purse

"Yes. Madam. Will that be all, your Ladyship?"

Lady Sarah nodded curtly. The housekeeper curtsied and left the room.

The staff were warned that anyone who gossiped or speculated about Maddie's sudden departure would be liable to instant dismissal. Then, following customary procedure, Maddie was, unceremoniously, sent home to her mother without further ado. She travelled to the Village in the covered trap with Mrs Mellish who accompanied her to explain matters to Mrs Benhope.

So far as Lady Sarah was concerned the matter was closed.

Maddie's mother, Hilda Benhope, was the daughter of Silas Beeching whose farm was on Wash Road, separated from Crannock's Farm by the Scolling Brook. Her father was a surly man who, never having been educated himself, considered his daughter should work on the farm. Standing in the dim lamplight of the farm kitchen he aired his views to his timid wife.

"A darter's place is 'ere; 'elpin' out wiv the farm work. What use is book larnin' and such to the likes of 'er? If yer wants ter learn 'er you do it arter she's finished 'er chores; but she b'aint goin' orff ter no fancy school"

So, although her mother managed to teach Hilda to read, write and do simple arithmetic, to her father she was a slave, to work for him as an unpaid cowhand - cum-milkmaid. Later, when her mother died, Hilda was given the task of housekeeper to add to her other chores. When Robert Benhope, the cowman at Crannock's Farm, started courting Hilda her father encouraged the relationship in the hope of adding a free cowman to his farm; but Robert, the only surviving member of his family, had inherited the freehold of a cottage in Black Hut Lane and did not need the tied cottage offered by Silas on their marriage in 1902. He took his bride away from her drudgery and they settled down to wedded bliss in Robert's cottage. Their daughter Madeleine (Maddie) was born in 1905. Silas Beeching never foregave Hilda for leaving him and refused to attend his granddaughter's christening. So no-one was sorry when he lost his farm to the Bank who foreclosed on his mortgage when an outbreak of foot and mouth disease wiped out his herd. Without a word to his daughter and nothing but the clothes he stood up in Silas left the Village and was never seen again. Beeching Farm, now the property of the bank, had remained unoccupied since his departure and the farmhouse and out buildings were now derelict.

Robert Benhope, caught up in the fervour of patriotism engendered by Lord Kitchener's appeal for men, volunteered for service in the trenches and was killed on the Somme in 1915. Hilda found it difficult to manage after his untimely death. Her small widow's pension from the Army did not go far but she eked out a living doing part-time domestic work for the wives of some of the local farmers. Maddie was her only child and it was a great comfort to Hilda that when she left school at 14 her daughter had found security in a steady live-in job at the Hall. So, now Hilda lived alone in her cottage, except for the company of a large tabby cat and two kittens from her recent litter; the others having been found homes in the village.

Hilda was surprised to hear the light steps of the pony on the gravel road outside her cottage in Black Hut Lane. Her usual callers would be on foot and she could not think who her visitor could be when she heard the knock on her door. Mrs Mellish was not one to stand on the doorstep awaiting an invitation. She walked straight in followed by a crestfallen Maddie carrying her few pitiable possessions in a bundle. Mrs Benhope ignored Mrs Mellish and hurried to her tearful daughter; taking her in her ample arms to comfort her.

"Why, Maddie dear, whatever *is* the matter?"
Maddie did not answer and just cuddled up to her mother crying softly. Mrs Mellish answered

"You might well ask, Mrs Benhope. Your daughter has brought disgrace upon us all"

Hilda Benhope looked astonished

"Why? How? She's always been a good girl!"

The Housekeeper did not relish her task but she did not soften her tone

"So her Ladyship thought when she graciously allowed the child to work at the Hall. But the girl has shown her gratitude in the most unacceptable way and she is dismissed without a reference"

Still cuddling her daughter Mrs Benhope spoke defensively.

"Whatever she has done it cannot deserve this. Look at the poor mite!"

Mrs Mellish huffed

"You might well look at her and as for 'poor mite' you could give a thought for the 'poor mite' she may be carrying!"

Her mother swung Maddie around and looked pointedly at her still trim figure.

"What *does* she mean?. What have you done? Have you allowed one of the servants to interfere with you?"

Still sobbing the girl protested

"No, Mummy, I haven't done anything! It was...."

She hesitated and looked at Mrs Mellish who regarded her sternly. Maddie straightened her back and continued defensively

"I think it was..."

Mrs Mellish interrupted before she could say more and took Hilda Benhope to one side. A quiet conversation took place out of the girl's hearing, with occasional glances in her direction. Something changed hands and the Housekeeper went to the door without looking at Maddie. She had done her duty as she saw it and the girl was of no further concern to her.

"Good afternoon, Mrs Benhope"

Without waiting for a reply the Housekeeper left.

Mother and daughter stood silent while they heard the clip of the pony's hooves as the trap drove away. Hilda Benhope looked sorrowfully at her tearful daughter and folded her in her arms.

"You poor love. Mrs Mellish explained and I know it wasn't your fault. I should never have let you go to work at the Hall. An innocent young girl isn't safe among the Gentry."

The girl sobbed afresh at her mother's expression of love and understanding. The mother searched in her bag and took out a large white handkerchief with which she attempted to dry the tears.

""Come now, dear! Let's get you settled in and tomorrow we'll talk about what's to be done"

The following morning Mrs Benhope rose at five and looked into Maddie's bedroom to see her lying there awake.

"I've got to go up to Hanshott Farm to help Lillian with the weekly wash. Do you want to come down and have breakfast before I go?"

Maddie had been lying awake most of the night wondering what was to become of her

"I'll come down now" she said

Surprisingly, Maddie found her appetite. They sat on bentwood chairs at a plain, scrubbed, wooden kitchen table. The simple, but substantial, breakfast of hot porridge followed by large slices of whole-wheat bread amply smothered in butter and homemade plum jam, was just what she needed to buck her up. She looked at her mother over the rim of her cup

"Can I come and help you? I don't want to be left here all day on my own".

Hilda regarded her

"Perhaps it would be best if you do come with me, dear. On the way we must think up a reason to tell people for your leaving the Hall"

It was late September and there was a nip in the early morning air so they each donned a cloak before leaving the cottage. They cut through to the Village Green by using the narrow footpath which ran alongside the General Store. It was about 6.30 am when they crossed the Green to the Scolling Road. At this early hour the Store had not yet opened and the only person they saw was Mr Studding, the Vet, who was exercising his large smooth-haired Labrador on the Green. The dog trotted up to Maddie and nuzzled her hand. She responded by patting the animal's head. Her mother did not pause or encourage conversation; but the Vet smiled at Maddie's obvious attraction for the dog although he called it back to him. He nodded to her mother as he passed.

"Good Morning, Mrs Benhope. I trust your cat has recovered satisfactorily after having her litter?"

Maddie looked sheepish and turned her head away. She felt as though he could see inside her and the allusion was being made to her own condition. Hilda Benhope pretended she had not heard the question and, not wishing to stop for a conversation, carried on past him with a nod.

"Good morning to you, Veterinary. Looks like being a nice day!"

The Scolling Road was empty. Mrs Benhope was considering the situation and she remained silent until she and her daughter turned left into Hanshott Lane. A plume of smoke was rising from the stone chimney of the Smithy at the corner; the still morning air carrying it straight up, to disperse in the chill atmosphere. There was no sign of Joe French, the blacksmith. But he was always an early riser and they could hear the ring of a hammer striking metal so he was no doubt already about his business. They carried on up the lane but looked back as a voice called after them

"Hilda! Hold on a minute"

It was Joe's wife, Anne, who was trying to catch up with them before they had passed out of earshot. They turned back and Maddie once more felt a pang of guilt at the sight of the buxom woman who was obviously expecting a child in the not too distant future. Hilda Benhope had often pondered on the wisdom of starting a family when one is past thirty; but Anne, who had been married for no more than a year, exuded such happiness when she learned she was pregnant that no woman in the Village could bring herself to intrude on that joy by commenting on her age. They stopped and waited while Anne, a little breathless, caught up with them.

"Joe told me to ask if you could spare an hour or two either this week or next to help me get the nursery ready? He fusses so and is worried that I might harm the baby if I do anything strenuous"

Seeing Hilda Benhope hesitate, she quickly added

"Joe says he can pay you your usual rate. Oh please say you can help me!"

Hilda had only hesitated because her mind was full of Maddie's predicament and it took a moment for her to adjust to a fresh line of thought.

"Of course, Anne, I'd love to help you. I could fit it in whilst Maddie's home. She can help too. Which day do you want us to come round?"

Anne smiled her gratitude

"Whenever is best for you, but I don't want to leave it too long."

She patted her ample stomach and smiled contentedly

"I can wait but he or she, won't"

Hilda returned the smile as she glanced down

"Alright, Anne. We'll come up on Saturday at about nine, if that suits you?"

Anne nodded and turned to Maddie

"Hello Maddie. Got some time off from the Hall?"

Silently Maddie nodded. She started and looked away when she realised she was, rather rudely, gazing at Anne's bulging midriff.

As they continued up the Lane, Hilda turned to her daughter

"There! Anne has given us an excuse for your being home. We'll say you have been sent home for a rest. At least, it'll do for the time being!"

The decision had been taken none too soon; because, as they approached Hanshott Farm, they were met by 27 year old Len Mundy, as he was about to cross the Lane from his cottage to go to work on the Farm. Len was around medium height, with a broad back and strong arms. He was dressed in a collarless khaki shirt, which he had obviously brought back from his war service, and old, brown, corduroy trousers. A pair of dirty army boots and an old felt cap, over his unruly brown hair, completed his working outfit. Len had been invalided out of the army in the early weeks of the war and lived with his wife, Bertha, in a thatched farm cottage which came with his job as Foreman at Hanshott Farm. He spoke with a broad Suffolk accent.

" 'mornin' Mrs Ben`ope! Washin' day 'ere again? Time do fly dunit?"

He was limping slightly and he stopped to rub his right leg as he spoke to them. Hilda showed concern

"How's the leg, Len?"

"Thankee fer askin', Mrs Ben'ope, but its comin' along nicely. The 'orspital's got the shrapnel out now and the Doctor there says that, given time, it's gonna be as good as new. Hello, young Maddie! did'n expect to see you up 'ere with yer Mum. Why b'aint you up at the 'all lookin' after them toffs?"

Before Maddie could speak her mother answered

"She's been run down lately and her Ladyship's kindly sent her home for a rest."

Len looked surprised

"Well that's sumpin' new. Didn't know 'er Ladyship cared about anyone but 'erself. Still, good luck to yer lass! Don't go back until they drags yer. Y'gonna 'elp yer Mum with the washing?"

Maddie didn't answer but she smiled and nodded. He gave her a wicked grin

"You'm better watch out for Reg. 'e always 'ad an eye for a pretty face afore 'e went off to the war an' 'e ain't changed much since t'my way 'o thinkin' "

Remembering what Jennie had said about Reg Hanshott and the night of the Memorial Dance, Maddie blushed which caused Hilda to look sternly at Len, who, seeing the look on Mrs Benhope's face, turned away with a hurried

"G'day to yer Missus"

As fast as he could Len limped across the road to open the five barred gate opposite. He passed through and turned back. Carefully avoiding the disapproving gaze of Hilda Benhope, he pushed the gate to and fastened it before disappearing behind the hedge on his way to the Farm. Maddie suddenly realised that this was the gateway through which Wilkin had driven the car on that fateful night and she felt a slight pang of fear that she might see him come driving down the lane; or, perhaps worse, see Mrs Mellish step out and take her to task for being a bad girl. How many times, over the years, had she walked up this lane with Jenny on their way back to Frensham Hall after their day out? For a moment she felt the tears rising again and her mother, sensing her daughter's distress, put her arm round her waist and murmured

"It'll be alright dear! Things will work out and you've always got me to take care of you"

Maddie clutched her mother's arm more tightly

"I *do* love you, Mummy"

They carried on past the five barred gate that led direct into the farmyard and entered by the small wrought iron gate which led through the, roughly trimmed, elm hedge and onto the path of paving stones set in the wide lawn in front of the house. Before them stood the Hanshott farmhouse. It had been the Frensham Manor House until Sir Francis Frensham, who had returned to England, in 1632, after making his fortune in India decided he wanted something more pretentious. He built Frensham Hall, on a hill about three quarters of a mile to the north east of the Manor House, as the new seat for the Frensham Family and occupied it in 1633. To John Hanshott, who had been with him in India and had once saved his life in that wild country, Sir Francis gave the freehold of the Manor House and several acres of surrounding farmland.

The Elizabethan origins of the farmhouse were evident in the timber frame design with small latticed casements let in the lath and plaster walls and in the bays on either side of the canopied front doorway. A student of architectural design would note the Stuart and Hanoverian influences in the red brick alterations and extensions that had been added over the years; and replacement of the original thatch with red clay roof tiles. But, to Maddie, such historical features meant nothing. She saw only a huge rambling building which she had glimpsed many times when passing but had never entered. It did not compare with the grandeur of Frensham Hall, of course, but it was impressive in its own way and she felt an intuitive sense of excitement as they approached the house; as though it was to play an important part in her future.

Two big mongrel dogs ran, barking, towards them but fell silent when they recognised Hilda. Lillian Hanshott, coming out to see what was causing the commotion, smiled broadly when she saw the pair

"Hello! Hilda. You're bright and early. And who's this you've brought with you?"
She took off her glasses and wiped away the steam that blurred her vision and, before Hilda could reply

"Why, it's you Maddie. Nice to see you, dear. But why aren't you up at the Hall?" Hilda Benhope answered for her daughter

"She's been under the weather lately and her Ladyship has sent her home for a rest" Lillian clasped her hands together

"Wonders will never cease! Never known her Ladyship to care what happened to servants before". Hilda smiled

"That's what Len Mundy said when I told him just now"
Lillian chuckled

"Did he now? Well, he'd better keep his thoughts to himself when Martha's around. Like all the old'ns she still thinks the Gentry can do no wrong"

Actually, Martha, Lillian's mother-in-law, wasn't as old as Lillian intimated. She was only 57 but had aged prematurely following the death of her husband, John, last year from pneumonia when he was no older than herself. Some said he had lost his will to live after the shock of hearing that his two elder sons, Joseph and

Mark, had been killed within days of each other at Flanders in 1915. Martha had coped better with the grief of losing two of her three children but since her husband's death she had become withdrawn and now kept very much to herself. She still lived at Hanshott Farm but seldom left her room at the back of the farmhouse. She left the running of the house to her son Joseph's widow, Lillian. The running of the Farm itself was taken over by John's surviving son, Reg, who had come through the war unscathed but who had never married.

Lillian, at the age of 19, was devastated at the loss of her husband, Joseph, so soon after their marriage. She was already six months pregnant when he kissed her goodbye at Dunchester railway station. She was lost in her grief, like any other young wife would be in such tragic circumstances, but the birth of her daughter, Joanne, shortly after she became a widow brought her such joy that she recovered from her grief quickly and, now, at the age of 25, she found great comfort in caring for her seven year old daughter.

They entered the farmhouse and Lillian took Maddie's cloak.

"Its lovely to have you here, Maddie". She hesitated for a moment but continued "I wonder? Would you like to do something for me while your mother and I get on with the washing?"

Eagerly Maddie agreed

"Of course, Mrs Hanshott, what do you want me to do?"

Before saying what she wanted Lillian asked another question

"Well! Can you drive a pony and trap?"

Maddie nodded

"Yes! One of the grooms up at the Hall taught me so that I could run errands for Mrs Mellish"

Lillian was relieved

"Good! It is Joanne, you see. I don't like her walking to school on her own and there are no other school children living right up here that she can go with. I usually take her myself but its always difficult on wash days. Your mother is very good and always says she can manage alone but, since you are here, perhaps you can take Joanne for me this time?"

Maddie did not hesitate

"Of course, Mrs Hanshott, I'd love to take Joanne to school in the trap and I can collect her this afternoon as well, if it will help"

Lillian thanked her

"It's nice of you to offer, dear, but I expect we shall finish the washing this morning and I should be free to collect her myself"

They had reached the big brick-built washroom. Lillian had started the fires under the stone coppers early so the water was already hot. Two corrugated iron scrubbing boards were set over tin baths, each with a huge chunk of Sunlight soap to hand. A short distance away two large tin baths, three quarters filled with cold water, had been set aside for blue-rinsing the white sheets when they came out of the washing and scrubbing procedure. A huge iron mangle, with two well-worn wooden rollers and a large winding wheel, had been dragged on its small iron wheels away from the wall and stood waiting for the first wringing of the water sodden sheets into a zinc bath. The dirty linen and other items were heaped on the ample wooden benches that lined the opposite wall. Lillian Hanshott had obviously been up early to have this all ready by the time her help arrived. Although the windows were thrown wide open to reveal the yard beyond, the washroom was hot and steamy. Maddie stood by the door watching her mother and Lillian sorting out the piles of laundry. She asked Lillian

"What time do you want Joanne to leave for school?"

Lillian paused in her work and thought for a moment.

"Oh! She doesn't have to be there until nine o'clock, so half past..... No! let us say quarter past eight should do"

Feeling useless Maddie leaned against the doorpost.

"There's a half hour to go yet. Can I do anything to help you in the washroom?"

Lillian looked up again

"No, dear, We can manage. This is a regular chore and your mother and I can probably handle it better by ourselves. Tell you what! You could make us all a cup of tea. How about that?"

Maddie brightened

"Of course, Mrs Hanshott"

"And stop calling me Mrs Hanshott. I'm not that much older than you. I'd like you to call me Lillian, if you don't mind"

"Yes, Mrs ...er... Lillian"

Bobbing along in the trap Maddie felt happy in the freedom that only those who have been in domestic service can know when away from their daily chores. Joanne was a happy little girl, bright

23

and garrulous. As soon as the pony began trotting down the Lane she started chattering. She hardly gave Maddie a chance to answer the questions her agile mind conjured up. But Maddie was content to sit, holding the reins lightly, listening to her. She did not find it necessary to direct the pony. He knew the way from constant practice and instinctively turned off the Scolling Road by The Bowman and along School Lane, over the bridge that crossed the Primrose stream, and on to stop outside the village school. Joanne reached up and planted a kiss on Maddie's cheek before jumping down lightly from the trap and, with a cheerful wave, running to join the other children lining up in the playground.

Maddie sat there watching the scene, remembering her own happy days at the same school. Charles Tremming had been in charge in those days and she could see he was still there, with his wife, Charlotte, watching the children filing into class. He, briefly, looked in her direction but did not seem to recognise her and he turned away to follow the children. When they had all gone in she sat there a little longer looking at the empty playground. For a moment she forgot her troubles and was a little girl again, playing with the other children and without a care in the world. She sighed and, slowly, turned the pony round. With a quiet "Giddy-up" and a light slap of the reins she urged Tom into a gentle trot back to Hanshott Farm.

There was no sign of the dogs when she got back to the Farm. They were probably out in the fields with Reg Hanshott and the farm hands; or perhaps patrolling the hedgerows in search of rabbits. Leaving the pony standing quietly in the farmyard, she walked over to the washroom window. Steam was still billowing out and she could see the two women, their sleeves rolled up and their aprons damp, taking it in turns to wind the mangle and feed in the sheets. They were singing together 'You are my honey honey suckle ....' and were obviously happy and content in their work. It was better not to interrupt them. Maddie returned to the trap. Walking the pony over to the shade of the large chestnut tree that stood over a barn she unhitched him from the trap and tied him to a rail. She found a bucket and half filled it with cold clear water from the hand pump in the yard; but she allowed Tom to drink only a little because the animal was still hot from his exertions. She wondered whether she should feed him but, like most country girls, she knew about horses and recognised that feeding should be left

24

until he had cooled down a bit. Looking around in the barn she found a large dry, but none too clean, towel. She rubbed the pony down and ran a gentle hand down his nose, allowing him to nuzzle her, before she left him to go back to the washroom window.

The women were still singing as they worked, but had changed to a different tune. Maddie watched them for a while but they did not look up so she walked round to the back door of the farmhouse. The top half of the white painted wooden door was open wide and held flat against the wall by an iron hook. She reached over and pulled the iron bolt inside to open the lower half and walked into the kitchen. The quarry tiled floor was surrounded by solid oak cupboards and shelves which displayed, willow-patterned, white crockery and brown earthenware jars containing cooking ingredients. Gleaming copper pans, iron kettles and stewing pots stood on shelves; or hung onto the stone chimney breast with copper and steel kitchen utensils. Beneath the open chimney, and recessed into the breast, stood a large black-leaded kitchen range which shone in the reflection of sunbeams that streamed through the leaded light windows.

Although it was a warm day a coal fire glowed in the grate and a large black kettle stood simmering on the hob above the ovens. The room had a comfortable cooking aroma about it which did not displease the girl; but, feeling the heat, she moved over to open the windows wide. A light breeze lifted the chintz curtains slightly as it gently disturbed the air. Maddie noted that only a few eggs lay in the straw lined basket on the sideboard. Looking around her she saw a reed-woven basket trough hanging on the wall. She took it down and walked out into the yard. She could hear the chickens clucking and, following the sound, she came across the chicken pen behind the barn where she had tied the pony. Lifting each wooden flap at the rear of the nesting boxes she felt for the warm eggs she expected to find among the straw. One brown mother hen was sitting on her clutch and she turned, angrily clucking, when she felt Maddie's hand touch her soft down. Leaving the warm eggs under the hen, Maddie quickly withdrew her hand and moved on to the next box. She carried the trough, containing two dozen brown eggs and one and a half dozen white eggs, back to the kitchen. After carefully placing the eggs in the basket on the sideboard she hung up the trough and, checking to see it contained sufficient water, moved the black kettle along the hob to boil over the fire. She stirred the burning coals with the iron poker and looked around for the teapot.

The two women were delighted when they saw the pretty knitted cosy covering the hot teapot on the table; together with three large white china cups on saucers, a jug of milk and a bowl of sugar. Maddie had found a large fruit cake in the cupboard. Someone had already made a start on it so she thought it would be alright if she placed it on a dinner plate in the centre of the table. Side plates and wooden handled tea knives, which she had found in a drawer, completed the scene. Lillian exclaimed happily

"Well! Look at that, Hilda. You <u>have</u> made yourself useful, Maddie. Thank you for taking Joanne to school. Did she behave herself?"

"Of course! She's a lovely little girl"
Lillian beamed at the praise, then saw the eggs

"Why, you've collected the eggs too. You really have been busy. I'll have my tea in a minute. I must unhitch Tom and rub him down"
Maddie interrupted her animatedly, pleased at having done something useful without being told.

"No need! I did that when we got back. I gave him a little drink of water but no food. Is that alright?"
Lillian smiled and nodded

"Of course its alright. You can come round here more often"

They were sitting at the kitchen table when Hilda looked shrewdly at Lillian

"I was wondering! You couldn't use some regular help on the Farm, could you?" Lillian put down her cup and regarded Hilda

"Well I suppose it would be nice to have someone here to give me a hand. But you have far too much on your plate to take on the job. In any case, although the Farm is doing well, I don't think we could afford to take you on full time. I'm sorry"
Hilda hastened to correct the wrong impression she must have given

"I wasn't thinking of myself, Lillian. It is Maddie, here. She doesn't want to go back to the Hall and you can see how handy she is"
Talking as though Maddie wasn't in the room, Hilda continued

"She wouldn't want much. Just her own room and live-in with

the family and a small monthly wage to cover clothing and to spend on her day off"

Hilda paused whilst Lillian considered the matter. Making up her mind she looked at Maddie.

"Well it *is* true I could use some help and you seem to get on well with Joanne. What do you think Maddie? Would you like to come and live with us?"

Maddie eagerly answered

"Oh! I'd love to. When can I start? I'm sure Mrs Mellish won't expect me back when I tell her I've got another job"

Maddie stopped speaking and blushed slightly at the untruth. But, after all, she thought 'It was only a little white lie, wasn't it? and in the circumstances............' She briefly wondered what Lillian would say in a few months time if....; but decided to ignore the problem for the present. Lillian turned to Hilda

"I must have a word with Reg first. After all he will be paying Maddie's wages; but I know he will agree. He *is* a bit of a bear, at times, but he usually does what I want. I'll come down to you on Sunday morning with the trap. About eleven do? We can discuss the arrangements and, if you are both agreeable, Maddie can put her things in the trap and we shall return to the Farm together. It is going to be wonderful to have someone young about the place and I am sure Joanne will love it"

True to her word Lillian arrived at the cottage in Black Hut lane on Sunday morning. Tom stood contentedly outside munching at the grass verge while Hilda entertained Lillian with a cup of tea. Joanne had come too. She was excited at the prospect that Maddie might come to live at the Farm and threw her arms round her

"Oh! You *will* come, Maddie, won't you? *Please* say you will. I'll die if you don't" Who could resist such a plea? The two women looked at each other. Lillian was the first to speak

"Well! That seems to settle it, Hilda. Do you have your things ready Maddie?" Maddie did not answer but rushed upstairs. Hilda turned to Lillian

"They've been packed all the morning. She's that excited! I would've liked her to stay with me for a bit longer but I think it best that she be with you because I'm out most days working and it would be lonely for her here"

Hilda did not mention the real reason for Maddie's departure from the Hall. Some things were better unsaid. And as for the future she thought 'lets cross that bridge when we come to it'.

CHAPTER TWO

1921

Lillian was looking out of the kitchen window watching Maddie fussing with the harness as she readied Tom and the trap for the daily school run. Reg Hanshott was sitting at the kitchen table eating his breakfast. He had been up since five and had just come in from milking; leaving the farm hands to clean out the milking shed and the yard. It was a hot Summer's day in mid July, 1921, so the kitchen window was wide open and Lillian could hear Len Mundy swearing at the herd as he prodded the cows out of the yard on their way to the fields. She turned to Reg

"Maddie seems to have settled in very well"

Reg looked up.

"Yes! She's a bright girl and not afraid of hard work. Martha says she's a treasure"

Lillian's brother-in-law had been noticeably less surly since Maddie arrived and Lillian found him much easier to get along with. Although he was only five years older than Lillian they seemed to have little in common. Before Maddie came to live with them Reg would hardly pass the time of day with Lillian. He had said nothing to explain his attitude but he seemed to sub-consciously resent her. It was as though he believed her marriage to Joseph was, in some way, to blame for his brother's death. But this might not be so for he loved Lillian's daughter, his niece, as though she were his own child.

Each day he would rise early and leave the house to help Len Mundy bring in the cows for milking. He would come back to the kitchen, wash his hands and, without thanking Lillian for preparing his breakfast, he would sit down to eat it in silence; leaving the dirty dishes on the table before going off, with no more than a grunt and a nod, to his work on the Farm. The same procedure followed at dinner time, except during the Summer when he usually ate out in the fields with the hands; Lillian or Joanne having brought out the meal to him in a basket.

Before Maddie joined the household, most evenings Reg would leave the house after tea and walk down to The Bowman where he would spend the evening drinking with his cronies. Lillian and Joanne were always in bed when he returned. Some evenings he stayed in, drinking ale with one or two of his village friends, but Lillian did not join them. The visitors always treated her cordially but she preferred to retire early or to spend the evening with Martha in her room at the back of the house; knitting or sewing and gossiping or listening to the wireless.

When Maddie came to Hanshott farm Reg changed his pattern of living. He began to appreciate the things the girls did for him. He smiled when he saw Maddie and he thanked Lillian for preparing his meals and doing his washing; things he had taken for granted before. It was a gradual change but very noticeable to Lillian. His evening visits to The Bowman became less frequent. He brushed aside Lillian's casual remark

"You don't seem to go to the pub so much these days, Reg".

She half expected him to tell her to mind her own business but he did not seem to resent the question.

"The evenings are drawing in and I can't be bothered to walk down there after a hard day's work".

Lillian shrugged and smiled to herself as she continued with her ironing. She did not comment that Reg's friends seldom came round either these days and suspected he had not invited them. Maddie was sitting in the corner sewing but she looked up and smiled at Reg when she sensed he was looking at her while he answered Lillian. He seemed content to sit in the kitchen keeping Maddie company; but saying little. Maddie was growing fond of him and, although he did not have the persuasive charm of Wilkin Frensham, she found herself attracted to his rugged good looks and strong physical appearance. He was quiet but she realised that, beneath that rough exterior, lived an unhappy shy man who wanted to talk to her but could not find the right words.

Lillian also sensed that her brother-in-law's change in behaviour was caused by an attraction he felt for the girl. She dismissed the intuitive thought that something might develop from their close association on the farm. After all, she said to herself, the girl can't be more than 17 and he is much too old for her to be interested in him. Nevertheless, she found herself staying up much later than in the past because she did not think it would be proper to leave young Maddie alone in the kitchen with Reg.

Lillian turned away from the window.

"Maddie is filling out, don't you think, Reg? Perhaps they didn't feed her too well up at the Hall. She certainly eats well now. It will do her good. She was such a slip of a thing when she came here"

Reg did not reply as he stood up. He shrugged on his old farm coat and went out into the yard. Maddie had finished preparing Tom for his trip and met Reg as she came round the side of the farmhouse. He stopped.

"Would you like to help me in the back barn later, Maddie? Len has got to go into Lavering Market and I need someone to help me hoist the bales of winter hay up into the loft. It isn't heavy work. You will only have to help stack them after I've lifted them on the hoist"

Maddie smiled at him

"I'd like that, Reg. When I come back from the school trip I'll ask Lillian if she can spare me"

It had been hot work and both Reg and Maddie had discarded their coats. Now they had finished and were resting, sitting on a bale of hay. He gently took her hand, now roughened by farm work, in his large fist and looked at it

"You had such lovely soft hands at the Memorial Dance. Now look at them! Is this what we have done to you?"

She had never heard such a caring remark from him before and she looked up into his face in surprise

"I don't mind, Reg. Its much nicer working here than it was at the Hall. I am very happy with you, Lillian and Joanne. I hope you will never send me away"

Reg looked closely at her and smiled. He put out his hand and stroked her long fair hair; looking down into her pretty young face. She did not pull away so, encouraged, he put his arm round her shoulder and drew her to him

"No I'll not send you away! I don't know what I would do without you, Maddie. I know you have only been here a few weeks but it feels as though you are part of my life. I would like you to stay here for ever"

She did not seem to object to the intimacy of his words or his embrace so he tilted her chin with his other hand and gently kissed her. She did not feel the fire of Wilkin's kiss. Reg's kiss was so gentle, sincere and loving that she placed her arm round his neck and kissed him back. Folded in each other's arms they leaned back onto the hay bale. For a while he was content to kiss her on the lips but, after a while, he began to nuzzle her neck. Maddie felt herself

31

responding and did not resist even when he began to stroke her body; but when his hand moved down to lift her skirts she involuntarily grasped his wrist.

"No! Reg, please don't"

Momentarily she wondered why she had stopped him. After all, was this not what she wanted? She regretted her impulse as he moved his hand away from the hem of her skirt and she let go of his wrist. The moment had passed and they lay still for a while in each other's arms. She reached up and pulled his head down to kiss him again, this time with more passion; and she did not resist when he resumed stroking her leg just above the knee. Maddie felt her resolve weakening but this time she let him go on. Emboldened, Reg, moved his hand up to her thigh and began to explore further. Again she, involuntarily, grabbed his hand

"No, Reg, you mustn't!"

He stopped the movement but kept his hand where it was

"I thought you liked me?"

She did not draw away

"I do, Reg"

He squeezed her thigh, sending a thrill through her body

"Then why won't you let me.....?"

She whispered, almost to herself

"I'm afraid"

He tried to reassure her

"There is nothing to be afraid of. I'm not going to hurt you. I love you"

She still hesitated, feeling guilty. She felt an impulse to tell him about Wilkin and her condition, but could not bring herself to confess in case he would not forgive her. After all she really *did* care for this bear of a man and she wanted him. Lamely she replied

"Do you! Do you really love me?"

She knew the answer because she could see it in his eyes. She hugged him closer

"But....But! Supposing I have a baby? What will become of me?"

He looked at her searchingly, astonished that she needed to ask the question

"Why we`ll get married, of course! You don't think I'd leave you do you? I told you I love you. I *want* to marry you"

Mentally, Maddie heaved a great sigh of relief but she did not let it show as she hugged him to her. She was going to be married and all her problems would disappear. She started as a thought occurred to her. It takes at least three weeks to arrange a wedding and, although her slim figure was not yet showing signs of things to come, she felt she could not wait any longer than was absolutely necessary. She pushed him away in mock surprise

"Well, Aren't you going to propose to me properly?"

Reg sank onto one knee

"Alright, if that is what you want"

He took both her hands in his

"Maddie, darling, will you marry me?"

She flung her arms around his neck, kissed him and replied breathlessly

"Of course I will and if you want to.....want to.....now. I do too"

Her voice trailed off as Reg effortlessly lifted her up and carried her over the bales of hay. He spread the coats out as a marriage bed and looked away as she undressed shyly. When he turned round Reg felt he had never seen anything so beautiful and he was afraid to touch her in case he broke the spell. Maddie reached out to him and helped him out of his rough farm clothes. The strong masculine odour of his warm body heightened the desire she unexpectedly felt for him and she was completely unresisting when he gently took her in his arms.

Afterwards, they laid there; too breathless to speak. She was thinking 'I know I don't love him now but he is kind and gentle and love will come'. He turned to her

"Maddie, darling, I think we should get married as soon as possible"

He chuckled happily as he playfully patted her stomach

"Just in case"

Maddie felt mean at deceiving him but she had become really fond of Reg and she promised herself she would make it up to him by being the best wife he could hope for as she answered

"I would like that, Reg. But I wonder what Lillian will say?"

He looked alarmed for a moment

"Never mind Lillian. It is your mother that worries me. You need your mother's consent to get married and I am so much older than you. Your mother might not approve"

Maddie reassured him

"Don't worry about my mother. She will be concerned only that I am happy. She likes you and Lillian and she will give us her

33

blessing. I'm sure of it. In fact, I can't wait to tell her"

Lillian looked up as they appeared in the kitchen doorway. She had been kneading dough in preparation for baking bread and her hands and arms were white with flour. Reg was smiling with a sort of smug look and had his arm round Maddie's waist. She looked sheepish but happy. They did not speak immediately but the expressions on their faces made Lillian stop what she was doing and regard them questioningly

"Well now! What have you two been up to in the hay loft?"

She was smiling as she spoke, giving the impression that she did not really believe they had been 'up to', as she put it, anything. Reg looked fondly down at Maddie as she nudged him.

"Go on, Reg! Tell her!"

He hesitated before he spoke. Then he blurted it out

"We're getting married"

Reg waited for her to explode but Lillian was speechless as she looked from one to the other. She regarded them seriously for a moment then recovered herself as she let her gaze fall on Maddie

"Is it true, what Reg says?"

Maddie had half expected this reaction from Lillian and felt nervous but she braced herself

"Yes, Lillian! We love each other and Reg has asked me and I have accepted; but I've still got to get Mum's permission"

Lillian ran forward and hugged them both

"I am so glad for you both. I just know you will be happy together"

But, inwardly, Lillian was pondering the implications. She recalled wondering about Maddie's sudden and unexplained departure from the Hall after working there for three years. 'Could she have been......?' she mused. The girl had certainly put on weight since she had been with them. Well, if so, she thought 'I doubt that Hilda will object in the circumstances despite the difference in their ages'. But, seeing the joy on Reg's face, she could not bring herself to say anything. Instead, with a mental shrug, Lillian regarded Reg and thought 'He is a grown man and he is happy; and I am not his keeper'. Lillian had grown very fond of Maddie and if it helped the girl to solve her problem, if any, and Reg was content, she had no intention of interfering. Without further hesitation she drew them to the kitchen table and they all sat down.

"I am delighted for you both and I would love to have you as a

34

sister in law, Maddie. But you must go down to tell Hilda as soon as possible"

Maddie answered

"I was thinking about that. Will it be alright for me to go down in the trap immediately after dinner, so that I can call in and see Mum before I go on to pick up Joanne?"

Lillian's reply was that of a friendly sister

"Of course, dear, you are practically part of the family now. You don't need my permission to go out when you want to"

Maddie smiled her 'thank you' and, releasing Reg's hand, she rose from her chair and walked across the kitchen to take down her apron from the wall hanger. Donning it she joined Lillian, who had resumed her bread making. Reg also rose, gave Maddie a quick peck on the cheek, and went out into the yard.

Hilda Benhope was surprised to hear the pony clip-clopping down the lane and stopping by her cottage. She looked out the window and, seeing her daughter coming up the path, she rushed to open the door

"Why, Maddie dear, what a lovely surprise"

The girl threw her arms round her mother and breathlessly burst out, tumbling over the words,

"I've got something to ask you, Mum. Please don't say No! I know you will think he is too old for me but I want you to let me marry Reg Hanshott"

She paused waiting for her mother's reaction. Hilda Benhope folded her daughter in her arms. Her immediate reaction was relief that a solution to Maddie's problem had presented itself; but she would rather suffer the shame of an illegitimate grandchild than have her daughter unhappy for the rest of her life

"Are you really sure you want to marry him? It's not just because of ....?"

She looked into Maddie's face, seeking reassurance.

"No, Mummy, I really *do* want to marry Reg"

Hilda looked relieved

"That is settled then. But we must start things moving without delay"

Maddie put her hand out to stop her mother shutting the door.

"Reg is outside in the trap. He is afraid you might not like the idea and would not come in until you said it would be alright. I'll go and call him"

Hilda stopped her for a moment

"You haven't told him anything about..........?"

Maddie began to feel guilty again

"No! Do you think I should?"

Hilda squeezed her arm

"Perhaps it would be better for his happiness that he never knows. Go and fetch him in"

The tall well-built farmer was obviously tense and hesitant. He addressed Hilda nervously

"Good morning Mrs Benhope. I hope you don't mind?"

He ducked under the lintel as Hilda beckoned him in.

"Come in Reg. Maddie has told me about your plans and I am happy for you both. Let us all sit down with a cup of tea to discuss things; I am sorry I don't have any ale in the place"

Still hesitant, Reg looked uncomfortable as he took a chair

"Thank you, Mrs Benhope, I prefer tea at this time of day"

Hilda took charge. She fetched a calendar and they gathered round the table to study it; Maddie and Reg cuddling cups of hot strong tea as they waited for Hilda to speak.

"Reg, how soon do you want to get married?"

She held her breath as she waited for his reply. In the circumstances, of which he was not aware, a long engagement would not be advisable. Reg looked at Maddie as he took her hand in his.

"Well! It is really up to Maddie. But, as for me, I'd marry her tomorrow if she'd have me"

Maddie squeezed his hand and said, eagerly,

"Tomorrow would make me very happy"

Hilda consulted the calendar

"Let us see, it is Thursday, 14th of July today. We need three Sundays for the banns to be read. That takes us to the first week in August. You must go to see the Vicar right away. Will you have time to go now before you have to pick up Joanne?"

Maddie spoke for both of them

"Yes, Mum, we don't have to collect Joanne until four so we have plenty of time to go up to the Vicarage first"

Reg nodded his head in agreement but remained silent. In front of Maddie's mother he felt embarrassed for what he had done to Maddie and would agree to anything rather than face the wrath he had expected from Hilda if she found out. He was, also, a bit scared of what the Vicar might say about the difference in their ages; but he need not have worried. The Rev. Paul Wykeham had served as an Army Chaplain in France and nothing surprised him any more. There were many reasons for hasty marriages and, though he suspected this was one of the more common reasons, he made no comment. Nor was he concerned at the difference in ages. It was quite common among farming communities for men to stay single until they were thirty or so and then to marry teenage girls; whose mothers were only too delighted to see their offspring wed to a substantial landowner rather than to a local farm boy with no future.

A couple of weeks before the wedding Hilda Benhope dug into the bag of sovereigns she was saving for Maddie's future and she, Maddie and Lillian, accompanied by little Joanne, went on a minor spending spree in Dunchester. The white satin wedding dress was 'off the peg' but it fitted beautifully once the back seam had been unpicked to let it out a little at the waist. Maddie ignored the space at the back, and the arch glance of the middle aged shop assistant, as she pirouetted before the mirror. Lillian gasped delightedly
"You look beautiful Maddie"
Joanne chuckled delightedly and clasped her hands to her chest
"I hope my bridesmaid's dress will look as lovely as that". And it did.

The wedding took place at Frensham Down village church on Sunday, 14 August, 1921. It was a simple affair. Gerry Stokes who ran the General Store, and whose second wife Catherine was a close friend of Hilda's, gave Maddie away; and Len Mundy was best man. After the obligatory photographs had been taken in the churchyard, Maddie tossed the huge bunch of white chrysanthemums, held together by white silk ribbons, to Jennie. Her best friend was the only one from the Hall to attend. Mrs Mellish, in a rare burst of emotional generosity, had given Jennie the day off and even lent her the pony and trap. Cook, who was always fond of Maddie, had baked the huge iced cake which Jennie brought with her in the trap, but she did not come to the wedding.
The reception, which was held in the farmhouse kitchen, was equally simple. Of the farm workers only Len Mundy and his

wife, Bertha, were present. Otherwise, apart from Jenny with Gerry and Catherine Stokes, it was only a family group that sat round the kitchen table; including, of course Reg's mother, Martha, and Hilda. When the wedding breakfast and the brief speeches were over, Jenny took Maddie to one side

"You *are* mean Maddie Benhope. You knew I was after Reg Hanshott and you pinched him from right under my nose"

Maddie looked slightly apologetic but answered mischievously

"Its Maddie Hanshott now!"

Jennie smiled and, punching her playfully, whispered

"What is he like in bed? I've often wondered"

Maddie giggled as she nudged her friend

"How would I know? We have only been married a couple of hours"

Jennie chuckled

"Oh yes! Tell me another...."

Reg had offered to take his bride away for a honeymoon but, accepting the demands of a working farm where there was no-one to take over during her husband's absence, Maddie sensibly declined; saying that she preferred to start her married life in, what was, she now realised, her own home. During the weeks leading up to the wedding Maddie and Lillian, with some help from Reg and lots of advice from Martha, had completely re-decorated the main bedroom at the front of the house; giving its previously austere look a feminine touch. New furniture, including a large double bed, had been installed and new cotton print curtains matching the bed cover added to the transformation. Naturally, the newly-weds moved into the room on the night of their marriage.

Technically, Maddie was now mistress of the house but it was not in her nature to make Lillian feel uncomfortable; so life continued at the Farm much the same as before with both women living in harmony in the kitchen and going about their daily chores. Joanne loved her new auntie and wanted to be driven to school by her every day; but, recognising that Lillian might feel Maddie was alienating her daughter's affections, she offered to pick up Joanne in the afternoon; leaving Lillian to take her to school in the morning. Hilda Benhope continued her weekly visit on washday and the three could be heard merrily trilling in the washhouse and be seen sitting round the table gossiping after the work was done.

One evening, three weeks after the wedding, Reg was sitting at the kitchen table pouring over some papers with a worried frown on his face. Maddie, who was at a loose end, came up behind him and put her arms round his neck.

"What is the matter, Reg?"

"Its nothing for you to worry your pretty little head about. Just one of the many problems farmers face these days"

"But, I'd like to help if I can. If you could show me how the farm works, Reg, I am sure I could help you with the paperwork and, if I understand what is going on, perhaps we could discuss problems together. It must be tiring for you to do so much after a hard day on the farm"

"You work just as hard as I do and you need some rest too"

"Perhaps! But Lillian does a lot of the housework and she looks after the hens"

"Alright! But first let me show you a plan of the farm so that you can understand the problem and what I am thinking of planning for this winter"

He fetched a roughly drawn plan from the wooden cupboard which served as his filing cabinet and spread it out on the table. He pointed to the upper boundary bordering Hanshott Hill Common; which spread across to Frensham Hall Parkland

"Over here, behind the yard and across to the Common is a large area of land where the cattle graze. We call this Three Field Meadow because, to control the feeding pattern of the herd, it is divided into three fields; the cows grazing on one field only at a time"

He pointed to the area above Three Field Meadow

"This is where the land is ploughed to grow potatoes. Since 1917 we have received a Government subsidy to encourage us to plant potatoes and, although there are rumours that the subsidy will finish this year, the market is still sound so it will pay us to continue with the potato crop. Also, we will continue to harvest hay, for winter fodder, in Home Meadow which skirts the Lane from here, the edge of the farmyard, to the farm cottages"

"So what's the problem?"

"Its the use of Lower Acre, here"

He pointed to the area behind the farm cottages

"As you can see, this covers all the land behind the cottages across to the Scolling Brook and nearly down to Scolling Road. It is a big piece of open land where we have been growing wheat and oats since the Corn Production Act of 1917 guaranteed prices"

"No barley?"

"There! You *do* understand something about grain production"

"My Dad worked on a farm before he went away to the war"

"Well! It is true a farmer would normally grow barley with the other cereals; but the Act didn't guarantee the price for barley so we have kept to wheat and oats. The problem is that the Act has been repealed and the bottom has fallen out of the grain market"

"If it is no longer profitable to grow cereals, what are we going to do?"

"That's the problem, but I think I can solve it by growing sugar beet. We would plough Lower Acre Field in the winter, as usual, and, after the frost has broken down the sods we could plant sugar beet in the Spring"

"Why would it be better if we grow sugar beet? Anyway, what *is* sugar beet?"

Reg smiled at the 'we'. He had been alone for so long in making decisions before their marriage and he welcomed Maddie's interest. He squeezed her hand, affectionately, and tried not to sound patronising

"Sugar beet is a root plant, rather like a swede, but when the root is pulped and processed it yields about 20% of its weight in pure sugar; equal in quality to the best cane sugar. Apparently, it has been grown extensively in France since the Napoleonic wars"

He showed Maddie an official looking pamphlet.

"It says here that, due to the current 'post war' depression, the Government wants to replace some of the expensive cane sugar imports with home grown beet sugar; so they are offering a 'price guarantee' scheme to encourage we farmers to turn over some of our land to sugar beet. We don't have much land to spare here; but I thought we might give it a go!"

"But, won't that mean more hard work and require extra labour to harvest the crop?"

"That is true! But, we can bring in casual labour to lift the beet; and there is, also, a bonus to growing it. As we lift the beets we lop off the tops with the leaves and the tails of the vegetable before we send the beets to the sugar factory. After they have been wilted, the leaves and the upper part of the beets, which we keep, provide better fodder for the cattle than hay. So we get the best of both worlds; a guaranteed income from sale of the roots *and* excellent cattle fodder to improve the milk yield. Mind you we shall have to plan carefully and divide Lower Acre into sections; rotating the beet crops with cereal grain because the buyers will insist on this to reduce the risk of pest damage to the beet. So we shall still be producing some grain though considerably less than this year's harvest"

"So we shall be selling sugar beets next year?"

"Well! No! Sugar beet is a biennial which means we can't harvest next Spring's sewing until August the following year. Of course, after the first sewing, with careful rotation, we shall have an annual crop to sell. In the meantime we must forgo that new tractor I had in mind to buy and watch the pennies. But, don't worry! It will pay off in the long run"

"I didn't know so much planning went into running a farm but I would like to learn more if you have the patience to teach me. At least I can help you with the milk records and accounts, if you will let me".

It was an early Monday morning in the first week of October when Maddie broke the news to Reg. He had dressed for milking and was sitting on the bed, drawing on his thick woollen socks, when she turned to him. Maddie had been standing, in her nightdress, looking at her figure in the mirror by the light of the oil lamp. She rubbed her stomach and took a deep breath as she turned to look across at him. Then she blurted it out

"I'm going to have a baby, Reg!"

He looked up, startled. Then a broad smile spread over his face and, in his stockinged feet, he crossed the room in two strides to take her in his arms

"That's wonderful, my darling! Are you sure?"

She smiled up at him

"I have suspected it for some time, but now I am sure"

He clasped her close to his chest, careful not to squeeze her too hard, and gently kissed the upturned face. His face was beaming with a self-satisfied expression. The delighted expectant father fussed around her.

"Now come and sit down. You must take things easy. I can't wait! When is it to be?"

Maddie had grown very fond of her gentle giant since they got married and she felt a pang of guilt when she answered

"You remember that time in the hay loft, when you proposed to me?"

His smile broadened as he anticipated her

"Of course. How could I forget our first time together? So you reckon it could be sometime in April?"

Maddie did not want to commit herself

"I expect so, but you can never tell. My mother said *I* was an early birth"

Once again a guilty feeling assailed her as she looked into the trusting eyes of her husband. She drew herself up on tiptoe and, with her arms clasped tight round his neck, kissed him hard on the lips. She was surprised to hear herself saying

"Dear Reg! You are so good to me and I *do* love you so"

And, suddenly, she realised she meant it. She really *did* love him and she sighed contentedly as she snuggled up to his massive chest.

He grasped her hand

"Come on. Get dressed. I want to tell Lillian. I want to tell Martha"

He was so excited that he almost shouted

"I want to tell the whole world I am going to be a father"

Maddie restrained his enthusiasm

"Not *everyone* yet, dear. Lillian and Martha, Yes! And, of course, my mother must know. But, so far as everyone else is concerned I want to keep it our secret for a while. Do you mind?"

He was so pleased he would agree to anything she asked

"Whatever you want, my lovely darling"

He returned to sit on the bed with a happy look on his face while Maddie was getting dressed. Then, together, they descended the stairs to the kitchen. Lillian had been up for some time; setting the fire under the copper and getting the laundry ready for wash-day. She seemed genuinely surprised at the news.

"Oh! Maddie. How lovely!"

If Lillian had any doubts she kept them to herself as she hugged Maddie and turned to congratulate Reg.

"Reg, you old dog! I didn't know you had it in you"

He stood there beaming; proud of his achievement. Then, realising he had a farm to run, he kissed Maddie on the forehead and went out into the yard. Hilda learned of developments as soon as she arrived for the Monday morning wash. Martha, who had been told before Hilda arrived and who never appeared on wash-day, as a rule, in case she got involved in the work, chose this day to join them; but only for the tea and gossip session after the work was done and the washing had been hung out to dry. Maddie found herself the centre of attention as the other three exchanged experiences and regaled her with advice. She must see the village midwife, Molly Wittle, as soon as possible, Martha insisted. Lillian asked

""Why not the doctor in Scolling?"

Martha was scornful.

"Can't trust them doctors to be there when you want 'em. Supposing it 'appened suddenly in the middle of the night. 'ow would you get the doctor 'ere? I can just see Reg driving over to Scolling in the pony and trap at three in the morning an' when 'e gets there, the doctor's out on another call. No! Far better to get Molly in. You can trust 'er to be there when the time comes an' she knows more about babies than any doctor; *and* she won't charge you a fortune like them doctors do! She an' 'er mother, an' 'er mother afore that, 'ave taken care of births in this Village for over a 'undred years an' never lost a single mother or child. So that's what you must do Maddie, my dear. If you wants my opinion, get Molly Wittle in"

Martha, who had never made such a long speech in living memory, lapsed into silence as the others regarded her mutely; stunned at her outburst. Actually, the reputation she accorded Molly Wittle and her forebears was a bit of an exaggeration but, in the end, it was agreed that Maddie and her mother would visit Molly Wittle and seek her advice on the subject. At Maddie's insistence they all undertook not to broadcast the news for the time being; although it was a bit optimistic to expect the garrulous Molly Wittle to keep quiet.

Surprisingly, the news did not get around although anyone seeing Maddie must have suspected her condition as Christmas approached. Jennie had not seen Maddie since the wedding and seemed genuinely surprised to see the change in her friend and to learn the reason for it from Maddie herself on Boxing Day. All the servants at the Hall were required to be on duty on Christmas Day and were expected to join in the domestics' party at the Hall in the evening. But most of them were free for the afternoon and evening on Boxing day to visit relatives and friends. Jennie had no local relatives so she spent her free time at Hanshott Farm. Maddie was concerned when she saw her friend because she feared Jennie might let it out that she had left the Hall under a cloud. But Jennie really was a good friend and, whatever she knew or suspected, she kept it to herself; merely expressing delight as she hugged Maddie close. She looked envious

"You *are* a lucky girl, Maddie"

Maddie was a little puzzled by the comment and momentarily wondered whether it had a double meaning; but Jennie smiled ingenuously, setting her mind at rest.

Reg, of course, kept fussing around his wife; not allowing her to do anything strenuous over Christmas. She became impatient with him because she was still young and wanted to help Lillian and Joanne with the decorations and other preparations; and to join in the boisterous games and general hilarity of the Season. Nevertheless, harmony was soon restored between them when the New Year dawned and she became more appreciative of the love and care he showed during the ensuing winter months.

The months of waiting seemed interminable to Maddie as January stretched into February and the wind howled round the farmhouse at night; occasionally causing a downdraft to send a small cloud of choking smoke drifting from the range into the kitchen and making everyone cough. Reg insisted that Maddie should have the most comfortable chair by the stove but still the dull ache in her back persisted. Joanne became peevish when her auntie, who hitherto had joined in most of her strenuous games, did not play with her in the snow and did not travel in the trap with her when school re-opened in the New Year.

After what seemed an age to Maddie the cold March winds abated and the deep blue skies of April encouraged the women to hang the sheets on the line outside to dry; only to rush out shortly afterwards to bring them in from the rain. The showers left the wide open flowers of the wild primroses dripping in the hedgerows; whilst nourishing the clusters of daffodils blooming in the farmyard garden and bringing new life to the earth. Reg and the hands were busy sewing beet seed in Lower Acre; where sparrows were busily collecting twigs to build their nests among the budding branches of the hedgerows. The whole of nature appeared to be preparing for the arrival of the newborn.

As though the seasons were controlling her biological clock Maddie responded to the demands of nature and began to show signs of an imminent birth. Everyone, except perhaps Maddie herself and her mother, was surprised when she went into labour in the early hours one morning in late April. At Maddie's insistence her mother had been staying at the farm for the past few days to help Lillian. When the signs started Reg called Hilda and Lillian before he harnessed the pony to the trap and set off at speed to fetch Molly Wittle. The midwife was not surprised. She had been monitoring Maddie's progress and knew, from experience, that the birth would be long before the prescribed nine months from the date of the wedding. It was not her business what these young people got up to before they were married; so she made no comment on the subject to Reg. Indeed, she was so busy holding on to the side of the trap that she would have found it difficult to conduct a conversation as he drove her back to the farm at breakneck speed.

Following early instructions from Molly a spare room had been prepared for the birth. Reg had put blocks of wood under the legs of the iron bedstead to raise it to the height specified by the midwife. A waterproof sheet had been spread over the mattress and fresh sheets were kept on standby for use when needed. When Reg returned with the midwife a fire was blazing merrily in the hearth of the spare room with a wire spark-guard standing before it and a brass-railed iron surround bearing clean towels and nappies. Hot water was ready in the large china jug on the marble topped washstand, with a large china bowl, soap and a bottle of disinfectant. Maddie had been moved into the room and was sitting up on the bed with her mother and Lillian taking turns to rub her back to ease the labour pains. Maddie, herself, was torn between warding off the pain and fear of the impending birth and she was relieved to see Molly Wittle walk in with a worried looking Reg. Hilda had been comforting her daughter but she stood aside as the midwife took control the moment she walked into the room.

"Well! Young lady this will not do, will it? Now, I only want one of you in the room when the time comes"
She smiled grimly at Maddie
"That is, of course, apart from you, my dear. We can't manage a birth without the mother, can we?"
The midwife turned to Reg

"You, young man, have done your bit so we don't need you anymore. But you can go downstairs and boil some water. Let Hilda know when it is ready"

Thus, she dismissed him and then turned to Hilda

"No offence, Hilda, but Lillian is younger and stronger than you are so she can help me. Anyway, it will be a little while yet so why don't you go and make us all a nice cup o` tea? Oh, and while you are at it, tell that young man to keep the water boiling. That will give him something to do"

It was nearly two hours later when Reg heard the thin wail of an infant coming from the house. He was out in the yard, checking that Len Mundy and the hands had been coping with milking despite his absence. At the sound he dropped the bucket he was carrying towards the cooling shed, spilling the foaming milk on the ground, and ran towards the house. He hardly noticed that the pan of water on the stove was still boiling away and forgot to remove his muddy boots as he charged up the stairs. Hilda barred the way

"Not yet, Reg!"

She caught his arm and turned him round

"Let us go down and make a pot of tea. I think they can all do with it; except your daughter, of course"

He tried not to show his disappointment that it was not a son

"A daughter? I've got a daughter? Is she alright? Is Maddie alright?"

The questions tumbled out. Hilda smiled broadly

"Everything went fine. They`re both fine but Maddie needs to rest, so you must give her a minute or two before you go in"

Maddie was sitting up with a knitted woollen shawl round her shoulders when they entered the room with the tea. She was, possessively, cuddling her well-wrapped daughter to her breast; smiling contentedly. She looked up

"Oh Reg. Come and see our lovely daughter. Isn't she beautiful?"

Reg lifted the corner of the baby's shawl and looked at the puckered little face. The blue eyes stared into space and the tiny mouth opened to emit a small cry.

"She's got blue eyes, just like yours"

Molly Wittle snorted at such ignorance

"*All* babies got blue eyes when they'm born!"

Reg ignored her comment as he said

"I still think she's wonderful"

He looked round, embarrassed at expressing his feelings so openly in public; but they were all smiles as the midwife took his arm

"Mother must get her rest now. She has been a good girl and we don't want to tire her out. But you can sit by the bed for a little, while I dispose of these"

Molly picked up a bundle wrapped in brown paper and left the room. Recognising that Maddie wanted to be alone with her husband, Hilda and Lillian, carrying the water basin, the enamel pails and the towels, followed the midwife out of the room. Maddie and Reg were pre-occupied with their daughter and did not notice them go. After a while Reg rose from the bedside chair. He kissed Maddie lightly on the forehead and, brushing her fair hair gently with his hand, he started for the door

"I won't be a minute, dearest. I've got something important to show you!"

She looked up from her daughter

"Well! Don't be long"

"I won't".

Reg returned quickly, carrying the family bible which he set down on the bed. It was a large leather bound first edition of the translation authorised by James 1st in 1604 and bore the publication date of 1611. The flyleaf was headed, in neat script, 'Hanshott Farm (Formerly the Manor House, Frensham Down) - In the year of our Lord 1633'. Below this appeared `John Hanshott (1604 - 1667)'. This was the ancestor to whom Sir Francis Frensham had given freehold title to the land and the Manor House. The Hanshott family tree followed. The handwriting was in various styles as each generation was added by a succeeding head of the family. Reg pointed to the last entry, which had been made by his fasther. It showed his own name, with the date of his birth, to which Reg had added a record of his marriage to Maddie Benhope.

"Now we have a new entry to make; but, first we must decide on a name"

Maddie thought for a moment

"I would like Sarah. It means Princess. But it sounds a bit starchy and reminds me of Lady Sarah at the Hall"

Reg did not comment. He was gazing admiringly at his new daughter while Maddie paused, deep in thought, then her face lit up

"I know! Let us call her Sally. It is short for Sarah but has a happier sound to it; and I would like Jennifer, after Jennie, for her second name" Reg smiled his approval

"I don't mind and I *do* like the sound of Sally. So the next entry in the bible will be Sally Jennifer Hanshott, born April 28th, 1922" He looked lovingly at his young wife and a wicked grin crossed his face

"But we must leave space for the rest of the family" Maddie punched his arm mischievously

"Give me a chance to get over this one first" But, within a year, Mark was born and Matthew followed a year later.

Sally Jennifer Hanshott was christened at St James Church following the Sunday morning service on 4th of June, 1922. Reg Hanshott stood proudly by while the child's godmother, Jennie Madieson, stood next to her friend Maddie. Jennie was holding the baby wrapped in the traditional gown in which Martha Hanshott (nee Crannock), Reg's mother, had been christened in 1864. The other Godmother was Lillian, mother of Joanne Hanshott, whose father, Dr Paul James Wykeham, Vicar of St. James, was performing the ceremony. Gerald Stokes who ran the General Store in the Village, and who had given Maddie away at her wedding to Reg, was in the congregation with his wife, Catherine. She was holding her eighteen months old daughter, Jean, who was to become Sally's best friend in later years. Len Mundy, looking uncomfortable in his Sunday suit and proud to be the child's godfather, stood next to Reg Hanshott wondering what he was supposed to do.

Most of the congregation from the morning service had remained to watch the ceremony; much to the chagrin of those farm labourers whose wives had insisted on staying and who would rather be in the Bowman 'wetting the baby's head' with a pint or two before Sunday dinner. The Vicar smiled fondly at his daughter as he took the baby from her to hold the infant over the font. Sally cried thinly as he made the sign of the cross on her forehead with holy water; and this set off Jean as though she had already developed an affinity with the baby Sally. Len Mundy managed to make his responses without a hitch, taking seriously the responsibility he was undertaking regarding Sally's future welfare.

As those invited to the christening party were following Maddie, Sally and Reg, who were riding in the trap, along Castle

Lane on their way back to the Farm they moved aside to make room for Wilkin Frensham as he rode by in the opposite direction on his way to exercise his horse on Castle Hill Common. He paused as he reached the trap and politely raised his hat.

"Good day to you, Mr Hanshott...er...Mrs Hanshott"

Something about the baby made him stare at it for a while; though, had he been asked, he could not have said why. He came to himself abruptly, and simply congratulated the proud parents

"It's a fine day for the christening. I wish the child well in the future!"

Reg thanked him but Maddie cast her eyes down and said nothing. As Sir Wilkin rode away she clutched Reg's arm fiercely

"I *do* love you so, Reg, and thank you for my lovely daughter"

"What brought that on?" he asked but she did not answer.

CHAPTER THREE

1932

The field was spread out, the Master and foxhounds well out in front, with the rest streaming along behind. Sir James Frensham was enjoying himself. He was now 67 and Lady Sarah had urged him to give up fox hunting. But following the hounds was in his blood and, although he found it difficult to mount Samson these days, he could not resist the January Meet at Selchester Towers. When he was younger he would always be in the fore, close on the heels of the Master of Hounds and would bathe in the admiration of the ladies as he unerringly jumped each hedge and ditch. He hated being in the rear and, when he realised the leaders were curving to the right, he decided to take a short cut across a ploughed field. In his younger days his keen judgement would have warned him not to attempt the hedge that loomed up before him but neither his eyesight nor his brain were as keen as in the past and he set Samson at the obstacle. At the last moment he realised the horse was jumping too early and he instinctively attempted to rein in. Samson's belly crashed down heavily on the thorn hedge and he screamed; kicking up with his hind legs. The unseated baronet flew clear over the hedge and fell headfirst into the ditch beyond. His head struck a lump of ice and his mind went blank. He was still unconscious when they found him, two hours later; but, though he had suffered nothing more than a bump on the head, a few bruises and a dent to his pride, his clothing was soaked by the icy water. They wrapped him in a blanket but it took another hour to carry the shivering knight back to Selchester Towers. By the time they got him tucked up in bed he was hot with fever and in delirium. The doctor was called and dosed Sir James with quinine; but all to no avail. Nothing could be done about the pneumonia which followed and a few days later, on 20th January, 1932, Sir James died in a paroxism of coughing.

With the death of his father the hereditary baronetcy passed to Wilkin Frensham and Lady Victoria took over from Lady Sarah as Mistress of Frensham Hall. Lady Sarah was five years younger than her husband and had enjoyed supremacy over the household since she moved into the Hall as a young bride 44 years earlier. She recognised the imminence of a clash of personalities when her daughter in law took over the reins and, ever the diplomat, decided she should move, in her Dowager status, to the Lodge at the entrance to the Drive. The Lodge had stood empty for some years so Sir Wilkin had it surveyed for structural damage and repaired where necessary. It was thoroughly cleaned, re-decorated inside and out, carpeted and furnished to her Ladyship's fastidious taste; also a telephone, including a direct line to the Hall, was installed. The small, unkempt, enclosed space surrounding the Lodge was given over to the attentions of Fullitt, the Hall's permanent gardener, to turn into, what would become in the summer, a neat pretty garden; which he and his lad would maintain.

In the meantime Lady Sarah accepted an invitation to spend a few months at Selchester Towers until the Lodge was ready for her to move in. Whether by coincidence or design the Duchess had, also, invited a distant cousin as a house guest, Lucy Watson.

Lucy was married to Victor Watson, a wealthy financier. Their only son was among the ten million young men who died in the Great War and, like so many grieving parents, Lucy and her husband found no solace in the platitudes that he had given his life for a noble cause. Victor tried to assuage his grief by absorbing himself in the development of the airship industry and he was proud to boast that he had 'sailed' at 2000ft over London in the R101, the biggest airship of her time, during her maiden voyage on 14 October 1929

Their comfortable lifestyle received a shattering blow on 24 October, 1929 when most of Victor's fortune was lost in the Wall Street crash. Following this disaster Lucy found her circle of friends in London Society dwindling as the childless couple were forced to give up their town house and move to a more modest dwelling in the country. The final blow to their marriage came when Victor was killed in the airship R101, which was on her first voyage to India, when she crashed into a French hillside near Beauvais on 5 October, 1930. When Lucy came to visit Selchester Towers she was living on a small annuity which had been set up by her own family before she married Victor.

Lady Sarah and Lucy were much the same age and from similar backgrounds, so it was not surprising they should find each other's company agreeable. They spent a great deal of time together during their sojourn at Selchester Towers. When Lady Sarah learned that Lucy's hobby was cooking she broached the subject that had been in her mind since she became aware of Lucy's financial difficulties

"My dear, do not be offended, but I wonder if you would like to come and live with me at Frensham Hall?"

"It is very kind of you, Sarah. I know we get on well together and I would love to spend a holiday with you. But I could not impose on your generosity by accepting a permanent arrangement; and there is the rest of your family to consider. They have not even met me"

"Oh! You need not worry about them. We would not be living at the Hall. My son, Sir Wilkin, is refurbishing the Gate Lodge for me, so we shall have a place of our own. It is a pretty little cottage and quite spacious. You would have your own room and we shall have one of the housemaids from the Hall living in to take care of us"

"But I don't see how I can pay my way as a permanent guest and still maintain my own house"

"You would not have to pay anything and your contribution would be to take care of the meals"

"It sounds lovely! But I...er...cannot accept charity"

"It won't be charity. You will be doing me a favour. I need a companion and I need a cook. Suppose I offer you the post of paid companion and arrange for a stipend to be paid by monthly instalments directly into your bank account? That way you can retain your independence and neither of us needs to be lonely again. I shall get one of the kitchen maids to come down from the Hall each day to do all the kitchen chores and help with the cooking. Come on! Why not give it a try? You have nothing to lose and I am sure we shall have a wonderful time. You can always go back to your own house if it does not work out"

"Alright, if you are sure! I would love to give it a try"

So it was that in March, 1932, Lady Sarah and Lucy Watson took up residence at the Lodge with a, live in, housemaid supplied by Lady Victoria.

There remained one matter of concern to Lady Sarah; that was the possession of the, so called, Agra Ruby. This priceless jewel, set in a gold pendant, had been given by Mumtaz Mahal, wife of Shah Jahan, Emperor of the 3rd Mughal Empire, in 1629, to Sir Francis Frensham for his wife to wear. It was now an heirloom, to be passed down to each Lady Frensham. Although it would one day pass to Lady Victoria, Lady Sarah insisted that the jewel remain with her while she lived. Sir Wilkin demurred

"No, Mama, it is too big a risk. If thieves were to learn that the Agra Ruby was at the Lodge they would not hesitate to break in. Why, for such a prize, a thief would not stop at murder"

"But, Wilkin, it is my right to wear the Ruby"

"No-one is disputing that, Mama; and you can still wear it when the occasion demands. But, otherwise, it is my responsibility to see that it remains in the safe at the Hall"

There were to be other changes at the Hall during that year; changes brought about by circumstances beyond Lady Victoria's control. Late in September Mrs Mellish, a woman of iron will and a constitution to match, took to her bed with a high temperature and a body aching all over. Fears that chaos would reign without the watchful eye of the Housekeeper to keep things in order were allayed when Jenny, now twenty eight years old and senior housemaid, took the initiative and stepped into the breach. Recognising the young woman's ability to cope Lady Victoria allowed her to continue and encouraged her by letting her handle the household accounts during the absence of Mrs Mellish. Unfortunately, what had been thought at first to be a common cold became worse and the doctor was called. When he diagnosed influenza panic ensued because the disease was often a killer and had been known to spread rapidly. Lady Victoria took stock of the situation and acted accordingly.

Lady Sarah and Lucy Watson were thought to be reasonably safe; isolated as they were at the Lodge. Nevertheless, Lady Victoria telephoned her mother-in-law warning them to stay away and to instruct her housemaid to avoid direct contact with anyone from the Hall. She also said that the daily kitchen maid would stay away from the Lodge for the time being and hoped they could manage without her. Twelve year old Julia and nine year old Willis were not a problem. They were both away at boarding school. However, fearing for the rest of the household, she insisted the invalid should go Dunchester hospital and Jenny was instructed to see that no member of the household came into contact with the invalid more than was absolutely necessary. Treatment for influenza was in its infancy and there was little the Hospital could do for their patient. Thus, it was no great surprise when the news came that the Housekeeper had died on the 2nd of October 1932.

Of all those who knew the stern Housekeeper perhaps Jenny was the most sad at her passing. After Maddie had left all those years ago Jenny seemed lost; as though she felt her friend had let her down in some way by leaving so abruptly. Mrs Mellish had sensed the distress in the girl and felt she was, in some measure, responsible for the gap in Jenny's young life. Within the strictures of the need to maintain discipline the Housekeeper had done what she could to help Jenny. In particular, she had encouraged the girl to improve her education by reading the right books and had taken the trouble to give elocution lessons to the girl in her spare time. The success of her efforts could be seen in the confident, well spoken, young lady into which her charge had developed as she moved up the scale to become Senior Housemaid and deputy to Mrs Mellish when necessary.

Lady Victoria Frensham lifted her eyes from the household books she had been examining with such care. Closing the books she removed her pince-nez and studied the young woman who stood before her on the other side ot the writing desk. Jenny blushed under the scrutiny but regained her composure as her Ladyship spoke

"You seem to have managed very well in the absence of Mrs Mellish. The household accounts and records are all in order and have been kept up to date. I am very pleased with you. Now that Mrs Mellish, rest her soul, is no longer with us it falls to me to appoint a permanent Housekeeper. However, before advertising the position, I discussed the situation with Cook whose opinion I value in such matters. She has suggested that I offer you the position"

She paused and regarded Jenny, waiting to see what her reaction was to the suggestion. But Jenny's face gave no indication of what she was thinking. Inwardly her mind was in turmoil. She could not believe that she, who had started work at the Hall when she left school at thirteen as a kitchen maid fifteen years ago, was about to be considered for one of the top positions in domestic service. Getting no reaction, Lady Victoria continued

"There is no doubt, in my mind, that you understand what will be required of you and that you have the ability to carry out your duties properly; but I wonder whether you are, perhaps, too young (you are twenty eight years old are you not?) for such responsibility. I could, of course, offer you the position on a trial basis; but that would not be fair to you. If it did not work out you would have to leave my service because you would not be able to work under the supervision of another Housekeeper once you had experienced the authority of being in charge of a household yourself'

Lady Victoria paused again and leaned back in her chair contemplating Jenny. She smiled and, for once, dropped her customary haughty demeanour. There were two cups on the tray before her and she poured tea in both. She pushed one over to Jenny and smiled

"Bring over a chair, Jenny, and sit down. Add your own milk and sugar. This is an important decision for both of us and I think it best we make it in a relaxed atmosphere"

Lady Victoria waited until Jenny had sat down and sipped her tea.

"What do *you* think? Do you think you would be happy in the new position? You can stay on as senior housemaid if that is what you would prefer; in which case I shall invite applications from outside. But I must confess I would be more comfortable to have a Housekeeper whom I know and one with whom the staff are happy"

Jenny was sitting uncomfortably on the edge of the chair. She sipped her tea and took a moment to compose herself before replying

"I am beholden to your Ladyship for offering me this opportunity but I could not accept if I did not feel confident that I could carry out the duties satisfactorily. During the past weeks I have learned that I can never be satisfied to be a housemaid again. So, if your Ladyship pleases, I shall gratefully accept the post of Housekeeper"

Jenny stood up as, rising from her chair, Lady Victoria walked round the table to face her. Her face beamed as she took Jenny's hand in a friendly clasp. Then she released her hand and reverted to her customary bearing as an employer formally addressing a servant.

"Very well, then! That is settled. From this moment you are Housekeeper at Frensham Hall and responsible to no-one but myself. You will carry on as you have been until I can present you to the staff formally in clothing more suited to your new status. However, your salary will be increased from today and you are to move into the Housekeeper's bedroom and sitting room immediately. I expect you might want to change the curtains and decor. The same applies to the decor of the room allocated for the

Housekeeper's office. Do whatever you wish in this respect, even changing the furniture if it is not to your liking; charging the expenditure to the household account"

She gave a sly smile as she continued

"My only concern will be when I check and approve the monthly accounts; but do not let that make you spoil the ship for a ha`porth of tar as I understand they say at sea. If you have problems of any kind that you cannot, or feel it is not your place, to resolve do not hesitate to come and see me. Should I feel the need to speak with you, I shall visit you in your office or call you on your telephone. At the end of each month I shall ask you to join me with the books to discuss the accounts and any household matters which require my attention; otherwise I shall leave you alone to carry out your duties as you see fit. You are free to determine your own comings and goings, provided you ensure these do not interfere with your duties. I trust it is not necessary for me to explain the extent of your duties?"

Jenny shook her head so her Ladyship continued

"I suggest you telephone the outfitters in Dunchester immediately and arrange for them to supply you, as soon as possible, with such clothing as befits your new position. Do not concern yourself with the expense. Charge your out-of-pocket expenses to the household account and buy whatever you need at our regular outfitters in Dunchester; charging your purchases to Sir Wilkin's account. By the way, the pony and trap which was used by Mrs Mellish is now at your disposal any time you need it"

Lady Victoria paused, considering what else she needed to say

"From now on, of course, you will deal with all trades people and staff matters. The only exception will be Cook. Although, technically, you are senior to her in the household, I prefer that she shall continue to run her own domain and daily menus will be decided by myself in consultation with her. Cook will also be responsible for ordering catering needs; but she will liaise with you regarding settlement of caterers' accounts"

Lady Victoria paused, then had a further thought "Another matter before you go! The Housekeeper should not be addressed by her Christian name. Let me see! Your family name is Madieson?"

Jenny nodded as her ladyship continued

"Further, a married name lends more dignity to the position and earns respect from the servants and trades people. So, in future, you will be addressed as *Mrs* Madieson. I shall inform the family accordingly and shall make this clear to the staff when I introduce you to them formally as the new Housekeeper. This is an essential to the maintenance of good discipline"

She smiled and again held out her hand

"Well I think that is all for now. Good luck to you, Mrs Madieson. I am sure we shall get on very well together"

She held the books out to Jenny who folded them to her chest.

"Thank you, Madam. Will that be all your Ladyship?"

Lady Victoria shivered as she nodded

"Yes, but it is getting quite dark and chilly in here. Would you kindly send someone in to stoke the fire, light the lamp and draw the curtains?"

Jenny moved towards the fireplace. Lady Victoria rebuked her sharply

"No! Not you, Mrs Madieson. Remember your position! You are the Housekeeper now and you must conduct yourself accordingly. You can never maintain discipline in the household if you do not remember your position"

Jenny stopped in mid-stride, alarmed at the reprimand. Lady Victoria smiled disarmingly

"There now, do not look so shocked. But remember what I have said and do not give me cause to regret my decision"

Lady Victoria suddenly had an after thought.

"By the way, Mrs Madieson, Sir Wilkin is thinking of buying one of those small motor cars, I think its called an Austin Seven, as a run-about and you might find it useful in place of the trap; particularly in the wet weather. I don't suppose you can drive, can you? I can't!"

Jenny shook her head.

"Well there cannot be too much to it. I understand you have to get one of those licence things from the post office and I am sure Mr Briggs can teach you. Alright run along now and, by the way, would you mind asking Cook to send up some more tea?"

Jenny dropped a brief curtsy

"Yes, Madam"

She left the room; almost colliding with Sir Wilkin who was about to enter.

Jenny descended the back stairs and entered the kitchen. Millie and Jean, two of the upstairs maids, were sitting at the table finishing their tea and chatting to one of the stable lads.

"Millie! Go up to the writing room and stoke the fire, light the lamps and draw the curtains. Remember to knock and wait for an answer before you go in. Her Ladyship is in there with the Master" The confident authority in Jenny's voice brooked no argument. Millie recognised something different in her tone and got up immediately.

"Yes! Jen........Miss!"

She took the large box of 'Ship' safety matches from the shelf and left the kitchen. Jenny turned to Ivy Baxter, the Cook,

"Well! Mrs Baxter, it seems Her Ladyship was pleased with the way I deputised for Mrs Mellish and, apparently thanks to your support, I am now Mrs Madieson, Housekeeper at Frensham Hall"

Ivy Baxter looked up from her pastry making and, her ample face beaming, she jovially thrust out two, flour covered, arms to grasp Jenny's hands

"I am that glad, my dear. You have been here a long time and have worked hard. You deserve it. And, since you have suddenly become a married woman in the quickest wedding I have ever heard of and without a husband, at that, you can drop the 'Mrs Baxter' and call me 'Cook', as becomes your new position. Then, I am sure we shall get on famously."

Jenny drew herself up and, smilingly, addressed Ivy Baxter formally

"Right, Cook, her Ladyship said she would like some more tea right away. She will need an extra cup for the Master"

Having despatched Jean, the other housemaid, with the tea tray Cook turned to the stable boy

"Go on! Be off with you, boy. I am sure you have plenty of work to do outside. If you haven't I shall soon find some for you in here" She turned to Jenny

"They hang around in here all day if I let them. I think it is more to get warm and the chance to get a piece of pie than the attraction of the girls; although young Millie thinks otherwise. Have you got time to sit down for a drink and a chat?"

Ten year old Sally Hanshott was taunting her teenage cousin

"Joanne's meeting a boy-oy!"

Maddie and Lillian smiled indulgently at each other while Lillian's daughter blushed and chased the elusive Sally round the kitchen

59

table.

"I am not you little wretch! Just you wait 'til I catch you" Maddie interrupted

"Stop teasing her, Sally!"

Then to Joanne

"You *have* taken a lot of trouble with your appearance for Sunday School, Joanne. Who is he?"

Joanne looked abashed as she defensively replied

"Nobody! I just like to look nice"

Sally meant no malice but she could not resist revealing Joanne's secret

"She is hoping to run into Johnny Studding!"

Lillian thought Sally had gone too far in her taunting

"Now that is enough Sally! It won't be long before you begin to show an interest in boys yourself and you would not want us prying then, would you? Anyway, the Vet's son seems a nice boy. Why don't you bring him home for tea sometime, Joanne. We would love to meet him properly, wouldn't we Maddie?"

Sally butted in, mischievously tormenting her cousin again,

"He wouldn't come. He is more interested in Betty Twist"

Joanne turned on her

"No he isn't and you are being mean. You wait, Sally Hanshott, I'll get you for that"

Lillian looked at the clock

"Come on you two. Stop bickering and collect the boys or you will all be late"

Joanne Hanshott, Lillian's daughter, was now seventeen years of age. She had inherited the rather heavy build of the Hanshott family; but her features, though not what one would describe as beautiful, held the serene charm that had attracted Joseph Hanshott to her mother. Both mother and daughter would always attract attention because they had a striking facial bone structure which defies the aging process. Perhaps rather tall for a girl, Joanne dominated the diminutive Betty Twist, but the latter's prettiness sapped Joanne's confidence in their rivalry for the attentions of Johnny Studding.

Joanne worked on the farm during the week but at weekends she and Betty were both teachers at the local Sunday school, which was held in the afternoon at the Village Hall at the bottom of the Green. It was a long way from the Church, which overlooked the Green from the top of Vicarage Hill, but it was more convenient for parents of the many very young children who regularly attended Sunday school to send them here. It would be an arduous task for them to drag their reluctant offspring up the steep hill to the church. Sally Hanshott had grown into a vivacious, albeit mischievous, ten year old and had been attending the Sunday school since she was five. One day, no doubt, she would be a teacher there like her older cousin. She was about average height for her age and had inherited her mother's prettiness, with pale blue eyes and long fair hair; the latter with a touch of auburn. In contrast, her two brothers, Mark (aged nine) and Matthew (aged eight), who had just entered the kitchen, both had their father's brown eyes and brown hair; though they, too, had inherited the more delicate features of their mother rather than the heavy good looks of Reg Hanshott.

Gathering the children together, Joanne had just reached the front door when someone knocked. She opened the door to find a tall young woman standing there. She was dressed in a smart, dark grey suit of jacket and skirt; the latter ending about five inches below the knee. A somewhat severely-cut cape protected her from the mid-October chill and she wore fine black leather gloves. Her neat fairish hair was cut in the latest short style and was surmounted by a dark fashionable hat, the brim drawn down above one eye. Black silk stockings, elegant black shoes and a fine black leather handbag completed the ensemble. She stood aside to allow the girls to pass with their young charges. Joanne did not recognise her but she acknowledged the courteous gesture with a polite

"Thank you, Madam"

As the Sunday school party carried on down the path Maddie came to the door. She gasped in surprise

"Why! Jenny! Is that really you? My! you do look smart! Come in"

Lillian looked up from her sewing; a query in her expression. Maddie laughed

"Lillian! Don't tell me you don't recognise Jenny?"

The light dawned on Lillian's face

"Why, of course. So it is. But what has happened? No offence, but we don't usually see you looking so elegant"

Jenny smiled and twirled on her high heels

"You see before you, not Jenny the housemaid, but Mrs

61

Madieson, the Housekeeper. I have taken over Mrs Mellish's old job"

Maddie could not contain herself and she rushed to clasp Jenny's hands in her own.

"Oh Jenny. How wonderful. Who would have thought..........?"

She trailed off and was speechless for the moment. Lillian rose, smoothed her apron and made a great show of dusting a chair. Then she, smilingly, addressed Jenny with mock respect

"Why, Mrs Madieson, it is so nice of you to drop in. Please sit down. Can we offer you a cup of tea and a slice of cake? It will not be up to your usual standard but we humble folk do our best"

Jenny took the proffered chair.

"Come off it, Lillian. I get enough of that at the Hall. I am among my friends now, am I not?"

Lillian was contrite

"Oh, alright, Jenny. Just having a bit of fun. Now come and sit down and tell us all about it; and what is all this 'Mrs'? You haven't got married without inviting us to the wedding have you?"

Sally Hanshott was standing on a chair, looking furtively through the window in the Village Hall. She gleefully glanced over her shoulder to Jean Stokes, her best friend,

"He is coming over!"

Jean was two years older than Sally. She was the daughter of Gerry Stokes who, with his wife, Catherine, ran the General Store on the south side of the Village Green. It was just after 3pm and Sunday School had finished. Jean's older brother, Alan, had already left to go home but Julian, her younger brother who was the same age as Sally, was hanging around with the Hanshott boys; wistfully hoping Sally would notice him and give him a smile. Jean looked up at Sally

"Are you sure he is not just walking the dog?"

Sally climbed down from the chair

"He has the dog with him. But I am sure he is coming over here. What a lark?"

Joanne and Betty Twist were in the porch, making sure the younger children did not stray before they were collected by their parents. Had she been asked, Joanne would have denied she was lingering in the hope of seeing John Studding; but she was very conscious of the fact that he was approaching with his dog. She turned casually to Betty, hoping she had not noticed John, "Why don't you go on home, Betty? There is no need for us both to hang around". But Betty had also seen John Studding approaching and she had no intention of leaving him alone with Joanne. She smiled sweetly at Joanne.

"It is alright! I have to wait for my brother. He is with your two and I thought we might all go together when all the littl'uns have gone. After all, we all go the same way home"

Sally and Jean, determined not to miss anything spicy, had joined the two older girls by the time John reached the porch. The boys, who had followed them, looked at each other in puzzlement as the little girls giggled together behind their raised hands. The large Labrador wagged its tail and, to Joanne's chagrin, ran up to Betty who held out her hand to him. However, Joanne brightened when John spoke to her rather than to Betty.

"Hallo Joanne! Sunday school finished?"

Before Betty could butt in Joanne answered

"Yes! What are you doing? Taking Ben for a walk?"

He reached down and patted the dog

"Well! Yes. I usually take him up to Castle Hill Common, but it is a bit muddy after the rain last week. There is no traffic on the Scolling Road on Sundays so perhaps I'll just give him a run along there"

Betty managed to get a word in

"If you are going in the direction of the garage I will keep you company"

She turned with a smirk to Joanne

"You just said you could manage here without me, didn't you Joanne? And you won't mind seeing David gets home safely, will you? He would prefer to be with your boys". Betty looked triumphantly at Joanne and, taking the initiative, linked her arm through John's, calling the dog to follow her

"Come on Ben. Let us go, John"

John Studding the, tall good looking 18 year old, second son of the Veterinary Surgeon, was conscious of the rivalry between the two girls and would probably have left them to it had he not come over specially to see Joanne. He had inherited his father's distinction for diplomacy and, gently disengaging Betty's possessive arm, he tactfully suggested a compromise.

"I am in no hurry! Why not wait until the last of the young

children has been collected and we can *all* go together?"

Betty could hardly conceal her annoyance as Joanne, with a triumphant smile at Betty, replied

"That is a good idea! Then you can help me with these little monsters after we have dropped Betty and David off at the Garage"

The fun over, Jean took her brother's hand and skipped off across the Village Green towards the General Store; tossing over her shoulder

" 'bye Sally. See you in school tomorrow"

Sally waved to her friend and turned to make a fuss of Ben.

John was walking as slowly as he could without making it too obvious. He felt a thrill at being, more or less, alone with Joanne and wanted to make it last as long as possible; he had taken the bold step of holding her hand and she had not objected. They were halfway up Hanshott Lane. Sally and the boys were some distance ahead trying to keep up with the dog which was running from side to side seeking out strange smells on the grass verges. Joanne broke the silence

"My mother and Aunt Maddie suggested you might like to come to tea?"

John resisted the question 'How did they know I would be meeting you, today?' Instead he squeezed her hand as he replied

"That would be nice. Do you mean today or later?"

She was surprised that he accepted so readily and wondered whether her mother would mind if she turned up with him unexpectedly.

"I suppose today would be as good as any other time"

He pondered for a moment

"Do you have a telephone? I will have to call my mother to let her know. She will be expecting me back home for tea and I would not want her to be worried"

Joanne was still a little overcome at the thought she would spend the evening with John and she answered somewhat breathlessly

"Yes, we do have a 'phone. So you *will* come?"

He squeezed her hand again and nodded, but had an after-thought

"What about Ben? Do you have any dogs at the farm?"

"No! Not since Hector died. Uncle Reg is thinking about getting another dog. He says a farm is not a farm without a dog. But he hasn't got around to it yet"

64

Maddie and Lillian should have been surprised that Joanne had taken up their suggestion so quickly but, remembering Sally's taunt about Betty Twist earlier, they were not surprised that Joanne had grabbed the first opportunity to cement her relationship with John Studding. He politely asked if he could telephone his mother, this concern for his mother finding favour with the two women, and was respectful to Reg Hanshott with whom he found it difficult to converse at first.

Making small talk, John commented on old farming families and the fact that the Lane was named after the family. There was some pride in Reg's voice as he talked about his family.

"Nothing strange about that, lad. It is only a lane and most lanes are named according to where they lead. The lane leads to Hanshott Farm so it is called Hanshott Lane"

He chose to ignore the fact that it also lead to Frensham Hall as he continued

"This land has been farmed by the Hanshotts for nigh on 300 years. Why young Joanne there has her name in the family bible. Starting with John Hanshott who died in 1667, you will find all the Hanshott's names written there. You just sit there, young man, and I will fetch the bible. I think you might find it interesting"

Reg fetched the family bible and spread it open at the first page on the kitchen table. He showed John the entries and launched into the history of the family. They all listened avidly as Reg talked about the time when the Farmhouse was a Manor House owned by Sir Francis Frensham who had made a considerable fortune serving as military adviser to Shah Jahan, Emperor of the 3rd Moghul Empire in India, in company with his friend and companion at arms John Hanshott. When they returned from India in 1630 Sir Francis built Frensham Hall and gave freehold of the Manor House to John Hanshott with several hundred acres of land. The latter forming the present Hanshott Farm. With his finger he traced the family tree, holding young Sally enthralled, and talked about incidents of which neither Lillian nor Maddie had been aware before that night. He stopped abruptly when he reached the period where his brothers were lost in the Great War and, closing the bible, changed the subject.

""Well! I must be boring you all. Sorry! Got carried away, I suppose. Would you like a pot of ale, John?"

Lillian turned to John while Reg was getting the drinks

"Don't you have an older brother, John? I seem to remember him in the Village when he was a boy but I haven't seen him around for a long time"

"Yes! my brother, William, is two years older than me. You probably haven't seen much of him because, after he left the Village school, he was sent away to boarding school until he was eighteen"

"And I suppose he went on to university after that?"

"Dad wanted him to go up to Cambridge and then to Veterinary College so that he could take over the Practice, in time"

"So he is up at Cambridge now. Which college?"

"No. Bill isn't at Cambridge. He had other ideas. He had done well in the school cadet corps and had made up his mind to make the Army his career"

"But if he was under twenty one, I thought he would need his father's consent to join the Army in peacetime?"

"That is true! And it was with considerable reluctance that Dad agreed to sign the consent form. Dad was disappointed that Bill had no interest in the Practice but he would not stand in Bill's way if he had set his mind on a different career"

"So. Where is your brother now?"

"He is at Sandhurst on an officer training course. Last time he was home on leave he said he wanted to go into the Royal Engineers and be posted to India; but Mum does not like the idea of him going to India because it will be for a five year tour"

John looked up at the kitchen clock.

"I really must be going. I didn't realise it was so late. I know you all have to be up early on a farm and I apologise for not leaving sooner"

Reg Hanshott shook him by the hand.

"Not at all, John. It has been a real pleasure to have you here. You must come again soon"

Joanne stood up.

"I'll see you to the gate"

Sally rose, intending to follow them, but Maddie interceded.

"It is time you three children were in bed. It is a school day tomorrow"

Sally continued towards the front door.

"And that means you, too, young lady"

"But, I was only going to......."

"No `buts`. Go on, off up those stairs now"

Sally said goodnight rapidly and tore up the stairs to peep from behind the curtains on the landing. She could see two figures standing close to each other in the shadow of the tree by the front gate; but nothing else of interest. She sighed, shrugged her shoulders, and skipped away to her own bedroom.

Joanne was standing close to John outside the wrought iron gate at the end of the garden path.

"Thank you for coming to tea"

"No! I should be thanking you for asking me. Its been a lovely evening. Your mother and aunt are nice and I particularly enjoyed talking with your Uncle Reg. Seventeenth and eighteenth century history is a particular interest of mine. In fact I shall be reading it at Cambridge next year, if all goes well. We cannot trace our family back beyond my grandfather and it is fascinating to talk with members of a family with a recorded history as old as yours"

"You must have struck the right note with Uncle Reg. He seldom spends time chatting to visitors unless they are old cronies of his from The Bowman. I have never heard him talk so animatedly before and it was lovely to learn so much about the family history. Perhaps you can get him to talk some more next time you come. I would like to write it down because Uncle Reg seems to be the only one left who knows all about it since my grandmother died in 1929"

He looked down at her

""So you are going to invite me again, then, Joanne?"

""Of course! If you will come?"

The moon broke through the clouds and shone on her upturned face. He caught his breath and felt a sudden urge to kiss her, but he resisted the impulse. Instead, he took both her hands in his.

"Joanne! I have been wanting to ask you this for a long time. Would you like to go out with me?"

She had been expecting him to kiss her and was a bit disappointed when he did not. But this was more than she dared hope for. Nevertheless, she could not help teasing him a little as she hesitated before she answering

"Do you mean be your regular girl friend? I don't know about that"

John was taken aback at her apparent reluctance

"But you must. I don't want anyone else"

She wanted to hug him for saying that; but her but pride got in the way

"What about Betty Twist? You seem to be smitten with her"

His denial was just what she wanted to hear.

"No, I *am* not! She chases after me but I am not interested. It is only you I want. Please say you will?"

Her heart was in her mouth and she had difficulty in not displaying her eagerness

"Oh, alright! Let us go to the Picture House in Dunchester next Wednesday. There is a Charlie Chaplin film on called 'City Lights'. It is supposed to be very funny"

John folded her in his arms and kissed her. She responded with her arms round his neck and it was a long lingering kiss. He reluctantly let her go

"See you on Wednesday"

He called the dog and, with jubilant step, set off down the lane. The moon was still out and he turned to wave. But he could not see her in the shadow of the trees by the gate. Joanne stood by the gate watching him until he disappeared in the darkness. Then, with a happy heart, she skipped up the garden path to the door.

She let herself in quietly, intending to go straight to bed, but she saw the light was still on in the kitchen so went in to say goodnight. Maddie and Lillian were ostensibly tidying up. Lillian broached the subject that was on both their minds.

"He seems a nice young man. Are you going to bring him home again one day?". Joanne did not answer. She smiled; the smile of a cat who has stolen the cream

"He is taking me to the pictures on Wednesday. I can't wait to see Betty Twist's face when I tell her. I am off to bed. Goodnight".

CHAPTER FOUR

1932 - 1937

Jenny was dreaming she was knocking on Maddie's door. She thought she was seventeen again and it was imperative that she woke Maddie up, though she did not know why. She could hear the knocking in her head but her balled fists were meeting no resistance as they pounded at the sheets. She gave up, but the knocking continued. Louder, more insistent, and she became half awake to realise someone was knocking at her sitting room door. It was not the timid knock of a servant attempting to rouse the Housekeeper; such a tapping would probably not have awakened her because the door of her bedroom, which led off her private sitting room, was closed. But this was the heavy thumping of someone in panic and, even though she was still half asleep, it invaded her mind. Her befuddled brain cleared and she became fully awake as she realised the banging was accompanied by a voice shrieking in fear

"FIRE! Wake up Mrs Madieson. Wake up! There's a FIRE"

As realisation of what that dread word could mean reached her consciousness Jenny threw off the blankets and leapt out of bed. Without thinking she, automatically, thrust her feet into her bed slippers and pulled on her dressing gown as she stumbled, still a little bemused by sleep, across her bedroom to turn on the light. But the wall switch did not respond and the bedroom remained in darkness; or rather semi-darkness because a red glow was coming through the window panes. In the faint flickering red light she found the bedroom door. The knocking and yelling became louder as she reached for the sitting room wall switch just outside her bedroom door but this did not work either. She called to the person outside

"Alright! I am coming"

The knocking ceased. Jenny stumbled as she bumped into an armchair but recovered herself and reached the sitting room door. Before unlocking the door she tried the other wall switch but to no avail. She paused to pull herself together. Jenny recalled Lady Victoria's words when she was appointed Housekeeper last year 'Always remember your position. It is the only way to maintain discipline', She threw off the rising panic and drew herself up as she unlocked the door and flung it open. A housemaid stood before her. The girl was trembling and distraught but calmed when Jenny took her by the shoulders.

"Millie! What do you mean by shouting FIRE like that. I cannot smell smoke. Calm yourself girl and tell me what is the matter"

"It is the stables, Ma'am. There's flames an' smoke everywhere. The 'orses is screamin' an'.........."

She trailed off and burst into tears. Jenny shook her

"Has Mrs Baxter been called? And Mr Johnson?"

Millie pulled herself together

"I don't know about Mrs Baxter, Ma'am, but Mr Johnson knows. He's out there with the stable boys and Mr Briggs"

Jenny quickly made up her mind

"You run along and call Mrs Baxter; then rouse the rest of the household staff. Tell them to get dressed in warm clothes and to gather in the back yard. Except for the men, who are to see what they can do to help Mr Johnson, otherwise everyone is to remain in the yard until I can address them. Tell Mrs Baxter that I am alerting the Family. Now, pull yourself together, girl, and do what I have told you. Run along now!"

. Having dismissed the housemaid Jenny returned to her bedroom and flung open the casement window. From her vantage point on an upper floor she could see along the back of the Hall and part of the north wing; beyond which the glow of the flames and the red tinged smoke could be seen rising over the roof. Though loud, the crackling sound of burning timber did not completely drown the hoarse shouts of the men fighting the fire; but the screaming of the panic-stricken horses was unnerving. Jenny returned to the sitting room. She picked up the telephone instrument connecting the Hall to the outside world and lifted the receiver. Getting no immediate response she jiggled the receiver lever several times. There was a pause while she waited for the operator to answer.

"This is the Housekeeper at Frensham Hall. We appear to have a fire in the stables. Will you kindly alert the fire brigade at once?"

For a moment Jenny wondered why the electric wall switches did not work; then she remembered that the generator was located in a shed next to the stables. She never really trusted the electric light system which had been installed only recently; and always kept a candle and matches in the drawer of her bedside table. Now, she took these out and, by the light of the candle, looked at her bedside clock. It was 4am. She fastened the lighted candle in a flat tin candlestick; then, placing this on the bedside table, she calmly walked over to the washstand, splashed some cold water in the hand basin, then briefly rinsed and dried her face. Jenny carried the candle stick into the sitting room and put it on the table. By the dim light she walked to the telephone instrument attached to the wall. The line would connect her with any part of the Hall and, if necessary, with the chauffeur's and chief groom's quarters; also to the Lodge. She dialled the number which would connect her with Lady Victoria's bedroom. While waiting for a reply she noted that the calendar on the wall showed it was 14th November, 1932. She could hear the vibration of the bell at the other end of the line, then a sleepy, irritable, voice answered

"What *is* it? Who is ringing at this ungodly hour?"

With proper deference Jenny spoke into the mouthpiece

"This is Mrs Madieson, the Housekeeper. I am sorry to wake you, Madam, but I am afraid we have a serious fire in the stables. I do not think it will spread to the Hall but I felt it only proper to let you know"

Not one to panic in a crisis her Ladyship took the news calmly

"Quite right, Mrs Madieson. I take it you have the matter in hand?"

Jenny was equally calm

"Yes, Madam, I have called the fire brigade and have alerted all the servants. Johnson and the men are doing what they can until the fire engine arrives. I have not called Nanny or any of the family. Do you wish me to call Sir Wilkin or anyone else?"

"No! Mrs Madieson, you can leave that to me. Sir Wilkin will be concerned about the horses and I am certain he will be there directly. Meanwhile, I suggest you look after things out there and see that the staff are alright"

Her Ladyship rang off abruptly. Jenny replaced the receiver and, forcing herself to remain calm despite the panic she felt rising in her chest, she returned to her bedroom where took a few minutes to dress and put up her hair. It would not do for her to appear outside improperly dressed in any circumstances. She donned a warm cloak and gloves and, still carrying the candlestick and matches, she left her room; carefully locking the door behind her. Shielding the dim light with her hand, and moving as fast as she could without putting the wavering flame out, she took the most direct route, via the main staircase, down to the entrance hall. In a cloakroom, off the hall, she found and lit two hurricane lamps. She left one lamp on the hall table by the front door with the, now extinguished, candle and matches. The other she carried out with her into the chill air of the early morning.

The stables were on the west side of the Hall and were separated from the main building by a wide gravel-covered yard. They were in a square U shape with the open end toward the Hall. The feed room and hay loft were to the left of the opening. From these five loose boxes stretched back to the tack room at the far corner. The closed end of the U was formed by a further four loose boxes, to the right of which was the spacious coach house. The right arm of the U comprised three two-storey cottages with slated roofs. The first of these provided living accommodation for the head groom, Mr Johnson; also his wife and two stable boys. The next cottage was occupied by the chauffeur, Mr Briggs and his wife. The third cottage was the home of Ken Fullit, the gardener; who lived there with his wife and fifteen year old Jeremy Styles, from Crannock's Farm. Jeremy, who helped the gardener and did odd jobs around the Hall, only lived-in from Monday to Friday. After he had finished his work on Friday the lad would bicycle home to spend the weekend with his parents on the farm, which was about two miles from the Hall on Wash Road; returning at 8am on Monday morning.

The lower part of all the buildings forming the stable complex was brick-built, but the upper walls were constructed of pitch-covered ship-lap timber boards. Even the roof was covered with pitch-washed wooden shingles; making the whole structure highly flammable. The fire had started in the brick shed which had been built alongside the feed room to house the electricity generator. This had already been gutted; accounting for the loss of electric power to the Hall. The fire was now raging through the roof of the hay loft, from which flames and red sparks were rising high into the night sky. The red glow reflecting off the low clouds must have been visible for miles. It was pulsing and growing as the fire spread along the roof above the left hand row of stalls as far as the tack room; threatening the rest of the stalls and the coach house.

Ignoring the showers of sparks the head groom, Mr Johnson, and the stable boys, with cloths wrapped round their faces, were concentrating on getting the horses out of the stables. Those furthest from the fire were frightened by the nearby flames but had

72

not yet panicked so could be handled with relative ease. With their eyes covered they had been led out of the yard to be let loose in the open paddock, well away from the stables. Julia Frensham's favourite mount, Delilah, was in a box close to the approaching fire. She was smashing her hoofs in her stall and screaming in panic as the smoke swirled round her and she could feel the heat and hear the crackling as the flames reached the roof above her. Several attempts had been made to calm her down so that she could be brought out but, each time, she kicked out with such ferocity that the men and boys were unable to take hold of her. One boy was sitting on the doorstep outside the chauffeur's cottage, nursing a broken arm, while another was standing beside him trying to staunch the blood which was pouring from a gash in his own arm where a flying hoof had caught him. Jenny called to Mr Briggs, the chauffeur, who, with the help of Ken Fullit, the gardener, and the two footmen from the Hall, was ineffectually attempting to stem the flames with buckets of water. He dropped his bucket and came over

"Sorry, Ma'am, there is not much we can do except try to stop it spreading"

She nodded

"Well! Do what you can. The fire brigade will be here shortly. Tell those two boys to come over to me"

The two injured stable lads followed Jenny to the yard where the rest of the servants were waiting. She handed them over to Mrs Baxter.

"Cook, will you take care of these two and make them comfortable in the kitchen until I can get the doctor? Oh yes! And her Ladyship would like to see you as soon as you are free. Would it be alright with you if I instruct Millie to take tea out to Mr Johnson and those helping him?"

Mrs Baxter nodded grimly

"And, if its alright with you, Mrs Madieson, and since there is nothing they can do out here, I'll tell the rest of the house servants to come into the kitchen for a hot drink before they return to their duties"

Jenny turned to the servants who were waiting in a group.

"There appears to be no danger to the Hall so you can go back. Millie, will you see that a kettle of tea, with mugs, is sent out to Mr Johnson and another to the fire officer and his men when the fire brigade arrives".

73

Daisy, the live-in housemaid at the Lodge, was awakened by the bell of the first fire engine as it turned into the drive. She looked out of her bedroom window, which faced the park, and could see the flames rising above the Hall. She tried the wall switch but the electric light did not come on. She fumbled around in the dark to find her dressing gown but gave up and felt her way out of the room in her thin nightdress to wake Lucy Watson. In her excitement she reverted to her Village accent

"There's a fire, Ma'am. Up at the 'all! It looks like the 'ole place is on fire"

Lucy remained calm

"What time is it, Daisy?"

"'bout 'alf past four, Ma'am. Shall I wake 'er Ladyship?"

"No! Not until I have telephoned the Hall to see what has happened. There is no need to alarm Lady Sarah unnecessarily"

Lady Victoria answered the telephone.

"No, Lucy, no-one is in danger here. The fire is confined to the stables and I am sure the fire brigade can take care of it. Is Lady Sarah distressed?"

"She is still asleep and I would rather not disturb her"

"I agree! There is nothing you can do to help. But thank you for calling me. Goodnight....or should I say 'Morning'"

Down at Hanshott Farm Reg Hanshott was up early, as usual, to do the milking. He was pulling on his socks in the bedroom when he heard the clanging of the fire engine's bell. He jumped up and flung open the window in time to see the second fire engine go tearing past on the way up to the Hall. Maddie rubbed her eyes sleepily when he shook her

"Wake up! I think there is a fire at the Hall. Two engines have just gone past up the Lane and I can't think where else they would be bound for. I am going to look out of one of the back windows"

Maddie joined him to look up the hill. They could hear the fire engines in the distance, as they turned into the Drive, and could see the flames shooting up; causing a red glow to spread across the low lying clouds. Maddie gasped

"Jenny! I must go up to see if she is alright"

Reg replied

"I'll get the truck started and we'll drive up"

Hearing the unusual bustle so early in the morning the others had joined them. Sally and the boys soon forgot to be sleepy when they

74

heard the cause of the commotion. A FIRE! How exciting! They jumped up and down, Sally crying out

"Can I come, *please*. Oh, do let me come"

Sally's plea was echoed by the boys. But Reg was adamant

"No! You will only be in the way. You can watch from here"

He turned to Lillian

"Perhaps you could keep an eye on the yard in case any sparks drift down on the wind? And, Joanne, would you mind telling Len Mundy where I have gone and that they are to get on with the milking without me? They won't be needed at the Hall now the fire brigade is there"

The firemen were drawing water from the lake and hosing down the part of the stables the fire had not yet reached when the truck arrived. Reg jumped down to see what he could do to help. Meanwhile, Maddie, who was relieved to see the fire was not at the Hall itself, sought out Jenny in the kitchen. Cook gave Maddie a cup of tea and Jenny sat down with her to relate what had happened.

"It is lovely of you to worry about me, Maddie, but I am fine. The fire brigade have taken charge outside but I think most of the stable buildings will be lost. Thank goodness none of the cottages have caught fire. The sparks have been bouncing off the slate roofs but I dread to think what would happen if they had been thatched"

Some smoke must have affected Maddie's eyes because she took out her handkerchief and rubbed them. Thinking it was the dim light from the oil lamps Jenny, apologetically, commented

"The fire started in the generator shed so we have no electric light. We've had to dig out all the old oil lamps"

Maddie chuckled

"Unlucky you! We don't have the luxury of electricity down at the farm so I did not notice the difference when I came in"

Having finished their tea, Maddie and Jenny went outside to the stable yard and joined Reg, watching the firemen at work. Maddie saw Sir Wilkin talking to Mr Johnson. Julia was dragging at her father's arm

"Daddy! You *must* do something. Delilah is screaming. Oh! Daddy, Please get her out!"

Mr. Johnson turned to Sir Wilkin.

"We can't get to her, Sir, and the fire officer says the roof is going any minute"

Sir Wilkin shook off his daughter's arm and strode rapidly back to the Hall. Julia shrieked after him.

"What are you going to do Daddy?"

But she knew what he was going to do and her fears were confirmed when he returned a few minutes later carrying his service revolver

"No Daddy, don't. Please don't shoot her!"

Julia clung to him but he shook her off. Jenny took hold of her arms from behind and held her. She still struggled

"Get you hands off me, Mrs Madieson. Who do you think you are? Let me go!"

But Jenny was much stronger than Julia and she hung on tight. Mr Johnson fetched a grain sack and slit the side. He soaked it in water and threw it over Sir Wilkin`s head as he walked cautiously towards the stable door. Ignoring the heat, Sir Wilkin shielded his face with his left arm as he raised the revolver. Taking careful aim he fired into the stable. The screaming stopped suddenly but the sound of the horse falling was drowned by the crash of the roof caving in. Returning to the group Sir Wilkin pocketed his revolver, threw off the steaming sack and, taking the towel that Mr Johnson handed him, wiped his face and head. The fire officer came over

"That was a brave thing you did, Sir"

The knight brushed it aside tersely

"Had to be done! Couldn't let the poor beast suffer"

Ignoring his daughter's tearful rage he turned away. It was then he noticed Maddie and stopped to stare at her, as though he had seen a ghost. He recovered himself and walked towards her

"It is Maddie Benhope, is it not?"

For a moment Maddie's mind flashed back to a dance hall in the distant past and she half expected him to ask her to dance. But the moment passed and she did not smile as she replied in an acid tone

"No! Sir Wilkin. I am Mrs Hanshott and this is my husband"

Sir Wilkin's face did not register the rebuff. He stood looking at her for a moment then, casually, he nodded to Reg and bid her farewell.

"Good morning, Mrs Hanshott"

He strode off; leaving her astounded that he had not even tried to comfort his daughter who was crying in Jenny's arms.

Sally answered the door. Sir Wilkin stood there looking down at her. Although he had reached the age of forty three he had retained the illusion of youth in his upright bearing and his charm was not lost on Sally, despite her tender years. Like her mother before her she was enchanted by his smile and easy manner. The difference was that, to Sally, the man who stood before her was a charming old man; not the captivating war hero of her mother's youth. She knew who he was and, concealing her surprise that he should call at the farm, she addressed him politely

"Good morning, Sir. Do you wish to see my father?"

He countered with a question of his own

"Are you Mrs Hanshott's daughter?"

She nodded and he continued

"And might I ask how old are you, my dear?"

"I shall be eleven in April, Sir"

He regarded her seriously for a moment, as though he was working something out in his head, then returned to her original question

"I would like to see your father but I expect he is busy on the farm. Perhaps I could have a word with your mother?"

Sally did not ask him in

"If you will kindly wait here, Sir, I will see if my mother is around"

She left him standing under the porch with the door open and walked away towards the back of the house.

Maddie was in the kitchen, with Lillian and Joanne, preparing the mid-day meal. Lillian looked up when Sally walked in

"Who was it, dear?"

Sally directed her answer to Maddie

"It is Sir Wilkin Frensham from the Hall. He wanted to see Daddy, but asked if you would see him as Daddy is not here"

Maddie hesitated, wondering whether she could ask Lillian to go instead; but, realising they would not understand the reason for her reticence, she took off her apron and, leaving Sally in the kitchen, went out to the front door. Until the night of the fire, Sir Wilkin had not seen Maddie for several years. He found it difficult to accept that this beautiful young woman was the same girl he had known as a housemaid all those years ago. Maddie was now twenty eight and, having thrust aside her guilt in a happy marriage, had developed into an assured person of standing in the farming community. Had he entertained any thoughts of renewing his relationship with Maddie, Sir Wilkin's hopes were soon dashed when, without inviting him in and with a cold edge to her voice, she addressed him primly

"Good morning, Sir Wilkin. My husband is out in the fields. Can I help you?". Recognising that his natural charm would be lost on this new, matured, Maddie, he also adopted a formal, though disarming, tone.

"Well! Mrs Hanshott. Her Ladyship asked me to call in to thank you for your concern and help the other night. You will be pleased to know that there were no serious injuries and, apart from my daughter's mare, none of the horses suffered any ill effects........"

He tailed off, not knowing what else to say. Maddie regarded him icily. She did not believe for one instant that Lady Victoria had said anything of the kind. It was not in her Ladyship's nature to express gratitude to the peasants which, in her Ladyship's mind, included the whole of the local farming community. Least of all would she ask her husband to carry out such a task. Had she thought of such a gesture, she would have dispatched one of the servants to convey the message. In fact, Maddie was convinced that Lady Victoria knew nothing of the visit. She frostily, replied

"Please thank her Ladyship; but assure her we would have done no less for any of our neighbours at such a time. Well! If that is all? Good day to you, Sir Wilkin"

He had meant to ask her about her daughter. But, without waiting for him to say any more Maddie firmly closed the door; leaving him staring, mouth open, at that solid symbol of rejection.

When he returned to the Hall Sir Wilkin was in no mood to put up with the tantrums of his twelve year old daughter.

"It is about time you grew up and learned the facts of life, young lady! Delilah would not have survived and I did what had to be done to save her from a horribly painful death. You should really be at school not mooning around here causing trouble for everybody. After Christmas you start at your new school, Millchester; but, until then, you can go and stay with your grandmother at Selchester Towers. She has a way of handling recalcitrant young ladies like you"

He looked pointedly at his wife who had been raised at Selchester Towers under the watchful eye of a stern nanny and an equally severe mother, the Duchess of Selchester. Julia looked appealingly at her mother but saw no reprieve in her eyes.

"Your father is right, Julia. I shall telephone your grandmother today and make the arrangements. I expect she will agree to Nanny accompanying you"

She paused and looked at her husband. Receiving an almost imperceptible nod from him she continued

"While we are on the subject of your future I might as well tell you what our plans are for you when you leave school. It is important for you to learn how to behave in the manner demanded by your position in Society"

Julia peevishly pouted as she looked at her mother questioningly.

"Your father and I have discussed this and we have decided that you shall stay at Millchester until you are sixteen, after which you shall go to a finishing school for young ladies in Paris. Do not look so petulant. I did the same thing when I was your age and it is not so bad. It will give you a chance to make new friends of your own class"

The month or so at Selchester Towers did nothing to improve Julia's temper; nor could the teachers at Millchester do much to rectify her petulant character. Nevertheless, as Julia grew older, she learned to curb her arrogance and contempt for those less fortunate than herself. Although she was mixing with other young girls, many of whom were from a similar background and had developed the same autocratic temperament as herself, she gravitated to a girl with a completely different disposition to herself who was to become her best friend for life. It was the influence of Michelle d'Ellysee that changed Julia's character to the extent that she became a much more likeable person.

Michelle, who came from Rouen in Northern France, was the same age as Julia. Her background was similar to that of Julia but, conversely, she had a gentle, friendly, nature. Because it was a long way for her to travel home to France during half-term breaks it became the practice for Michelle to spend the short holidays with Julia at Frensham Hall. It was during one such break from Millchester that the Village veterinary surgeon, William Studding, happened to call at the Hall to tend one of the horses. The Vet's eldest son, also named William, had been home on leave, having recently been granted his commission in the Royal Engineers, and, before reporting to the Royal Engineers' base at Chatham, he was accompanying his father on his rounds that morning. The twenty two year old subaltern saw only two schoolgirls, looking pretty in

79

their summer dresses. But, to the girls, he was a dashing hero. This tall young officer in his smart new uniform, the belt buckle on his polished leather Sam Browne seemingly attempting to outshine the highly polished uniform buttons and the single brass pip on each shoulder flap, fascinated them. While his father was busy with the horses William chatted to the enchanted   young girls, who responded animatedly. Egged on by Michelle, Julia persuaded William to give her his address in Chatham and, when they returned to Millchester, the two girls, giggling together at night in the dorm, composed a joint letter which they posted with some misgivings. After all, it was not the sort of thing a young lady should do! But it was fun, was it not, they giggled; thus justifying their action.

If he had been asked, William could not have said *why* he answered the letter. Perhaps he was flattered to receive a letter from the daughter of Sir Wilkin. After all, he had been raised to look up to the gentry and he was aware of Lady Victoria's contempt for the lower classes. Whatever the reason, he *did* reply; and, addressing his remarks directly to Julia, told her all about his days in the Barracks at Chatham and the plans for him to join a regiment in India. Michelle was a little put out that William seemed more interested in Julia than herself, but she pocketed her pride and helped Julia to compose a reply.

Thus grew a regular exchange of correspondence as from one friend to another and Julia found herself looking forward to his, much too infrequent for her liking, letters. When William was posted to India Julia would watch for the postman, anxiously. His letters were full of news about the exotic sub-continent and his, exaggerated no doubt, exploits on the north-west frontier. Now and again he would enclose photographs of Indian scenes which she would proudly show around to her school friends; particularly those depicting William, looking every inch the dashing hero in his khaki drill uniform. Despite their pleas she refused to read out excerpts from his letters, letting the envious schoolgirls think they were too intimate; although the real reason for her reticence was that the letters contained no endearments at all. Michelle was aware of this but kept her own counsel; although she was still annoyed that William did not write to her.

April in Paris, 1937. The trees were in bloom along the Avenue des Champs Elysees and, although the storm clouds were gathering on

80

the political horizon, the customary air of gaiety was still to be seen in the fashionable spring dresses that brightened the boulevards and decorated the tables outside busy cafes. Hitler was flexing his muscles in Germany and sending his air force to help Franco in the desperate fighting that was going on in Spain. But, in Paris, the talk among the bourgeoisie was on more light-hearted matters such as the Spring collections and the self-imposed exile of the Duke of Windsor and his domicile with Mrs Simpson in France.

Julia Frensham sat with her friend, Michelle d'Ellysee, at a pavement table watching the world go by. They were both in their second year at the finishing school; but had escaped the eagle eyes of their mentors for the afternoon. They would probably find themselves in trouble, once more, when they returned but, for the present, they were enjoying these stolen moments to themselves. All the tables were occupied and they objected at first when the waiter asked if they minded sharing their table with another couple; but, seeing one of them was a well dressed, tall, good looking young man in his late twenties, Julia graciously waved them to sit in the other two chairs. The young man held the chair for his companion to sit down; then, straightening, he gave a slight bow to the girls and clicked his heels together before seating himself. With difficulty he addressed them in French, made worse by a guttural accent, and thanked them; also apologising for the intrusion. Usually rather aloof with strangers, it was surprising that Julia was the first to speak. She thought she recognised the man's origins and addressed him in fluent German, but with a slight English accent

"You and your companion are very welcome. Am I correct in assuming you come from Germany?"

It was clear that Michelle did not understand what Julia had said so the young man smiled and, in much better English than his French, asked Michelle if she understood him now. She nodded brightly for, though she came from Rouen, she had spent much of her childhood in England and spoke the language without a trace of accent. Having established a common language the young man continued in English by answering Julia's original question

"Actually we are Austrian and we come from Innsbruck. Permit me to introduce ourselves. My wife also speaks English. Her name is Eva and mine is Ernst Mittelburg. My wife is a nursing sister and I am a doctor; although neither of us is working at present"

There was a pause in the conversation while the waiter came over to take the order. Ernst asked if the girls would like to join them in another cup of coffee and they graciously accepted; leaving the way open for a continued conversation. It was a bit one-sided because neither Eva nor Michelle joined in, content to sit there listening to Ernst talking to Julia.

"We are, hopefully, on our way to England. We have been in Paris for two years trying to get permission to live in England. Now, for the first time, there is hope. We spent this morning at the British Embassy and, because we are both qualified medical practitioners, they think there will be no problems this time. Meanwhile, we are kicking our heels - is that the right expression? - in Paris until the Embassy receives approval from London. The problem is that we have no friends in England and, although I have enough money to set up in private practice, we do not know where to look"

Michelle exclaimed delightedly

"There, Julia, you can solve the problem in your village"

She turned to Ernst

"Julia lives in a village in the countryside of East Anglia. It is called Frensham Down. When I visited her home last summer we needed a doctor but the nearest one was about fifteen miles away"

Julia was not enthusiastic but she nodded her head as Ernst turned to his wife

"That could be the answer. Thank you, Mademoiselle. We shall certainly look into the possibilities there"

The conversation continued with small talk until Julia stood up, Ernst politely rising also.

"We must be getting back. I hope all goes well for you"

They shook hands, Ernst clicking his heels instinctively, and the girls walked away leaving the others to order another cup of coffee. It was not until they were out of sight that Ernst realised the girls had not given him their addresses. Which was just as well because Julia was berating her friend for telling them about Frensham Down.

"My mother will have a fit if they turn up at the Hall. You did realise Eva is a Jewess?"

Michelle stood back, appalled,

"So what! *I* don't have any prejudice against Jews and nor should you"

Julia took her friend's arm

"No! *I* don't, but my mother does. In fact, if she were in Germany she would probably be a Nazi!"
Michelle, with Julia's arm linked through hers, carried on walking but changed the subject.
"Have you heard from William lately?"
Julia stopped and fumbled in her handbag to draw out an envelope. It bore an Edward VIII stamp with India printed at the bottom and was date-stamped New Delhi. She took out two photographs and handed them to Michelle
""He *was* in Lahore but now he has been posted to Delhi"
The first photograph showed William, in tropical uniform with two pips on each of his shoulder epaulettes, relaxed and sitting on the ornamental wall of a huge stone basin into which cascaded water from an enormous fountain. Behind him rose the impressive British Government administrative buildings with their twin towers. The other photograph, taken from the opposite direction, showed William pointing down the long vista of public lawns, lakes and gardens to the Gate of India war memorial which straddled Kingsway a measured mile away. Michelle was impressed.
"It looks as though he has been promoted. Gosh! I would love to go to India one day"
Julia took the photographs back
"So would I"
She gave a little sigh as she replaced the photographs in the envelope.

CHAPTER FIVE

1934 - 1937

It was an early evening in October, 1934, three years before Ernst Mittelberg and his wife, Eva, met Julia Frensham and Michelle d'Ellysee in Paris, and the back streets of Munich were quiet. Lights were beginning to show in the windows of the dingy houses as darkness fell. The afternoon rally of Black shirts in the nearby park had broken up. The hated Brown shirts had been disbanded by Hitler earlier that year but many of these thugs had joined the Black shirts, as part time troopers, and small bands of these were wandering the streets of Munich looking for trouble. Ernst had chosen a back street route to avoid the wandering bands and he was walking slowly along with his fiance, Eva Goldschmit, on their way back to the hospital where they both worked; he as a doctor and she as a nursing sister in the English speaking Department. They turned into a cul-de-sac at the end of which a flight of stone steps led to another street and were about to ascend the steps when three youths, each with close cropped fair hair and wearing the Black shirt uniform with the sinister swastika armband, appeared at the top of the flight. By the light of a wall lantern Ernst recognised the leader who, though barely twenty himself, appeared to be older than the other two. It was Hans Kluger, an assistant porter at the hospital, and he was wearing the stripes of a Korporel. He frequently worked in Eva's ward and, although Ernst did not know Kluger well, he had always suspected him of being a bully. Ernst knew Eva resented the sullen way in which Kluger carried out her orders; and, more than once, Ernst had caught the youth eyeing her lasciviously when he knew she was not looking.

Now Kluger stood there arrogantly, with feet apart and hands grasping the waistband of his leather belt, obviously intending to look menacing. It was clear the Black shirts had no intention of moving aside so, not wanting a confrontation, Ernst grasped his fiance's arm and turned her round to retrace their footsteps. As he did so he found three more youthful Black shirts cutting off their retreat. He turned back to the leader

"Alright Kluger, we do not want any trouble. If you will kindly move aside we shall be on our way"

The Korporel stood his ground as he addressed Eva

"Well! well! If it isn't the Jewish whore from the hospital. You cannot order me around here can you, Miss Goldschmit?"

He spat the family name out sarcastically as though it were a dirty word. Ernst rose to her defence.

"Now Kluger! I shall overlook your rude remarks to Miss Goldschmit if you move out of the way"

The youth laughed, as he swaggered down the steps to confront Ernst, followed by the other two; while the three youths behind came up to form a rough circle round the pair. He continued to sneer as he looked up at Ernst

"Did you hear that, boys? So Mr high and mighty doctor here thinks he can protect his Jewish slut"

Ernst was at least four inches taller than any of them and considerably heavier. He attempted to push Kluger aside but the two thugs standing immediately behind him grasped his arms and held him. Another took hold of Eva's arms. Kluger leered at her. He turned to the youths holding Ernst

"Take him over by that wall and hold him tight. If you let him get away it will be the worse for you"

He reached out and dragged Eva's scarf from her neck and tossed it to the group.

"Here, take this and gag him"

Ernst struggled to break away but, despite his superior height and weight, he was no match for five of them. So he could do nothing when Kluger grabbed the protesting Eva and dragged her over to the shadows of a doorway opposite, pushing her hard against the closed door.

"'It will not be long before we have complete power in Germany and you Jews will all be rounded up and made to work for us, the true Aryans"

Ignoring her protests he was fondling her breasts while he hissed the words

"Any girl who is not bad looking will be sterilised so that she cannot produce any more Jewish bastards and will be sent to a brothel to be used by any true German who wants her. But where you are concerned I do not intend to wait for that day. I am going to have you now"

All the time he had been speaking he had continued to fondle her breasts and was breathing heavily into her face. Now he undid his trousers and let them fall to the ground as he reached down to lift her skirt.

"What is going on here?"

The Korporel, engrossed in his attempt to rape Eva, recognised the voice of authority, which was unmistakable, but he did not look round as he flung over his shoulder

"Mind your own business!"

The voice spoke again; this time addressing the Black shirts who were holding Ernst.

"Let that man go!"

At the order the youths restraining Ernst let him go and sprang to attention. Ernst ripped off the gag and rushed over to Eva; brushing the intruder aside. He grabbed Kluger, spun him round effortlessly, and raised his fist to strike him in the face. But, the Black shirt officer grabbed his arm and pulled him away. Meanwhile the Korporel, now realising that the voice belonged to his superior officer in the Black shirts, had sprung to attention. He looked ridiculous with his arm raised in a Nazi salute and his trousers sagging down to his boots; but there was no humour in the seriousness of the situation. Eva was sobbing as she straightened her clothing and joined Ernst, holding tightly onto his arm. Ignoring Eva, the officer addressed Kluger.

"Tidy yourself up, Korporel, collect your men and go straight to headquarters. I shall expect you to report to me there within ten minutes so you have no time to cause further trouble here. Now move!"

He offered no apology to Eva and ignored Ernst as he marched away up the steps; confident that the Korporel would obey his orders to the letter. Kluger had appeared to be subservient in the officer's presence and he collected his men together. But there was a malevolent gleam in his eyes as he turned to the, still sobbing, Eva and hissed.

"Do not go away, whore, I have not finished with you yet. I shall be back for you"

Kluger turned to the five youths with him

"You, Wilhelm, and you, Herman! Stay here and make sure these two don't get away. I shall be back soon and it will be the worse for you two if she is not here when I return"

He glared at Ernst

"And if you think she can escape me she cannot. Whereever she goes I shall find her and finish what I started tonight"

He marched the others off.

Ernst looked down at the two boys. Neither was more than seventeen and Ernst towered over them. Gently disengaging Eva's arm, he walked casually up to taller boy and, with his left hand, grabbed him by his belt. Pulling the scared youth toward him he slapped him hard on either side of his face.

"Now run along home to your mother, Sonny. You have finished playing soldiers for tonight"

The youth hesitated and looked at his companion who made no move to help him.

"Go on now, the pair of you, before I change my mind and beat you both to a pulp". The boy turned and ran; the other one tearing after him.

Ernst took the trembling Eva in his arms and tried to comfort her but only for a brief moment because he did not know when Hans might return with more bully boys. He urged her to move quickly.

"We must get away at once"

"What do you mean, Ernst. Away to where? The hospital?"

"I don't think that would be a good idea. But, even if we do go to the hospital, we must come out sometime to find Kluger and his thugs waiting. Its no use going to the police or the hospital authorities because neither is likely to lift a finger to protect you in the current political climate"

She looked up at him tearfully

"But I am scared, Ernst. That man is horrible! I never want to see him again! What can we do?"

"Well! I have been thinking for some time that we should leave Germany before things get too difficult for you. This incident has brought matters to a head. So, I think we should go now; while we still can"

"But *where* can we go?"

Ernst had already considered that question and was ready with the answer.

"I can take you home to your parents in Innsbruck. You will be safe in Austria; at least for the time being"

Eva brightened

"I would love to go home but what about our things at the hospital? And the money we have in the bank here. We can't the money out until the bank opens tomorrow"

"Forget our things at the hospital. Let us go straight to our lodgings. We can decide what to do about money on the way"

They were walking quickly along a main road, keeping a watchful eye open for any Black shirt bands, when Ernst hailed a roaming taxi. He ordered the driver to take them to the lodging house where they both had rooms. Paying off the driver he ushered Eva up the stairs to her room.

"Pack everything you can into no more than two cases and bring all your personal papers. Make sure you leave nothing behind by which they can trace you; like the address of your parents. Everything else you must sacrifice. It will be best if we don't stay here tonight because Kluger might know of this address. When I have packed my things I will knock on your door like this. We must sneak out without rousing attention. I will write a note to the landlord saying we have been called away suddenly on family business and will write him later to say when we shall be returning. I will enclose a month's rent for each of our rooms to give the impression we have not gone for good and leave the envelope on the hall table when we leave. That should delay any official enquiries about our abrupt departure"

Eva was happy to leave all the arrangements to her fiance, whom she trusted implicitly, but she wanted to know whether they were catching the night train from Munich.

"No! We shall stay at an hotel tonight and get a taxi to the bank first thing in the morning so that we can withdraw all our money as soon as the bank opens. We will take our bags with us in the taxi and go straight to the railway station from the bank. By noon tomorrow we should be in Innsbruck"

Eva was still frightened

"But what about Hans Kluger?"

"I do not think he is bright enough to outguess us but, even if he does, it is unlikely that he can do much on the station concourse in broad daylight. After all, the civil police are still in charge; although I wonder how long it will be before the Nazi Gestapo, will have overall power?"

They had chosen a hotel near the financial centre of the City and, checking out soon after breakfast, they took a taxi to the bank. It was just opening when they arrived and they lost no time in closing their accounts. Ernst asked if they could have the money in Austrian Schillings but the manager would allow only half to be paid in this way. There was nothing sinister in this. It was only, said the manager, that the bank did not like to part with such a large amount from their limited stock of foreign currency in one transaction and would they mind taking a bank draft in Austrian currency for the balance. Alternatively he could arrange for a transfer to an Austrian bank. However, Ernst decided it would be better to cut their tracks so, rather than disclose the name of a bank in Innsbruck, he accepted the draft made out in his own name. It would not be prudent to take a draft in the name of Goldschmit.

Ernst thought it safer to alight from the taxi in a street behind the station; but his precaution proved unnecessary because there was no sign of Kluger or his companions when they bought their tickets. The half hour wait for the train to leave seemed interminable but, eventually, the whistle blew and, billowing steam, the huge locomotive slowly hauled the train out of the station. Eva was still suffering from the shock of her ordeal and timidly tried to hide in the corner of the carriage behind the bulk of Ernst; but she relaxed once they had passed the border town of Kufstein and had entered Austrian territory. When they alighted at Innsbruck she was visibly relieved. She spread her arms wide and she cried to the hills around her

"Oh! How lovely it is to be home again!"

Eva did not tell her parents why they had returned to Innsbruck so suddenly. Her mother assumed they had planned to bring forward the date of the wedding so they decided to humour her. Ernst was in favour of the change

"It would be wise for us to get married as soon as possible. There is some anti-Semitic feeling in Austria, although it is not as bad as in Germany. Hitler has banned mixed marriages in Germany and mixed couples, married or not, are being arrested. We should get married here and make plans to leave for Switzerland as soon as possible"

It was not necessary for either of them to work, because the Goldschmit family were very wealthy. But Ernst insisted that he find a temporary post at a local hospital. Meanwhile, Eva and her mother spent the next month or so preparing for the wedding. So it was that Eva and Ernst were married at a civil ceremony in Innsbruck on the second of August, 1935.

Joseph Goldschmit, Eva's father, was a man of average height and build. He was born in 1879 and, not wishing to join his father in industry, chose to be an officer in the Austrian army. He was serving as a captain/adjutant with the Austrian Military Commission in Bosnia during the annexation of that Country by Austria in October, 1908, when he was injured in a road accident. At the military hospital he was tended by an attractive young nurse who was from Zurich and serving with the Swiss Red Cross. They fell in love and Joseph married Magda Zeiss when he was invalided out of the Army. The happy couple set up home in Innsbruck where their only daughter, Eva, was born in December, 1909. Joseph joined his father's firm and, when his father died, in 1912, he and his brother, Jan, continued to run the business and to build it up so that, when Jan was killed on the Western Front in 1917, Joseph had become a very wealthy man.

Attempts by Ernst to persuade Joseph and Magda Goldschmit to leave Austria with them fell on deaf ears. Joseph had considerable business interests in the country and he refused to believe that Nazi-ism would flourish in Austria.

"You must do what you think is best for you and Eva, but I think Magda and I will be quite safe here"

"But what if the Nazis take over Austria?"

"I doubt that they will bother me or my family. I have powerful friends in the Government and I am not a practising Jew"

"But aren't you concerned about Mrs Goldschmit's safety"

"No! She is Swiss born and she is not a Jew"

"That will not make any difference to the Nazis"

"Well! I appreciate your concern, Ernst, but I think I shall leave the matter for the time being and watch developments. If, as you think, Austria shows signs of becoming part of the Reich I will think again"

Despite his protestations, Joseph Goldschmit could not have been really as convinced of his safety as he led the world to believe because, while the happy couple were in Innsbruck, he began a process of converting his capital assets into cash and transferring the money to a bank in Zurich.

Ernst was not deterred by his father-in-law's arguments regarding Austria's independence from the Nazi threat and, refusing to take the risk of exposing his wife to any further humiliation, made plans to take her to Switzerland as soon as possible. With the help of Magda's sister, who lived the German quarter of Zurich and whose husband was a doctor, he obtained a post at a Swiss hospital and the couple moved to a house on a hill above Zeestrasse, looking out over the lake. Once the couple were settled in Switzerland Eva's father transferred a considerable part of his fortune to Eva's personal bank account in Zurich. When she protested he justified his action with

"You are my only daughter and the business will come to you one day, anyway, so you might as well have some of the money to use now when you most need it"

With typical male pride Ernst continued to work at the hospital. He did not resent his wife being wealthy, but he considered it was his duty to support her and any children that might come along in due course. When she pointed out that what was hers was also his he parried it with

"I am a doctor and my patients need me. Its nice to know we shall never want for money but I must keep practising medicine"

Eva did not share his moral sentiments about medicine and was content to run their home without the pressures of a hospital ward.

Nevertheless, despite his convictions, Ernst recognised the freedom presented by the fortune that Eva now controlled. They had been in Zurich for only a short time when Ernst suggested they move again. They both spoke French, albeit with a somewhat limited vocabulary, so found little difficulty communicating with hospital colleagues and patients; although social occasions spent with Eva's aunt and her husband encouraged them to keep company with German speaking acquaintances. Ernst did not believe Switzerland was in danger of Nazi domination, but there were enough Nazi sentiments expressed in the German quarter for him to feel uneasy. He suggested to Eva

"We should go to America or England. It is difficult for Austrians to enter America, but we could try both. What do you think?"

Eva was thoughtful for a moment

"Well! We both speak good English and I don't mind where we live so long as I am with you. I leave it to you, Ernst. Do whatever you think is best"

As Ernst had suspected, the American Consulate held out no hope. They were not, technically, political refugees so could not expect priority in a very long list of hopeful applicants. The British Consulate was equally un-cooperative, but a sympathetic official privately suggested they might stand more chance at the British Embassy in Paris. Taking his advice Ernst resigned his post in the

Zurich hospital and they moved to Paris. Ernst pestered the officials at the British Embassy for a year before they learned anything to their advantage. During the long wait Ernst was itching to get back to medical practice but could not commit himself to anything while they daily expected to receive permission to live in England. It was during this time that they, briefly, met Julia Frensham and Michelle d'Ellysee and thought of Frensham Down as a possible place to settle.

Ernst and Eva forgot about the casual meeting when, on returning to their hotel, they found a message requesting them to call at the British Embassy, without delay; and to ask for a Mr Wilton. It was still early afternoon so they took a taxi and, having reported to the Embassy reception, they were escorted to an office where Mr Wilton was waiting. He came straight to the point

"I have some good news for you, Herr Mittelburg. We have received word from London that your application for residency has been approved; on condition that you are prepared to become naturalised British subjects and continue to practice medicine"
Eva was sceptical

"What does 'naturalised' mean?"

"It means, in effect, that we would welcome you in the UK provided you renounce your Austrian citizenship and become British"
Ernst was proud of his Austrian background and asked

"Why is this condition necessary? There are no political differences between our Government and yours"
Mr Wilton, ever the polite diplomat, answered

"I do not make the rules. That is the condition for your entry into England as anything more than a temporary visitor; but I suggest, strongly, that you accept without delay. It is my opinion that you have been granted the concession because of your medical qualifications and I suspect the concession will not stay open for long"
Eva had remained quiet but now she asked another question

"Will we have to change our names?"
Mr Wilton smiled

"No! not if you do not want to, but you might consider it advisable. You both speak excellent English and you should merge easily into an English community without question regarding your origins. But the name Mittelburg will sound German to the English

93

ear and, in the present political climate there is unease among my countrymen regarding German nationals"

Eva protested

"But we are not German; we are Austrian"

"*You* know there is a difference and *I* know it too; but, to the average Englishman, Germans and Austrians are the same people and are regarded with the same suspicion"

Ernst thought for a moment then turned, questioningly, to Eva who shrugged her shoulders in resignation and nodded her approval. She took Ernst by the hand and squeezed it as he turned back to Mr Wilton.

"We understand the position and we accept. We have brought our papers with us. What is the procedure now and how soon can we leave?"

Mr Wilton pressed a button on his desk. His secretary knocked politely before entering the room. He told her to bring in the senior clerk. While they were waiting he rummaged amongst the papers on his desk and produced two large forms covered with neat entries.

"I hope you do not mind, Herr Mittelburg, but I took the liberty of having my secretary complete the forms for you from the information you supplied earlier. Perhaps you could read them through now to see that you agree the entries are correct?"

By the time they had completed reading, and had returned the forms to Mr Wilton, the secretary had re-entered the room accompanied by the senior clerk. Mr Wilton addressed Ernst and Eva in turn.

"Please place your index finger on the red seal and read the words on this card aloud in English so that the witnesses can hear and understand"

He waited until each had completed the formal declaration

"Now, kindly sign, here, and here"

The documents were then passed to the witnesses for their signatures. The two witnesses shook them by the hand, and wished them well, before leaving the room. Mr Wilton addressed the couple again

"That completes the formalities for your entry permit and short term residency, so far as you are concerned. But I need to retain your papers for a day or so to obtain the Ambassador's signature and to complete the procedure for issue of your entry permits"

In answer to the unasked question in Eva's eyes Mr Wilton said

"This does not make you British citizens so I cannot issue you with passports. You will enter Britain as Austrian citizens with visas which allow you to remain there for up to a limited period of time. You have agreed to apply for naturalisation and you must do this within a short time after you arrive. The documents you will receive with your visas will tell you how to do this. Since you appear to have ample private means I suggest you will find it more convenient to stay at an hotel in London while you apply for naturalisation. Because you intend to stay in Britain, as soon as you have settled in at your hotel, you must register without delay at a local police station and report there at regular intervals until your citizenship has been approved. If you fail to register, or fail to apply for naturalisation, your entry permit will be revoked and you must leave the Country immediately"

He stood up and came round the desk. He shook them both by the hand

"Welcome to Britain! I hope you will find happiness in our Country. If you come back to the Embassy at noon the day after tomorrow you will find your entry permits and papers waiting at Reception for your collection"

Mr Wilton produced two temporary identity cards which he asked each of them to sign in his presence.

"Take these with you for now. You will need to produce them the day after tomorrow as evidence of your identity when you sign for your papers at Reception. If you have any further problems while you are in France please feel free to contact the Embassy"

He shook hands again as he ushered them to the door of his office.

Ernst and Eva were busy on the day before they were due to pick up their documents. While Eva spent the day shopping and preparing for the trip, Ernst made arrangements for them to travel first class from Paris to London by train and ferry. He also booked accommodation, by telephone, at a good hotel in the West End of London. The next morning at noon he telephoned the Embassy to make sure the documents were awaiting collection; then they checked out and took a taxi to La Gare du Nord, calling at the Embassy on the way.

The trip was uneventful and they settled down in their London hotel while the formalities were being completed for naturalisation. To while away the time, as much as anything, they attended a local language school to perfect their accents. As soon as they had changed their names by deed poll to Ernest and Evelyn Middleton they moved, without leaving a forwarding address, to a small hotel in North London. They registered at the hotel in their new names, while they considered the future. Only two formalities remained. They opened a current account at a London bank in their joint names and Eva arranged for 80% of her funds in the Swiss bank to be transferred to their London account. The balance she left in the Swiss bank account to be available should she need to finance her father and mother if they fled to Switzerland. Ernst registered with the BMA as Dr. Ernest Middleton so that he could set up his own general practice in the United Kingdom. Eva wrote to her parents giving the name of the London bank for any reply. Some sixth sense warned her not to divulge their English names or their plans in England at this stage. Instead she arranged for the bank to place any letter addressed to Mittelberg in a fresh envelope and to address it to Mrs Middleton; then to retain it to await collection.

It was now mid-summer in 1937 and Eve was fed-up with waiting for developments in their hotel room. Ernest suggested a break from hot and dusty London.

"Let us go away for a few days. We can stay at a small hotel and explore the local countryside"

"That is a good idea. Why not try to find that place the two young girls in Paris mentioned? What was it called? Something like Frenchman Down? They said it was somewhere in East Anglia"
Ernest bought an ordnance survey map of East Anglia.

"This must be it! It is called Frensham Down and the nearest large town is Dunchester, which is about 20 miles from the village. It is not a very big place; but, if they still need a doctor, it could be ideal for us"

The few days they spent in Dunchester convinced Ernest he was right. A Dunchester solicitor, Philip Golding, who happened to live in Frensham Down, was a great help. He confirmed the need for a doctor in the village and, at Ernest's request, arranged for the purchase of a newly built, detached, bungalow on the Scolling Road at the corner of the Village Green. Ernest engaged a local builder to extend the property by adding a surgery and waiting room and, as soon as this was ready for occupation, he set up his practice there. Once they were settled in Eve wrote to her father giving him their new names and address so that her parents could find her if they escaped from Austria. Ernest added a postscript requesting Joseph not to pass this on to anyone else and to destroy the letter. Joseph Goldschmit carried out Ernest's request by burning the letter but, not trusting his memory, jotted down their English names and their Frensham Down address on a piece of paper, which he kept in his wallet; a mistake which was to have dire consequences in the future.

Sally Hanshott stood on a chair to change the date in the roller calendar which was held in a wooden box fixed to the post office wall behind the counter. It was Wednesday 8th September, 1937. Sally had been working there for a year and a half, ever since she left the secondary school at Chetsford at the age of fourteen. She was alone in the post office because Mrs Higgins, the sub-postmistress, had taken to her bed with a high temperature. Sally could not leave the place unattended until one o'clock, when the post office closed for the day, although she had locked the door for ten minutes to make a cup of tea for Mrs Higgins.

Sally climbed down from the chair and returned to her sear behind the counter, where she continued to browse through the glossy magazine Mrs Higgins had just received. It was a new publication called 'Woman' and this was the first issue. Sally thought it expensive at 2d a copy. She only earned eight shillings a week and, by the time she had given five shillings to her mother her pocket money did not go far; certainly not far enough to waste 2d a week on a magazine. Reg insisted it was good for her character that Sally should feel she was helping with the household expenses. He said to Maddie

"If you do not need it for the housekeeping, save it for her future". So Maddie did just that and, unbeknown to Sally, a nice little sum was growing in the biscuit tin box, marked SALLY, which lay hidden in Maddie's bedroom.

It was early closing day and Sally would have the afternoon off. She looked wryly through the window at the rain sweeping across the Village Green; thinking she would get wet on the way home. On the other hand, she did not see how she could leave Mrs Higgins alone in her present state of health; but she would think about that when the doctor had been.

Doreen Higgins was a war widow. Her husband, Joseph, was sub-postmaster at Frensham Down when she married him at the tender age of sixteen and came to live at the post office. When he joined the army, in 1916, a temporary sub-postmistress was appointed in his place; but she did not 'live in' and Doreen remained there as caretaker/assistant in the post office. She was too young, at seventeen, to take over when they learned that Pte Higgins had been killed at Ypres, in 1917; but the sympathetic authorities allowed Doreen to stay there, with the temporary sub-postmistress in charge, until she was old enough to run the small post office alone. She had no children and, after many years of loneliness, Doreen employed young Sally to assist her in the Post Office she treated the girl like a daughter. Doreen encouraged Sally to improve her education and, accompanying her to the library in School Lane, introduced her to a world of literature she would probably never have discovered without her employer's guidance.

Sally looked up as the doctor opened the door, causing the small warning bell to ring on its spring. He entered, carrying his medical bag and a large black umbrella. He held the open umbrella outside while he shook off the surplus water; then closing it, he deposited it in the stand by the door before looking across at Sally. His beaming smile lit up the dull room

"Hello Sally! Not a very nice morning! I never expect rain at this time of year and it usually catches me unawares. It is only 100 yards from the surgery and I would have come out without the umbrella if Eve had not thrust it in my hand as I was leaving"

Sally liked Doctor Ernest Middleton. He was in his late twenties, tall and well built. The long face, with its neatly trimmed moustache, reminded her of William Powell, her screen idol; except that Doctor Middleton had fair hair. He was always charming and considerate with his patients and Sally felt at ease with him. His wife, Evelyn, was very nice too. She was a little younger than the doctor and she had dark hair which she wore in a bob. Since they opened the Practice a couple of months ago Eve Middleton had become involved with the other village wives in all the communal activities and was popular with everyone; her pleasant manner breaking down the guarded reserve with which English country folk usually treat strangers. Sally thought she noticed a slight accent in their speech but, although she was familiar with the many different accents in East Anglia, she could not place it; she assumed they were from somewhere in the west country. Sally came round from behind the grill to undo the catch and lift the hinged section of the counter and open the small door beneath; allowing the doctor through. He thanked her.

"There is no need for you to come up, Sally. I know the way and I am sure you should not leave the post office unattended"

Although the villagers tended to address him, formally, as 'Doctor', Ernest Middleton had formed a habit of addressing his patients among the villagers by their Christian names. He looked down at Mrs Higgins, after examining her,

"It is only an autumn chill, Doreen; but I think you should stay in bed for a couple of days until your temperature comes down. Take these two tablets with water and you will feel more comfortable. I will ask young Sally to pop along to the surgery when she closes downstairs to pick up a bottle of medicine for you. It will help you sleep and reduce your temperature. I will call again on Friday but I shall expect to see you much better by then. It would be best if you could eat something. I shall have a word with Sally before I go"

Sally attached a note to the window pane in the Post Office door 'Back in 10 minutes' and locked the door. She found a packet of soup in the larder and made it up in a bowl. With the soup on a tray, accompanied by bread and butter, she climbed the stairs to Doreen Higgins' bedroom.

"The doctor says you are to eat this all up and that, except when I go to collect your medicine, I am not to leave you alone in the house. So I have telephoned my mother and she says I can stay here tonight. Is it alright if I sleep in the spare bedroom?"
Mrs Higgins smiled her gratitude

""Of course, dear. It is very nice of you to take care of me. But it is your afternoon off today? I know! You can have the whole day off next Wednesday to make up for it. How is that?"

Actually, Sally did not mind. There was not much she could do on a wet afternoon and she would only be kicking her heels in the farm kitchen; that is, of course, unless she contrived to run into Mike Grey from Church Farm. He worked at the farm, which was on the other side of the Scolling Road, right opposite the Village Green. He, also, had Wednesday afternoon off. It was an odd co-incidence that Michael always seemed to want a postage stamp just on closing time on Wednesday, or he would be hanging around at the top of the Green when she came out. She looked up at the clock. The hour hand stood at one and he had not come in. She consoled herself with the thought that the rain was keeping him away. Never mind, she would be going up to the surgery for the medicine in a minute and who knows...?

Mike was standing under the bus shelter, wearing a raincoat, when Sally came out of the surgery. He walked over to her.

"Well! Hello Mike! Fancy seeing you here"

Sally was feeling playful

"If you are waiting for a bus there isn't one until four o'clock"

He looked at her with concern on his face

"Are you ill, Sally?"

She laughed

"No, it's not me. I have just been to the surgery to collect some medicine for Mrs Higgins"

He kissed her on the cheek and took her hand

"Can I walk you home?"

Sally teased him

"Of course, but its only a few yards. I am staying with Mrs Higgins tonight. She is alright but the doctor says she must not be left alone"

They were standing outside the post office door which Sally was about to open. She pushed him back

"No, you can't come in. Mrs Higgins would not like it"

Mike squeezed her hand

"Why? Don't you trust me?"

Sally was adamant

"It is not a question of whether or not I trust you, and I am not so sure that I do, but my mother doesn't and she would go mad if she found out I had let myself be alone with you in there"

Mike put on a mock crestfallen expression and she almost relented; but, instead, she compromised

"Tell you what! It has stopped raining, so you go and sit on that seat over there and, after I have seen to Mrs Higgins, I will come and join you".

They were sitting on the bench under one of the shelters that dotted the Green, holding hands, and looking across the Green at nothing in particular. To tell the truth there was not much to see.

The tea room in Primrose cottage had closed for the winter so there was no sign of the cyclists and hikers who would be hanging around there in the Summer months. The war memorial looked stark in the clear post-rain air. Perhaps the thought 'lest we forget', as was engraved in the granite, should be in the air; but the young pair had seen the stone obelisk there all their lives and they had no memories of the war to forget so they ignored it. Absorbed only in each other, their concern was for the present not the past and who could say what the future had in store for them.

CHAPTER SIX

1938

During the Spring of 1938 the Nazi party strengthened its grip in Germany and occupied Austria. The British Government, sensing approaching hostilities, had taken the unprecedented step of planning to issue free air raid shelters to every home in London and were drawing up plans to evacuate mothers and children from London into the countryside immediately on the outbreak of the war they hoped to avoid. The war drums were beating in Europe for those not too deaf to hear. As the Spring gave way to Summer, the English public at large chose to ignore the warnings as, during that long hot summer, they carried on as though all was right with the world. Len Hutton beat Don Bradman's record with a 364 innings at the Oval; the beaches were thronged with holidaymakers and the London parks were crowded with office workers seeking a tan during their lunch breaks. In common with the national lethargy, the villagers of Frensham Down carried on as usual whilst the Primrose Tea Gardens did a roaring trade as the trend for keeping fit brought passing cycle clubs and hikers to the Village.

It was a hot Sunday afternoon in August, 1938. As in so many English villages nothing much stirred in Frensham Down. The two youths by the bridge could just hear the rippling of the water as the Scolling Brook flowed over the gravel bed further upstream but here, below the bridge, the water was deeper and it flowed smoothly and quietly beneath the single stone arch. A duck, quacking agitatedly, paddled quickly out to rescue one small struggling brown duckling that had been caught in the mainstream and was in danger of being swept away. She fussily nudged her offspring to join the rest of her brood among the rushes by the bank, while her mate placidly watched and occasionally up-ended his tail as he dipped deep into the water to catch a passing morsel of food.

They leaned their bare forearms on the stone parapet, idly watching the ducks. Michael Grey sighed and, turning to face the road, heaved himself up to sit on the parapet. He looked at the indentations made by the rough stone in his arms and rubbed them as he muttered, almost to himself

"I am bored!"

Oliver Twist did not answer. Mike looked up the road in the direction of Scolling but the road was empty for as far as he could see. A green painted box hand trailer had been hauled onto the grass verge. The letters on the side, DRDC, showed it to be the locked toolbox left for the weekend by road workmen from Dunchester Rural District Council who had been patching the road. The heat of the sun had moistened the tar in the repair work causing a shimmering heat haze to hover over the road surface. Michael turned his head to look in the other direction towards the Village Green. The road sloped downward and there was no heat haze, but the Scolling Road was equally empty in that direction of both traffic and people.

"I am bored!"

Oliver had joined Mike sitting on the parapet. Mike punched Oliver playfully in the arm.

"I just said that"

"Well! I am. And this place is dead. I wish we could go into Dunchester"

Mike was idly watching a crow pecking energetically at something in the road

"There is nothing much open there either; and, in any case, how would we get there? There is no bus today and no trains stop at Frensham Halt on a Sunday"

Oliver looked down towards The Bowman, the inn that stood opposite Church Road and next to the garage where he lived.

"There is always the pub but it doesn't open until seven o'clock on Sunday evening"

Mike shrugged

"They wouldn't let me in anyway. Angus McKuy knows I am under age"

They sat quietly for a while, each wrapped in his own thoughts. The silence was broken by the sound of singing in the distance. It was carried on the still air from St James church on the hill above the village. Oliver looked towards the sound

"That will be the christening service for Amy Golding's baby, June"

Mike grinned as he chided his friend.

"You should be there, shouldn't you? We are sitting right next to Brook House and you wouldn't like Philip Golding to catch you here when they return from the church"

"It wouldn't matter. I know he is my Boss when I am in the Dunchester office but my time off is my own"

"You are not usually so brave! You weren't invited, were you?" Oliver pretended to ignore him and Mike changed the subject."

"The bells give me an idea. We could go to church this evening?" Oliver was not enthusiastic, to say the least,

"What? and sit with all those old biddies chanting and singing? Do me a favour!". Mike looked at him, a wistful expression on his face.

"Church bells remind me of Sally Hanshott. I once followed her when she was with her mother on the way to evensong and sat beside her. We held hands until her mother said something to her and she let go"

Oliver shrugged

""You and your Sally. Don't you ever think of anyone else? I prefer her friend Jean Stokes; she has more meat on her. Does Sally still work at the post office?"

Mike nodded, subdued for a moment by his friend's remarks. Oliver jumped down and turned back to lean on the wall to watch the ducks again. They had settled back into the nest among the reeds and, apart from the bright colours of a dragonfly flitting over the surface, there was nothing of interest to see. Mike was still sitting on the wall day-dreaming about Sally. Her two younger brothers had the dark hair and heavy looks of their father, Reg Hanshott, but Sally had inherited her mother's slim figure, pretty face and long fair hair; but with a touch of auburn which made her stand out. There was something about that auburn touch in her hair......? But the thought eluded him.

Oliver resumed his seat on the parapet.

"You got any money, Mike?"

Mike fumbled in the pocket of his shapeless grey flannels. A none too clean handkerchief dragged out a sixpence which fell and rolled into the road. He looked in his palm to see a two florins, one shilling and four pennies.

"Five and four, that's all!"

He jumped down to retrieve the sixpence in the road

"Five and ten pence"

Oliver brightened up.

"That is enough to buy us a cream tea at Primrose Cottage"

Mike looked at him in disbelief

"Come off it!. This has to last me the week. You earn more than I do. Why should I buy *you* anything? Haven't you got any money of your own?"

Oliver shrugged his shoulders and grinned at his friend

"Actually, I have about six shillings, but I have got to pay my bus fare to work and back out of that, so I am worse off than you are. Still! It was worth a try. Let us go down there anyway! Perhaps the Miss Henshaws will treat us. After all, they owe me a favour for cutting their grass last week"

Oliver was about 5ft 9ins tall and four months older than, the slightly shorter, Mike. He was lean and looked smart in the latest style of grey gabardine slacks, which he had bought with the 10 shillings, his father (Garage owner, James Twist) had given him last September on his 18th birthday. Actually, his given name was David, but everyone, except his mother, called him Oliver; a sobriquet which he picked up early in his schooldays and which had followed him ever since. He had matriculated at the grammar school in Dunchester but his father could not afford to send him to university so he was working in the Dunchester office of Mr Golding, the solicitor, who lived at Brook House on the Scolling Road. Oliver had plans for his future and to this end was studying law books in his spare time.

Mike's father was Thomas Grey, the tenant farmer at Church Farm. Mike was intelligent but did not have the educational advantages of his friend. They had both attended the village school but Mike had received little encouragement to study from his father. The result was that, whereas Oliver had passed the scholarship examination and had gone on to the grammar school at Dunchester, Mike had failed the exam and been sent to the secondary school at Chetsford. It was there that he came to know Sally Hanshott. She was a year behind him in the school but she looked up to him as her protector and always contrived to be in the same carriage on the train between Frensham Halt and Chetsford. When Mike left school, at the age of fourteen, and began work on the farm with his father, he put young Sally from his mind; or so he thought. 'After all she is only a silly schoolgirl' he said to himself. But his interest was re-kindled when he saw her, now grown into a pretty teenager, working at the post office counter. Compared with Oliver he had little to offer her. He received a minimal weekly wage, as pocket money, from his father and relied on his mother, Anne, to buy his austere clothing on weekly credit from a mail order book. Mike sighed and decided not to think of the future as he climbed off the wall to follow Oliver who was already strolling along the Scolling Road towards the Village Green.

They jumped, hastily, onto the grass verge as the triple call of a bugle horn sounded behind them. Turning, they saw a white open-topped Bentley Tourer bearing down on them. The driver, a young man of around twenty-two years, would not have looked out of place on the playing fields of Harrow; dressed, as he was, in a fashionable ribboned coat with a silk scarf streaming behind him. His short fair hair was uncovered but one could imagine him, in a straw boater, cheering his college boat on the home stretch at Henley. His passenger was a teenage girl with long auburn hair which was blowing in the wind behind her, despite the restraining flowered headband she wore. She had attractive, aristocratic, features which broke into an easy smile when she saw the boys. She raised a slim bronzed arm to wave to them as the car swept by.

"Who was that?"

Mike turned with a surprised look to Oliver who replied

"I don't know the chap but the girl is Julie Frensham"

Recollection dawned as Mike commented

"I haven't seen her in the village since she went away to boarding school"

"Nor had I until I met her outside the station in Dunchester last week. She looked familiar but she obviously did not remember me. When she asked where she could get a taxi to Frensham Down I introduced myself and she told me who she was. Apparently she has been away at finishing school in Paris and she said, with her nose in the air, that she was on 'la vacance d'ete'. When I replied in my limited French she became less reserved and offered me a lift back to Frensham Down in the taxi. That is how I know who she is. But you do not stand a chance with her! She is a stuck up little madam!". Mike shrugged

"I am not interested anyway. It is Sally for me and she is not the least bit stuck up"

They watched the Bentley slow at the corner and disappear into Hanshott Lane. A little later they heard the driver accelerate as he reached the hill. This triggered off a thought for Mike

"It is early yet, let us stroll up Hanshott Lane"

Oliver smirked

"So you are not interested in Julie Frensham?"

Mike was affronted

"No! I was hoping I might see Sally"

"Not much chance of that; but, OK, if that is what you want to do"

The Smithy on the right was quiet as they entered Hanshott Lane. The sun was still high and the oak tree cast a short shadow on an empty yard. On the left hand corner of the lane the police bungalow was recognised by the official notice board by the gate. Constable Bell, in uniform trousers and light blue shirt, with sleeves rolled up, looked up from his lawn mower and eyed them, speculatively, as they passed. Feeling unaccountably guilty for being idle the boys increased their step.

The strip of grass fronting the ancient tiled almshouses on their left, as they passed, was maintained by old Pat Crannock, who was employed by the Parish Council as the public hedger and ditcher. With the dry weather the grass had not grown much and Pat had left it for the past two weeks. As a result it was a mass of daisies, dandelions and buttercups lifting their bright flowers to the sun and the bees; unaware that Pat would shortly be along, with his old 14 inch mower, to cut off their heads. Opposite the almshouses was a row of white-walled, thatched, farm cottages; fronted by high hedges bright with white and green convolvulus bells and pink dog roses, which hid the fact that the front gardens were given over, mainly, to the growing of vegetables.

The boys slowed their pace when they reached the fairly steep hill where the Bentley had accelerated. Here, the hard roadway surface gave way to a narrow tar and gravel track with passing places at intervals. It was kept in good condition by Reg Hanshott to support the constant stream of farm vehicles which traversed Hanshott Lane on weekdays. Today it was empty. The passing of the Bentley had left a faint smell of burnt petrol which was at odds with the natural fragrance of the blackberry bushes. These, with the small clusters of white fruiting flowers intermingled with pale pink dog roses, hung over the buttercups and nettles which lined the ditches by the sides of the lane.

Unlike most of the farm workers Len Mundy, foreman at

Hanshott Farm, grew his vegetables at the back and kept a pretty garden of country flowers in neat beds at the front of his cottage. He was trimming the low front hedge in the old fashioned way with a stick and sickle as the boys approached.

"Hello! Len. Nice day!"

Len looked surprised to see them but a grin spread over his brown weather beaten face as he offered a welcome

"Mike, Oliver - What be you two doin' up 'ere?"

Oliver looked innocent but Mike blushed

"Just out for a stroll. Nothing else to do"

Len's grin widened

"No you b'aint"

He looked pointedly at Mike

"You be looking out for young Sally. You'm better not let the Mistress see you. She will take 'er broomstick to your backside"

Oliver raised his eyebrows in query as he looked at Mike

"Why, what have you been up to?"

Mike was defensive

"Nothing! I wouldn't harm Sally for the world"

For a moment Len looked speculatively at Mike as though he was wondering whether he should continue.

"I b'aint sayin' as 'e 'as been up to anythin' and I b'aint sayin' 'e aint. But anyway, good luck to you, son, if 'n that's what she wants. I only wish 'appiness for the lass an' that goes for me missus too, I be sure. But don't let 'er Mum catch you. I reckon she don't trust you. She knows what you young country lads is like when you gets an innocent young girl alone and she b'aint far wrong to my way o 'thinkin'"

Having stopped work and always ready for a chat, Len put down his sickle and stick. Then he lit his pipe as they all crossed over to lean on the five barred gate looking across the newly mown field. Oliver sniffed

"I love the smell of new mown hay"

Mike looked at Len and commented

"So you got the hay in early this year. My Dad will be pleased to know that. He relies on Hanshott farm to keep him in winter fodder"

"Yes, Mike, it is all bundled up and stowed in the Dutch barn away from the weather"

Oliver asked "Did you get many rabbits?"

Len was filling his pipe and he waited until he had lit it before answering. He blew a cloud of aromatic smoke out across the field

"Bruce 'ere........."

He looked down at the mongrel dog, which had followed them across the lane and was lying on the grass verge beside him. The dog wagged its tail and lifted its head at the mention of its name. Len bent down to pat him and repeated the dog's name

"Bruce. 'e caught three and Joe brought down four with 'is gun. That'll be good for a few stews an' pies when they'm finished 'anging!"

Len Mundy blew another cloud of smoke and seemed content to remain silent while he leaned on the five barred gate. Mike was next to him with one foot on the bottom bar. His thoughts were on Sally and he did not want to share them with his companions. Oliver climbed up on the gate and sat on the top bar; facing the lane and supporting himself with his hand on the hinge post. A distant drone caused them to look up.

"Over there. Can you see it?"

Oliver pointed with his free hand towards the ruins of Benley Castle. The others turned round and, leaning against the gate, shaded their eyes as they scanned the clear blue sky above the trees in the direction of Castle Hill. It was too far away for them to distinguish the RAF roundels on the bi-plane which appeared in the distance and, by the time they had identified it as an RAF fighter, they saw the second bi-plane following about a mile behind. As they idly watched the planes Oliver turned to Len Mundy

"Do you think there will be a war, Len?"

Again Len puffed out a cloud of smoke from his pipe before he answered

"Dunno! But I bin readin' the papers and listenin' to the wireless. It don't look too good! I reckon that there 'itler b'aint gonna be satisfied now 'es got the Rhineland and Austria without a fight. Mark my words it will be Czechoslovakia next and there aint gonna be no stopping 'im after that if we don't step in and teach them Germans another lesson like we did last time"

Oliver was still watching the bi-planes carrying out mock attacks on each other

"Can you see Hitler taking us seriously when the RAF relies on planes like that?"

Len was defensive

"They was good enough to do the job for the RFC and RAF in the last war"

Mike interposed

"Yes, but this is different. I saw a news reel at the Pictures showing the weapons the Nazis had when they moved into Austria and their planes in action over Madrid. If we threaten them with weapons from the last war they will just laugh at us"

Len was not to be deterred. He defended his corner

"Well, at least we beat the Germans 6 - 3 at football last May so we've got the spirit if not the weapons. I b'aint gonna worry too much 'bout it! Anthony Eden an' Winston Churchill are war-mongerin' an' badgerin' the Government but good ol' Neville Chamberlain won't let us get into a war. In any case, they won't want me! I am too old and I'm needed on the farm. I'll leave you young'ns to worry. It's gonna be your problem!"

They fell silent, each lost in his own thoughts, as they watched the planes soar and swoop high up above the ruins of Benley Castle. Oliver broke the silence by changing the subject

"Did you see that advertisement in the window of Cook's Tours office in Dunchester? They are offering an eight day holiday on the French Riviera for £8.17.6; including return fare"

Mike laughed

"There is your chance, Oliver. You can polish up on your French and impress Julie Frensham"

Oliver scoffed

"Whose got eight quid odd to spare? That is more than a month's wages and I have already had my two weeks' holiday for this year. Mr Golding would have a fit if I asked for an extra week"

Len had not been paying much attention to the banter but he looked up on hearing the Frenshams mentioned.

"Wouldn't 'ave nothin' to do with them Frenshams if I was you, lad. They'm a stuck up lot. Particularly that Julie!. Went past 'ere in a bloody great car just before you come along. Nose in the air! Stuck up little cow!"

Oliver grinned

"That's what I told him"

There was a sudden stuttering noise in the air. Len looked up, startled.

"One of them's firin' 'is guns"

Mike reassured him

111

"No he isn't, but he *is* in trouble. That is his engine about to cut out"

The aircraft in difficulties was near the top of a loop when its engine cut out. The plane side-slipped into a `falling leaf` spiral towards the earth. They could hear the pilot frantically trying to re-start the engine which spluttered and sprang into life just in time for him to level out and lift the plane over Frensham Hall. The engine cut out again, but the pilot now had the plane under control, and the boys and man at the gate watched as the powerless bi-plane glided down to bounce along the rough stubble in the field and tip up, its propeller snapping as it churned up the hay stalks in a cloud of dust, before burying its nose in the hedge.

For a moment they remained where they were, in stunned silence. Then, without a word, they hastily climbed over the five barred gate and ran towards the wrecked machine. Bruce, the dog, tried to climb through the bars to follow but gave up and ran along the hedge until he found a hole through which he scrambled then ran at full speed to catch up with his master.

The pilot, a young man of about twenty-five years, climbed out of the cockpit. Oliver was the first to reach him.

"You alright?"

A little shaken, and somewhat embarrassed, though otherwise unruffled, the pilot took off his goggles and leather flying helmet

"Oh yes! Just a bit of a prang. Nothing to worry about"

The drawled, almost bored, Oxford accent was not lost on Len, who instinctively felt he was expected to touch his forelock (had he had one) to this aristocratic stranger. Len had little respect for the gentry and his first impulse was to walk away and let the stuck up b....d get on with it; but he just stood there silently watching. Oliver, who was displaying the usual interest of a young man for the aircraft, looked back at the pilot.

"Last war, job?"

The pilot turned to him

"No! It is a Gloster Gladiator. Only came into service last year"

He looked up at the other plane which was circling low over the field

"So is that"

He took off his white silk neckerchief and waved it

"Just to let Jerry know I am OK"

The pilot of the other plane waggled its wings in acknowledgement and flew off. The crashed pilot continued

"It is not a bad machine. Easy to fly, but bi-planes will soon disappear if a war comes. Monoplanes are faster and more manoeuvrable"

Mike, who was not particularly interested in aircraft, became aware that people were running over from the farmhouse but he only had eyes for Sally. She had been sunbathing and he thought she looked wonderful in a pair of longish white shorts and a loose floral-patterned blouse which she was hastily buttoning up as she ran. Mike was relieved to see Maddie Hanshott was not in the group. Reg Hanshott was there but he took no notice when Sally sidled up to Mike and silently took his hand. For a moment they watched the pilot busying himself with the airplane. Then Sally quietly whispered

"It is Jean's eighteenth birthday today and my Mum says I can cycle down to the General Store to spend the rest of the afternoon and the evening with her. I reckon I should be there in about an hour's time"

Mike smiled at her

"What a happy coincidence. Oliver and I were just going down to have a cream tea in the Primrose Tea Garden"

Oliver, who had heard Mike's comment, looked across at him

"Were we, then? I thought you were broke"

Sally flashed Oliver a quick smile but otherwise ignored him as she assumed a conspiratorial expression and dropped her voice

"You go down to the tea garden, Mike, and we'll come over and join you. Are you sure Oliver won't mind?"

Mike looked across at Oliver, who was now out of earshot looking over the crashed plane.

"No! He likes Jean"

She relinquished Mike's hand and started back towards the farm.

Constable Richard Bell, looking officious, now joined the group near the plane. No amount of urgency would discourage him from his duty to represent the law properly dressed. Before toiling up the hill, wheeling the official police bicycle, he had changed his shirt and dressed in his full uniform which was, despite the heat of the day, buttoned up to the neck in proper regulation fashion. Only in his mid-thirties, but overweight from lack of exercise, the constable was breathing heavily and perspiring freely after his long climb. His face was florid but he did not remove his helmet

"Now, then, what have we here?"

In the circumstances it seemed a rhetorical question, so no-one answered. As he took out his notebook and pencil, the constable addressed the pilot

"You cannot land a plane in a field here without official permission. What is your name and rank? Where do you come from?"

The pilot broke off his resumed conversation with Oliver and gave the policeman a long suffering look. He raised his eyes to the sky momentarily, then winked at Mike. His drawled answer was clearly intended to entertain the onlookers and to discomfort officialdom

"I am afraid, constable (that *is* your rank, is it not?), you seem to have misunderstood the situation. I have obviously landed here, as you succinctly put it, so it is not practical for you to point out that I *can't* land in this field. I have just proved to you that I *can!* Nevertheless, be that as it may, any fool can see that I have crashed my aircraft in the field and I assure you that was never my intention. You ask for my name and rank? I am Flying Officer William Lavington of the Royal Air Force. That is, Lord Lavington to you"

He paused and looked at the assembly, as though he expected everybody to bow. Richard Bell was busy writing in his note-book and did not seem to be either ruffled or impressed. The pilot continued in the same high-handed tone

"Is that sufficient identification for you, constable? As for where I come from, as you crudely put it. If you mean to ask where I am stationed, that is currently a security matter which I am not at liberty to divulge"

The arrogance of the pilot was not lost on the rest of the onlookers, none of whom represented the gentry, but who held respect for law and order as embodied in their village constable. Embarrassed by the pilot's irritable outburst Oliver and Mike, somewhat disillusioned, turned away and, joined by Len Mundy, made their way back to the gate. The others were also leaving when the pilot, finding himself being deserted except for the constable and addressing no-one in particular, spoke again

"I need a telephone!"

He looked across at the telegraph poles leading to Hanshott farm. But Reg Hanshott, who had also turned away, was not prepared to accommodate him, simply flung over his shoulder.

114

"You will find a public call box outside the post office down in the village. You look quite capable of walking a couple of miles. If you ask him nicely the constable might point you in that direction"

As they walked back to the gate Len turned to Mike "If that is a sample of our gallant air force God help us, if a war breaks out" Oliver asked
"Do you mean the plane or the pilot?"
"Both!"

"Ouch!". Sir Wilkin Frensham rubbed his forefinger briskly to alleviate the sharp pain of the rose thorn. He turned, irritably, to his wife, who was collecting blooms from her rose garden nearby,
"Damn your roses"
Lady Victoria Frensham did not look up
"You should wear gloves like I do when you are gardening"
Sir Wilkin snorted
"I am only doing some weeding to give my dahlias and chrysanthemums a chance. Shouldn't need gloves for that. If Fullitt took more care in pruning your roses he would not leave thorns in my flower beds. I shall have a word with him next time I see him!"
They were pottering among the neat beds alongside the lawn that fronted Frensham Hall. A wide gravel driveway separated the lawn from the imposing facade of the magnificent Elizabethan building. Sir Wilkin grew dahlias and chrysanthemums as a hobby. He kept part of the extensive greenhouses in the grounds of Frensham Hall as his own domain for developing the plants which produced blooms of such quality that they regularly took first prize at the village flower show and, more important to his pride, at the County Show each year. He left the rest of the greenhouse and grounds to the care of the full time gardener, Ken Fullitt, and 15 year old Jeremy Styles, from Crannock's farm, who was employed at the Hall to help Fullitt and to do odd jobs for the cook.
Sir Wilkin heaved himself up from his kneeling position. He rubbed his finger once more, brushed the loose dirt off his fawn corduroy trousers and removed the frayed old wide-brimmed straw hat to mop his brow with a clean white handkerchief. He looked across to his wife, who had finished her chore and, having placed the trough with the blooms in it on the ground for a servant to collect, was lounging in a deck chair on the lawn.

In his 49th year Sir Wilkin was showing the usual signs of middle age. He had retained his handsome features and the auburn hair, that had so enhanced his looks in his youth, was darker, thinner and streaked with grey at the temples. His once trim figure had put on some weight and he would find it impossible to squeeze into the smart RAF uniform which he had last worn at the Memorial Dance in Frensham village hall in July, 1921. He looked across at his reposing wife and regarded her angular features thoughtfully. He had never considered her to be a beautiful woman but she had held some feminine attraction for him in her slim figure; which was still lean but beginning to broaden at the hips. Lady Frensham was aware of her advancing years and she constantly watched in her mirror for tell-tale grey hairs which appeared all too frequently. Sir Wilkin was unaware of the latter because his wife discreetly gave her hair a regular rinse of her natural dark brown colour to retain the illusion of youth.

In common with the practice among the aristocracy of the day Wilkin Frensham's marriage to Lady Victoria Lavington had been an arrangement between two Society mothers and a marriage between two titled families; little account being accorded to the feelings of the main participants. When Wilkin married Victoria he sought no more from her than was to be expected from a dutiful wife. She, in turn, was prepared to accept her fate, think of England, and do her duty; which she found not unpleasant with the handsome war hero she had managed to capture. Wilkin had resigned himself to frigidity in a girl of her background and then was surprised by Victoria's passion on their wedding night. Years of repression in a girls' boarding school during her formative years had only served to make her pine for an outward expression of her suppressed natural instincts. In Wilkin she found a physical attraction beyond her dreams and she responded to him with an ardency that surprised and delighted him. Over the years she had never ceased to amaze him with her competence in most things she did. He had to admit he could not have found a finer wife.

Dropping the trowel he had been using, Sir Wilkin walked over and sat down in the other deck chair next to his wife. "It is hot today" he muttered, but Lady Victoria had her eyes shut under her floppy white linen hat and did not answer. He pulled the straw hat over his face and composed himself for a nap.

They both looked up at the sound of the Bentley coming,

noisily, up the Drive from the Lodge. Seeing them on the lawn, the driver swung the vehicle round on the wide gravel surface and stopped a few yards from where they were sitting. The girl jumped out and, her face beaming, ran lightly over to give them both a perfunctory kiss on the cheek.

"Mummy! Daddy! Gosh, its hot!"

She swept off her headband in a careless gesture, letting her auburn hair flop down across her face in abandon. She laughed gaily

"Look after Freddie for me. I am going in to change before we play tennis"

Her mother called after her retreating figure "On the way, Julia, pop into the kitchen and tell Cook to send out some tea, will you?"

Julia did not reply, or look back, but acknowledged her mother with a brief wave over her shoulder. Freddie Frobisher came over and sat on one of the white-painted iron garden chairs which were arrayed round an ornate, white-painted, iron garden table. Sir Wilkin, reluctantly and with obvious effort, rose from the deckchair to join him

"Hello Freddie, that is some machine you have there. It is not yours is it?"

The drawl, with a slight lisp, held a bored, almost insolent, tone

"No! It is Pater's. I sold my old bus to one of my college chums and I am waiting delivery of a new SS standard"

Sir Wilkin knew little about motor cars.

"Airplanes are my thing. I am not much up on cars. Is that a new type?"

Freddie was only too willing to enlighten him

"Yes! Its made by some new company. Their name is Jaguar, I think. The Jag SS100 is going to be all the rage among the smart set and I want to get in first"

Frederick Frobisher came from a wealthy family which farmed extensive acres in Norfolk. He doted on Julia Frensham, but to her he was no more than a lapdog; there to cater to her every whim. He got on alright with Julia's father but always felt embarrassed in the company of Lady Frensham. She had made no effort to acknowledge his presence and did not join them at the garden table. Her haughty, unwelcoming, demeanour would never let Freddie forget she was the daughter of a Duke of the Realm and she did nothing to set him at ease. Conversation with Julia's father having petered out Freddie rose from the chair

"Excuse me, Sir!"

He almost bowed to Lady Frensham as she looked up

"I think I should see what is keeping Jules"

Victoria shuddered at the diminutive and, acknowledging his presence at last, she tossed over her shoulder

"See what has happened to the tea while you are about it!"

Actually, Lady Frensham was not deliberately ignoring Freddie. Her thoughts had been miles away. She had lifted her floppy hat and was, idly, watching two airplanes circling around each other in the distance. They directed her attention to the spire of St James' church. The aircraft reminded her of Wilkin when she first met him. In her mind's eye she could see him, so tall, smart and handsome in his uniform, when her mother had first introduced him to her at Selchester Towers at the end of the war. The Duchess of Selchester had organised a Victory Ball as a welcome home for officers returning from the Front and had, shrewdly, combined the occasion with a 'coming out' for her 18 year old daughter; aptly named, considering the occasion, Victoria. Though he was many years older than Victoria, the Duchess had decided Wilkin Frensham should be bestowed with the honour of becoming the father of her grandchildren. So when, following his father's instructions, Wilkin sent round his card and asked permission to 'call on' Lady Victoria the Duchess replied that her daughter would be pleased to receive him and, after a short courtship, his proposal of marriage was graciously accepted.

Lady Victoria Frensham sighed as she remembered the wedding which took place on 19th July, 1919. The Cathedral at Selchester had been gutted by fire, and was still in a state of repair, so the ceremony was held at St James Church, Frensham Down. Practically every county notable seemed to be in the village church; the men dressed in their fashionable morning suits and carrying grey top hats; whilst their ladies wore long summer dresses suited to the occasion with matching wide-brimmed hats. There were few pews available for the regular Sunday congregation but, practically, the whole village turned up to stand outside and witness the occasion. The Vicar himself was only a member of the congregation because Her Grace, the Duchess, had insisted that the Bishop of Selchester should officiate at her daughter's wedding. Never had there been so many flowers in the church. The dark haired bride, her rather plain face hidden by a long white veil, looked angelic in a dazzling white satin dress in the latest high neck fashion, specially commissioned and designed by a top French couturier, as she glided down the aisle on the Duke's arm. Two small page boys, looking uncomfortable in miniature copies of an RAF officer's uniform, tried not to trip over the long train which they were supposed to be preventing from trailing in the ingrained dust of the old grey stones, inset with several medieval brass burial plates, that paved the aisle. Six teenage bridesmaids, in pairs, took up the rear of the procession; looking pretty in alternate blue and pink dresses set off by matching posies of blooms. The Groom, nervous despite his age and experience, held out his hand to his bride as she approached. At the insistence of the bride's mother he was wearing his RAF 'parade dress' uniform; with sash and sword. The best man was similarly uniformed, as were several fellow officers in the congregation.

The ceremony completed, the newly-wed couple left the church and, showered with confetti and rice, passed under an arch of honour, formed by swords held aloft by the bridegroom's companions at arms; to be assisted into the waiting open white carriage by grooms wearing the Duke's livery. Two grooms, seated on the box, controlled four magnificent greys, each sporting a cockade of white plumes. The Duke and Duchess followed and were, in their turn, assisted by grooms into the Duke's emblazoned official coach, which was drawn by four matching black horses. Sir James and Lady Sarah Frensham travelled with them. The nobility among the guests each had their own carriage and, as the cortege proceeded slowly along Castle Lane, on the way to Frensham Hall, the villagers followed, mostly on foot, to enjoy the largesse provided for them in the grounds of the Hall. Lady Victoria sighed to herself as she recalled the occasion.

CHAPTER SEVEN

1938

Left to himself at the garden table, Sir Wilkin had, also, noticed the circling aircraft but his thoughts were elsewhere. He was reminded of the last time he wore his RAF uniform and the night of the Memorial dance in the village. Then there was Maddie!! 'Ah! Maddie' he sighed to himself. He had not seen her since the chance encounter at the stable fire had encouraged him to seek her out at the farmhouse at Hanshott farm. That was more than five years ago and, although Maddie had rebuffed him in no uncertain terms, he could not forget the little girl who had answered the door and had left him standing there while she called her mother. Was that a touch of auburn he saw in the child's hair? He had asked her age and it seemed to be about right? Could it be that she was.........? His mother, Lady Sarah, had never mentioned a child; but it would explain the sudden disappearance of Maddie from the Hall while he was away. It had been too delicate a subject to raise at the time, so he had not spoken of his suspicions to Maddie when she came to the door; not that she gave him much chance to say anything. Nor had he mentioned the matter to anyone else, with the exception, that is, of Lady Sarah, who interrupted his half-spoken question with an imperious wave of her hand

"The least said about that episode in your life, Wilkin, the better. Now what about re-decorations for inside the Lodge. I have decided I would like........."

Sir Wilkin had tried to dismiss the matter from his mind and would probably have succeeded had he not seen Sally again, recently, quite by chance. He had called in at the Village post office to make an enquiry concerning his gun licence and there, behind the counter, stood the same child. She was now a teenager but he would recognise her anywhere. Her mother's pretty looks were unmistakable and there was still that touch of auburn in her hair. His impulse was to speak to her when she smiled at him but, his business with Mrs Higgins concluded, he merely smiled back and left. Again it troubled him. If she was, as he suspected, his daughter, he wanted to know her better, Strangely, he felt no guilt about his part in bringing her into the world; more a feeling of sadness that he had no part in bringing her up. Now, he felt a need to protect her and give her a better chance in life than she could have as the daughter of a farmer. But, what could he do for her? Sally almost certainly knew he was Sir Wilkin Frensham, he thought; but it was obvious, that she knew nothing of his connection with her mother. Further, he was certain that Reg Hanshott knew nothing of any relationship; indeed there had been no relationship, in the ordinary sense, between himself and Maddie. He felt it would not be wise to approach the girl on the subject; nor would it be discreet to broach the matter with her mother after all these years. Nonetheless, he was now determined not to forget Sally. One day the time would come, he was sure, when he could do something for her; even though she might never know who was her benefactor or the reason for his regard. He would leave it at that for the present but he resolved to call in at the post office from time to time, without appearing to be too obtrusive, to watch her growing up.

Sir Wilkin was awakened from his reverie by the stuttering engine of one of the aircraft. The engine had cut out at the top of a loop and the plane was spiralling towards the ground. To no-one in particularly, Sir Wilkin, snorted

"Damn fool! Where does the RAF get its pilots from these days. In my day I would have had him up in the orderly room for at least a reprimand....."

His thoughts changed to concern and he watched, aghast, as the plane, its engine now failed completely, swooped down to disappear behind the Hall. For a moment there was silence as Sir Wilkin held his breath. Then, with a sudden roar, the plane re-appeared as the pilot lifted it over the building. With shock the knight realised that the aircraft had only just missed the roof and his hat fell off as he raised his head. Again the engine mis-fired, stuttered and cut out as the machine, its pilot clearly visible, swept low over Sir Wilkin and Lady Victoria. As it banked to the right, the plane looked as though it might crash on Hanshott Hill Common; but the pilot seemed to be in control of the silent aircraft as he levelled out and took it into a long descending glide. Forsaking his criticism, Sir Wilkin muttered "Good man! Now gently does it"

The plane glided down to bounce across the stubble in the field beyond the common and Sir Wilkin thought he saw the tail tip up as it ran into the hedge.

The maid, who had been bringing out the afternoon tea, started at the sudden noise of the aircraft engine almost on top of her and dropped the tray; the silver teapot spilling its contents onto the gravel and the fine porcelain crashing into fragments on the ground with the remnants of bite-size sandwiches and cream cakes. Julia, who had changed into a pleated tennis skirt and white blouse, dropped her racket as she followed Freddie at a run across the gravel to the car. Freddie called to her as she ran

"What a whizz!"

Freddy was excited as he started the Bentley. Julia turned to her father as she leapt into the passenger seat.

"Gosh, what a lark. We are going down for a look-see. Do you want to come, Daddy?"

Sir Wilkin shook his head, but Freddy had not waited and the car was already well away down the Drive to the Lodge. Lady Frensham took no notice of her daughter's abrupt departure. She was busy admonishing the maid for her carelessness and the maid was in tears.

The Bentley drew up as Len Mundy, Oliver and Mike were climbing over the gate into the lane. Julia nodded at Oliver, ignored Mike, and addressed Len

"Anyone hurt, Mundy?"

Len was not impressed at being addressed thus, but thought it discreet to be polite

"No, Miss"

Instinct made him wait to be dismissed. Julia, ever haughty like her mother where the peasants were concerned, tossed her head.

"Right, Mundy. That will be all!"

Len turned away to join the boys and muttered

"What did I tell you? Stuck up little bitch"

Julia and Freddie were standing on the lower bar of the gate when the pilot, accompanied by Constable Bell, approached. The light of recognition spread across Julia's face as she shouted with delight

"Willie!"

"Jules?"

The pilot ran forward and climbed the gate to embrace her. Julia turned to Freddie

"You don't know my cousin Willie Lavington. Do you?"

She turned back to the pilot

"Willie, this is Freddie Frobisher"

123

The two men regarded each other suspiciously but they clasped hands with the customary rhetorical greeting

"How d'you do?"

"How d'you do?"

Julia butted in excitedly

"What happened? What are you doing here? Were you coming to visit us?"

The questions tumbled out. Willie held up his hand

"All in good time, Jules. Thanks for your concern...."

The last rather sarcastically, since she had not enquired after his health. He continued

"But I am OK; although the aircraft has taken a bit of a bash. Is that Frensham Hall up there? I did not recognise it from the air; but then I had my hands a bit full at the time trying to get down in one piece. I say, that is a nice looking bus. Have you got a telephone?"

Julia was only too ready to offer her lap dog's services

"Of course. Freddie won't mind giving you a lift, will you Freddie?"

She looked at Freddie, daring him to contradict her; which, of course, he did not.

"At your service! Jump in the back."

Freddie added the latter quickly because the pilot was heading for the driving seat.

The car reversed into the gateway to turn and, narrowly missing Len Mundy's dog, it roared away up the Lane back to the Hall. Mike and Oliver had already left on their way down to the Village Green, so Len Mundy and Constable Bell stood alone watching the road monster disappear belching a noisome cloud of blue smoke. Constable Bell sniffed

"Shouldn't allow those things on the road. Afternoon, Len! Got to finish my mowing!"

He mounted his bicycle and rode off down the Lane. Len Mundy watched him go for a moment then picked up his sickle and stick.

"Come on Bruce!"

He closed his front gate behind them. The dog following, Len walked, meditatively, down the path to the panelled white door of his pretty cottage. His wife, Bertha, smiled affectionately at him as she stood aside to let them both in. He nodded to her as he entered.

"Stuck up! The lot o' them"

She did not answer; she guessed who he was talking about. He closed the door.

Sir Wilkin and Lady Frensham were sitting at the garden table when the Bentley returned. The maid had picked up Julia's racket and taken it into the porch. She had brought fresh tea and cucumber sandwiches; but these had been consumed leaving only the empty teapot, cups and plates on the table. Julia ran lightly over to the table dragging the pilot by the arm while a sullen Freddie followed obediently behind her. He had expected to have Julia to himself for the afternoon and resented the intrusion of this cousin of hers, no matter what the circumstances. Recognising her nephew, Victoria Frensham stood up to greet him

"Why, Willie, what are *you* doing here?"

She did not embrace him but held out her hand rather limply as though she expected him to bow and kiss it. Instead Willie boisterously grabbed her by the shoulders, planted a kiss on her cheek, and said, in that almost insolent drawl of his,

"Watcha! Auntie, how are you old thing? Hope you don't mind me dropping in, so to speak?"

He guffawed but Victoria only shuddered at his familiarity and snorted

"Your manners have not improved, young man, since you inherited the Lavington peerage. I suppose it is too late to have a word with your mother about it?"

She looked across at the maid who was clearing the cups and plates away. Her nephew did not endear himself to her. He was too much of a fop for her taste but her good manners prompted her to order the maid to fetch some more tea and sandwiches. She turned back to Willie

"I suppose you would like to stay and have some tea?"

Willie was not in the least offended at her tone. He knew his aunt very well; but he answered with a hint of apology

"Well! I was rather hoping I could wash up, use the phone and...er..."

He hesitated, looking appealingly at Sir Wilkin for support,

"Perhaps I could stay the night?"

Lady Victoria did not look at all accommodating. Sir Wilkin shared his wife's opinion regarding Willie's character, but he was too much of a gentleman to let it show. He answered Willie's question

"Of course, my boy, you may stay as long as you like"

Willis, Julia's fifteen year old brother came pedalling up the drive. He skidded to a halt on the gravel and, dropping his bike to the ground, joined the group at the garden table

"Hello! Cousin Willie. What are you doing here?"

Without waiting for an answer he continued impetuously, as young boys do, "Did you see the plane crash?"

Willie grinned

"As a matter of fact I didn't see it. I was in it!"

Willis was delighted

"Oh I say, how wizard, what was it like?"

His mother intervened

"Where have you been, Willis? You have grass stains on your trousers. Go and change and come back here for some tea. Now go along with you"

Sir Wilkin called him back

"And do not forget to take your bike with you. Hold on a minute!"

He turned back to Willie as Willis paused

"Now, you wanted to use the telephone didn't you, Willie? Run along with Willis, he will show you where it is"

Willis Mark Frensham, Sir Wilkin's only son and heir, picked up his bicycle and moved off, chatting animatedly with the pilot. He was relieved not to be detained to answer his mother's question concerning his activities; for he had been spending the afternoon on Castle Hill Common with Cherry French, the blacksmith's fourteen year old daughter. They had been friends since they were little children and, as Cherry had grown, despite retaining some of her puppy plumpness, into an attractive teenager, their friendship had developed into a secret adolescent romance. Willis was home from school for the Summer. He took after his father rather than his mother; with the same auburn hair and a promise of aristocratic good looks. There was no doubt that he would develop into a tall, slim heartbreaker. Willis wished to say nothing to his family about his afternoon's liaison because he knew neither his mother nor his sister would approve. As for his father he was not sure, so he kept the friendship with Cherry a secret from him also.

Their mild flirtation was disturbed by the stuttering of the airplane's engine as it swept low over their heads. Willis and Cherry watched while the engine picked up as the plane flew away to the north and banked round to disappear behind Frensham Hall. Willis gasped, excitedly, as it re-appeared only just above the roof of the Hall.

"Gosh! That nearly hit the Hall"

They were too far away to hear the engine cut out again but they could see the plane turn towards them as it glided down out of sight behind the trees. Willis jumped up and picked up his bike.

"I reckon that 'plane crashed. You can see the other one circling over Hanshott Farm. Let us go and see what has happened"

Cherry had been hoping he would be bold enough to kiss her and would rather have stayed where they were; but she, resignedly, picked up her own bike to follow him down the hill. They took a short cut through the alley that led them onto the Scolling Road and cycled along to Hanshott Lane. They had dismounted at the foot of the steep hill and started to wheel their bikes up the Lane when they saw Constable Bell free-wheeling down towards them. He stopped, but ignored Willis for the moment

"And where do you think you are off to young Cherry? Does your Dad know you are out with him?"

He nodded towards Willis, who broke in to lie convincingly

"We only just met, down there. We are going up to see the airplane crash"

Although he felt it to be his duty to keep the public away from the crashed aircraft, the policeman had no intention of spending his afternoon off in the field alone until the RAF decided what should be done; nevertheless he was not going to encourage sightseers.

"No you are not. It is on private property and you would be trespassing. I think you had better come along with me young Cherry. I shall see you home before this young man leads you into more trouble. As for you, my lad, you had best get back to the Hall where you belong"

He looked sternly at Willis who, with a cheeky pout of his lips, smiled a hasty goodbye to Cherry. Willis thought about examining the wreck by himself but, when he saw Reg Hanshott and Len Mundy had returned to the scene, he decided it would be more diplomatic to carry on home.

As his son was retreating across the gravel with Willie Lavington Sir Wilkin stood up. He stretched his shoulders as he addressed his wife

"I do not want any more tea. Think I shall go for a ride over by

Castle Hill Common. Might blow the cobwebs away"

Lady Frensham did not look up or answer him. So, without further comment, he walked away towards the stables to tell Johnson to get his horse ready while he returned to the Hall to wash his hands and change his clothes.

Reg Hanshott was back at the farmhouse when the phone rang. Maddie answered it

"It is for you Reg. I think it is somebody from the RAF about the 'plane crash"

Reg listened for a minute or so then exploded

"No! I will *not* send any of my men to guard the wreck. For one thing they are not here, seeing as its Sunday, and another thing they have plenty of work to do on the farm when they *are* here. If you want the plane guarded you must send some of your own men. And tell them to mind how they go. I do not want my field churned up with lorry tracks. And another thing! Get your airplane off my property before I start charging you rent"

He slammed the receiver down on its hook and turned to Maddie

"Bloody cheek! I don't care if he *is* Squadron Leader whatever his name is. He is not ordering me around on my own farm"

He looked round the kitchen table

"Where is Sally? Doesn't she want any tea?"

Lillian looked up from cutting the bread

"She has gone down to Jean Stokes' birthday party"

A group of cyclists was leaving as Mike Grey and David (Oliver) Twist approached the Primrose Tea Gardens at the side of the Village Green and behind The Bowman. It was a pretty spot and a favourite haunt for cycling clubs out for the day from Dunchester. Occasionally hikers would discover the Village Green as they strode along the Scolling Road and would welcome a cream tea or a glass of lemonade in the Gardens. Primrose Cottage took its name from the Primrose Stream, so called because its banks were smothered with wild primroses in the Spring, which flowed along the back of the Gardens. A natural spring fed a large pond at the side of The Bowman and, from this, a small waterfall lead to a short, pebble bedded, ditch to join the Primrose Stream so that rippling water could be heard on two sides of Primrose Gardens; a pleasant accompaniment to the sound of the birds in the tall elms that overlooked the edge of the garden.

The two storey, white faced stucco and thatch-roofed, cottage was built in 1601 by the Frensham family as accommodation for the incumbent vicar of St James church and was occupied by succeeding vicars until 1785. When the Church Council built the Vicarage next to the church the cottage was sold to Douglas Henshaw, the second son of the wealthy Henshaw family of Dunchester and a gentleman of independent means. Whilst retaining the Elizabethan character he refurbished the cottage and, following his marriage to Miriam Alrich, from Oxford, occupied it as their family home. His wife died in 1881, at the age of thirty-six, while she was giving birth to their second daughter, Miriam, and Douglas raised his two daughters alone, apart from the help of a woman who came in daily to clean and cook for the family and a village girl who looked after the children in his absence.

As the sisters grew up they took care of their elderly father in return. He died in 1915 from a heart attack at the age of seventy-five and left the freehold cottage and grounds to his two daughters. His small fortune, mainly from foreign investments, was eroded by the 1914-1918 war and left a limited income to support his heirs. So, at the end of the war, and in anticipation of the much lauded move towards outdoor activities, the sisters turned the extensive grounds of Primrose Cottage into the Primrose Tea Gardens which they opened to the public during the summer months; partly as an interest for themselves and partly as a means of supplementing their income.

Now, in 1938, the two ladies were in their late fifties and were both staunch supporters of local community activities; but, apart from that, they were as different from each other as chalk is from cheese. Miriam had grown up reasonably content with the hand fate had dealt her and was as sweet and gentle a lady as one could hope to meet. Her mode of dress and hair style, which were neat but not fashionable, gave the impression that she was older than her years but suited her composure. Her sister, Marianne, was two years her senior and dressed severely in Edwardian style. Her manner was equally severe and she tended to dominate her younger sister. Being little more than a baby when her mother died, she could not really remember her yet, as she grew older, Marianne felt a deep sense of deprivation; particularly when she saw maternal love bestowed on other children in the village. Inwardly, she blamed her father for giving her mother the baby that killed her. As a result she felt a deep resentment against all men, although, if asked, she could not have explained the reason for this. Nevertheless, she never had a good word to say for the men of her world and rejected the few attempts they made to woo her in her younger days. In her infancy she also resented the baby who had been the instrument of her mother's untimely demise. The child, Miriam, was unaware of her sister's animosity and, as she grew older her love for her elder sister was akin to love for a surrogate mother. In her bitterness Marianne resented this attachment, as though she thought it was an attempt by Miriam to ask forgiveness for being born. But she would not admit, even to herself, the deep seated bitterness she felt against her younger sister. Nonetheless, it was there, lurking in her sub-conscious, waiting for the trigger which would bring it to the surface.

A close observer would recognise one such trigger in the attitude of Marianne to her younger sister's few suitors. One could see that, in their younger days, Miriam had been the more attractive of the two girls; a fact which only added fuel to Marianne's animosity. Whether it was jealousy, in this respect, or her natural distrust of men which prompted Marianne's treatment of the young men Miriam brought home to seek her approval, one cannot say; but her distant manner acted as a deterrent to their approaches to her sister and she drove them all away. Perhaps it was simply that Marianne could not bear to see her sister happy when she herself was not. Strange to say, Miriam did not resent her sister's interference in her love affairs or even recognise it as such; assuming it was, perhaps, misguidedly intended for her own good.

Miriam crossed the grass to greet Oliver and Mike . She addressed Oliver "I was hoping you would come to see us, Oliver. We want to thank you for cutting our grass"
She led them over to a table with two chairs and wiped down the table and chairs with the cloth she took from her waist band
"Now, sit down both of you. What would you like? How about a nice cream tea as an appreciation for helping us?"
Oliver thanked her and she bustled off. As soon as she was out of sight Mike turned to his friend
"Let us move over to that table"
He was pointing to one near the fence that bordered the path alongside the road. Oliver looked surprised

130

"Why? What is so special about that table?"

Mike grinned

"It has four chairs. Sally is over at Jean's place and I am expecting them to join us over here. You don't mind do you?"

Oliver did not answer, but shrugged his shoulders in acceptance. Miriam returned with the scones, cream, jam and tea. She looked towards the empty table, then her eyes swept the gardens in search of them. She came over

"So there you are! Anything wrong with the other table?"

Oliver grinned

"It was *his* idea. I think he is expecting company"

Miriam smiled but said nothing as she placed the tea tray on an adjacent table while she took out her cloth and wiped the table. It was none of her business, she thought, as she laid out the tea things on the table and, with a cheerful "Enjoy your tea", she left them to return to the cottage.

Mike had made sure he was facing down the Village Green towards the General Store. He could see a bicycle leaning against the white picket fence outside the shop-cum-bungalow. After a while the girls came round the side of the bungalow and walked across the Village Green towards him. They smiled at the boys as they passed their table, on the other side of the low picket fence which bordered the Gardens, and walked along to come in by the small wooden gate. The boys stood up and Sally lightly touched Mike's hand with hers as she sat down on his left, facing towards the Green. Jean looked at Oliver

"You didn't mind me coming. Did you, Oliver?"

Oliver smiled and waved her to the other chair

"Of course not! It is your birthday, isn't it? Many Happy Returns!"

He then added, wickedly,

"Mike has offered to buy you a cream tea for your birthday, haven't you Mike?"

Seeing Mike was embarrassed, Sally squeezed his hand and smiled sweetly at him; but she parried Oliver's suggestion with

"What he means is that *I* will buy a cream tea for Jean and myself"

Before anyone could reply Jean interrupted

"No! It is *my* birthday so, seeing that you two already have yours, I shall treat Sally!"

Mike was still embarrassed and, feeling a little guilty, was about to protest; but, remembering the paltry five shillings and ten pence in his pocket, and the week stretching ahead, he breathed an inward sigh of relief and said nothing.

Marianne came over and, glancing sourly at the two boys, smiled at Sally as she took Jean's order. She was thinking it was just like boys to have a free meal and leave the girls to pay for their own. She glared at these young representatives of the detested male sex as she walked away. Fortunately, it was Miriam who returned with the tray because her sister's manner had not escaped Oliver and the sarcastic comment that he had composed for Marianne's return remained unspoken as he politely thanked Miriam for her service.

Jean Stokes was nearly a year and a half older than Sally so when Maddie took Sally to the village school at the age of five it fell to Jean to watch over her in the playground. This was mainly, perhaps, due to their family connections. Jean's mother, Catherine, was Sally's godmother and her father, Gerald, had 'given away' Sally's mother, Maddie, at her wedding to Reg Hanshott. In fact, so close were the two families that, although there was no blood relationship between them, Sally had been raised to respect Catherine and Gerry Stokes as a sort of aunt and uncle and the two girls looked upon their own relationship as that of cousins. As they grew older the difference between their ages was less apparent and they had become firm friends. Jean worked in her parents' shop and, when the post office was closed for lunch on weekdays, Sally would often carry her sandwiches across the Village Green to spend her break with Jean. During the summer months they could be seen, at lunchtime, laughing and gossiping as they sat on one of the benches on the Village Green

Oliver was stirring his tea when he turned to Jean

"I haven't seen your older brother lately, Jean"

She put down the scone she was about to spread with cream before answering

"No! Alan has joined the Air Force. When he reached eighteen last year he asked Dad for permission to sign on. He has always been interested in airplanes and the room he shared with Julian is full of those boys' magazines and paperbacks with lurid covers showing planes fighting each other during the war. He fancies himself as a fighter pilot but he cannot get a commission because he

didn't go to grammar school. The nearest he has got to flying is driving a military truck at Hornchurch RAF station in Essex"
She paused and Sally took over the conversation
"I have been telling Jean about the crash at the farm. Do you think *that* plane came from Hornchurch?"
Oliver answered
"We don't know where it came from but, apparently, the pilot is some Lord or other and knows the Frenshams"
Mike chuckled
"He might be one of the gentry, but he did not get much change out of Reg Hanshott, Jean. When he asked for a telephone Sally's Dad told him to use the call box outside the post office. Told him a two mile walk would do him good! Actually, he probably didn't need to use the call box in the end because Julie Frensham turned up as we were leaving. She was in a big fancy car and I expect she took him back to the Hall to make his 'phone call"
Jean looked surprised
"I thought Julie Frensham was in France?"
Mike, did not answer because he had just caught sight of a horseman on the other side of the Green
"Well! talk of the devil ! Isn't that Julie's father over there?"
Sir Wilkin had brought his horse down from Castle Hill Common, taking the same alleyway that his young son had used earlier, with the intention of allowing his mount to drink at the pond outside The Bowman. Realising the animal was hot after its gallop over the common he had dismounted and was walking the horse round the Village Green to cool it off before allowing it to drink. He was on the far side of the green when Mike saw him and he could see people sitting at tables but, not having the youthful eyesight of Mike, he did not recognise any of them at that distance. Had the inn been open he would have gone in for a drink but, seeing the Gardens were occupied he decided he might get a refresher there. So he re-mounted and walked his horse slowly across the green. He intended to dismount and tether the horse to the picket fence but hesitated as he passed the group seated at a table near the fence when he realised Sally was among them. For one moment he was tempted to join them but, discretion dictated this was not the time for such a move and they might misconstrue his motives. So remaining mounted, and with no more than a slight pause, he raised his hat and nodded. Ignoring her companions, he

133

addressed only Sally

"Good afternoon, Miss Hanshott. Pleasant day, what?"

Sir Wilkin continued the horse's slow pace to the pond outside the inn. He did not look back; otherwise he might have seen them all staring after him. Oliver was the first to speak

"Well I never! So his Lordship has taken notice of our little Sally"

Sally blushed and Jean rose to her friend's defence

"Come on! Don't be mean Oliver. He was only being polite and he happens to know Sally as the daughter of his next door neighbour"

Sally spoke up

"He probably knows me from the Post Office. He has been in once or twice lately. In any case, he is old enough to be my father"

She had an uneasy feeling she should not have said that and glanced at Mike. He made no comment but he was gazing thoughtfully at the auburn touch in Sally's fair hair.

Sir Wilkin did not allow his horse to remain long at the pond for it was best that the animal should not drink too much on such a hot day; especially as they had some way to go yet and uphill, at that. The inn would not be open for a couple of hours or more so he ignored his own thirst and started walking the horse slowly along the Scolling Road. He had intended to retrace the way he had come, back to the Common, but changed his mind when he reached the Alley. The unexpected encounter with Sally, brief though it was, had given him pause for thought and he wanted more time to himself. So, continuing along the Scolling Road at a walking pace, he passed Hanshott Lane and carried on until he reached the stone bridge where Mike and Oliver had been sitting earlier that afternoon. Immediately after crossing the bridge he turned left and down the slope onto the bridle path which led him alongside Mill Road to Frensham Mill. The brick-built mill had not been used for more than half a century and was in a sadly dilapidated condition. There were gaps in the roof where the winds had blown away the clay tiles and an oak tree had grown, unchecked, through the rotten floors to burst out through what was left of the roof and spread out to cast a heavy shadow over the scene. The waterwheel had long since jammed; although the mill stream still pushed vainly against the rotting wooden paddles and gurgled as it flowed through the spaces in the broken wood. The devastation of the mill-house was relieved by the colourful flowers of the briars that might once have been cultivated roses climbing against the walls. Now they were wild and in such profusion that their thorns prevented human access to any part of the derelict building; leaving it as a haven for the wild life of Frensham Woods which bordered the stream.

Mill Road crossed the stream and skirted the old mill to cross the Scolling Brook onto Hanshott Common. But Sir Wilkin did not take this route home. He wanted more time to himself to think so, instead, he took the longer route; continuing past the Mill and along the bridle path beside the mill stream until it re-joined the Scolling Brook; and then following the Brook until he could cross it by the old stone bridge which connected Frensham Woods with his own parkland. This was the Frensham Down from which the Village derived its name.

Sir Wilkin was in no mood for social chit-chat with the company whom he knew would still be at the Hall because he could see Freddie Frobisher's Bentley standing on the gravel outside; so, skirting the private lake, he dismounted by the boathouse and let the horse loose to graze. For a moment he considered taking out one of the rowing skiffs that were moored by the jetty but decided it was too hot for such strenuous exercise. Instead, he sat down on a wooden bench in the shade under the eaves of the boathouse. Loosening his stock he relaxed, taking in the beauty of the scene. The lake was man-made. It was a large, kidney shaped, expanse of water with an island in the centre of the widest part at the end nearest the Hall. The water was clear because it was fed from a natural spring. It overflowed via a small dam into a shallow stone-bedded stream in which it babbled away down to the Scolling Brook. Clumps of trees bordered the lake and patches of reeds and bull rushes, in the still water by the banks, housed a myriad of water life and provided nesting places for wild ducks and moorhens.

Contrary to the belief of Hilda Benhope, Sir Wilkin was not the hard, unyielding, selfish man she thought him to be seventeen years earlier. He actually regretted bitterly his actions on that drunken night and, when he had sobered in the morning, he remembered only flashes of what must have happened. He had made no further attempts to approach Maddie at the time and, with his father's encouragement, had taken himself off to London the next day; remaining there for three months. When he returned to the Hall, in some trepidation at the shame he knew he would feel when he saw Maddie, he found she had gone. He was admonished by his mother, and ostracised by his wife for some time, but of Maddie's fate he had learned nothing. He told his mother that he wanted to do something to help Maddie after she left the Hall but his mother told him she had taken care of that and the best thing he could do for the girl was to leave her alone. The secrecy with which the outcome of his association with the Maddie had been conducted by all those concerned had left him in ignorance of the probable existence of a child and it was not until he saw Sally on her mother's doorstep that the possibility occurred to him. He recognised that Maddie had found her own solution and needed nothing from him but, for five years, he had puzzled over how he could help Sally without revealing the secret of her birth. From the rare and brief conversations he had managed to have with her at the post office he was sure the girl herself was unaware of her ancestry and believed Reg Hanshott to be her father. After an hour of meditation Sir Wilkin was still no nearer a solution to his problem but he was determined not to forget the responsibility he felt. He resolved to go to London and seek the confidential advice of the family solicitor and with that he re-mounted his horse and made his way slowly back to the stables.

CHAPTER EIGHT

1938 - 1939

It was half past seven on the evening of the crash that the driver of the 30cwt., canvas covered, RAF truck noisily changed down through his crash gears as he slowed to negotiate the sharp left turn into Hanshott Lane. He pulled onto the grass verge outside the police house and switched off the engine. Corporal Jack Mills climbed down from the passenger seat and, reaching back into the cab, brought out his tunic and peaked cap. Once he had donned the cap, buttoned up his tunic and fastened the brass buckle of the tunic belt, he walked round to the tailboard and addressed the four aircraftmen who, jacketless and with shirt sleeves rolled up, had been sitting on the rolled-up bell tents in the back; they were now standing by the tailboard preparatory to climbing down

"Stay where you are lads! We are not there yet"

Aircraftman Fred Finch was thirsty

"Come on, Corp. We just passed a pub back there. How about a pint?"

Then, coaxingly, "I'll buy you one"

But with Corporal Mills duty came first

"I'll 'old you to that, Finch, when we have settled in an' sorted out the stags. But, for now, stay where you are"

He walked over to the police house and knocked at the front door. It was opened by Valerie Bell, wife of the village constable. Her seven year old daughter was hovering behind her, curious to see who was calling on a Sunday evening.

Corporal Mills was always polite to civilians and particularly to attractive ladies when confronted by them. He smiled disarmingly and, speaking in what he considered to be his 'posh' voice, said

"I would like to see the constable if 'e is in, please"

Valerie returned the smile but did not ask him in. She called over her shoulder

"Richard, it is for you"

Then, taking her daughter by the hand, she moved back into the bungalow as Richard Bell took her place at the door. The constable had expected their arrival and asked only one question

"Good evening, Corporal. Do you know your way to the crash

site?"

"I've got a driver who knows the area an' 'e knows the way to 'anshott Farm but we don't know exactly where the crash site is"

Constable Bell did not really want to spend any more of his Sunday off on this incident but he thought it best to co-operate with the authorities

"I'll stand on your running board and show you the spot. Hang on a minute"

He went back inside to collect his uniform jacket and helmet; then came out, shut the front door, and went round to the back of the bungalow. He returned with his bicycle

"You can toss this in the back of your truck"

It was a statement, rather than a question, but the corporal did not demur. He waited while the constable passed up his bike to the airmen in the truck. Then they walked round to the cab. The driver was talking to Hazel French, the blacksmith's elder daughter. She had been in her bedroom at the rear of Glebe Cottage when she heard the sound of the truck turning the corner. She looked through her window when the truck pulled up and was surprised to recognise the driver so, welcoming a diversion on a boring Sunday evening, she hurried out to chat to him. It was not by chance that Leading Aircraftman Alan Stokes, brother of Jean Stokes, had been chosen for this job. The sergeant who had given the orders was aware of LAC Stokes` knowledge of the district, so he was the natural choice. But Corporal Mills had no intention of allowing a mere LAC to take an advantage over himself where the local girls were concerned. He believed rank should have its privileges and this meant first pick of the local females available. He grinned at Hazel and, making it clear he was in charge, ordered the driver to start up the engine.

"Come on Stokes. Get this wagon moving. You're going to be too busy when we get there for dilly dallying down 'ere"

Before walking round to the front of the truck to take the passenger seat the corporal turned to Hazel

"See you later, darling!"

She ignored him and addressed Alan

"So long, Alan. Mum and Dad would like you to come in when you are free"

She tossed her head at the corporal and walked away; enjoying the attention of the lads in the back who were whistling as she went.

138

Corporal Mills found that the police constable had already installed himself in the passenger seat and was chatting to Alan Stokes. There was no room for three in the cab and the constable showed no signs of giving up his advantage; so the corporal had no choice but to stand on the running board clinging to the window frame of the door.

When they arrived at the entrance to the field Corporal Mills jumped down and, walking round to the back of the truck, ordered one of his men to get down and unfasten the five barred gate, and swing it wide open. Meanwhile, another of the airmen handed down the constable's bike. Richard Bell pointed out the crash site to the corporal then joined Len Mundy who had come out to see what all the noise was about. The corporal did not even thank the constable and ignored Len Mundy as he climbed back into the passenger seat of the truck. The airman who had opened the gate guided Alan Stokes into the field, then followed the truck on foot as it was driven slowly over the stubble to the crashed aircraft. The constable watched them go, then, closing and fastening the gate, he crossed the lane and leaning his bike against the hedge, joined Len Mundy. As if by common consent, without saying a word and with Bruce padding along behind, the two men crossed the lane and leaned on the gate. Len's pipe had gone out and he made a show of relighting it as they, silently, watched the RAF at work. The airmen were busy unloading and erecting two camouflaged bell tents. Len blew out a cloud of aromatic smoke and turned to Richard Bell.

"Thought they was goin' to move the wreck?"
Richard shook his head

"No! They are only here to guard it. I expect most of them will be in the pub later if you want to find out more. By the way, young Alan Stokes is driving the truck"

"What! Gerry Stokes' boy? Well I never! It be a small world b'aint it?"

It was about half past eight when Sally opened the kitchen door to see LAC Alan Stokes standing there. He had called to ask permission to draw water from the pump outside in the farmyard. She looked happily surprised

"Why, Alan? Jean and I were talking about you only this afternoon. Now you turn up here like a bad penny"
She asked him in to be greeted by Lillian, Maddie and the boys. Reg Hanshott was down at The Bowman; no doubt regaling his

cronies with the aircraft incident and getting the odd pint on the strength of it. Over a cup of tea Alan told them that the aircraft had, indeed, come from Hornchurch and that Corporal Mills and his crew had been hastily assembled for the long drive up to the crash site. Fifteen year old Mark Hanshott was avid for news on anything vaguely military

"Have you got a machine gun?"

Alan laughed

"No, and there isn't one in the aircraft. We only have Lee Enfield rifles and, come to think of it, no ammunition for those. Still! That is probably a military secret, so don't go spreading it around among your school mates"

Lillian intervened

"What is the point of carrying guns without bullets when you are supposed to be to guarding something?"

"When on a job like this each airman is issued with a rifle and bayonet, which he has to keep clean and ready for use at a moment's notice. Officers and warrant officers carry revolvers and other ranks have rifles. But we don't have any bullets for the rifles. They only issue us with ammunition during firing practice. I suppose they think we might shoot somebody by mistake"

He had an afterthought

"Oh! There *is* one exception. When on guard duty at the gate of an RAF station, or other important military site, each sentry carries one clip of five rounds (that's air force jargon for bullets, Mark) but only in a pouch attached to a webbing belt. The sergeant says the sight of one of us carrying a gun is enough to frighten anyone off. I reckon he is being sarcastic and means we are not to be trusted with a loaded rifle. Come to think of it, he might be worrying about his own safety. And don't go spreading that around either, Mark. I probably shouldn't have told you! I reckon it is one of those things that the RAF likes to keep quiet about"

Lillian asked what they were doing for food but Alan assured her they had all they needed in the truck, including a camp cooking stove. "All we need is water and, if you don't mind, use of your outside toilet? Otherwise we shall have to dig a latrine and I don't suppose Mr Hanshott would like that in his field"

He stood up

"Well! I had better be getting back. John will probably be feeling lonely on his own down there"

Sally looked surprised

"Are there only two of you, then?"

He paused at the door as he answered

"No! but, after we had unloaded the equipment and put up the tents, Corporal Mills drove the truck down to the Village so that he could phone in his report to headquarters. He took the others with him to The Bowman. I don't suppose they will be back until after the pub closes"

Mark's younger brother, Matthew, wanted to come down to the impromptu camp

"You can come down now, while I am in charge, if you want to; but Corporal Mills will probably chase you away when he gets back"

Maddie was concerned

"You two can go down with Alan for a while but you must be back before it gets dark"

Alan Stokes grinned at the boys

"You need not worry Mrs Hanshott. I will make sure they get back alright"

Sally had another thought

"Why didn't your corporal ask to use *our* phone? It is nearer than the Village call box"

Alan grinned and winked

"Knowing our corporal he probably *would* have come up here if he had known a pretty little thing like you would be here. As it was I didn't tell him about you and the call box is near the pub, if you see what I mean"

Sally was thinking about Jean

"It is Jean's birthday today. Are you going down to see her while you are here, Alan?"

"With all this business I had clean forgotten it was her birthday. Haven't even sent a card! I will try to pop down tomorrow, if I can get away. But if I don't make it will you apologise to Jean for me?"

But Alan's parents were destined not see their son because the next morning an aircraft recovery vehicle lumbered up the lane and, with great difficulty and some damage to the five barred gate, turned into the stubble field. It was followed by another truck loaded with airmen, dressed in air force blue denims and forage caps. They proceeded to detach the wings and, with the aid of a hoist, lift the body of the wrecked aircraft onto the transporter;

followed by the wings which were strapped alongside the body. Meanwhile, the guard, under the direction of Corporal Mills, struck their tents and loaded their gear onto the truck that had brought them to Frensham Down. The whole job was completed, and the cargo lashed tight, within a couple of hours. The five barred gate, its hinge post dragged out, was left lying on the ground with two bars and both hinges broken. Its latch-post was leaning drunkenly to one side. Taking no heed of the damage their vehicles had done, the RAF convoy turned into the Lane without so much as a thank you to Maddie or Reg; the latter left fuming when he discovered the state of his gate and the deep ruts in his field. He vented his anger on Gerry Stokes in The Bowman that night

"It was your boy, Alan, who was driving the truck when they arrived and I reckon he is to blame for the damage. He should know better; seeing as how he was brought up here"

"How do you know it was Alan. He didn't come down to see his mother! Did you see him?"

"No! But Sally and Maddie did"

Joe French, the blacksmith, butted in

"That's right! My Hazel told me! Apparently, she had a chat with Alan while the first RAF truck to arrive was standing outside my place. They were only up at the farm for a couple of days and I don't suppose Alan could get away to come down to the general store"

"Well! He might have made the effort; seeing as it was Jean's birthday on Sunday. But, I suppose that is kids for you today. Alan never remembers his sister's or anyone else's birthday"

Len Mundy put down his pint mug

"Come to think of it, the RAF Corporal an' some of 'is lads was in 'ere on Sunday night; but Alan weren't with 'em. S'pose 'e 'ad to stay be'ind to watch the wreck"

Reg was still not happy

"Alright, Gerry, perhaps it wasn't your Alan's fault, but somebody among that lot cost me a farm gate and they don't come cheap. I won't be satisfied until the RAF puts the matter right"

But this was not to be the last brush Reg was to have with the military authorities that year; for, only three weeks later, the sound of a heavy truck engine was again to be heard in Hanshott Lane. But this time it was late at night and Reg awakened by the noise, reluctantly, got up to look out of his bedroom window. He saw only the headlight beams and the red tail lights of two three ton trucks, each towing a, canvas-covered trailer, as the convoy disappeared up the Lane on its way to Hanshott Hill Common. Muttering to a, still sleeping, Maddie he returned to his bed. He had to be up by five for milking and could not be bothered to investigate any disturbance that did not directly concern the Farm. He would have been more concerned had he known that the Royal Engineers sergeant in charge of the searchlight unit, armed with emergency authority, took it upon himself to break through a wired up gap in the hedge further up the Lane and to drive straight across three meadow field. Shooing the herd of cows out of the way, the sergeant broke through the opposite hedge to reach the Hanshott Hill common; leaving two huge gaps through which a few cows, perhaps more curious or less sleepy than the others, strayed before the morning milk round-up began.

An hour or so after Reg had been disturbed by the arrival of the trucks at Hanshott farm the landlord of The Bowman, Angus McKuy, was also woken by the sound of heavy vehicles turning opposite the pub into Church Road. This time it was a Territorial unit of the Royal Artillery who were in convoy with heavy trucks, towing a battery of four four-point-five anti-aircraft guns up to a pre-arranged (though National security ensured that none of the locals knew of such pre-arrangement) site on the open ground by Benley Castle.

That night, while the nation slept, throughout the Kingdom the Territorial Army air defence reserves had been mobilised; young men receiving messages, as they arrived home from work, to report immediately to their respective local TA headquarters. Following a well-drilled procedure, they collected their arms and equipment and proceeded immediately to their allocated defence battle stations; thus, placing England on full alert in case Mr Chamberlain's negotiations in Munich for peace failed.

As it happened the Prime Minister returned with a piece of paper, signed by Adolph Hitler, which was intended to guarantee peace between Britain and Germany during the lifetime of the current generation. The public were not aware of the fact at the time, but this was a ploy on Hitler's part to keep Britain off his back while he pursued his expansion plans in Eastern Europe in an attempt to dominate the communist States. It is not known how much faith Mr Chamberlain, himself, placed in that signature but it is a fact that the air defences remained on standby for another two weeks before the TA were stood down. To the relief of anxious mothers with teenage daughters in the vicinity of the camps, the soldiers returned to their humdrum jobs in civilian life. Frensham Down resumed peaceful normality, at least for the time being; except, that is, for the rage of Reg Hanshott when he found the damage caused to his hedges and field by the searchlight unit. Once again he vented his feelings to all and sundry in The Bowman

"It is about time the Army and Air Force realised we civilians have rights. They cannot barge in, damaging gates and hedges and ruining farmland, just when they feel like it"

Philip Golding, the solicitor who lived at Brook House on the Scolling Road, took issue with the irate farmer

"I am sorry, Reg. But I am afraid they *can*. At a time like this the Government takes emergency powers by which they can occupy any land for military reasons without giving prior notice, and without explaining their actions to anyone. Mind you, you might be entitled to claim compensation for damage caused to your farm; but I don't know how to go about applying for it or how much you will get, if anything"

Reg was not to be placated

"We were lucky not to lose any cows but it took the hands quite a while to round up two of the Friesians, Daisy and Lupin, who were wandering over the common, and one of the Jersey cows, Pansy, was nigh on down to the Scolling road by the time we caught her. Can't have her running about upsetting her full cream milk because it is her cream that helps to keep up the butter-fat quality of the herd's yield"

Len Mundy chuckled

"Pity we didn't 'ave old Dutch, the bull, loose in the field. As it was 'e were tethered to an iron stake down by the brook. Pity 'e weren't loose. Can't imagine what might 'ave 'appened if 'e was to get onto the common. That would 'ave given they soldier boys somthin' to think about"

Few people believed in the Munich agreement. Except for some vociferous pacifists, who were prepared to accept Nazi domination of Europe in exchange for an uneasy peace at any price, the population at large could be heard in pubs, factories and offices declaiming that allowing the Germans to occupy the Sudetanland, the German speaking part of Czechoslovakia, in return for Hitler's assurance that he would make no further territorial demands, was untenable. As history was to show, Hitler had no intention of attacking Britain at that time and would have been content to keep peace with the Allies if they would not interfere with his plans for Eastern Europe and Asia. In any event, those who knew the depleted strength of the British army and air force recognised that the United Kingdom was in no position to use force against the Nazis and that, with the Munich agreement, the Prime Minister was buying time to build up the armed forces. So, while British arms factories went into full production, the Nazis, unopposed, occupied the Sudetanland in October 1938. Almost immediately, Polish troops moved into the Teschen-Silesian area of Czechoslovakia to provide a military buffer zone between themselves and the Germans; an ineffectual move, as it turned out, because Hitler used this forced occupation later as an excuse to invade Poland. The Spanish civil war looked like ending with the creation of a Fascist state under General Franco and it was becoming, increasingly, clear that Mussolini would join forces with Hitler in an unholy alliance. It was in this state of unrest, with Fascism dominating a major part of Europe, that the year ended and, as 1939 dawned with the clouds of war gathering, the toast for the New Year throughout the Kingdom was a plea for peace above all else.

Len Mundy, ever the harbinger of doom, was having a New Year drink with his friends in The Bowman. He drank deep from his pint mug and proclaimed to the bar at large, and Gerry Stokes in particular,

"I've said it before and I says it again that there 'itler b'aint gonna be satisfied. Now 'e 'as got 'is jackboot into part of Czechoslovakia; next thing 'e will 'ave the rest of the Country. Then it will be Poland's turn. You see if I b'aint right, and, since we've got a pact to protect Poland, we will 'ave no choice but to go to war"

He paused while he drained the ale from his mug

"You mark my words, there'll be a war afore we sees another Christmas!"

Gerry Stokes agreed

"You may well be right, Len. But my Catherine won't be happy about it, with Alan in the RAF"

" I reckon 'e is better off there than in the army. At least 'e won't 'ave to go into the trenches like what we did in the last lot"

He looked, pointedly, at his empty beer mug

"...an' mine's a pint of ale, Gerry, if'n you is buyin'"

Gerry was taking back the empty mugs for a refill when William Studding, the Vet., walked in and headed for the bar. Gerry intercepted him

"I'm in the chair, Bill. Your's a pint? I am with Len Mundy over there"

Bill thanked him and changed direction to sit at the table with Len. When Gerry returned with the ale Len was still expounding his views on the political scene; this time with Bill Studding as his audience

"We was just sayin', Veterinary. I reckon there'll be another war afore long. Gerry, 'ere, was sayin' 'is Catherine won't be too 'appy with a son in the air force. What does your missus think about your two boys? Both orfficers, ain't they?"

"Yes, at least Bill is. He is a lieutenant in the Royal Engineers but we never see him these days. He is out in the Far East doing a five year tour of duty. The last we heard Bill was in Delhi; but he was expecting to be posted to a place called Roorki, in north west India, where he will be with the Royal Indian Engineers. If that posting comes through, it is not likely they will bring him back to Europe if war comes. They will need British and Indian troops out there to protect the Empire. Mind you, it will be different in young John's case"

"What do you mean, it's different for John. He's an orfficer too, bain't 'e?"

"Not really! He is still in training as an officer cadet in the RAF. What I meant was that John will certainly be in the thick of it if war breaks out in Europe"

Gerry Stokes did not comment. He was thinking of his own son, as a ranker in the RAF, and the difference between his opportunities and those of the Vet's son.

Alan Stokes had enlisted in the ranks of the RAF earlier in 1938, at the age of nineteen, partly because he was fascinated by flying machines. His main reason, however, was that he had been bored with village life since his older brother, Charlie, had joined the merchant navy and gone away to sea the year before. John Studding, on the other hand, was five years older than Alan Stokes and had little in common with the grocer's son. He had left

146

grammar school at eighteen, in April 1932, and, to his delight, was accepted at King's College, Cambridge. Five months later, when he found himself installed among the ancient buildings of Kings, he was in his element, for the College was an ideal setting for someone with his love of historical buildings. Throughout the next three years Cambridge was his life and, not wanting to come down to the outside world at the age of twenty two, he welcomed the opportunity to stay on for an extra year to take an honours degree in engineering. When he came down eventually, in 1936, he was torn between taking up engineering as a profession or complying with his father's wish that he should carry on studying for the qualifications he would need to take over the veterinary practice in due course. With a mother's intuition Valerie Studding was conscious that something was troubling her son and she asked her husband to find out what was wrong. He tackled John after surgery one evening.

"Your mother is worried about you, John. Is there something on your mind?"

"Well! Yes, Dad, there is. I know you are not going to like this but, although I am not certain about my future, I am pretty sure I am not cut out to be a Vet. I have a degree in engineering and I wonder whether I might be better suited to something in that line"

William did not answer at once and John pressed on

"I know you have spent a lot of money on my university education and I am grateful for all you and Mum have done; but I would like to have some time to think what I would like to do in the future and feel free to make my own choice"

He paused, waiting for his father's reaction. But William said nothing as he regarded his son thoughtfully. He had already suffered the disappointment that his eldest son had chosen the Army as a career rather than join the Practice. Now John, too, seemed reluctant to join him. He was not a martinet and was sympathetic to his son's dilemma. He consoled himself with the thought that his third son, Henry, who was still up at Cambridge might view the Practice differently.

"I take it you have discussed this with Joanne? What does she think?"

"She says I should honour my obligation to you, Dad"

William was touched by her sense of duty; although, had he known it, Joanne ws considering her own interests. She would rather John

147

stayed in the Village and became a Vet. William pondered for a moment, then offered John a compromise

"You don't have to start your veterinary studies straight away. So why not take your time? Bear with me! Spend a year or so helping me on my rounds and, if, after that, you decide it is not for you I will support your decision; whatever it is. Can we agree on that?" John's face lit up as he clasped his father's hand.

"Joanne will be pleased that we have not fallen out over this"

"So will your mother"

Joanne Hanshott became engaged to John Studding in August, 1938. At that time he was still helping his father in the Practice. He had not yet made up his mind about his future; although he was beginning to persuade himself to give up the idea of an independent career in engineering, and to comply with his father's wishes. It was in October that year, and during this period of indecision, that John received the letter from his older brother, Bill, which was to decide his future.

Lieutenant William Studding, Royal Engineers, was stationed at Government House in Delhi, India. He had written, at length, urging John to consider his position in the event of war. He had pointed out that, despite the Munich agreement, it was almost certain there would be a war and this would mean conscription, either before or immediately upon the outset of hostilities. He said that anyone who wanted a choice of service, and particularly those who wanted a commission, would be wise to volunteer now while they still had that choice.

When John showed the letter to Joanne, and asked what she thought of him volunteering, she had mixed feelings.

"If you want me to be honest, darling, I would prefer you to stay here, marry me, and join your father's practice. But I can see your brother's point. Do you really think there will be a war?"

"Yes! I think it is almost certain we shall be at war with Germany by next year and I agree with Bill. When that happens all men of my age will be conscripted; mostly into the Army. If I want any choice of service I must volunteer soon; before it is too late"

"But, if you joined your father's practice, wouldn't you, as a Vet, be exempt from military service?"

"A Vet *might* be; but I doubt that I would be qualified by the time conscription starts and I would be called up and sent into the Army without a commission"

Joanne hugged him close, possessively

"I am afraid for you, John. My Dad was a sergeant in the Army when he was killed at Flanders. Mum told me about the terrible time he had in the muddy trenches. I would hate to think of you being out there. If you must go, I would prefer that you were in the RAF. I don't know if serving in the Air Force would be any better but it could not be worse"

"I agree, and if I *must* join the forces, I would rather be in the RAF than in the Army; and I would rather serve as a commissioned officer than in the ranks"

"Well! If you think it is best to volunteer now do so, but I hope it does not stop us getting married next Spring?"

John was not certain about that, but he reassured her

"I don't think so. Plenty of RAF officers are married, but we might have to defer the wedding until I finish training and get my commission"

Joanne was reluctant to defer the wedding but she would agree to anything that kept her John away from the dreadful experience of trench warfare.

So, with his fiance's reluctant blessing, and the unwilling acceptance of his father and mother, John applied for a commission in the Royal Air Force at the age of 24; giving his preference for service as a fighter pilot. The RAF at that time was desperately seeking young men with the right academic background to train as pilots and navigators. Earlier criteria, which followed the class system and demanded, amongst other things, that commissioned officers be from a public school background, were being waived. So, with his academic qualifications and a reasonably acceptable background, John Studding had no difficulty in persuading the interview board of his suitability to hold the King's commission. Having signed on the dotted line, and taken the oath, Officer Cadet John Studding was allowed home for Christmas; after which, armed with a travel warrant, he was required to report to an RAF base in Berkshire.

The first six weeks were not what John had expected. Kitted out in an, ill fitting, rough serge uniform the realisation dawned that, if he failed the tasks set for him, he would remain in the RAF for seven years, but as an ordinary airman; unless fate decreed he should climb the non-commissioned promotion ladder. Thus, with little complaint and filled with determination to succeed, he endured a regime which consisted almost entirely of squad drill and strenuous physical training under the orders of sadistic sergeants and corporals; whose sole aim in life appeared to be to humiliate him and his fellow cadets by placing them in situations designed to provoke rebellion. Instead the cadets uncomplainingly submitted to orders which demanded instant compliance, irrespective of their relevance to the situation, on pain of what they considered to be unreasonable punishments.

John may not have appreciated it at the time but the purpose of this hard regime was to toughen his body and to instil a sense of discipline which would make it second nature for him to obey orders blindly in time of crisis. It certainly achieved the first of these criteria, as evidenced by the lean healthy airman who emerged at the end of the course. The second aim seemed to have limited effect as the future was to prove that blind obedience to orders was not in the nature of some fighter pilots. Sleeping thirty to a hut in close proximity with others, who had come from comfortable homes to the harsh rigours of camp life and with a common resentment against the authority of the NCOs in charge of training, achieved a third aim. By mixing with others in common adversity John learned the value of comradeship; an essential ingredient of any successful fighting unit.

Officer training school was only slightly less strenuous. Hard physical training continued; but interspersed with leadership exercises and other outdoor activities together with classroom lectures which John enjoyed. He passed out second in his group and was pleased to see his parents and Joanne in the crowd of relatives watching the passing out parade in February, 1939. Proudly wearing his new blue uniform with a single thin ring on the sleeve, Pilot Officer John Studding went home with his parents and fiance, immediately after the passing out parade for a few days leave before being posted to an FTS (Flying Training School) in Sussex.

Since January British aircraft factories had been in full production, supplying aircraft to the RAF at the rate of 400 per month; which was about two thirds of the rate at which Germany was re-arming the Luftwaffe. Improvements in fighter plane design, from the old bi-planes, high-wing monoplanes and low-speed low-wing monoplanes to the new high-speed hurricanes and, later, the super-marine spitfires meant retraining for every operational flying officer in fighter command. Similarly, new designs in multi-engined bombers and transport aircraft demanded retraining for air crews. Reservists were mobilised for six months training and re-training courses. However, not for John or his colleagues the impressive hurricane. His initial training, along with that of his fellow embryo flying officers at the FTS in Sussex, was confined to learning to fly in Tiger Moth trainers and the occasional Gloster Gladiator.

"I say, mind what you are doing"
John Studding was at the bar, in the Officers' Mess, trying to catch the eye of the bar steward, when another young officer, turning away from the bar next to him with a tray of drinks, caught John's shoulder with the edge of the tray; toppling the glasses and spilling whisky over John's, relatively new, uniform.

"Terribly sorry, old chap. Let me buy you a drink"
The offender turned to the bar steward and handed him the tray

"Sorry about that, steward! Clear this lot up, there's a good fellow. Then pour out another round and take it to Freddie's crowd over there. But, before you go, a couple of double whiskies for my friend here and myself. Put the lot on my tab!"
He held his hand out to John

"I am Willie Lavington"
John took the outstretched hand

"John Studding. What are you doing with our crowd? I see already have your wings but I noticed you with one of the rookie groups out in the field today. I thought perhaps you were one of the instructors?"
Willie chuckled

"Now, therein lies a story! I pranged a Gladiator near a village called Frensham Down last August and my CO sent me here as sort of punishment, don't y'know. Told me the RAF would never trust me with one of their new fighters if I did not take a re-training course with you chaps. I'm not complaining. It is a bit of a doddle really and, when I have done my stint, I am hoping to get posted to a hurricane training group"
He paused to take a sip from his glass and John interrupted

"Did you say Frensham Down just now?"
"Yes! Why, do you know it?"

"Do I know it? That is where I live"

"In that case you should know my cousin, Julia Frensham?"

"Not really! I know who she is but we don't move in the same circles. My father is the village veterinary and the nearest I have been to Frensham Hall is a visit to the stables with him"

Willie clamped his arm round John's shoulder

"Never mind! We are not as class conscious in the RAF as my relatives are at the Hall. I reckon we are all equal, except, of course, where senior rank is concerned. Got to show a bit of respect to Wing Co's and above, I suppose. As for the Frenshams, my aunt is a bit of a snob but the old boy is alright; so is young Willis. Jules takes after her mum a bit, but she is not so bad when you get to know her. I am thinking of going over there on my next leave. If you can get away at the same time I shall introduce you to the family properly"

He nudged John conspiratorially and grinned

"Perhaps we can get you off with Jules. That would upset her Ladyship when she finds out you are one of her peasants, as she calls the villagers"

John accepted the spirit of camaraderie and tried not to look offended

"You would be wasting your time. I am already engaged"

Willie regarded him with mock astonishment

"Really? What is she like? No! don't tell me. She is the most wonderful girl in the world and you have no intention of introducing her to me because you have heard of my scandalous reputation with women; which I must confess is all true"

John decided he liked this outgoing young man and was pleased when Willie invited him to join the group at Freddie's table. But he became embarrassed when he found himself in the company of a group of experienced flying instructors; two Squadron Leaders and two Flight Lieutenants. John had not yet started his flying training so he knew them only by sight. Willie was unabashed and, ignoring the fact that John might already know them, introduced him as a newcomer to the Mess

"Chaps! I want you to meet my new friend, John Studding. His Dad is a Vet so if you need that mongrel of yours put down, Jeremy, he is your man. Still! We won't hold that against him, will we? He is a good bloke really and the only thing not in his favour is that he is....wait for it.....he is engaged. Yes, you heard me right, he is engaged to be married"

They all smiled, as they groaned at the last statement, and stood up to shake John by the hand. Willy did the honours

"Freddie Stent, Squadron Leader, Jeremy Swift, Squadron Leader, Ronny Bridges, Flight; and, last but not least, Jerry Wilson, Flight"

Freddie Stent took the initiative

"Welcome to the Mess, John! Don't take any notice of Willie's banter. He has no respect for anyone's feelings. I take it you are here to get your wings?"

John resisted the temptation to stand to attention and salute

"Yes, Sir. I hope so, Sir"

Freddie Stent raised a deprecating hand

"No 'Sirs' in the Mess, if you please. In here I am Freddie to my friends. On duty, of course, rank must be observed. Willie is the lucky one! He is only here for a short while. When he returns to his station at Hornchurch they will probably post him to Group Fighter Training in Wales for a course on hurricanes. As for the rest of us we won't get a chance to go for fighter training until they bring in civilian flying instructors or reservists to take our places as instructors"

Willie was irrepressible

"John will probably beat you to it. P'raps I can take him under my wing, so to speak, and make him a fighter Ace before you get away from here"

Jeremy Swift butted in "You would be wise, John, not to learn anything about flying from Willie. His only achievement to date is to wipe out one of His Majesty's best aircraft in a hayfield"

So the banter went on and, by the time John staggered back to the darkness of his hut and fumbled past complaining bodies to his bed, he felt he was at last where he belonged and could not wait to earn his wings and join that illustrious company as an equal, more or less.

If John had expected to jump into the cockpit of an airplane straight away when he arrived at FTS he was sadly mistaken. The would-be flyers spent hours in the classroom mastering the mysteries of such matters as aero-dynamics, weather patterns, cloud formations and their effect on aircraft, navigation, aircraft construction and behaviour and a hundred and one other things; some of which seemed to bear little relevance to flying. There were the practical exercises, such as split-second recognition of aircraft appearing briefly on a screen in silhouette. As the instructor, wryly, commented "You don't want to find yourself saying 'Whoops, sorry' when you have just shot down one of your chums by mistake, do you?"

Then there was recognition of geographical terrain from photographs taken from the air. Outdoor training included map reading exercises in all weathers, often combined with instruction in survival techniques, parachute drill both from a tower and from an aircraft; and, when there seemed to be nothing else on the agenda, there was always the interminable physical training to keep them fit.

In view of the grave political situation, and the need to build up air defences quickly, no home leave was allowed during training. So John had to content himself with the letters he received, almost daily, from Joanne. She told him any news from home she thought would interest him but her letters were mainly concerned with her desire to have him with her and regularly included questions regarding how soon they could be married. His replies were just as endearing but it is doubtful whether she found solace in his enthusiasm for the Air Force life.

Conscription came much earlier than John had predicted. For, in April, 1939, the British Government introduced compulsory conscription to military service for all 20 year old males for a minimum period of six months or duration of the war; if the latter should commence during that time. A National Service register was also compiled for all males between the ages of 18 and 21 for use if it became necessary to extend of the conscription programme. When the first group of conscripts had served for a period of six months training they were to be co-opted into Territorial Army regiments or, in some cases, Naval and RAF reserve units; so that they would provide a pool of trained civilians to be mobilised instantly on the outbreak of a war. This action confirmed William Studding's prediction and, in John's mind, justified his own voluntary enrolment in the RAF.

The order to wear uniform on duty and off had not yet been introduced and the trainees found it a relief to change into civies when they had time off to go outside the Training Camp. Nevertheless, their social life, apart from the occasional afternoon or Sunday trip into the nearby town to the cinema, seemed to revolve around the local pub, which was in a village some three miles from the camp. John's association with his colleagues on such occasions depended on whether he could cadge a lift from a fellow officer who owned a car. More than once he was stranded when the pub turned out because the only MG available was crowded with bodies and he found himself with an uncomfortable walk, often alone, on a winter's night back to camp; so he elected to stay in the Mess most evenings keeping company with Willie and his friends, at least until Willie left to go back to his unit. He was sorry when Willie left because they had become firm friends; but he found some consolation in exchanging regular letters with Willie which kept them in touch. As the Winter of 1938/39 gave way to Spring, and the dogs of war bayed in Europe, the trainees yearned for the day when they would finish the preliminary training course which was designed, partly, to weed out those whom the RAF considered were not suitable for flying duties. Joanne's dream of a Spring wedding faded as John could not get leave during training, but he wrote reassuring letters saying that he had obtained permission from his CO to marry, a military formality, and that he hoped to get leave for this purpose in the Summer.

By June, 1939, conscription to the Army had started in earnest, and the spider huts of training camps could be seen filling up with twenty year old trainee soldiers throughout the English countryside. At the same time the instructors at the RAF flying training school decided that John's class was ready to learn how to handle an airplane. It was a much smaller party that was handed over to the fighter plane instructors; of the original class of thirty only a handful remained. Some of the class had not passed the preliminary courses and had been posted elsewhere because they were assessed as being more suited to support crew as navigators, wireless operators or observers. Some had simply fallen by the way had been posted to non-flying roles in the RAF, more commensurate with their talents.

John's first flight was in a twin seat, dual control, trainer with his instructor sitting in the rear cockpit and flying the aircraft. After a while the instructor allowed John to take over once the plane had levelled out, but he was not allowed to take off or land until he had mastered control in the air. His first take off went very smoothly but his landing was spectacular. The aircraft bounced back into the air as soon as the wheels touched the ground and all but crashed as it kangarooed along the grass landing field. He was shamefaced when he climbed out of the cockpit but felt less embarrassed when each of his fellow pupils did the same. As June progressed the signs of impending war grew and training was speeded up. Within a very short time John's group had diminished to eight and John found himself flying solo. He managed to get himself lost on a couple of occasions as soon as he was out of sight of the field but he kept his head and found his way back when from 600ft up he was able to make out familiar landmarks. Nevertheless, he satisfied his instructors and, following an armament practice course, John was awarded his wings early in July, 1939.

Pilot Officer John Studding was allowed only five days leave after receiving his wings. During this leave he and Joanne Hanshott were married, by special licence, in St James church, Frensham Down. It was a very quiet affair and guests were kept to a minimum. William Studding was still in India and John's younger brother, Henry, who had been caught up in the first wave of conscription, could not get leave for the wedding. So John asked Willie Lavington to be his best man. Willie managed to get only three days leave and caused a stir when he turned up late at night on the eve of the wedding in his new sports car. He had taken Freddie Frobisher's advice and bought one of the new jaguar convertible sports cars in white. Its enormous twin headlamps, which decorated the front grid, lit up the whole of the village green as, sounding his clarion horn, he swung the car off the Scolling Road and headed for the vet's cottage. He had resisted the impulse to drive up to Frensham Hall to show off his new toy; and had accepted John's father's invitation to move into Henry's room. To the delight of the village boys, who had never seen anything like it, Willie parked his gleaming new motor outside the Vet's cottage on the Village Green.

Sally looked delightful in her bridesmaid's dress and Reg Hanshott was proud to be giving Joanne away. John and Willie both wore their dress uniforms and Jennie Madieson supplemented the official photographer's pictures with snaps from a box Brownie. Both Lillian and Maddie wept a few private tears at the reception in the Hanshott farmhouse; Lillian emotionally affected as a mother and Maddie fondly remembering her own wedding reception there seventeen years earlier.

John still had a couple of days leave to go which the happy couple were spending with his parents. But the day after the wedding Willie had to go back to camp. John, who was leaning on the passenger door of his friend's car outside the vet's surgery, said.

"I'll be reporting to Group Fighter Training in South Wales at the end of my leave"

Willie was sitting at the wheel with the engine idling. The top was down and his bag was perched on the back seat

"I say, what luck, I have been posted to St Athan, too; so has Freddie. He has got away from flying instruction at last!"

He grinned with the impish look that had charmed so many girls; but it had no effect on Joanne, who was standing beside John holding his arm

"I s'pose its a bit much to ask you to give up your last two days with your new wife and come with me now? There is plenty of room in the old bus"

Seeing John's expression, and the disapproval on Joanne's face, he smiled, disarmingly, and added quickly

"No! I doubt that is a good idea"

He reached across and shook John's hand with a firm clasp

"See you in a couple of days"

He blew a kiss to Joanne and roared off round the village green. Stopping to give a wave when he reached The Bowman, he turned right and disappeared. They could still hear his engine accelerating into the distance up the Scolling Road.

It was early morning when, two days later, John Studding kissed his bride of a few days goodbye at Dunchester Railway Station. Lillian, who was there with John's parents, could not help remembering kissing Joanne's father goodbye on the same spot in 1915. He had never returned to her and there was a lump in her throat as she clasped John in a farewell embrace.

John made a good connection in London but the train ride to Cardiff seemed never-ending. There was no direct line to St Athan; the nearest railway station being at Merthyr Dyfan which was on the local line to Barry. So, before he joined the train to Barry, John asked the RTO (Rail transport officer) at Cardiff to telephone the RAF station and ask Willie to arrange for him to be picked up at Merthyr Dyfan. It was late in the afternoon when John stepped off the train and, as he left the small railway station, he was relieved to see Willie had come, himself, to meet him.

"Well there you are, old boy! I have been waiting here for half an hour"

Willie, looking every inch the dashing fighter pilot with his coveted wings sewn on the breast of his blue uniform and a long silk RAF scarf slung round his neck. His cap perched jauntily on the back of his head, he was sitting on the ample wing of his sports car with his arm round the waist of the pretty teenager standing beside him

"This is Rosie! We have just met. I am giving her a lift as well; but I don't know where to yet"

He looked inquiringly at the girl, who simpered

"I don't know about that, Willie. I don't really know you or your friend. In any case my uncle is supposed to be picking me up in a minute so I must wait for him"

"Oh well! Suit yourself, old girl. Sling your bag in the back, John, and we'll be off. So long Rosie. See you around"

Willie did not look back or wave as the car roared off; leaving the lone figure standing in the lengthening shadows outside the station. In Willie's philosophy she was just another pick-up, to be forgotten if there was no hope of a quick conquest, and he had already dismissed her from his mind.

"Hang on tight, John. We'll be there in no time"

Freddie Stent was in the Mess waiting for them. He held out his hand

"Welcome to hurricanes, John. I knew you'd make it. Willie tells me you are bunked down with him. I am not sure that is a good idea. They tell me he snores!"

"Come off it, Freddie. *You* are the one who snores. The guard commander has complained that you keep his sentries awake at night"

Once again with his old friends John felt at home and he experienced an undeniable thrill next morning when he reported for duty and saw the hurricanes he and his friends were to learn to fly lined up on the field. Training in handling the aircraft and standard fighter command tactics took a month but it passed without a hitch. So, by the end of August, 1939, the three friends had become operational fighter pilots and were eagerly anticipating the possibility of active service overseas in the near future. They were not to be disappointed, for the Territorial Army and other Reservists had been mobilised and everyone knew war with Germany was now inevitable.

CHAPTER NINE

1939

It was Friday, 1 September, 1939. The hot summer had held and the weather forecast promised an Indian Summer which, at another time, would probably have been the most important thing to occupy the minds of the people in Britain; particularly the farmers who were gathering in the last of the grain harvest. But this summer was different. The Navy, Army and Air Force put on full alert and all reservists had been mobilised. School children were being evacuated from London, and other major cities, to homes in the comparative safety of the English countryside where some would be greeted with open arms and others would be reluctantly accepted by their temporary foster parents; the latter having been forced under the emergency powers regulations to take in their quota.

The LNER Special steamed slowly into Frensham Halt and, with a hiss of steam from the braking system, stopped with a jolt. Children of all ages could be seen leaning out of the windows; some shouting to each other and others gazing silently at the unfamiliar countryside. The doors of three compartments opened and an adult from each compartment helped the occupants, with their few belongings, to alight safely onto the platform. The children stood there in a bewildered group, five girls between eight and ten years of age and seven boys between seven and nine years of age. Some with cardboard cases and others with brown paper bags and parcels; but each with a small cardboard box containing a gas mask which hung by a string from their necks. They stood huddled together for mutual comfort as they, silently, waited to see what was to happen next. Two of the escorts, women teachers from a London school, stood by with the children while the third teacher, a briskly efficient woman of around 35 years, checked the name tab of each child against a list she had attached to a clipboard. Satisfied, she approached the three ladies who formed the reception committee. Mrs Charlotte Tremming, headmistress of Frensham Down junior school, stepped forward.

"Good morning, Mrs....?"

"You must be Mrs Tremming? Good morning to you! It is Miss actually. I am Miss Amelia Wallace from Central Park School, East Ham. Here is a list of the children for your village. They are all

161

under eleven so that they can attend your local school. We have already dropped some of the older children off with the group at Chetsford and there are others remaining on the train until we reach Dunchester. It is preferable that the children be placed in homes around the schools they will attend"

She paused and pointed to one ten year old girl who was clutching the hand of a tearful small boy.

"Peggy Jones, there with her brother Tom, has an older brother and sister. Twins of thirteen years whom we dropped off in Chetsford. The authorities will be in touch within a few days to let you know where the twins are living. We do not want families to lose touch with each other. However, in case of difficulties, here is my address and telephone number and the East Ham address of the children's mother. We have some parents on the train; but none of *these* little ones have their parents with them. There were plenty of tears at Liverpool Street station when they were seen off by their mothers but we have managed to cheer the children up during the journey. Each child has a name tab pinned to their coat. Perhaps you could check the names off on this list and sign it to show I have handed them all over to your care?"

Mrs Tremming walked over to the group of children and, nodding a brief 'Good morning' to the other two women teachers, she bent down to speak comfortingly to each child, in turn, while she checked the names off on the list. She signed the list and handed the clipboard back to Miss Wallace; who lifted the page and signed a copy which she withdrew from the clipboard and handed to Mrs Tremming.

"This is *your* copy. I hate to be formal, but I must be assured that you have made the necessary arrangements for the care of these children?"

"Oh yes! You need not worry! We have found comfortable homes for all of them. They will all be attending my school and my husband, the Principal, will be monitoring their progress. When the children have been installed in their new homes I shall write to their parents to give them the addresses. Let us hope it will not be for long. They say that, if war comes, it will be all over by Christmas"

"I am not so sure about that prediction; but, either way, I am glad these little ones will be out of harms way if things in London get difficult. Well! We must get back on the train. The driver and guard will be getting impatient. We still have a lot of children to place

162

around Dunchester before we can call it a day. Goodbye, Mrs Tremming. Thank you for your help and please thank these good ladies, also, for their help and convey our gratitude to all those kind people who are taking in our children"

Miss Wallace turned to the children. There was a hint of a tear in her eye as she hugged each of them

""Goodbye, children. Now, behave yourselves and do as Mrs Tremming tells you. I shall be hearing how you are getting on and I do not want to have any bad reports waiting for me to deal with when you return to Central Park. Look upon this as a holiday in the country and I know you will be happy here"

The three teachers boarded the train. The guard blew his whistle and waved his green flag. With a few rapid puffs of steam and smoke the engine took the strain and the train slowly gathered speed as it left Frensham Halt on it way to Dunchester.

The group on the platform were watching the departing train and no-one saw the figure that had, furtively, jumped from the baggage car onto the down line while they were busy on the opposite side of the train. He had hidden himself among the bushes by the side of the track and now crouched down there watching the group on the opposite platform. Charlotte Tremming turned to Valerie Bell, the police constable's wife, and Maxine Wykeham, the vicar's wife

"Well, we had better get this little lot down to school and feed them"

Little Mary Smith tugged at Charlotte's skirt

"I wanna go to the lav"

"I am sorry, dear! There are no toilets here. You will have to wait until we get to the school. Come along now. The sooner we get in the bus, the sooner we shall get there"

The ladies led their small charges over the footbridge and Valerie and Maxine ushered them onto the small single-deck bus that had been hired for the occasion; while Charlotte counted them and rechecked their names against her list as they boarded the vehicle. She returned to the downside platform and looked both ways to make sure no-one had been left behind. Satisfied, she returned to the bus.

The man was about to emerge from his hiding place in the bushes beyond the end of the platform, but he crouched down as the party came over the footbridge to his side of the line. He watched as Mrs Tremming came back to check the empty platform but remained crouching there until he heard the bus drive away. Then he, cautiously, emerged and looked around him. He could hear the bus making its noisy way up Station Road to the Scolling Road; but there was no-one in sight. He was around 25 years of age and of average height and build, with blond hair and a small moustache. He was wearing crumpled grey trousers and a tweed sports jacket. He removed a pair of horn-rimmed spectacles from his breast pocket and put these on. Anyone looking through these would see the lenses were of, slightly tinted, plain glass and realise the stranger was wearing them for effect or in an attempt to hide the hard, sinister, look in his bright blue eyes. He took a piece of paper from his the inside pocket of his jacket and unfolded it to reveal a roughly drawn map. Orientating himself with the spire of the church on the hill in the distance, he determined the direction he would need to travel. Replacing the map, he picked up his light leather suitcase and walked back along the track, towards Chetsford, for about half a mile until he crossed the small stone bridge where the railway passed over the Primrose stream. Then, stumbling down the embankment by the bridge he climbed over the low wooden-railed fence which lined the rail track. There was still no-one in sight as he followed the stream until he reached Black Hut Lane. Here, he paused for a moment while he leaned on the five barred gate, listening and looking around him. Above the sound of babbling water he could hear the low murmur of voices coming from behind the hedge on the opposite side of the lane. Consulting his map again he saw that the hedge hid the Village cricket pitch and decided he need not be concerned about the voices . Nevertheless, he moved silently as he climbed over the gate. No-one was in sight when the stranger crossed the stone bridge by the Black Hut and, quietly opening the front gate of number 25, walked up the garden path to let himself into the terraced cottage with a key which he took from its hiding place above the lintel.

Hilda Benhope was out shopping at the time so she did not see her next door neighbour arrive. Had she done so she would have maintained nothing more than a passing curiosity because she had recently received a visit from a post office representative asking if she wanted a telephone line installed at the same time they would be connecting a telephone to the furnished cottage next door.

The GPO man did not name the new tenants and had only mentioned them so that Hilda would not be alarmed when GPO engineers arrived at number twenty-five. Hilda had only recently paid for connection to the electricity service which had, at last, reached the village and could not afford the additional connection to the telephone service yet. She, idly, wondered whether her new neighbours, when she got to know them, might allow her use of the instrument in an emergency. But, she dismissed the thought as being presumptuous, almost immediately it occurred to her, and decided not to raise the matter with her neighbours; at least not for the time being. But it would be nice to know Maddie could contact her, wouldn't it?

The stranger carried his case up to the back bedroom and unpacked it. Taking his washing materials he descended the stairs to the small kitchen at the back. He flicked the light switch on the wall to check that the electric power was connected. Then he filled the electric kettle and plugged it into a wall socket above the draining board. While he waited for the kettle to boil he unbolted the back door and paid a visit to the outside toilet. Returning, he removed his jacket, tie and shirt before adding hot water to the bowl of cold water in the sink. Then, with the aid of a small shaving mirror, a safety razor and the bar of Lifebuoy soap he found lying on the draining board, he shaved off the stubble from his face and washed himself. Still drying his face on the kitchen towel, he walked into the front living room and crossed to the sideboard. Dropping the towel on a chair he picked up the upright telephone instrument. Holding its post in his right hand, he lifted the earpiece with his left and used the fingers of his right hand to joggle the lever to attract the operator's attention

"Could you connect me to a London number, please?"

"Yes Sir. What number are you calling from?"

He looked at the disk let into the base of the instrument

"Frensham Down 435"

. "That is a new number. Isn't it?"

"I think so! I have only just moved in"

He was not in the mood for small talk and was getting impatient

"Well! Can you put me through or not?"

"What number do you want?"

"Maida Vale 3843, please"

There was a pause then a female voice answered. The operator came back on the line

"You are through, caller"

"Is that Maida Vale 3843?"

"Yes! Who is calling?"

"It is your cousin Harry calling from the cottage"

There was a guarded pause before the woman gave the expected response

"I have no cousin Harry. Go away!"

The line went dead. The stranger replaced the receiver, then sat down in an armchair and waited. He checked the time with his pocket watch. It was exactly three minutes later that the telephone bell rang. He picked up the instrument and put the earpiece to his left ear; but said nothing. The same woman's voice spoke.

"Good morning, George"

It was his turn to give the expected response

"Who is George?"

"Georgie, Porgie, Pudding and pie. Kissed the girls but they didn not cry"

"Alright! Winkler said you have the package for me?"

"It was despatched yesterday for you to collect at Dunchester Railway Station. A rented car is waiting for you to pick up at the garage on the Scolling Road. Identify yourself with your driving licence. Have you made contact with the subject yet?"

"No! I shall wait until I have collected the car and the package"

Without further comment he replaced the earpiece and returned to the kitchen. He picked up his coat and tie and climbed the stairs to the bedroom. Rummaging among the clothing left in his suitcase, he withdrew a Luger automatic pistol. He slipped out the clip to ensure it was fully loaded then replaced it in the butt of the gun. For a moment he contemplated whether he should carry the weapon but decided it was not necessary for the present and might require explanation if it were to be found on him. He replaced the pistol and, locking the case, thrust it under the bed. Returning to the kitchen he picked up a straw shopping basket and consulted his map again before leaving the cottage.

The stranger turned right, retracing his footsteps along Black Hut Lane until he had crossed the bridge. The he turned left to drop down onto the footpath, which ran alongside the Primrose Stream, skirting the cricket pitch and school playing fields until he reached School Lane. As he entered the lane the evacuees' bus, now

166

empty, passed him on its way to the garage at the top of the lane. He followed it and, reaching the garage forecourt, casually looked towards the driver who was standing idly by the bus while James Twist filled the petrol tank. The driver looked casually in his direction but, to the stranger's relief, he gave no sign of recognition. So the driver had not seen him leaving the train? He waited by the garage door until the bus had driven away, turning left to go back down School Lane. James Twist turned to him.

"What can I do for you?"

The stranger produced his driving licence

"I understand you have a car for me?"

James looked at the red linen-covered licence. It had an East London address shown inside for the holder.

"Yes! Mr Grimble. If you will kindly follow me into the office we can sort out the paper work"

They entered the grubby office. It smelled of oil and grease. The garage owner's wife, Catherine, was seated at the desk working on the accounts. She looked up and James Twist smiled at her as he wiped his hands on a piece of rag and reached round her into a drawer to fish out a paper contract which had already been filled in. She looked at the stranger but James did not introduce his wife, so she said nothing as she moved her books to make space for James to spread out the contract on the desk.

"I see the car was hired for you by Murphy's, the estate agent in Dunchester, and the full deposit and one month's hire money have been paid in advance. There is no local address given here for yourself?"

"No! I expect to be travelling around the area and I am not sure where I may be staying at any one time. You have seen the London address on my driving licence. Is a local address also necessary?"

"Not really! Please sign here ...... and here"

James compared the signatures with that on the driving licence and, satisfied, he passed the original hire contract to his wife and handed the copy to Fred Grimble.

"When you have finished with the car please return it to the Dunchester garage at the address shown on your copy of the agreement. If that is not practical, telephone the garage to tell them where the car is so that they can arrange to pick it up. If you need the vehicle for more than one month you will need to contact the Dunchester garage to arrange the extension and pay the extra rental

167

charge. Well! I think that is all! If you will kindly wait outside I will fetch the car for you and fill her up. The rent includes a full tank of petrol. By the way, do not forget to contact the car hire people about petrol coupons. You are alright for a couple of weeks but after 23 September, when rationing starts, you will need coupons"

"Thank you, but that will not be a problem. My firm will see that I get the coupons in time"

James drove the black Hillman Minx saloon car out onto the forecourt and filled the petrol tank. He handed over the keys and watched the car being driven slowly away down the Scolling Road towards Dunchester. James Twist returned to his office and addressed his wife.

"Odd sort of cove! Never smiled and hardly spoke a word. When he did speak there was a strange clipped tone to his speech. Another thing! Did you notice that his clothes were a bit crumpled? Almost as though he had been living rough. And where did he come from? There *is* no bus at this time of day. And why pick up the car from here? He had no gas mask and no luggage but he said he had no local address. I thought he might be staying at the Bowman but he drove right past the pub when he left here. Anyway, I'll ask Angus when I see him tonight. If Mr Grimble is staying in Dunchester I would have thought it would be easier to collect the car directly from the Dunchester garage?"

He stroked his ear reflectively

"And another thing, he seemed unfamiliar with the controls. I would have thought a commercial traveller would be used to driving any make of car. It is all rather odd! I hope I haven't let someone who found the driving licence steal the vehicle. No! It must be alright. How would a thief know the car was waiting here to be collected?"

Charlotte Tremming had spent a tiring afternoon sorting out the children and dispatching them to their new homes. School was still out for the summer holiday so, apart from her own daughters, there were no other children for her to worry about while she dealt with the newcomers. When they alighted from the bus at the school the evacuees had sat around on the grass bank beside the playground to consume the sandwiches and lemonade brought to them by Charlotte's thirteen year old daughter, Angela. Eight year old May

168

Smith sat apart from the others rocking to and fro; her long fair hair dropping down to cover her face and mingle with the fair hair of the doll she clutched. She was sobbing quietly to herself. Charlotte's younger daughter, Josie, was the same age as May and, at her mother's request, she sat down next to the child and attempted to make friends and comfort her. She had little success, but May's tear-stained face brightened with interest when she heard the clip clopping of hoofs and she saw the pony and trap which Melanie French, the blacksmith's thirty-nine year old sister, had driven into the schoolyard. Melanie and Cherry, her fourteen year old niece, jumped down to be greeted by Charlotte Tremming who took them over to May.

"This is May Smith. As you can see she is unhappy to be away from home but I am sure she will brighten up now she has met you both and knows where she is going"
She turned to May.

"Come along, May, and bring your things. This is Miss French and she is going to take you for a ride to her lovely cottage where you will be staying with Cherry, here, and her sister, Hazel. I know you will be very happy there"
May gazed apprehensively at the animal

"Its an 'orse an' cart! I aint never ridden in an 'orse an' cart"
Melanie French was not put off by the cockney accent. She smiled at May.

"Actually, dear, it is called a pony and trap. You need not look so worried. The pony is called Gypsy and he is very gentle. I think you will like him when you get to know him. Look, he is already trying to make friends with you"
Melanie French climbed back into the trap and took the strain on the reins to settle Gypsy while Cherry helped May to climb up the two iron steps into the two wheeled vehicle. Cherry followed, to seat herself next to May, while Melanie reached over to give the child a comforting hug.

"Don't worry, love. Your mummy will be coming down to see you before you know it. You are just going to have a nice holiday with us. I am sure you will love it when you see the room you are sharing with Cherry. Is that all the luggage you have?"
May did not answer but nodded her head.

"Never mind. We shall soon fix you up with anything else you need.   'bye Mrs Tremming and thank you. Gd'up Gipsy"

Angela Tremming sat on the grass beside Peggy Jones and Tom, her seven year old brother, waiting for the other evacuee children to leave. Charlotte had made an instant decision to take personal responsibility for contacting their older brother and sister at the Chetsford address Miss Wallace had given her and had determined it would be easier if Peggy and Tom were given a home in the residence next to the schoolhouse. The small guest room was unoccupied, so Charlotte decided Peggy should share her daughter Josie's room and she would put Tom in the guest room; though she was not aware, at the time, the problems this would create because little Tom had never slept alone before.

Maisie Moore was a streetwise tough little seven year old and had taken the move in her stride. She had managed to restrain the call of nature until they reached the school and, after rushing off the bus straight to the 'lav', as she put it, in the playground she had joined her nine year old brother, Billy, on the grass with the others. Maxine Wykeham had taken the pair under her wing and they were to stay with her at the Vicarage. Later, when the vicar collected Maxine and her two charges, in his little Austin Seven, there was no indication of the consternation this arrangement was to raise, in a few months' time, when Rabbi Moore and his wife visited their children at the Vicarage.

The bus, which had returned to the school after its petrol trip to the garage, was to take the remaining seven children to their new homes. Charlotte Tremming left her husband, Charles, to keep an eye on the children at the school while she accompanied the remaining evacuees on the bus. The vehicle turned right out of the schoolyard and, then left into Wash Road. The children were delighted by the wave of spray that rose either side of the bus as it splashed through the 'wash' at Scolling Brook. It pulled up outside the Crannock Farmhouse. Ten year old Gilly Wells and her nine year old sister, Maggie, loved animals and were ecstatic to learn they were to live on a real dairy farm, with cows and everything. Mary Styles came to the gate with two of her four children to welcome them. Her fourteen year old daughter, Betty, greeted them cordially but her brother Jeremy, a year older, was not so friendly. His first, caustic, comment was intended to put the intruders off

"I 'ope you likes farmwork, 'cos me Dad'll 'ave you out collectin' eggs, milkin' the cows, muckin' out an' all that, like 'e do the rest of us"

170

Neither child was deterred by his unwelcoming comments. Both girls were reasonably well spoken, apart from dropping an aitch here and there, but Gilly put on her best cockney in reply "Oi! We're gonna to love it 'ere. Aint we Maggie?"

The bus continued up the road to turn left onto the Scolling Road and right into Hanshott Lane. The children could see the pony and trap standing under the oak tree in the Smithy yard and waved to May Smith who had turned round on hearing the bus come round the corner. The vehicle continued up the hill to stop by the garden gate at the Hanshott farmhouse. Maddie and Lillian came out to greet Charlotte Tremming and the boy who was to stay with them. But, eight year old Dick May was reluctant to leave his best friend, Jimmy Horn. He pleaded with Charlotte

"I want to stay with Jimmy"

"Jimmy won't be far away and you will see him in school every day. It will be just the same as if you were at home"

"No it won't. We lived next door to each uvver in East 'am"

Charlotte looked despairingly at Maddie

"Well! It is up to you, Mrs Hanshott. The regulations only require you to take in one child"

"Where is the other boy supposed to be going?"

"Tom and Anne Grey are expecting him at Church Farm. But I know Anne is worried about room space. I understand their son, Mike, is not happy at sharing his room with a small boy"

Maddie looked enquiringly at Lillian, who nodded her agreement. She turned back to Charlotte.

"We were going to put Dick in Martha's old room on his own; but, if he is happy to share the room with Jimmy, we have no objection to taking in both boys. They will be company for each other and can walk to school together"

Charlotte hesitated.

"Can I use your phone to call Anne Grey. I am sure she will welcome the change but I must talk to her before I can leave the boy with you"

Ann Grey was relieved to be released from the responsibility and raised no objections. So Dick and Jimmy, all smiles, climbed down from the bus together and followed Lillian into the farmhouse. Maddie walked down the lane and opened the five barred gate which allowed the driver to reverse into the field and turn the bus round to face back down the lane. When it had completed the manoeuvre she shut the gate and stood waving towards the back of the retreating vehicle.

It was a short journey to the next stop outside the police cottage at the corner of Hanshott Lane. The children had seen May Smith in the yard at the blacksmith's cottage when the bus first turned into Hanshott Lane. So, when Charlotte called eight year old Harry Moon forward, he thought, at first, that he was to stay with May Smith. The Smithy looked an interesting place and Harry was disappointed, and not a little anxious, when he realised Charlotte was leading him past the Police notice board and up to the front door of the Constable Bell's cottage.

Valerie Bell was not at all happy at having another young child thrust upon her. She already had her ten year old son, Dicky, and her seven year old daughter, Primrose, to look after and had not planned to add to her responsibilities. When Richard Bell had told her they had been requested by his superintendent to take an evacuee, as an example of their patriotic spirit, she felt she had no choice in the matter. Nevertheless, she remonstrated with her husband

"Don't you think I have enough to do looking after you, Dicky and Primrose without having another lot of washing and cleaning up after a strange child?"

"It is not my decision, my dear. There are many farmers around here who are not happy to have crowds of town-bred children roaming around, leaving gates open, trampling crops, disturbing the animals and generally intruding on their lives. But they would not want these little mites left in London when the bombing starts. In any case, Inspector Rose says that we, in the Force, have a duty to set a good example and, where we can, we should take in at least one evacuee"

"But we don't have the room. Where is he, or she, to sleep?"

"Both Dickie and Primrose have a large bedroom each. So the single bed the authorities are supplying can be set up in whichever room is practical"

"Well, I suppose I shall have to put up with it. Primrose is too young to object and will probably look upon the newcomer as someone to play with. Dickie keeps saying he'd rather have a brother than a sister so perhaps he will be happy if it is a boy"

Valerie turned back to her dusting, but not before she added a parting shot

172

"They are coming from the East End of London aren't they? I only hope they don't bring fleas with them!"

Despite her misgivings Valerie Bell could not help feeling sorry for the little boy who stood on her doorstep clutching Charlotte Tremming's hand. Like most East End schoolboys, Harry had experienced minor brushes with the law and more than once had received a clip on the ear from the constable on the beat for some misdemeanour. His teenage brother had only escaped a prison sentence, a few years earlier, by agreeing to sign up in the Army for seven years. So Harry had no reason to expect gentle treatment from the occupants of a police house. But he came from stern stock and, little though he was, he braced himself; determined not to be intimidated by circumstances. His face was impassive as he looked at the woman who opened the door. Her two children were standing in the hall behind her. Harry found it disconcerting when Valerie, despite the feelings she had expressed to her husband earlier, smiled at him

"Come in Mrs Tremming. Is this the young man who is coming to stay with us?"

"Yes, Mrs Bell. His name is Harry Moon and he is eight years old. He is a bit tired after a long day travelling from East Ham in London. It may take him a little while to settle in but he has two of his school friends staying at Hanshott Farm and a little girl of his own age, May Smith, has moved in with Melanie French across the road from you so he won't have any trouble finding someone to play with outside school hours. But, of course, I was forgetting, you have your own two and your Primrose must be around Harry's age?"

"She is a little younger but, between them, I am sure Dicky and Primrose will keep Harry occupied. I think you will like them, Harry. You will be sleeping in Dickie's room"

Dickie, peeking from behind his mother skirt, poked his tongue out at Harry, but the evacuee decided to bide his time and did not return the greeting.

May Smith was looking out of the bedroom window when the bus pulled up outside the Police Cottage. She glanced over her shoulder and spoke to Cherry French.

"Looks like that 'orrid little 'arry Moon is goin' to live across the road"

"Who is Harry Moon?"

"A nasty little creep what was in my class at Central Park School. Got a bruver what got sent away to the Army by the judge an' a Dad what's always bein' taken away by the cops. Fancy 'arry goin' to live in a cop shop! I can't wait to tell Maisie Moore when I see 'er. The copper over there 'ad better watch out! 'arry'll steal 'is 'elmet an' anyfink else 'e can lay 'is fieving little 'ands on"

Charlotte Tremming was relieved when the bus reached its last delivery point outside the general store at the bottom end of the village green. She helped down the remaining two children as Catherine Stokes and Jean came out to greet them. Catherine was required by the emergency regulations to take only one child but, when Charlotte telephoned her from the school and told her nine year old Steve Graham had a small brother, she immediately insisted they both share her spare room. Reg Graham, an apprehensive, seven year old, was tired from the long journey and near to tears when Jean Stokes, now eighteen years of age, gathered him in her arms and gave him a huge welcoming hug. Nine year old Steve considered himself too grown up to show his emotions in public. He shrank back, involuntarily, as Jean's mother, Catherine, approached him; thinking he was to receive the same affectionate treatment as his brother. But Catherine's smiling face as she looked down at him reminded him of his mother and he relaxed as she took his hand gently in hers. Saying goodbye to Charlotte she led him into the shop to join his younger brother.

Actually it was a coincidence that Fred Grimble was on the evacuees' Special. He had intended to catch a fast train to Dunchester and to find his way from there to Frensham Down. However, when he arrived at Liverpool Street station the concourse was milling with children and their escorts. A notice stated that, during the day, all main line services had been curtailed while the evacuation was in progress. He heard one child ask another where Frensham Down was and watched to see which train that child was joining. Probably thinking he was one of the escorts, no-one paid Fred Grimble any attention when he attached himself to the end of the group as they passed onto the platform. As the teachers were ushering their charges into the Special he looked around and, seeing no-one was looking at him, he, quickly, crossed the platform and climbed through the open door of the baggage car; where he hid behind some cases destined for Dunchester. For a moment he wondered whether he might be drawing unwanted attention to himself by his action but, while he was debating this, the guard closed the door to the baggage car and the train was on its way. As it turned out this was a good way to enter Frensham Down without curious observers wondering who he was.

Fred Grimble drove straight to Dunchester after he left the garage. He parked the car in a side street off the main shopping centre and carefully locked the doors and boot before strolling through the streets to familiarise himself with his surroundings. While he was doing this he bought groceries and other things for the cottage. He also bought a portable wireless receiver, a large electric torch and a selection of clothing to add to his limited wardrobe; returning to the car periodically to stow his purchases on the back seat. On his last trip to the shops Fred Grimble bought a map of the area at a newsagents; also a daily newspaper and a local newspaper, both of which he browsed through while having a meal at Lyons tea shop in the High Street. Returning to the parked car he located the railway station on his map and drove there; parking as close as he could to the pull-down shutters that indicated the luggage bay. Entering the station he found the `left luggage` counter and, presenting his drivers` licence, he identified himself to the attendant; who told him to wait outside by the shuttered entrance. After a while the shutters were lifted and the attendant appeared wheeling a medium sized cardboard box, marked `Fragile - Handle with Care`, on a two wheeled luggage trolley. He helped Fred Grimble to, carefully, lift the box into the car and, receiving a florin tip for his trouble, returned happily to the luggage bay.

Fred Grimble decided to wait until it was getting dark before returning to Frensham Down; so he parked the car near the local cinema and, making sure the vehicle was securely locked, went to the pictures. Although his Teutonic taste did not, normally, appreciate American humour he laughed at the antics of the Charlie Chase comedy that preceded the main film. He also found some amusement in the stilted, propaganda-dominated, commentary that accompanied the Pathe news film on the current situation in Germany. But the brooding looks and sombre performance of Laurence Olivier in 'Wuthering Heights' brought him back to his previous thoughtful mood.

Driving out of Dunchester in the twilight Fred Grimble

travelled the twenty miles of unfamiliar and unlit Scolling Road safely to Frensham Down. He carefully turned right by the village green and right again into Black Hut Lane. Driving slowly down the lane he drifted quietly to a halt outside his cottage. He would have preferred to park the car round the back but, it being the centre building in a three cottage terrace, there was no side entrance to the back of his cottage. He compromised by parking on a patch of gravel by the high hedge that fronted the large garden of number eighteen opposite, which happened to be empty. Thus, a passer-by, seeing the car, would not be able to determine to which cottage it related. He knew what was in the package and, rather than risk damage to the contents by lifting it himself, he decided to leave it locked in the car for the time being. His purchases he removed and carried into the cottage.

CHAPTER TEN

1939

Dread anticipation was in the air as Sunday, 3rd September, 1939, dawned to a clear blue sky and a light mist hovering in the valley along the Scolling Brook. Hitler had been warned that Britain would not tolerate further invasion and demanded that he give an undertaking to immediately withdraw all German forces from Poland or a state of war would exist between Britain and Germany. Everyone knew Hitler would ignore the ultimatum so it came as no surprise when the Prime Minister, Neville Chamberlain, announced in a nationwide broadcast at 11am that Great Britain was at war with Germany. Although it was expected, the declaration was met with mixed feelings. There were those among the older generation for whom the thought of war conjured up memories of the horrors in the trenches during the Great War; many consoling themselves by muttering with more hope than conviction.

"It won't come to anything. Hitler will back down and it will all be over by Christmas"

Less optimistic listeners, probably influenced by scenes in the recent film of H. G. Wells' novel 'The Shape of Things to Come' and believing the exaggerated claims of the Nazi propaganda machine, braced themselves for an immediate onslaught from the air. Their fears were re-enforced when air raid sirens sounded across the Country shortly after Mr. Chamberlain's announcement but they were, no doubt, relieved to learn later that it was a false alarm triggered by an over-enthusiastic air sentry who could not identify a lone aircraft approaching the south coast. For the younger generation, in their 'teens and early twenties, who had no previous first-hand experience of war, it was a time of excitement; a release from the growing tension of the past few months and a promise of change from the dull routine of everyday life.

The outbreak of war was not the only important event scheduled for that Sunday; for it was also the day of the annual cricket match between Frensham Down and Lavering Market. Len Munday was in The Bowman at 11am and, after listening to the Prime Minister's broadcast in the public bar, he quelled the doubts of his fellow cricketers in his role as their captain

"Drake finished 'is game of bowls when the Armada was in sight of Plymouth an' I don't see why we should cancel the match this a'ternoon on account of ''itler. We stands a fair chance o' takin' the cup this year with young Mike Grey's bowlin' on form and young Charlie Bramley, best bat at the College last year, in the team"

As it happened, neither Mike nor Charlie had their minds on the game because they were daily expecting their call-up papers to arrive. To Len Mundy's disgust, Frensham Down were all out for 62 by tea time and the visitors, having been refreshed with an excellent meal provided by the village ladies, jubilantly knocked Mike's best efforts all over the field to make 81 runs for 4 by the close of play. Sally Hanshott, who had been watching the game with Jean Stokes, consoled Mike

"Never mind! There is always next year"

The Hanshott evacuees, Dick May and Jimmy Horn, had been impressed with Mike's bowling and were regarding him with something like awe when he answered

"Next year? We'll be lucky if we are here next year to play. The war situation is serious. It is clear the Government is expecting an air raid at any time. The anti-aircraft guns have returned to the hill by Benley Castle and the searchlight site has been set up again behind your place on Hanshott Hill Common........"

He was interrupted by the evacuees who chorused,

"Soldiers be'ind the Farm? Can we go up to see them Sally? Oh please let us go up there now?"

"You will have to ask my Dad when we get back but I don't think he will let you go up there this late in the day. Why don't you look out from your bedroom window when it gets dark. They'll probably test the light like they did last night when you were asleep. Anyway, I expect the soldiers will be here for a long time, so there's no hurry"

The Graham boys, the evacuees Jean Stokes had brought along to the game, made no comment. They were thinking about their father who was already at sea in a Royal Navy destroyer and their mother whom they had last seen holding back the tears at Liverpool Street station as the Evacuee Special pulled out.

Gilly Wells turned to her younger sister Maggie.

"Not much of a school. Is it?"

It was Tuesday, 5th September, 1939, but it would take more than a declaration of war to change the routine of an English village. So the school was open, as usual, for the first day of the Michaelmas term and the School year. The early morning mist had lifted from the Scolling Brook and it was a clear warm day when the two evacuee girls left Crannock's Farm to walk, unaccompanied, to school. No school uniform was required and, hatless, they were dressed simply in cotton floral dresses with white socks and brown sandals. They had taken off their sandals and socks to paddle through the wash where the Scolling Brook crossed Wash Road, rather than take the small foot bridge provided for pedestrians, and, giggling at their naughtiness, had padded along the dusty road barefoot before donning their socks and sandals again outside the school gate. Now, the girls were sitting, with the other newly arrived evacuee girls, on the grass bank at the side of the playground waiting for Mrs Tremming to tell them what to do. It was Peggy Jones, who was lodging in the schoolhouse with the Tremmings, who answered Gilly

"Well, it *is* only a village school. You can't expect it to be as big as a London school. There aren't many local kids here and it looks like they have only got three teachers"

The observations by the new arrivals would have been true for any village school; for the building that housed Frensham Down School was one of hundreds built to a standard design in villages across the UK with the intention of providing 'board school' elementary education; and implementing the Education Act of 1870 which was introduced to combat nationwide illiteracy. The Act required that elementary education be provided for all children from five years to thirteen years of age; but the designers of the school building at Frensham Down seemed to have had little regard for the small number of children within that age group residing in the catchment area. As a result, although the school building could take up to 60 pupils, there were seldom more than 35 children there at any one time. In 1902 Frensham Down School was placed under the control of the County Education Authority and the leaving age was reduced to ten years; after which the children were transferred to the new secondary school in Chetsford to continue their elementary education until they were 14 years of age. Thus, by the time Charles Tremming took over the School in 1914 there were seldom more than 25 children being taught at any one time. When he first arrived Charles was assisted by a nineteen year old junior teacher, Charlotte Benwick, who travelled to the school daily from

Scolling. During the summer holiday of 1919 Charles married his assistant and she moved into the school house. Charlotte continued to run the lower school, mainly teaching the children to read, write and do basic arithmetic. When they were 8 years old the children would move into the upper school, under Charles` care, to learn basic Geography, English history and English grammar until they left to go to Chetsford secondary school.

However, when the Benley Council Estate, a small development of some fifty houses located to the north of the Scolling road and to the east of Battle Wood road, was built in 1936 the catchment area was expanded and the village school was, additionally, required to provide primary education for the children from the council estate. The influx doubled the number of pupils at Frensham Down and Charles remonstrated with the authorities; demanding assistance with the teaching. He was disturbed to learn that the move was intended only as a temporary measure until Dunchester Rural District Council erected a new school building in the village of Plaisham, some five miles north of Frensham Down, to which the council estate children would go in due course. His fears regarding the possible demise of the Village School, when the new school building was completed, were allayed when he heard later that, due to shortage of funds, the Council had decided to postpone their plans to expand the Benley estate and, consequently, the County Education Authority had deferred erection of a new school building for the time being. Nevertheless, Charles still pressed for the addition of at least one more teacher and was rewarded for his efforts by the arrival of Betty Twist, the daughter of garage owner Gerald Twist.

Betty was no longer the plump teenager who had vied with Joanne Hanshott for the affections of John Studding and was now a small, slender, pretty woman of twenty-four. She had plenty of admirers but had never found anyone who, in her opinion, matched the charms of John Studding. So, having lost him to Joanne, she had remained emotionally unattached. After leaving Dunchester Grammar School at eighteen, Betty had enrolled at the Garnet Teacher Training College, in London, for a full-time course; and, when she graduated three years later, she had decided to seek employment as a teacher in foreign languages. To this end, and with her father's financial support, she spent two years doing casual work in the principal cities of Germany, Austria and France;

socialising and conversing with the local inhabitants to perfect her command of these European languages. She also spent some time in the Italian speaking area of Switzerland and in Northern Italy to add to her command of foreign languages. When she returned to England in August, 1938, she was fluent in German, French and Italian but she felt she still needed practical experience in handling children and in teaching. When she learned that Charles Tremming was looking for a junior teacher she applied for the job partly to remain at home with her parents for a while and partly to gain practical experience in the handling of children. Betty had no intention of abandoning her planned career but taking the job as a temporary measure allowed her time to assess her options, constructively, while she looked around for a post more suited to her talents. She had been at the school for a year, now, and looked after the younger children most of the time but she, also, taught elementary French to the older children. During August, 1939, Betty had become re-acquainted with Charlie Stokes, Jean's brother. She had known him during her own school days at Frensham Down and they had become very close during his leave from the Merchant Navy. Charlie had returned to sea and Betty was apprehensive for his safety when she heard the declaration of war.

With commencement of the Michaelmas term, in 1939, Charlotte was teaching the middle group of children aged between seven and eight years; while Charles Tremming continued to concentrate on the children who were in their last two years before they moved on to the secondary school at Chetsford. The younger children were in the hands of Betty Twist who, on this bright morning in September, had met the mothers bringing their apprehensive five year olds to school for the first time. Betty had taken both the parents and the children into the assembly hall while she sorted out the registers and pinned a name tag on each child. She eventually persuaded the worried mothers to say goodbye to their offspring and had just ushered them out of the hall when Charlotte came in

"Have you sorted out the newcomers yet, Betty?"

"Yes, Mrs Tremming, but I don't want to leave them alone. Do you think you could bring in from the playground what is left of my group from last year?"

"I was just going to suggest that, to get them out of my way while I organise the older children"

"Are you alright, Mrs Tremming? You don't look yourself this morning"

"It is just one of those mornings. But I expect I'll survive"

Charlotte Tremming was not in a good mood. She had been up half the night with her eight year old daughter, Josephine, who had complained of toothache and had been taken into Dunchester by her father to see the dentist. Normally the School bell rang for classes at 9.00am but, on the first day of the school year, allowance had to be made for re-organisation and seat allocation. On this occasion her husband's absence had thrust the whole burden onto Charlotte. On top of the usual chaos she had twelve evacuee children to integrate into the classes. Having taken in the younger children and left Betty to deal with her own group, Charlotte returned to the playground and surveyed the scene. The five evacuee girls were sitting on the grass together as were the seven evacuee boys, but each in a separate group. The local children were playing various games and had made no attempt to make friends with the evacuees. Charlotte blew her whistle for attention.

"Peggy Jones and Gilly Wells. Come here!"

The two evacuees rose apprehensively to their feet and approached the teacher. Had someone told her about them paddling in the wash?

"Now all children aged nine or ten join Peggy and Gilly. The rest of you carry on with what you are doing until I return. And behave yourselves!"

She led the older children off to join the group in the classroom used by Charles and, appointing 10 year old Maxine Wykeham, the vicar's daughter, to take charge, she gave each child in the group a copy of Oliver Twist to keep them quiet until Charles returned. The seven remaining evacuees were destined for the middle school and, with the locals who had come up from the lower school and those not yet old enough to move into Charles' class, she had a group of 36 children to contend with. It had been already decided that she would need two classrooms to accommodate them and she had just got the children settled in the classrooms according to their ages when she was relieved to hear her husband's Morris Minor chug into the yard outside. Charlotte had recognised a leadership quality in Dick May so she gave him the responsibility for keeping the class of seven to eight year olds in order. Angela Tremming had been helping generally and Charlotte asked her daughter to keep an eye on the class of seven year olds while she went through the building to greet her husband.

"Thank goodness you are back. I've had a hell of a morning! If it hadn't been for Betty and Angela I don't know what I would have done"

She turned to her younger daughter who was holding her handkerchief to her swollen jaw.

"How are you, dear?"

Charles answered for Josephine

"He took out the tooth. She won't be able to speak much until the cocaine wears off."

Charlotte took her daughter's arm

"Come along, dear. I'll take you indoors". To Charles she said "Would you go and see to your class? I have left them reading Oliver Twist to themselves with Maxine Wykeham in charge but they are much too quiet for my liking. While you are at it, would you look in on my lot? I've left one of the new evacuee boys in charge of the seven to eight year olds and Angela is watching the others"

But Charles did not go into the classrooms. He looked up at the clock in the entrance porch and, seeing it was 12 noon, he picked up the hand bell from the table in the corridor and rang it for the dinner break.

Wally Tanner and Freddie Smith lived on the Benley council estate. They were both nine years old and considered themselves streetwise compared with the country bumpkins from the surrounding farms. They recognised a kindred spirit in Harry Moon and, although Harry was younger, they joined him on the grass to swap sandwiches and find out some more about him. Wally offered Harry half of a corned beef sandwich and accepted half of a cheese and pickle sandwich in return

"Where do you come from, then?"

"East 'am"

"Where's that?"

"Next to West 'am"

"Don't be funny! I don't like funny kids"

"Don' care what *you* don' like. D'you wanna a fight then? Anyway East 'am and West 'am is next to each uvver on the east side of London. Not far from the docks. That's why we was sent dahn 'ere. So's we wouldn't get in the way when the bombing starts"

"You scared then?"

"I aint scared of nobody nor nuffin. You wanna fight, then?"
Freddie Smith intervened

"No we don't want to fight. At least not in the playground where
old Tremors will catch us and give us the cane. You're staying in
the police house, aren't you? Well! You'd better watch out. Dickie
Bell, the copper, is no pushover"
Wally was looking across at the Graham brothers who were busy
munching Mars bars. He turned to Harry.

"Those two. Who are they and where do they get chocolate bars
for dinner?"

"Oh! Them's Steve an' Reggie Graham. They was both in my
school in East 'am but Steve's a year older'n me and 'is bruvver's
only a kid so I don' 'ave much ter do wiv 'em. Anyway, me Mum
says them's a stuck up fambly. I 'spec they get the choclit fer
nuffin' from the general store in the village 'cos them's stayin'
there"

"I'm going over to talk to them. It would be useful to have
someone in our gang who can get their hands on chocolate bars
when they like"
Wally got up and walked over to the Graham brothers. Steve gave
him an unwelcome look.

"What d'you want, then?"

"I wondered which way you came to school this morning?"

"We walked up to the main road...The Scolling Road aint
it?...Then past the pub and down School lane"

"That way it probably took you over half an hour. Would you like
me to show you a short cut? You can get home in ten minutes from
here if you know the way"

"OK. But what's in it fer you?"

"Nothing. Just being friendly. And I thought you might like to
join our gang?"

"Not if that tow-rag Harry Moon is going to be one of the gang"

"Never mind him. Freddie Smith over there is my mate. We'll
meet you out the back here when the bell goes at four"

Steve Graham was waiting in the playground when he was
joined by Wally Tanner and Freddie Smith. Wally took his arm and
pulled him.

"Come on. We don't want to hang around here for old Tremors to

184

catch us going out the back way"

"Hold on. I've got to wait for my brother. His class hasn't come out yet"

When Reggie came running out to join them he had Maisie Moore in tow. Steve told his brother to let go her hand

"Maisie can't come with us, Reggie. She is supposed to be collected by the lady she is staying with"

"But I want to go with Reggie!"

"Well, you can't. We are not going your way home. Anyway, here comes that Maxine who was in charge of our class this morning. She's going to see you get home alright, Maisie"

Maxine Wycliffe looked suspiciously at the boys as she took Maisie's hand.

"Come along, Maisie. You don't want to hang around with this lot. They will only get you into trouble"

The boys watched Maxine and Maisie disappear round the corner, then Wally led them out by the back gate and across to the corner of the playing field. A dilapidated wooden fence provided plenty of gaps for the boys to scramble through onto the footpath that ran alongside the Primrose Stream. A hundred yards along the path, behind and just past the cricket pavilion, a wooden footbridge crossed the stream. The bridge had been built by the Parish Council to connect the cricket pitch with the village hall. But, today, the crossing was inaccessible because the bridge was undergoing repairs and all the middle slats were missing. Wally was not to be deterred.

"We could balance on the edge but your little brother might fall in the stream. There *is* another way we can go. At least you know the short cut now because the village hall over there is right next to the general store. Come on!"

They continued along the footpath to the stone bridge in Black Hut Lane.

"This is only a little bit further and its still quicker than the way you came this morning. I wonder what that car is doing there? I've never seen a car down here before. None of the people who live round here can afford a car. Let us take a look see"

The boys walked round the car; peering through the windows and trying the locked doors and locked boot. Freddie looked across the road.

"I thought the place next to Hilda Benhope's was empty, but there

is someone watching us from the upstairs window. We'd better go!"
They ran off up the road, to disappear up the footpath that skirted
the general store and led to the village green.
Jean Stokes greeted the Graham brothers

"So here you are then. Did you like your first day at the village
school?"
They nodded, but her eyes narrowed as she saw the two boys
accompanying them

"Well! What do *you* two want?"
Steve answered for them

"Wally and Freddie showed us a quick way home"

"Did they now? But I saw you come up the sideway. There is a
quicker way than that. When I went to the village school I used to
cut round by the village hall and over the footbridge"
Freddie had been very quiet. Now he spoke up for a change

"We tried that way but the footbridge is being repaired"
Jean was still suspicious of the escorts' motives, but she was
prepared to give them the benefit of the doubt

"Well, I suppose you *have* gone out of your way to do a good turn
for once. Here is a Double Six bar for you to share"
Freddie grabbed the gift but Wally did not seem happy

"I don't like dark chocolate! Can we have a MARS bar instead?"

"No you can't. You'll take what I give you. And don't think this
means you can come around here thieving when I am not looking.
Knowing you two, I can guess the real reason why you brought the
new boys home and I shall be watching you when you are next in
the shop. Now be off with the pair of you!"
When the other two boys had gone Steve turned to Jean

"Why did you talk to Wally and Freddie like that?"

"I don't think my Mum and Dad would like you going around
with them. They are not to be trusted and they will get you into
trouble"
Reggie Graham looked from one to the other, a puzzled expression
on his face.

"I like Maisie Moore. Can I play with *her* or will *she* get me into
trouble?"
Jean smiled down at him and gently patted his blond hair

"I don't know Maisie Moore. But if you like her I expect she is
alright for you to play with"
Steve thought he should explain

186

"Maisie is from our school in London. She came down with us last week and she is staying up at the Vicar's house. She is OK and she's the same age as Reggie so she's in his class at the Village School"

"Well! I expect I'll meet her at the Sunday school"

"I don't think so. She didn't come with us to the Methodist sunday school in London. She and her brother, Billy, went to the Synagogue on Saturdays"

Jean smiled as a thought occurred to her

"Did you say she is staying at the Vicarage?"

"Yes! And her brother, Billy, is with her"

Jean chuckled

"I wonder whether the Vicar knows they went to the synagogue? Well, why don't you two go out to the garden at the back of the house to play until tea is ready?"

"Can we have a chocolate bar?"

"No! It will spoil your tea"

Jean raked among a bundle of papers stored behind the counter and brought up some back numbers of Tiger Tim, The Magnet and The Wizard

"But here are some old comics you can have to read. Don't leave them lying around to clutter up the place or my Mum will get cross. When you have finished with the comics bring them back here"

Fred Grimble watched the four boys run off up the road and enter the footpath that led alongside the general store to the village green. He stayed at the window for half an hour to see if they returned. Then he descended the stairs and made to open his front door; but he shrank back when he heard his neighbour's front door slam shut. He closed his door quietly and moved to the front room window, from where he saw Hilda Benhope walk down her garden path carrying a shopping bag. He did not know it but she was on her way to the Post Office to meet her grand-daughter, Sally Hanshott, and to accompany her home on a visit to Maddie; nor that she would not be back until later that evening. Fred Grimble watched her follow in the footsteps of the children then, once again, he waited for a while to see if she returned. When he was satisfied no-one was about he left his cottage door open while he crossed the road and checked the car. All was secure so he returned to the cottage.

He sat in the armchair thinking of his plan of action. It was

187

really time to make a move but his orders were to remain as inconspicuous as possible. So far he had done exactly that by staying out of sight in the cottage since returning from Dunchester on the day he arrived. But the car was a problem. It had obviously excited the interest of the children and he had no doubt that his next door neighbour must be wondering who he was and where he came from. She was likely to become more and more curious if she saw nothing of him. Perhaps he should move the car, he mused. But where to? He certainly could not leave it where anyone could pry into the boot. He made a decision. He would make contact with the subject after dark that night and get rid of the package in the boot. Then he would feel free to dispose of the vehicle if need be. He picked up the telephone.

"This is Frensham Down 435. Please connect me with a London number. It is Maida Vale 3843"

"Please wait a moment"

A female voice answered and the operator came back on the line.

"You are through, caller"

"Is that Maida Vale 3843?"

"Yes. Who is calling?"

"It is your cousin Harry"

"I have no cousin Harry, Go away"

The line went dead and Fred Grimble replaced the receiver on its arm. While he waited he checked the minute hand on his watch. Exactly three minutes after he had hung up the telephone bell rang. He put the earpiece to his left ear but said nothing as he waited for the woman to speak

"Good afternoon, George"

"Who is George?"

"Georgie, Porgie, Pudding and Pie. Kissed the girls but they didn't cry"

"Give Winkler a message. All is quiet. I intend to make contact with the subject tonight. Please confirm connection time at six today. Will use code two next time"

He hung up the ear piece and went into the kitchen to make himself a meal. Precisely at 6pm the telephone rang again. He picked up the receiver and listened. The same female voice said

"Affirmative. Connection 11pm"

Fred replaced the ear piece and climbed the stairs to his bedroom. He drew the curtains across the window before he switched on the light. Taking out his battered old suitcase from under the bed he dropped it on the counterpane. From the suitcase he withdrew the Luger pistol and a small cardboard box of greased ammunition. Rummaging amongst the contents of the case he found a lightweight harness with a shoulder holster attached. He left all these items on the bed while he changed into the new white shirt and trousers of a nondescript dark-grey suit he had bought 'off the peg' in Dunchester on the day he arrived. He put on the black socks, black shoes and dark tie he had also bought that day. Then he donned the shoulder harness; which he covered with the suit waistcoat; leaving the empty holster dangling outside the waistcoat under his left armpit. He picked up the Luger and withdrew the clip from the butt. Now it was unarmed and he pulled the trigger several times to check the action. He checked the clip was fully loaded, before slipping it back into the butt of the gun and fastening the safety catch. Satisfied, he slid the gun into the shoulder holster and tested the speed and smoothness with which he could withdraw it; should circumstances make it necessary for him to use the weapon. He slipped on his jacket and wrapping eight spare bullets in a piece of greaseproof paper he put these in his right hand jacket pocket before tucking the cartridge box under the clothes in his suitcase. He put on his, clear-glass, tortoise-shell framed spectacles and critically examined his reflection in the long mirror which was attached to the inside of the wardrobe door. It was getting chilly in the evenings so he wore the dark overcoat and black trilby hat which he had also bought in Dunchester. Quietly he let himself out of the cottage and crossed the road to the car.

Hilda Benhope had returned to her cottage before it got dark. Sally, who was going to see Jean Stokes, had wheeled her bike from Hanshott Farm as she walked back with her grandmother to make sure she reached home safely. She left her bike leaning against the, white-painted, picket fence while she joined Hilda for a cup of tea before cycling back to the general store. They heard the car start up outside but they were listening to a comedy programme on the wireless and could not be bothered to get up to look out of the window. Sally turned to her grandmother

"Have you met your new neighbours yet?"

"No! But I think there is only one person and that a youngish man. I saw him in the back garden once a couple of days ago. But he didn't seem to hear me when I called out because he walked quickly back into the cottage without looking at me. These walls are very thin but I haven't heard him moving about; although I am sure he is there. Perhaps he is shy"

It was growing dark as Fred Grimble drove away in the opposite direction from the village green and down Black Hut Lane. He crossed the bridge over the Primrose stream and, passing the cricket pitch and Beeching Common, turned left into School Lane; then up, past the school buildings, to the Scolling Road, where he turned left and onto the forecourt of the Bowman. Nobody was about and he saw no other vehicles. It was completely dark when he switched off the lights, parked the car and locked the doors. He double-checked to make sure the boot was still locked, then walked along the Scolling Road to the bus shelter. It was a dry night but the crescent moon, whilst visible, was partly obscured by thin traces of cloud so it gave little more than ambient light and cast only vague shadows. In the darkness of the shelter, he was aware that he would be nothing but a dark shape to a casual observer; as he stood still watching the Doctor's cottage at the opposite corner of the village green.

He had been there for twenty minutes when a middle aged couple came out of the Surgery door and walked towards him. They stood under the shelter with him but did not attempt to engage him in conversation. After about ten minutes a single-decker country bus, its headlights shielded and windows curtained, came along and stopped by the shelter. The man turned to Fred

"This is the last bus for Dunchester tonight. Don't you want to get on?"

"No, Thank you! I am waiting for someone from Scolling. But they don't seem to be on the bus"

The bus trundled off and left Fred Grimble standing alone in the darkness. He presumed the car standing in the driveway by the surgery belonged to the doctor. So he was home and, no doubt, his wife was there too. They would be surprised, if not shocked, to see him and he did not want any patients to be present to witness the meeting. So he stayed in the shelter for another half hour or so before straightening his shoulders and striding purposefully across to the doctor's cottage.

Fred Grimble checked his step at the cottage gate and opened it quietly. He crept stealthily up to the door marked 'Surgery Waiting Room'. Gently turning the door handle, he pushed the black-out curtain aside and peeped into the lighted room. Chairs were set around the sides of the room and there were various notices pinned to the walls. He felt a welcome warmth from a small electric fire, which stood in the fireplace, but the room was empty of people. Just as softly, he entered the room and quietly turned the key to lock the door behind him. He walked over to the surgery door and listened. There was an almost inaudible sound of conversation between a man and a woman in the other room. He took a deep breath then, moving across to the mantle-piece, he pressed the bell push and waited.

Dr Ernest Middleton was at his desk writing up his notes when he heard the waiting room bell ring. He looked up at his wife, Eve, who was tidying the surgery.

"I thought the last patient had gone. Would you see who that is, dear? I hope it is nothing urgent because I fancy an early night tonight"

Eve put down the bowl she was drying and, involuntarily, put her hand up to, unnecessarily, straighten her hair before she opened the door to the waiting room. She saw a rather sinister looking stranger standing there, dressed in a long dark overcoat and with a black hat pulled down to shield his eyes. She did not recognise him but there was something familiar about the stranger. She heard herself saying.

"Surgery is closed for tonight. Unless it is urgent could you come back tomorrow?"

"No! I must see the Herr Doktor now."

That voice! She knew it but could not place it. But the use of the German address! She felt panic rising and hastily turned to go back into the surgery; back to the protection of Ernst. There! She was even thinking of her husband in his Austrian name.

"Ernst!" she gasped.

Dr Middleton stood up suddenly and stared over her shoulder at the man who had followed her into the surgery. He reached across the desk to pick up the telephone but the stranger was quicker and, pushing Eve to one side, he grabbed the instrument first, with his left hand, while he drew the Luger with his right

"I would not do anything hasty if I were you, Herr Doktor. Now sit down and listen to what I have to say. You too Fraulein Goldschmit. Or is it Frau Mittelburg now?"

Ernest Middleton had recovered himself and, now he had

recognised Hans Kluger, his memory went back to that time in a Munich back street so long ago and he had fears for his wife's safety. He decided to hide his fears and take no action, if indeed such action were possible in the face of the heavy gun Hans was pointing at him, until he had discovered the reason for the visit.

"Why are you here, Kluger? You know you are an enemy alien in England and liable to be shot as a spy if you are discovered by the police. Why don't you hand over that gun and surrender yourself as a prisoner of war? At least you will survive that way"

"And why don't *you* shut up, sit down and listen? Before you do anything I think you might like to know that a Jewish family called Goldschmit was arrested by the Gestapo at the Austrian border two weeks ago as they attempted to escape to Switzerland. Papers in their possession show they are your parents, fraulein?"

His gloating look stunned Eve into silence. The thought of her dear Mama and Papa in the hands of the Gestapo was almost too much to bear and she clung to the patients' chair for support. It was Ernest who spoke

"How do we know what you are saying about my wife's parents is true?"

"We thought you might want proof. So here it is"

Hans Kluger reached into the inside pocket of his jacket and withdrew an envelope. He handed it to Eve who, opening it with trembling fingers, took out a locket on a gold chain. One of the links of the chain was broken as though the locket had been snatched violently from the neck of the wearer. She gasped as she opened the locket to reveal two miniature portraits. One showed her parents together. The other was a photograph of herself as a teenager, but she had not changed so much that the German failed to recognise her. She held the locket out to her husband.

"Look, Ernest. It is Mama and Papa"

The doctor took the locket from his wife and looked at the pictures

"Where did you get this, Kluger?"

"I took it from the woman myself when the Gestapo brought them to the SS office for interrogation. We traced you because your father, fraulein, had foolishly made a note of your address in England in his diary"

Ernest ignored the fact that Hans consistently addressed his wife as though she were unmarried. Perhaps it gave the thug some sort of perverse pleasure to keep up the pretence that she was still the innocent he knew as a nursing sister in Munich. He struggled with himself to remain cool while he considered the evidence.

"Alright! Suppose what you say is true, and I am still not convinced that I believe you. You did not come all this way and risk your neck simply to deliver a message which you knew would cause my wife distress. You must have some other motive. Get to the point, man. What do you want?"

"What do I want? I want to get even with you for getting away from me in Munich and I want to finish what I started there with the fraulein"

He looked lasciviously at Eve who backed away in fear. Ernest started up from his chair.

"Sweinhund!"

The intruder waved the gun menacingly and Ernest moved back, although he remained standing, as Hans, unperturbed by the outburst, continued

"Speak in English. It will excite less attention should anyone hear us in conversation. You ask what I want, but this is not about what I want. I am here as an agent of the Third Reich and my controller wants you to work for the Reich in England. So long as you do as you are told, the Goldschmits will stay alive. Do you understand me? If my controller does not hear, today, from me that you have agreed you will never see or hear from your parents again"

He was glaring straight at Eve as he made the last remark; and she had tears in her eyes as she looked appealingly at her husband

"Poor Mama and Papa! You must do what he says, Ernest"

There was a triumphant look in Hans Kluger's eyes as the doctor sank back in his chair and shrugged his shoulders in resignation.

"What do you want me to do?"

"Well, the first thing is for you to move your car out of the driveway so that I can back mine close up to the waiting room door. After that we will go to the forecourt of The Bowman to collect my car. Then you must help me unload the package from the boot. So come along with me now. And while we are gone, fraulein, I suggest you make a pot of tea and I advise you not to telephone anyone about this; or you know what will happen!"

Len Mundy was walking towards the Public Bar when he saw Ernest Middleton about to get into the passenger seat of a car

"Evenin', Doctor"

The doctor paused and looked over his shoulder

"Good evening, Len"

"Not comin' in for a pint then?"

The driver, whose face was hidden by the gloom in the car, said something which Len did not catch and Ernest turned back to Len

"Sorry I can't. I have to go out on an urgent call"

"Well! There'll be one waitin' for you when you gets back, if you wants it"

"Thanks! But I don't know how long I shall be"

Len watched the car drive off and turn onto the Scolling Road in the direction of Lavering Market. 'That's odd' he thought 'Never known the doctor to be so short with me; and who was that driving the car? 'e kept 'is 'ead down; an' I didn't recognise the car neither. P'raps its a worried father-to-be from that lot up on the Benley estate come in 'is own car to pick up the doctor. But why didn't 'e collect 'im outside the surgery? Odd!'. He turned away and, entering the pub, ordered a pint from Olivia McKuy who was serving behind the bar

"Doctor Middleton been in 'ere tonight, Olivia?"

"No, Len! Why?"

"Oh nothin'. Just saw 'im outside gettin' into somebody else's car an' I wondered if 'e didn't wanna drive 'cos he'd been drinkin'. But, if 'e didn't 'ave a drink?...."

Olivia bustled off to serve another customer; leaving Len looking into his pint mug and muttering to himself

"Mm......odd!?"

CHAPTER ELEVEN

1939

Hans Kluger reversed the car up the driveway alongside the doctor's surgery and got out to unlock the boot while Ernest got out of the passenger's seat and entered the surgery via the waiting room. Leaving the room light off and sliding the black-out curtain to one side, Ernest propped open the waiting room door with an old flat-iron. Kluger warned him to take care as they lifted the cardboard box from the boot and placed it on the gravel driveway; while Kluger locked the car boot and doors. The box was more awkward than heavy and, once they both had a firm grip on the hemp binding, they found it easy to carry the box through the waiting room and into the Surgery; where they hefted it onto the examination couch. Kluger returned to the waiting room, locked the outer door and switched off the light. When he returned the doctor was still standing looking at the box

"What is it?"

"It is a long range wireless transmitter and receiver; capable of sending and receiving messages between here and the Republic of Ireland. A smaller, battery operated, set would have been more convenient but, since neither of you are trained in the use of morse code it was necessary for the controller to supply you with a set which allowed you to speak into a microphone when transmitting. This set works off the mains electricity supply and you will need to string the aerial inside the loft of the cottage. Before I leave you tonight I want to see it set up and operating"

Ernest had no intention of endangering either Eve or himself by spying for Germany during wartime, but he decided it best to appear to co-operate with Kluger until he could find a way out of the dilemma in which he and Eve had found themselves.

"Suppose an aerial in the loft doesn't work?"

"Then you will have to rig up a temporary aerial under the roof gutter behind the cottage. There will be fixed times for transmitting and receiving once each day. But it will be best if the set, complete with its aerial, is kept in the loft where no-one can come across it by accident. Is the loft fully boarded and do you have stairs leading to it?"

"It is boarded but there are no stairs. When we want to get into the loft we use a pull-down ladder which is concealed above the hatch"

"All the better. No-one else is likely to go up into the loft by mistake. Is there an electric power point up there?"

"No, but an electric light bulb hanging from one of the roof beams can be switched on from the hall"

"That will do for the time being. The set operates on a low amperage and the power lead can be plugged into the light socket. I don't suppose you know anything about electricity, do you?"

Actually, Ernest was quite knowledgeable on the subject but he did not intend to make matters any easier for the German than he had to. So he shook his head but did not comment. Kluger continued.

"In that case you will have to use a torch for light in the loft until I can run a lead from the power circuit down here up to the loft"

Eve, who felt revulsion each time she saw Kluger (she could not bring herself to think of him by his first name) looking at her, was keeping out of the way in the kitchen while her husband, reluctantly, obeyed the German's instructions. He switched on the loft light and, using a pole with a hook on the end, released the hatch cover and pulled down the ladder. Kluger climbed up into the loft and Ernest held up a small table which normally stood in the hall for Kluger to haul into the loft. This was followed by two kitchen chairs. Kluger paused while he looked round the loft to assess its potential. Apart from a few cardboard boxes, some odd items and a static water tank, the roof space was empty.

"I shall get you two chairs and a table from a second hand shop in Dunchester to replace these. It would not do for a regular visitor to notice these ones are missing and to, unnecessarily, excite interest"

Kluger climbed down and fetched from the boot of the car the strong tow-rope and the heavy torch, which he had purchased in Dunchester. They fastened the rope round the package; securing it to the hemp bindings. Carrying the loose end of the tow-rope Kluger climbed back into the loft and, standing on a chair, he passed the rope over one of the roof beams and stepped down from the chair. Then, with Ernest climbing the ladder to steady it, Kluger hauled the package up onto the boarded floor. Ernest followed into the loft and together they manoeuvred the package to the centre of the roof space and unpacked it. Using the table and chairs to gain height they strung the aerial as high as they could reach along the roof beams, leaving the plug end loose to dangle down to floor

196

level, near the table.

Once the set was assembled on the table and the aerial lead had been plugged in, Ernest watched silently as Kluger earthed the metal chassis of the set to the static water tank and fitted a bayonet plug to the set's power lead. He switched on the electric torch and set it down on the table. Wrapping his right hand in a cloth to avoid being burned, Kluger stood on a chair to replace the bulb with the bayonet plug. Climbing down, he switched on the wireless set. When the valves began to glow he switched the set to 'receive'. Immediately, a loud sound of 'mush' came from the two sets of headphones. Kluger turned down the sound until it was only faintly audible. Then he donned one set of earphones and carefully tuned the set to the required frequency and wavelength. He turned to Ernest

"Make a mental note of those numbers. Never leave the set switched on or tuned in when you are not here. What is the time now?"

It was a rhetorical question because he looked at his own wrist watch

"It is 10.20. The call time tonight is 11.00 so we might as well go down and have that cup of tea"

Kluger switched off the wireless, spun the tuning knob to a random set of numbers, and placed the spare valves and other accessories in the table drawer.

Half an hour later they were back in the loft seated by the wireless. Kluger switched on the set and waited for it to warm up. He donned one set of earphones and gave the other set to the doctor to wear. At exactly 11 pm he switched to 'send' and spoke into the microphone.

"Zeta calling. Zeta calling. Acknowledge"

He turned to Ernest.

"There will be no immediate reply. We have to wait exactly thirty seconds and call again with a different call sign"

He consulted the second hand on his watch. When the 30 seconds were up he spoke into the microphone again

"Willard One calling. Over"

He switched over to 'receive' and again consulted his watch. After exactly 15 seconds delay a voice, with a strong southern Ireland accent, came from the earphones

"OK, Willard. Receiving strength nine. Over"

197

"Willard receiving loud and clear. All is in order this end. Subject is co-operating. Will listen in as agreed schedule but will not transmit, except to acknowledge, unless we have message for you. Over and out"

He switched back to receive. The voice sounded again

"OK. Out"

Kluger switched off and spun the tuning knob. He turned to address the doctor

"Each day you must carry out the same procedure at the prescribed time and write down any message you receive. The messages will be in code so you will not understand them. Simply acknowledge receipt. I shall contact you daily to learn of any messages. If any messages are to be sent from here they will be transmitted only by myself, in code, and you will not be present. The prescribed times are 15 minutes earlier each day; commencing each week at 11.30pm on Sunday; hence the time today was 11 pm, and ending at 10 pm on Saturday. There is nothing else for you to do; but I must impress upon you the consequences to your wife's parents if you do anything to sabotage this set-up or if anything happens to myself"

"But suppose something happens to you, Kluger, which is nothing to do with us?"

"That would be most unfortunate for you. So, you had better pray it doesn't"

"Where can I contact you, if necessary?"

"You cannot. I shall give you no warning of when I might turn up. So expect me at any time, day or night; and you and your wife had better co-operate, or you know what will happen!"

"Leave my wife out of this, Kluger. I will do whatever you want but keep away from my wife"

Kluger smiled with his mouth, but not with his eyes.

"She is still a very attractive woman, the fraulein. I am not sure I can resist her charms. But you will just have to wait and see, won't you? If she wants to co-operate in other ways besides operating the wireless I shall not object"

"You touch her, Kluger, and I will kill you"

"And you know what would happen then, don't you? I do not think your wife would ever forgive you if you do anything to harm her parents"

Eve was waiting when they returned to the surgery. Kluger eyed her

198

up and down and she cringed under his gaze. Ernest tried to hold his temper; his hands clenched at his impotence. He tried to keep his voice calm

"Kluger is going now he has set up his wireless station"

The German agent paused for a moment; still looking at Eve contemplatively. 'She will keep' he thought. Shrugging his shoulders, he put on his overcoat and hat and left by the waiting room door. Eve rushed to lock and bolt the door after him before collapsing into her husband's arms.

"What are we going to *do*, Ernest? We can't let them harm Mama and Papa. But we must not do what they are asking. There must be a way out of this. Can't we go to the police and let them deal with Kluger?"

"No! If he is arrested or anything happens to him your parents will suffer. In any case we would fall under suspicion as Austrian born citizens; even though we are naturalised British subjects. I don't see what we can do for the present. It is all too sudden! We must think about it and pray there is some way out of this mess. In the meantime we must carry on as usual and let Kluger think we are co-operating with him. But you must keep away from him. Don't let him into the house when you are alone and, when he *is* here, try to keep out of sight"

It was close on midnight when Hans Kluger parked the car on the gravel patch opposite his cottage. He was relieved that the vehicle no longer contained anything incriminating but he still locked the doors and the boot. He let himself quietly into the cottage and, despite the late hour, picked up the telephone. The operator connected him with the Maida Vale number. A sleepy voice answered. He did not want to excite the curiosity of the bored operator by having returned calls that late at night so he waived the preliminaries.

"George reports everything in order and Paddy responded"

"OK. No messages. Goodnight"

Feeling self-satisfied with his efforts he retired for the night. He awoke early next morning to the sound of Hilda Benhope singing to herself next door as she prepared to go out to one of her daily jobs. Mentally he re-assumed his alias of Fred Grimble as he looked at the bedside clock. It was 7.30am. 'Early yet' he thought, as he lay back looking up at the cracked ceiling. He waited until he heard

Hilda Benhope close her front door then he rose and, clad only in his night clothes, descended to the kitchen where he shaved, washed and made himself a light breakfast of buttered toast and black coffee. He switched on the portable wireless receiver he had purchased in Dunchester. The news was all about the war. Hitler continued to consolidate his success in Poland. The 'SS Athenia', a passenger ship bound for the USA with many women and children on board, had been sunk off the Irish coast by a German U boat with a considerable loss of life; but President Roosevelt had been quick to allay any fears by his countrymen that America might be enticed into the conflict by re-iterating the neutrality of the USA. Conversely, the British Commonwealth countries were all declaring their support for Britain. Fred Grimble switched off the wireless and returned to his bedroom to tidy the bed and dress in an open necked white shirt, with a tweed sports jacket and grey flannels with brown shoes. He stowed the Luger and shoulder holster out of sight on top of the wardrobe and looked round the room to ensure nothing suspicious was on view before donning his spectacles and leaving the cottage.

It was raining when Fred Grimble pulled into the forecourt of a garage just outside Dunchester and filled the petrol tank. He drove on to park outside a gentlemen's outfitters in the High Street where he purchased a rainproof gabardine trench coat, a brown tweed trilby style hat and a black umbrella. When he came out of the shop, wearing the hat and raincoat, it had stopped raining so he did not open the rolled umbrella which he left in the car when he parked it in a side street near a newsagents. He bought a daily paper to browse through while he took a leisurely coffee in Lyons teashop; casually glancing around him from time to time to ensure he was not being watched. No-one followed him out of the teashop but he still wandered the streets aimlessly for a while before entering a second hand furniture shop. He bought two bentwood chairs and a sturdy, but small, table with a large drawer and screw-in legs. Leaving these to be picked up when he had brought the car round to the shop, he visited an electrical shop and purchased fifty feet of flexible domestic power cable with a round-pin power plug attached to one end and a wandering lead socket attached to the other; also a separate three-pin power plug. He continued shopping for milk, bread, groceries, fruit and vegetables. Then he returned in the car to the furniture shop shortly before it closed at 1pm. By removing the legs he was able to stow the table behind the front seats of the car with one of the chairs. The other chair he stowed in the boot.

Fred Grimble did not want to return to Frensham Down in daylight with his purchases exposed to the view of passing school children who might display further interest in the car outside his cottage; nor did he wish to rouse the curiosity of his nextdoor neighbour unnecessarily. However, it was Wednesday and early closing day in Dunchester so most of the shops were shut for the afternoon. He considered wandering round the empty streets window-shopping but decided it was too small a place for him not to attract the attention of any curious policeman who happened to be about. So he parked the car in another side street while he had some lunch in a small back street cafe; then drove to the local cinema and parked behind the building. This time the main feature was "Beau Chumps" with Laurel and Hardy and there were several supporting short films but the show only lasted two hours. It was a continuous programme so he stayed in the cinema but, after seeing the show through twice, he noticed the two usherettes were looking in his direction and whispering together so he thought it was time to move. But when he walked out he found it was still light. Strolling casually along the High Street he noticed the Library doors were still open so he went inside. Going to the Reference Room he selected a book at random and sat at a table idly turning the pages. It was a book on Ladies' Fashions through the Ages and he was about to return it when a woman next to him remarked

"Why! It is Mr Grimble, isn't it?"
He was startled and was about to deny his identity, but he regained his composure and murmured

"Er! Yes. But I do not think I have the pleasure.....?"
"Of course, you don't remember me do you? I am Muriel Twist"
Seeing his puzzled look she added
"I am not surprised. You only saw me for a few minutes last week when you came to my husband's garage to collect your car"
"But of course. How could I forget? I am sorry"
"We decided you must be a travelling salesman since you said you would be moving about"
Fred Grimble did not want to prolong the meeting but he was thinking to himself 'Is she just making idle small talk or is she prying for some reason?'. He decided to encourage her to talk but

he must be careful not to reveal anything that might sound suspicious or unusual. He asked

"Have you been shopping?"

"Well, yes and no. It is early closing day and my sister works in Woolworths in the High Street. So I caught the early bus into town and spent the morning going round the shops before meeting her for lunch when the store closed. I came in here to look up something for James, my husband, before going back to my sister's place for tea. There she is now"

She called to a woman who had just entered the library.

"Joan, over here. This is Mr Frederick Grimble. He is new to the district"

"Really! How do you do, Mr Grimble? Where are you staying?"

He was thinking that Muriel Twist had even remembered his first name and the idle enquiry nearly caught him out. But he recovered, to lie convincingly

"I travel around a lot but, for the present I have a room in Chetsford. I have been in Dunchester this morning on business. Forgive me, Ladies, but I really must be going. It has been nice to meet you"

The two women watched him hurry away. Joan turned to her sister

"What a strange man. He seemed nervous; as though he had something to hide"

"That is what James said when he called at the garage last week"

Joan giggled

"Perhaps he is a German spy?"

"No! He is too short and looks too ordinary"

"Well, he has dropped something on the floor. Perhaps it is a code or something"

Muriel picked up the piece of paper. Written on was '3843 MV Middleton'. She put the scrap of paper in her bag

"If I see him again I'll give it to him"

"Did you find what you were looking up for James?"

"Yes. I have finished in here"

"Alright then! Let us go home to my place for tea. I bought some fresh cream doughnuts at the dairy"

"Ooh! Lovely. Come on then. I must catch the nine o'clock bus home"

Fred Grimble was feeling discomfited as he drove along the

Scolling Road. The chance encounter with the two women had unnerved him. He had tried to appear inconspicuous and, suddenly, out of the blue he had been greeted by someone who knew him. It was only a coincidence and of no great consequence in itself; but he could hardly melt into the background if people were noticing him and remembering his passing. Frensham Down was a very small place and he must finish his task there before more curious villagers noticed his presence and wondered.

He parked the car opposite his cottage and switched off the lights. Although it was still raining he wound down the driver's window and sat there listening. The fact that he could see no lights in the cottage windows meant nothing because the new black-out regulations were in force. There could still be people up and about behind the curtained windows; but the rain had kept most people indoors and there was no-one abroad in Black Hut Lane. He wound up the window, got out and, picking up the umbrella held it over him as he locked the car doors and boot. There was a chill in the air when he entered the cottage, so he switched on the electric fire in the front room. Hanging his raincoat and hat on a peg attached to the front room door, and leaving the rolled umbrella in the corner, Kluger looked at his watch. It was 9 pm. He had a while to go before the scheduled call time so, making a cup of black coffee and a cheese sandwich, he took off his shoes before sitting in an armchair and switching on the wireless.

Hilda Benhope had been doing some sewing while she listened to the Henry Hall music programme. She was an early riser so she switched off at 9.30pm and began to prepare for bed. She could hear music coming from the wireless next door but the sound was not loud enough to bother her. As she entered her bedroom about twenty minutes later the music stopped and shortly afterwards she heard the faint sound of a door clicking shut. The rain was streaming down the window pane as she looked out from her darkened bedroom to see her next door neighbour, huddled in a light coloured raincoat, cross the road to his car. She could not see his face or the soft hat he was wearing because these were hidden by the umbrella he held up to ward off the rain. 'Now I wonder where he is off to at this time of night?' she mused. 'It can't be the pub because the Bowman closes at ten'. She turned back the sheets and climbed into bed 'Oh well! It is none of my business. But it *is* odd'.

Hans Kluger took the long way round, as usual, entering the Scolling Road from School Lane. The Bowman was just closing and one or two people were hurrying away in the rain while Angus McKuy, the landlord, stood by the door waiting to shut and bolt it after his last patron had gone. The forecourt was empty but Hans decided it would draw attention to himself if he left the car there, while the landlord was watching, and just walked away. Instead, he continued on, past the pub, past the bus stop, and turned left into the road that skirted the Village Green. There was no car parked outside the doctor's cottage so he continued down the road to park outside the Post Office. Anyone noticing him would think he had stopped to use the telephone. That gave him an idea. He got out of the car and entered the public call box which was in darkness; the light bulb having been removed to comply with blackout regulations. Kluger lifted the receiver and listened.

"Number please?"

"I do not know the number but I want the doctor in Frensham Down. Can you put me through?"

"Hold on"

There was a pause before the operator's voice sounded again.

"Insert two pennies in the box"

The receiver gave a small clank sound as he inserted each coin; a ringing tone sounded at the other end of the line.

"Doctor's surgery. How can I help you?"

Kluger recognised Eve's voice. He pressed button A to make contact and heard the coins drop into the box. Holding a handkerchief over his mouth to disguise his own voice he spoke quietly

"May I speak to the doctor?"

"I am sorry but I am afraid he is out on a call. Can I help, I am the doctor's wife and a nurse?"

"No. I must speak to the doctor tonight. I will call again later. Do you know what time he will be back?"

"No. But it will not be for three hours or more. If I cannot help, can I take a message and a number where he can call you back?"

"No. That will not be necessary. But thank you for your trouble. The matter cannot wait so I shall have to call another doctor in Dunchester. Good night"

Kluger got back into the car and drove it up to park in the doctor's driveway.

Eve Middleton replaced the telephone receiver and returned to the sitting room. She looked at the clock on the wall. It was 10.10pm. It looked as though Ernest would not be back in time to make the scheduled call but they were resigned to carrying out Kluger's instructions and her husband had shown Eve what had to be done. She put aside her book and went into the hall where she switched on the loft light to provide power for the wireless set. She did not hear the car arrive outside; in any case, had she done so, she would have thought it was Ernest. She was about to open the trap door, with the pole hook, when there was a knock at the front door. Whoever it was she must get rid of them quickly so she hastened to the door and, without thinking, opened it. Before she could stop him Hans Kluger had pushed his way inside and shut the door behind him. She gasped in fear but managed to control her breathing

"What do you want?"

"I have come to make the scheduled call"

"I thought you were leaving it to my husband to make the calls?"

"But the Herr Doktor is not here"

"How do you know that?"

"His car is not outside. In any case I called you on the telephone to check"

Her eyes widened in fear

"So it was you who called just now?"

"Yes! Are you not pleased to see me?"

He did not wait for an answer

"But I have more important things to worry about for the moment. Let us get that ladder down and then we shall go out together to bring in the things from my car"

It took but a few minutes to bring in the things Kluger had purchased that afternoon. Leaving these in the hall, Kluger returned to the car and drove it back to the Post Office; it would not do, he thought, for the doctor to return early and be warned of his presence by the sight of the car in the driveway. Eve considered whether she should lock him out; but she was too frightened of upsetting him so she stood by the door until he returned.

Kluger made no move to molest Eve as she climbed the ladder first; to take the table and chairs he handed up to her. Then he plugged the electric lead into the power socket on the skirting board in the hall and, carrying the lead, followed her up the ladder. By the light of the torch he removed the bayonet plug from the light socket and replaced it with the electric bulb which he had left in the table drawer. Now he had light to change the bayonet plug for a conventional three pin power plug which he pushed into the socket on the wandering lead. He turned to Eve

"Now, remember! Each time you finish with the scheduled call, and switch off the set, you must disconnect this lead and take it downstairs. We do not want inquisitive visitors wondering why a power lead stretches from the hall to the loft"

Kluger looked at his watch.

"There are five minutes to go. I want you to show me you know how to make the call. So sit on this chair, put on the earphones and set the frequency and wave length"

Eve did as she was told and waited. Kluger was standing behind her. She felt him slide his hands under her armpits and fondle her breasts. She tried to push him off but he was too strong. He murmured in her ear.

"Are you going to be nice to me tonight?"

"No I am *not*. Leave me alone!"

"Oh! I think you will. You do not know what horrible things can happen to your mother if you do not"

"But I ...I....just *can't*"

He let go of her and, sitting in the chair next to her, he put on the other set of earphones. Reaching across he switched the set to 'send' and spoke into the microphone

"Zeta calling. Zeta calling. Acknowledge"

He watched the second hand on his watch dial; his left hand moving up and down on Eve's thigh. Eve tried to arrest the movement but with no success. She tried to get up but he pushed her down roughly, and held her hand tight to keep her there, while he spoke into the microphone

"Willard One calling. Over"

He put down the microphone and switched over to 'receive'. A man's voice with an Irish accent came over the air

"OK. Willard receiving strength nine. Do you have any messages for me?"

Kluger slid his left hand between Eve's thighs as he switched to 'send' again.

"Yes. It is about the female hostage. But just a moment...."

He looked at Eve and mouthed "Well?" She let go his wandering hand and, as he slid it up under her skirt, she gasped, involuntarily; but, realising she must play for time, she nodded. He returned to the microphone.

"Sorry about the delay. Cancel that last message; but stand by in an hour. I might need to call you again. Over and out"

Kluger switched off the set and stood up. He disconnected the power lead and dropped it through the hatchway to land on the hall floor. Eve shuddered as he cupped her breasts once more before he turned and descended the ladder; but she did not brush his hands away. He was waiting at the bottom when she came down and he swung her round, so that her back was against the ladder, while he kissed her savagely on the lips. His right hand slipped under her skirt and lifted it to her waist. She pushed his hand down. She must delay him as much as possible in the vain hope that Ernest would return early. She tried to control her voice

"No! Not here. If you are going to do this you must do it properly. Wouldn't you like that?"

Eve had a half formulated plan in her mind but, for the time being, she must make Kuger think she wanted his attentions. She slid her arms round his neck and kissed him wantonly. 'So she really does want me', he thought, 'this gets better and better'. He relaxed his grip and Eve pulled away from him; wrinkling her nose.

"You need a bath first. I can't enjoy going to bed with you while you smell as though you have not had a bath for weeks. You go into the bedroom and undress and I'll run you a hot bath"

Kluger was naked when he came out of the bedroom to find Eve bending over the bath testing the heat of the water. She suppressed a shudder as he slipped a hand up her skirt and between her buttocks; but she forced a laugh as she gently disengaged his hand

"Now! Now! Not yet. You get in the bath and I'll wash your back"

She washed his back and told him to lie down while she soaped his body. If her plan was to work she must get him excited and incautious. As she looked down at him she could not resist teasing him

"I can see *you* are ready. I don't think I can wait"

She reached down and grasped him; but, as he made to get up, she let go and pushed him back as she said, coquettishly,

"Now, you stay there while I get undressed and I will join you in the bath. Don't go away now!"

When Eve returned she wore a large bath towel wrapped round her waist. She had both hands behind her holding the towel up. Kluger gasped as he saw her naked breasts approaching. He sat up and reached for her

"Come on. Don't be coy. Drop the towel so that I can see all of you"

She chuckled and backed away

"You try to take it off me"

"So it is to be a game then? Come here"

Kluger half rose, reached out and grabbed the loose edge of the towel. He pulled but she laughed as she, teasingly, pulled back still holding the towel tight behind her. He pulled harder but still she held on. Again he tugged and, seeing he was off balance, she suddenly let go. As he fell back he saw her standing there naked. But it was the last thing he was to see in this life for, as he pulled the towel under the water, he also pulled the power socket of the lead that she had pinned to the underside of the towel. There was a loud bang from the fuse box in the hall as Kluger's body convulsed and, with staring sightless eyes, he slid beneath the water. The light circuit did not blow and Eve stood there, her hands to her mouth, looking down at the lifeless body. She turned away and, dropping to her knees, was violently sick in the toilet basin. When she recovered she grasped the rubber knob on the end of the chain and flushed the toilet. Then, trying not to look at the body in the bath, she went into the hall and, although she was sure it was no longer live, she pulled the plug from the power socket in the skirting board. She could not bring herself to return to the bathroom so she washed her face in the kitchen sink, before putting on a dressing gown. Going into the sitting room, she huddled down, with her knees up, in an armchair.

CHAPTER TWELVE

1939

After unloading the car Hans Kluger had driven it down the road to park outside the Post Office, so there was nothing to warn Ernest Middleton of his presence at the cottage when the doctor returned home an hour later. Eve was still sitting, crumpled, in the armchair when Ernest let himself in by the front door. He came into the room and, seeing her tear-stained face, gathered her up into his arms

"Why! Whatever is the matter, darling?"

She could not answer but just clung to him and burst into tears once more. She was trembling violently and Ernest held her close, whispering soothing words in her ear. As she calmed and moved away from his embrace, her dressing gown fell open and, for the first time, he realised she had nothing on under the garment. A terrible thought occurred to him.

"Kluger hasn't been here. Has he?"

Eve nodded, mutely, and Ernest exploded

"What has that swine done to you? Is he still here?"

Again she nodded through her tears.

"Where is he? I'll kill the bastard"

Eve pointed towards the bathroom

"He is in there but.........."

Ernest did not wait for more. He charged through the hall and burst into the bathroom to be brought up short by the sight of the body in the bath. He stood stock still taking in the situation. Without touching anything he traced the lead back to the hall and saw the plug had been disconnected. Although he was content that the power was no longer being conveyed to the bath, he went into the surgery and donned a pair of rubber surgical gloves before he returned to the bathroom. Then, pulling the chain that held the bath plug, he watched the water drain away. When the last drop had gone he carefully lifted the power lead and, unpinning it from the towel, dropped it to the floor. He checked the body for any sign of life and, finding none, he straightened up and returned slowly to Eve. He took her in his arms once more.

"You are in shock, my darling. Come into the kitchen and I'll make you a cup of hot sweet tea"

Eve sat at the kitchen table and, haltingly, told her husband what had happened. He listened without interrupting her until she had finished. Then he took her hands and murmured

"You poor darling! What a terrible thing to go through. But thank God you are not hurt and it is over. Now we must think what is to be done!"

"But Mama and Papa. What is to become of them? Kluger said they would suffer if anything happened to him"

"Well, somehow we must contrive things so that his death appears to have been caused by an accident some distance away from here. You must be brave because we must move quickly and I shall need your help. Do you think you are up to it?"

Eve pulled herself together and nodded. Ernest continued.

"Good girl! The first thing we must do is search through everything he brought with him to make sure there is nothing to connect him with us. Didn't he come in a car?"

"Yes. But he moved it down the road to the Post Office"

"Well! I must bring it up here and search that too. But let us go through his clothes first because I need his car keys"

At Ernest's insistence Eve, also, put on a pair of surgical gloves to avoid leaving fingerprints on any shiny surface. Then she collected Kluger's clothes from the bedroom and, bringing them into the kitchen, she dumped them on the table. Remembering that Kluger was a spy, Ernest checked the shoes for any features out of the ordinary, such as a concealed compartment in the heel; but found nothing. The underclothes, socks, shirt and braces were equally innocent; as was Kluger's hat. In one pocket of the raincoat there was a ticket stub with the word 'Regal' and the price printed on it. Ernest replaced this where he found it. The other pocket held a receipt for money paid to a Dunchester electrician for purchase of the length of power cable and its attachments. For the moment Ernest placed this at one side. In the trousers pockets he found a crumpled white handkerchief and a small leather change purse. Replacing the handkerchief, Ernest placed the purse with the electrician's receipt on the table. From the righthand side pocket of the jacket he withdrew a simple plain key-ring with two keys attached and a tag bearing the name and address of a Dunchester Garage. 'Ah! The car keys' Ernest thought, triumphantly, as he put these to one side. In the other side pocket he found a key for a Yale lock; it was attached to a metal spring ring to which was also attached a torn piece of card. This puzzled him for a moment but he shrugged and placed it with the other items on the table. From the left inside jacket pocket he withdrew a wallet and from the other inside pocket he took a notebook with a pencil in the spine sheath. Both these items joined the others on the table. He examined the hems and linings of all the garments but could feel nothing suspicious so he dropped them in a heap to the floor.

Now Ernest turned his attention to the items on the table. He picked up the car keys and put them in his pocket. He would need these to move the car. The other key still puzzled him. There must have been some sort of label attached to the ring. If so, where was it? He looked at the ring thoughtfully for a moment. Then he bent down and picked up the jacket again. This time he felt the lining of the side pocket more carefully. There was a small hole at the bottom. Fetching a pair of large tweezers from his surgery, he carefully withdrew a piece of crumpled card which had fallen through the hole in the lining. As he suspected the torn edge of the card matched the torn piece attached to the key ring. He spread the card out on the table to read '25, Black Hut Lane'. So that was where Kluger had been living. He had heard Hilda Benhope mentioning to Jean Stokes, in the general store, that she had a new neighbour. Jean had commented that he never came into the store for groceries. Ernest had thought it just idle gossip and had paid no attention to it at the time. The recollection gave him pause for thought. Then, still using the tweezers, he carefully replaced the crumpled card in the place where he had found it. 'That will give the police something to think about' he chuckled. The change purse contained nothing but a few English coins; but Ernest gasped when he opened the wallet to reveal more than £1,000 in small denomination English banknotes. On such a sum the average workman could maintain himself, his wife and a small family for several years. There was, also, a driving licence in the name of Frederick Grimble. He showed the licence to Eve

"So that was the name he was using. Have you heard anyone in the village talking about a Fred Grimble?"

"No, but perhaps he wasn't living around here"

"I am sure he was. This key is for the cottage next to Hilda Benhope's"

Ernest doubted there would be any English record of the driving licence because, in the circumstances, it was, probably, a professionally made forgery supplied to Kluger by his masters; so he replaced it in the wallet. After checking carefully to ensure there was nothing trapped between the notes and nothing written on any of them, he replaced these, also, in the wallet. Ernest was startled to find a piece of paper in the wallet with his own name and address written on it in a gothic hand; this he dropped in an ashtray and put a match to it. He stirred the ashes thoroughly then emptied the ashtray into the grate of the open fireplace. After making such a vital discovery he searched the wallet more thoroughly for anything he might have missed. Feeling a slight bulge in the lining he found a concealed compartment in which was Kluger's Nazi Party card. 'Foolish of him to carry that around', he thought, as he replaced it. He, then, turned his attention to the notebook. There were various entries, most of which were in German. This gave him no difficulty because it was similar to Austrian, his native tongue; but, although he could find nothing to directly incriminate him or Eve, he decided it would be safer to destroy the notebook in case he had missed something. So he put it on the draining board to be dealt with later. Ernest picked up the clothes and replaced the wallet, purse and electrician's receipt where he had found them.

A thought suddenly occurred to Ernest. He turned to Eve, who was standing beside him during the search

"Where is Kluger's wrist watch? I know he wore one because he looked at it last night when we made the call and he must have been wearing it tonight for the same reason"

"Yes, he looked at it when he made the call tonight". Eve also pondered "Where are his glasses?"
They found both the watch and spectacles on top of the bathroom cabinet. The watch was a Swiss made seven jewelled movement; the sort of inexpensive watch any man might wear be he English or German. Ernest carried both items into the kitchen. The watch he dropped it into Kluger's right hand jacket pocket and the folded spectacles he tucked into the breast pocket.

"I must be more careful. A little mistake like missing spectacles or a missing watch; or a watch on the wrong wrist could arouse interest from the police when they find the body"

Ernest moved his own car from the driveway onto the road. Then, disguising himself in Kluger's hat and raincoat, he picked up the car keys from the table and left the cottage. Making sure no-one was about, he drove his own car down to the Post Office and parked it in front of Kluger's car. Locking his own car, he entered the Hillman Minx. Fortunately, it started first time and he was able to drive it up to the cottage quietly. Once the car was in his own driveway, Ernest searched it, using Kluger's torch which he found on the passenger seat. Anyone seeing him would think he was looking for something in his own car. He returned to the kitchen with the map he had found.

"So far as I could see, there was nothing in the car except for the usual tools, an electric torch, a black umbrella and this map of Dunchester and district"

Pushing aside the clothes, which Eve had picked up from the floor, Ernest spread the map out on the table and examined it minutely for any markings Kluger might have made. He could find none so he refolded the map and set it to one side; to be put back in the car.

Ernest was still wearing the surgical gloves when he returned to the bathroom and, using a flannel, he washed Kluger's body to remove any fingerprints Eve might have made on it. He spread a layer of dry towels on the tiled floor, then lifted the body out of the bath and dried it thoroughly. He carried the body to the kitchen and laid it on some old curtains Eve had fetched from her linen cupboard.

"If my plan is to work there is no need to dress the body. We will just wrap it in the curtains while we move it. But we must not forget to bring the curtains back here. We must be very careful in handling the body and we must avoid knocking it against anything. A carcase bruises easily and there must be no bruises on the body when it is discovered"

Ernest stood up and went into the hall to replace the burnt-out wire in the fuse box while he pondered the next stage of the deception.

Being aware of Kluger's address in Black Hut Lane made things so much easier. Ernest remembered a second-hand one-bar electric fire which they had bought in a London street market before coming to Frensham Down. They had not used it in the cottage and had kept it stored in the garden shed. Ernest fetched the fire into the kitchen and checked to see that the plug fitted into the socket on the wandering lead Eve had used as a murder weapon. He carefully wiped every surface of the fire to remove or smudge any fingerprints there might be on the appliance; paying particular attention to the power plug which he took apart and reassembled. He took the fire over to the body and pressed Kluger's right hand round the handle for a moment to imprint his fingerprints on it. He did the same with the plug and switch. Ernest picked up the wandering lead and, remembering Eve had handled it with bare hands, he carefully wiped its length and wiped both the plug and socket. Recognising that, by so doing, he had erased Kluger's fingerprints also, he impressed Kluger's right hand prints on the lead, plug and socket before rolling it up. Leaving aside the raincoat and hat, Eve folded Kluger's suit and placed this with his other clothing to make a bundle. She then helped Ernest carry the bundle, shoes, power-lead, map and electric fire out to Kluger's car.

It was not raining when they lifted the wrapped body and carried it out to lay it on the back seat of Kluger's car. Eve was wearing a dark blue jumper and a pair of dark trousers; also Kluger's raincoat and hat. She was still wearing a pair of surgical gloves. Ernest had put on a dark overcoat and a dark trilby hat. He was, also, still wearing surgical gloves. Ernest turned to his wife.

"We have assumed Kluger was living alone at the cottage but it is possible someone else lives there with him. So we must be careful. Hilda Benhope lives next door at number 23 but she has to get up early in the morning so she should be asleep at this time of night. Number 27, on the other side, is empty because Harry Smith and his wife have gone away to visit their daughter in Nottingham and won't be back for a while. I will drive Kluger's car down to the cottage and investigate. You take our car and drive by the Scolling Road and down School Lane to the other end of Black Hut Lane. Park the car in the lay-by at the bridge in Black Hut Lane. Switch off the lights and wait until I signal the 'all clear' by flashing my torch. I will give two quick flashes followed by a pause, then one longer flash. When you see the signal lock the car doors then walk up to meet me. I will be waiting in Kluger's car opposite his cottage. If anyone comes along walk right past the car without looking at it and continue up and into the alley by the general store. I will join you there while we decide what we can do. Are you alright now? Are you sure you can do this?"

Eve nodded with a nervous smile. Ernest took her in his arms and held her tight for a moment before she walked down to the Post Office, got into their car and drove off. Ernest started up Kluger's car and drove off in the opposite direction, to turn right into Black Hut Lane. He looked at the dash-board clock. It was two o'clock in the morning on Thursday, 7th September, 1939.

Ernest considered driving without lights but he realised this would attract the attention of a casual observer because a person on an innocent errand would drive down an unlit country road at night with the, black-out shielded, headlights on. He saw no-one and the black-out curtains hid any light from the windows of the cottages that lined Black Hut Lane. As he was approaching Hilda Benhope's cottage he slowed right down and coasted the last few yards to park on the patch of hard gravel opposite number 25. He switched off the engine and waited in the car until he saw the shielded headlights of Eve's car coming in the opposite direction. When her car had stopped and she had switched off the lights Ernest opened his car door and picked up the torch; then he lifted out and opened the umbrella before heading for the cottage. He was thankful for a slight drizzle because it gave him an excuse to take cover under the umbrella, hiding his face, as he walked stealthily up the garden path. Under the porch he closed and lowered the umbrella. He left this leaning against the porch wall while he, quietly, inserted the key in the Yale lock. Hoping it would not squeak, he gently pushed the door open and stepped inside. He stood still for a moment, listening, but all was quiet.

Ernest knew the lay-out of these cottages because many of his patients lived in the same type of building so it did not take him long to search the place to make sure it was unoccupied and that only one bed was in use. As he checked each room he made sure the black-out curtains were drawn before switching on the torch. He decided not to use the room lights because he was not sure how effective the black-out curtains were and he did not want to attract the attention of an officious ARP warden. Making sure he still had the latchkey in his pocket, Ernest returned to the front door. He picked up the umbrella and, using it as a shield against the rain, he brought in Kluger's clothes and shoes, the electric fire and the wandering power lead. Leaving the umbrella in the hall and the key in the lock, with the front door ajar, he returned to the car and looked about him. There was nothing to cause him concern so he gave the signal to Eve; then climbed into the driving seat and waited.

It was too dark for Eve to see either her husband or Kluger's car from the bridge; but she recognised the torch signal. so she locked the car doors and walked up Black Hut Lane, as they had agreed. In case anyone was watching she did not slow her pace until she was level with the car. Ernest jumped out to join her.

"It is all clear and I have left the front door open. Let us get this thing out of the back and into the cottage. Don't switch on any lights and, whilst we are in there, we must not speak except in a whisper because the dividing walls are very thin and we don't want Hilda Benhope suspecting more than one person is in the cottage"

It was more difficult to get the corpse out than it had been to put it into the back of the car; but, somehow, they managed to remove it and to carry it across the road into the cottage. Leaving the corpse, still wrapped in the old curtains, on the living room floor Ernest went back and locked the car doors. When he returned he took the key from the front door lock and, with the car keys, placed it on the dresser in the kitchen.

The plan Ernest had devised required the presence of a bath but there was no bathroom in the cottage. For a moment Ernest felt panic rising then sudden relief as he remembered that farm workers usually bathed in a tin tub before the kitchen fire. He quietly let himself out into the backyard. Yes, there it was. A large tin bath suspended by a hook to the back wall of the cottage. Careful to avoid any noise he lifted it down and carried it inside to deposit it in the middle of the kitchen floor. Returning to the back door he closed it quietly and locked it; leaving the key in the lock. Moving slowly to cut down the risk of noise they unwrapped the naked body and placed it in the bath. Ernest rolled up the curtains and took them into the hall, leaving them by the door.

Eve took off Kluger's raincoat and hat; which she hung on the hook in the hall. Ernest collected the car keys and the latchkey from the dresser and replaced them in the jacket side pockets where he had found them. Then he carried the jacket, socks and shoes up to the bedroom. He left the jacket on the bed and the shoes, with the socks tucked into them, by the foot of the bed. The remainder of Kluger's clothing they draped over a kitchen chair after fastening the braces to the trouser buttons. Ernest picked up the electric kettle and looked at it meditatively. He noted there was no safety cut-out and thought about using the kettle in place of the electric fire but it was a chilly night and he could not imagine Kluger taking a bath in a cold kitchen; so he decided to stick to his original plan. Eve dropped a face flannel into the bottom of a large enamel jug to deaden the sound of the water while she filled the jug from the kitchen tap. It took a while to get the bath a reasonable depth.

216

Meanwhile Ernest boiled several kettles of hot water to add to Eve's efforts. It was essential that the water be hot enough to dissolve sufficient soap to make it look like bathwater. Ernest had to make several trips, unplugging the kettle each time because the lead would reach no further than the draining board by the sink. Eve found a packet of soap flakes in a cupboard and stirred some of these into the water to make it soapy; then she fetched the soap dish from the draining board with its, partly used, bar of Lifebuoy soap. Ernest placed Kluger's fingerprints on the dish and, after washing the bar of soap in the bathwater and replacing it in the dish, he set these down on the floor beside the bath. Eve dropped the face flannel into the bathwater and fetched a large white bath towel from a cupboard, which she draped over the clothes on the kitchen chair; another, smaller, towel she draped over the edge of the bath so that one end trailed in the water. As an afterthought, Ernest rubbed some soap on the flannel and bathed Kluger's eyes. He wanted it to appear that Kluger groped blindly for the bath towel to rub the soap from his eyes. He dropped the flannel back in the bath. By the light of the torch Ernest looked around but could think of nothing they had not taken into account. He fetched the power lead he had brought in and unrolled it. Leaving the kettle on the draining board, Ernest unplugged the kettle lead from the wall socket and inserted the plug on the wandering power lead in the same socket. He placed the second kitchen chair next to the bath, alongside the small towel, and set down the electric fire on it with the single filament bar facing towards the bather. He plugged the fire lead into the socket on the wandering lead and switched the fire on. Almost immediately the filament started to glow. All seemed to be ready.

Ernest whispered to Eve to stand clear while gave the fire a shove from behind. It toppled over and fell with a sizzle into the bathwater. Eve almost screamed when the corpse convulsed as though it were alive and a loud bang came from the fuse box under the stairs. Ernest held a finger to his lips in warning but no sound came from Hilda Benhope's cottage.

Telling Eve to wait in the front room, Ernest took the torch and climbed the stairs. He, gingerly, switched on the bedroom light. The room remained dark but he left the switch in the 'on' position. It would appear the light had been on when the 'accident' had blown the main fuse. By the light of the torch he searched the upstairs rooms for any incriminating papers. Then, before coming down, he made sure the landing light switch was also in the 'on' position. He carried out the same procedure in the front room, kitchen and hall.

They left the torch on the kitchen dresser and, going into the hall, Ernest brought in the umbrella and left it by the door. Gathering up the old curtains to take back with them, they silently let themselves out and, pulling the front door shut behind them, they walked as quietly as possible along the lane to their own car. No-one saw them go. Hilda Benhope, who did not know what had awakened her, looked at the luminous dial on her bedside alarm clock and drowsily noted it was three in the morning before rolling over and going back to sleep.

There was a large incinerator in the back garden of the Middletons' cottage and Ernest had decided he should burn the curtains in case they had some tell-tale stains on them. It would be best if this was done right away and, in normal circumstances, his neighbours should not be surprised to find him burning contaminated bandages and other discarded material connected with his profession. But he remembered the new black-out regulations. Everyone was a bit jittery in those early days of the war and anyone who observed the fire in the middle of the night would be likely to report it to the ARP warden. Ernest did not want to attract attention so he piled the curtains into the incinerator and splashed some paraffin oil over them, ready for him to drop a lighted match into the unit first thing in the morning. He tore Kluger's diary into shreds and, recognising that charred pages might rise from the chimney in the heat, he wrapped the pages in an old cloth toilet bag before he threw them in after the curtains. Finally he added the surgical gloves he and Eve had worn that night; then re-entered the cottage to join Eve for a coffee in the kitchen. Eve rose from the table and threw herself into her husband's arms

"Thank you, darling. I don't know what would become of me if you weren't here"

"There there! It is all over now and you must try to put it out of your mind"

"But I *can't* forget. That wretched wireless is still in the loft and I am worried what will happen to Mama and Papa"

"Well! There is nothing more we can do tonight. Let us go to bed and try to get some sleep. Perhaps the light of day will bring some fresh ideas"

"Alright, darling. But I don't think I can sleep"

But she did; the deep sleep of someone so exhausted that her brain simply shut off. It was Ernest who lay awake until it was nearly dawn. Then even he drifted off into a fitful dream where he was being chased by an English policeman with a swastika badge on his helmet and a face that looked remarkably like that of Hans Kluger.

When he awoke, at seven in the morning, the first thing Ernest did was to put on a dressing gown and go outside to put a match to the debris in the incinerator. He stayed there until he was sure everything was turned to ashes. Then he re-entered the cottage and made a pot of tea. When he took a cup in to Eve she was lying in bed gazing up at the ceiling.

"I would like a bath. But I don't think I can ever use that bath again"

Ernest could think of nothing to say. So he just held her tight in his arms.

It was around eleven o'clock that same morning, thursday 7th September 1939, and Ernest Middleton was about to go out on a call, when the manager of his bank in Dunchester rang.

"Is that Dr Ernest Middleton?"

"Yes. Who is calling?"

"This is John Templeton, manager of the Westminster bank, Dunchester"

"What is the trouble? Is there something wrong with my account?"

"No, doctor. It is nothing like that. I have received a letter from our Regent Street branch, which is addressed to Dr & Mrs Middleton, care of the Dunchester branch. The envelope is marked 'Private and Confidential' so it is being held here for your instructions. I recall that you and your wife had an account with the London branch and that you transferred this to my branch when you moved to Frensham Down. I understand the letter was despatched to the London branch by a bank in Zurich and is marked for urgent attention; so they forwarded it to me immediately. Do you wish me to enclose it in an envelope and post it to you or will you or your wife call in to collect it?"

"I have a call to make in Lavering Market this morning so I will drive on to Dunchester and pop into the bank before I return home"

"Very well, Doctor. Ask for the chief cashier at the desk. He will be holding the letter for you. But don't forget the bank closes at three o'clock this afternoon"

"Thank you for reminding me. But I expect to be with you before lunch"

Ernest replaced the receiver and picked up his bag as he left the surgery. Eve was in the kitchen, preparing lunch, when Ernest walked in.

"I am off now"

"I know I should not ask you to be here all the time but I still feel nervous on my own; although I know you will say there is no longer any reason to be afraid"

Ernest embraced his wife

"Irrespective of how we feel, outsiders must see us carrying on as usual. So try to put it all behind you and act normally. Last night never happened! It was only a dream; or perhaps I should say it was a nightmare. The more you can push it to the back of your mind the more unreal it will seem. I will try not to leave you alone more than is absolutely necessary; but the mid-wife would think it odd if I don't call in on Mary Tivot in Lavering Market to see how she is getting on after her delivery yesterday"

Eve kissed him on the cheek and eased herself from his arms.

"You are too good to me and I will try hard not to let you down. So you will only be about an hour. Would you like a coffee before you go?"

"No thank you, dear. I must be on my way. Actually I shall be a bit longer than an hour because I have just received a call from the bank manager in Dunchester. He says he has a letter for us from Zurich and I told him I would call in and collect it. But, if you would rather I came straight back after my call, I'll leave the matter of the letter until Monday"

"No. You must collect the letter right away. It is probably about the account I left open for Mama and Papa to use"

Tears appeared in her eyes as she thought of her parents and Ernest drew her once more in his arms to comfort her. But Eve pulled herself together and dabbed her eyes with the handkerchief she kept in her apron pocket.

"Go along with you. I am alright. I'll wait lunch until you come back"

It was just after noon when Ernest drew up in front of the

bank. He left his bag in the boot, locking this and all the doors. It was an old car and was probably not worth more than £20 so it was unlikely to be stolen; but a doctor had to take special care not to leave drugs and valuable instruments vulnerable to the opportunist thief. Going to the bank, he had to wait a few minutes until the tiny queue cleared and he faced the only cashier on duty.

"I would like to see the Chief Cashier, please"

"Can I have your name, Sir?"

"Doctor Middleton"

"May I ask the nature of your enquiry, sir?"

"I understand he has a letter for me"

"If you would care to take a seat over there, doctor, Mr Maplesfield will be with you shortly"

Ernest sat on the polished bench idly reading the posters on the opposite wall. They seemed to be mostly concerned with new emergency war-time regulations; some regarding the conduct of banks and others concerning more general matters, such as air raid precautions, use of gas masks and national registration. Ernest could not help wondering how the authorities had managed to produce, print and distribute posters and notices on such a variety of subjects within a few days after the outbreak of the war. Obviously the Government departments concerned with such matters had been planning and working ever since the 1938 Munich crisis to be ready for the inevitable conflict. He started from his reverie to find a small, dapper, man who was carrying an envelope and addressing him fussily

"Dr. Middleton?"

"Yes"

"May I ask your first name and where you live?"

"Ernest Middleton of Frensham Down?"

"And your wife's first name?"

"Evelyn"

"Do you have your driving licence with you, sir?"

"Yes, here it is"

The cashier examined the licence, then returned it to Ernest

"Thank you, sir. I am sorry to be so formal; but one has to be so careful these days"

"No offence taken. I hope everyone is as security conscious in these troubled times"

"Mr Templeton has asked me to give you this letter. But he has

221

another matter he would like to discuss with you and, considering its source, he suspects the contents of the letter might have some bearing on the subject. In the circumstances the Manager has asked that you read the contents now; after which he will join you. If you care to follow me you can read the letter in privacy"

The chief cashier unlocked a side door and led Ernest into a small private room. The door swung shut behind them and locked itself automatically. Seeing the concerned look on Ernest's face the cashier was quick to reassure him.

"It is a Yale type lock which can be opened from outside only with a key; but you can open it from this side by turning the knob. Bank security, you know. I shall leave you now. Please press this bell push when you are ready to see the manager. Can I send you in a coffee, sir?"

"That would be nice, thank you. White with one sugar, please"

Ernest sat, meditatively, turning the envelope over in his hands; but he did not attempt to open it until after a young girl clerk had brought in the coffee. The envelope bore the Logo and address of the same bank in Zurich where an account for a substantial fortune had been opened by Eve's father in the name of Eva Mittelburg. When they came to London the couple opened a joint account in the names of Ernest and Eve Middleton at the Regent Street branch of the Westminster bank; the same branch that had forwarded the letter to Dunchester. To this account Eve (as Eva Mittelburg) had transferred all but a fairly large balance of the Swiss funds. The balance they had left in the Zurich bank to be made available to Eve's parents should they successfully flee Austria and need financial help. Ernest stirred the coffee and, now he was alone again, he opened the envelope and withdrew another envelope with an accompanying letter from the bank. The letter was in French and was addressed to Herr and Frau Mittelburg c/o the Regent Street branch of the Westminster bank. It was a simple message. The enclosed envelope had been handed in at the counter at the Swiss bank with the request that it be forwarded to England. The envelope held no clues regarding the sender but the Zurich bank had stamped a receipt date as 28th August, 1939. The address on the envelope was in German and read 'Please forward to Herr & Frau Mittelburg, Westminster Bank, Regent Street, London'.

The letter in the envelope was, also, written in German. There was no address but, when Ernest turned to the last page, before reading the text, he saw it was signed by Joseph Goldschmit, Eve's father. The last line read 'Your mother and I are quite well and you need not worry about us now that we are safe in Switzerland'. Ernest breathed a sigh of relief. So they were safe after all. So Kluger had been bluffing! But he was still puzzled that Kluger had found out their address in Frensham Down and had, somehow, got hold of Magda Goldschmit's necklace. Well, it didn't matter now, but Ernest had a logical mind which could not accept loose ends for which he could not account; and he did not like to think that their address might be in the hands of other German agents. He must do something about disposal of the wireless set in his loft; and the sooner the better. He returned to the beginning of the letter and found it to be an account of what had happened to the Goldschmits.

CHAPTER THIRTEEN

1938 - 1939

When Hitler marched into Austria in March, 1938, Joseph Goldschmit was still convinced that his industrial and financial power would protect him from the excesses of Nazi persecution. Although he had transferred a major part of his fortune to a bank account in Zurich in the name of his daughter he was still a relatively wealthy man of high standing and influence among the population of Innsbruck. He had heard of the assaults by Nazi thugs on Jewish shopkeepers in the poorer areas of Vienna, and even in the working class areas of Innsbruck, but he chose to ignore the implications for a long time; despite pleas from Magda, his wife, that he should take care.

The first indication that the Nazi Government's attitude toward Jews might affect him came in early December, 1938, when he learned that the German Economics Minister, Walther Funk, had recommended to Adolph Hitler that all Jews be forbidden to operate bank accounts and that their business operations should be disposed of and the proceeds go to the State. Upon hearing of this proposal Joseph took immediate steps to convert such of his assets as were still freely transferable to cash in the form of Swiss Francs; which he wrapped in a parcel and hid in the house to be carried in his baggage when the time came to flee the country. He assigned his business interests to Austrian friends, who were not so vulnerable as himself, and withdrew all the cash from his current and deposit accounts with the bank. He accepted the first offer, low though it was, for his house and furniture but he could not bring himself to part with his Mercedes motor car, which was practically brand new.

Realising the Nazi border guards would be on the alert for Jews attempting to escape Joseph refrained from attempting a border crossing immediately. Instead, he strapped two pairs of skis to the roof rack on his car and, with a limited number of suitcases, he and Magda drove towards St Anton; hoping they would be inconspicuous on their journey among the many skiers going to that popular winter sports area. However, after travelling some 60kms without incident they turned south off the main road at Landeck. It was essential that they should avoid staying at hotels where their papers would be demanded so, by pre-arrangement, they lodged at the farmhouse of Jean and Marie Leblanc, a sympathetic Swiss couple of around their own age, who had lived in Austria for several years and with whom they had made friends on previous holidays. They felt much safer, now, away from Innsbruck and amongst friends whose Swiss nationality protected them, to some extent, from visits by the Austrian police who sometimes, though rarely and with little heart for the task, made searches for Jews in the district.

Once she had settled down to the rural life Magda was happy on the farm. Snug in the warm farmhouse, with the every sound muffled by the deep blanket of winter snow outside, she felt at peace with the world and had no desire to move on. Even the tumultous roar of the river which flowed swiftly in the fields below the farmhouse, as it tumbled over the boulders in flood, swollen with the melting snow coming down from the mountains, failed to upset her equilibrium. Spring came and went and the warm sun of early summer brought an atmosphere of tranquillity which it seemed would last for ever. But Joseph knew it was an illusion and it would not do to wait for another winter.

They were still there, on 19th of August, 1939, when the Swiss Government gave an undertaking to the German Government to return any Jew who crossed over the border illegally. Joseph now realised they had left it too late to make a normal crossing and that they must either stay where they were and take their chances, or attempt to cross over into Switzerland at some remote part of the border and hide away from the authorities.

It was during an evening in August when things came to a head. The sun was high over the mountains to the South-West and, although it was beginning to cast shadows on the snows between the peaks, Joseph and Magda were still bathed in the warmth of the evening glow. They had enjoyed an excellent meal with their hosts and were sitting, alone, on the river bank. He was drawing leisurely on his pipe while she lazily watched the water rushing urgently between the boulders on its way down the valley. The water made a gentle gurgling sound which mingled pleasantly with the occasional tinkle from a cow bell as the herd moved across the pasture behind them. Joseph drew deeply on his pipe and puffed out a cloud of aromatic smoke. As he watched it drift lazily on the still air there was the sound of motor engines on the road above and behind them which led to the farm. A stand of trees and bushes blocked their view of the road so they were unaware that a police patrol was visiting the farm. After a short while they heard the vehicles leave the farm and the sound of the engines faded in the distance. When they returned to the farmhouse in the twilight they found their friends, Jean and Marie, in an agitated state. Jean spoke, apologetically,

"I am afraid you cannot stay here any longer, my friends. We have just been visited by a police patrol with two German soldiers and an SS officer. They left us a form on which we must give the names and nationalities of every person on the farm. I don't think they are suspicious and it is probably only a routine check-up; but the form will be collected by the end of the week and I can't risk harm coming to my family or my workers by concealing your presence, so you must move on before then. I am so sorry, but you *do* understand, don't you?"

Marie was crying as she folded Magda in her arms; but Joseph squared his shoulders

"This was inevitable, with a major war looming, and it will not be long before the Nazi patrols replace the police along the frontier. So we must not delay any longer in our bid to reach Switzerland. We have no idea how long a war may last and we cannot expect you, our friends, to support us indefinitely even if there were no danger for you. The limited Austrian funds we have will not last much longer and questions will be asked if Jean attempts to change large numbers of Swiss francs for us locally. Magda turned to Marie and clung to her as she cried

"We have been so happy here. I wish there were some way we could stay?"

Joseph took his wife's arm

"No, I am sorry my dear, but it is no use. We cannot endanger Jean and Marie. We must make a move tomorrow"

The next day, after a tearful farewell, Joseph and Magda set off in the Mercedes, after dark and with dimmed lights, for, what was to prove, an eventful journey into Switzerland. They took the country road which ran up the valley alongside the river. This was a risky route because the road criss-crossed over the stream at several points, at any of which they might encounter a check-point on the bridge, but it was preferable to the main highway and the, almost certain, border posts at Plunds and Naudus. They met no traffic and were not challenged on the road. After travelling about 40kms they entered the tiny village of Bielerhohe which, according to the map, was some 8kms from the Austro/Swiss frontier. Seeing an inn by the side of the road, Joseph stopped the car and suggested they should take a beer while he consulted the map.

The bar-room was practically empty and the landlord did not seem unduly surprised that he should see strangers so late at night. Joseph carried two mugs of beer over to a table under a light and spread out the map. The road they had been taking ran more or less parallel with the Swiss border but at the nearest point the border was at least 5kms from the road and there appeared to be no side road which would take them across into Switzerland. If they continued the way they were going they would be moving away from the frontier and would probably end up in Liechtenstein. Joseph did not know what the position was in this independent State; but, even if it was not already occupied by the Germans, he was sure there would be a concentration of Nazi patrols on the roads leading to the State. He took a deep drink from his mug and looked despairingly at Magda. She had been following the road on the map with her finger and she pointed to a side road, a little way past St. Gallenkirch

"Look, Joseph, there is a road that goes down to......I can't quite see the name of the place........"

They were startled by the gruff sound of the landlord's voice over Joseph's shoulder

"Gargellan. That is the name of the place you are looking at. Its a small hamlet; but, if you are looking to cross the border there in the dark, you will need some help because the frontier is three kilometres beyond the end of the road and a crossing place is not easy to find"

Magda and Joseph looked up at him; stunned by the casual way he mentioned crossing the border as though it were an everyday occurrence. He grinned

"Do not look so shocked. We get many fugitives coming this way. We don't much like the Nazi's round here, so you need not worry. From your accents I would guess you are Austrians and, of course, you are not Jews are you?"

He shook his head with his lips pursed as he asked the rhetorical question. Joseph simply nodded and shook his own head in one movement

"Can you help us?"

228

"Well, I cannot help you personally. But those two over there probably can"

He pointed across the bar at a rather disreputable looking couple who were crouched by the fire. Although it was difficult to tell, the man was, probably, in early middle age. He was shabbily dressed under a heavy short coat. He wore scuffed leather boots and sported a thick head of dark hair with a straggly beard. The woman, who must have been around the same age, was only recognisable as such because she wore a skirt from which peeped a pair of scruffy brown boots. Her unkempt dark hair, over which she had tied a dark-cloth scarf tied in a knot under her chin, practically covered a weather beaten face as it dangled over an amply-filled blouse which had seen better days. Despite the heat from the fire, she was wearing a threadbare coat. Magda shuddered at the sight of them. The landlord continued

"I don't know much about them and, from what I have heard, I would not recommend them for you to cultivate as friends. But I know they frequently cross the border on......well, sort of, business, you might say. The type of business where you do not want the Customs involved. I can ask them for you if you like, but I expect they will want payment"

Joseph nodded and said "Thank you. I would like to speak to them"

The landlord brought over the unsavoury couple.

"No introductions, please. It is best you don't know these two and best they don't know who you are. I will leave you to it. I don't want to be involved in anything you arrange"

The landlord returned to the bar as the woman spoke up in a croaky voice

"I am thirsty; so is he"

She pointed across at her companion, who was slouched in a chair, eyeing them speculatively. Joseph went over to the bar and brought back two mugs of beer for the strangers. He came straight to the point

"Can you help us across the border?"

It was the man who answered.

"You don't beat about the bush do you? What makes you think we know anything about crossing the border? We are law abiding citizens, are we not?"

The last was addressed to the woman, who nodded her head and took a deep swig from her mug. Joseph hesitated for a moment,

229

then withdrew the small bundle of Austrian banknotes he had been clutching under his coat

"This makes me think you might be able to help us"

"Well! That is different. Why didn't you say you had the right documents all the time?"

The man finished his beer, then, picking up the banknotes and stuffing them in his pocket, he walked to the door. As the others followed, Joseph looked round to the landlord

"Thank you!"

But the landlord ignored him and walked into his back room. As the group stepped outside the light from the inn doorway reflected off the gleaming Mercedes. The guide looked at it enviously.

"Nice car. I would not mind having one like this for myself"

Joseph did not respond. The sky was overcast and it was beginning to rain. He said, abruptly, "You two get in the back".

He started the engine and drove the Mercedes off along the road in an easterly direction, following the line of the valley and still hugging the stream as it changed direction to north east; away from the frontier. During the twenty kilometres to St Gallenkirch they passed through two hamlets but saw no-one about. Neither of the passengers had spoken during that time but, shortly after passing through St Gallenkirch, the man banged Joseph, heavily, on the shoulder

"Slow down here and watch out for a small road going off to the left. It cuts back and you can easily miss it in the dark. You are nearly there so slow right down. Look, there it is. Turn sharp left"

Joseph swung the car left and down a short gravel covered gradient onto a, roughly surfaced, narrow road which wound between trees and over rising ground. The sky was still overcast and a gentle drizzle did nothing to improve the sinister looking scene as the shaded headlights picked their way between the towering trees which overhung the road in places. Fortunately they encountered no other vehicles for there were few places where they could pass. After several kilometres of uncomfortable driving Joseph saw the shapes of a few houses ahead. It was now very late and no lights were to be seen in the windows. He stopped the car and, switching off the headlights, turned to his passengers

"Well! What do we do now?"

"Drive on between the buildings until your way is barred by a farm gate; you will see a rough track beyond that. Do not switch on your headlights again until I tell you. Drive quietly now until we reach the farm gate. Then mien Frau will get down and open it for you to drive through"

Joseph followed the instructions and waited on the other side of the gate for the woman to rejoin them. The track was over an open stretch of scrub land, with clumps of bushes either side, and Joseph was keyed up with fear for Magda's safety as he drove slowly along it for what seemed an age before he was faced with a line of trees. The man banged him on the shoulder once more

"Stop here and get out. You too, lady. No! leave the keys in the ignition"

Startled by the sharp tone of the stranger's voice, Joseph looked round quickly to find he was gazing into the muzzle of a pistol about an inch from his face. He turned to Magda and said as calmly as he could

"We had better do what he says"

They climbed out of the car; the man and woman following them. The man was still brandishing the gun and Joseph was not inclined to argue with him.

"Walk ahead. That will do. Stop there and don't turn round"

Joseph could hear the man talking to the woman behind him.

"Go round to the front and search them, while I cover them from here. Bring what you find back here"

To Joseph he said

"The pistol is pointed at your wife. Any tricks and she gets it first"

Magda stood quietly while the woman ran her hands lightly over her clothing. Finding nothing she took the handbag Magda was carrying. Magda gasped as the woman bruised her neck when she broke the gold chain to rip off the locket which contained her precious family pictures, but she still said nothing. The woman took Joseph's wallet and his passport from an inside pocket of his coat; also the bundle of Austrian banknotes from which Joseph had paid the man. She returned to the man and gave the items to him. He handed the gun to the woman while he searched Magda's handbag. He kept her passport but, otherwise, found nothing of interest. He tossed the handbag with its other contents intact across to land beside Magda

The man tucked the money, Joseph's wallet and the two passports into his pockets; and gave the gold chain to the woman, who wrapped it round her wrist. He waved the gun towards the trees

"You wanted to cross the Swiss border? Well, there it is! You only have to climb two wire fences and you are in Switzerland"

"But what about my car and our luggage?"

The man gave a derisive laugh

"I don't see how you are going to lift the car over the fences, do you? And there is no road on the other side. Only forest tracks. No, you had better leave it here. It is a nice car, as I said earlier, and I shall look after it for you. You can collect it from me when you come back; *if* you come back, that is. As for your luggage. I am not an unreasonable man and I am feeling generous tonight. Here you are! You can have one bag. I don't know what is in it but you will find it hard enough carrying a small bag like that. You are no youngster and any more would only make it too difficult for you in the forest. So I am doing you a kindness by not burdening you with more than you can manage"

He laughed sardonically.

"Do not worry. Your other bags will all be here in the car for you to collect. That is, if the Gestapo let you have them when they catch you. Now go! Before I change my mind and leave you both here with bullets in your heads"

Magda bent down to collect her handbag while Joseph picked up the bag that had been thrown to him. They stumbled away through the darkness. The man in the car was laughing as he watched them go. They heard him turn the car round but did not look back. The line of trees looked formidable in the rain swept darkness but, fortunately, the fences were no more than four feet high and there was no barbed wire.

The man and woman were jubilant as they drove back across the scrubland. They passed through Gargellan without stopping to close the farm gate and continued down the slope between the trees; but their joy was short-lived when they saw the rear lights of an army patrol vehicle which was blocking their path as they were about to emerge from the side road. The man had no choice but to stop the car and, as he did so, a second army vehicle pulled off the verge and came up behind the Mercedes; its headlamps lighting the scene.

The German patrol surrounded the Mercedes. A sergeant, carrying a machine pistol, shone his torch over them.

"Well! What have we here? Papers, please"

The man tried to bluff

"We come from the farm on the hill and we don't have our papers with us"

"Get out of the car and stand facing this truck. Put your hands on the side of the truck, lean against it and spread your legs. Yes, you *too* woman. Search them"

The latter order was addressed to the troopers who soon found the bundle of banknotes, the passports and the wallet; also the chain and locket and the gun. The sergeant was delighted. He could not see the passport photographs very clearly in the dark but, using his torch, he read the names without difficulty

"Jews, eh?"

The man started to protest, but lapsed into silence as the sergeant waved the muzzle of his machine pistol menacingly in his direction. The sergeant hefted the man's pistol.

"Planning to make a fight of it were we? You wouldn't stand much of a chance against my men with this little pop-gun. SS Intelligence will be pleased to see you two. Come along. Get back in your car, start it up and follow me. And no tricks or we will deal with you on the spot"

The sergeant climbed into his own vehicle and led the way onto the road. His driver turned to the left and stopped; expecting the Mercedes to follow, with the other truck taking up the rear. However, the driver of the Mercedes had other ideas. As he reached the road he swung the steering wheel sharply to the right. The rear wheels skidded on the gravel surface, momentarily slowing the vehicle, as the driver stamped hard on the accelerator. Suddenly gaining purchase, the car shot forward but the moment's delay had given time for the sergeant to leap from the passenger seat of his vehicle. He steadied himself and brought the machine pistol up in one movement; sending a savage burst of fire after the fleeing Mercedes. The car bucked violently, as the driver lost control, and spun off the road; hitting a tree head-on with a grinding metallic crash. Flames began to lick the underside of the car as the troopers ran towards it; but, before they could get there, the vehicle exploded into a fireball. The sergeant spat on the ground.

"Well! There are two less Jews to pollute the world. I wonder why they were coming *away* from the border? Still! We will never know now"

He looked at the bundle of money the troopers had found.

Shrugging his shoulders he thrust about half the bundle into his inner tunic pocket. The rest he handed to his troopers to share. Having second thoughts, he took out a few notes and stuffed them in the wallet. Then he placed the wallet, passports and gold chain with its locket. He muttered to himself "They won't need these anymore. I'll pass them on to Herr Kluger of SS Intelligence. Perhaps he will find them useful".

Joseph and Magda looked around them. They could see little in the gloom under the trees and could hear nothing but the dripping of rainwater from the leaves and the sound of their own shoes squelching through the wet loam underfoot. They were following a path that headed directly away from the wire fence and, after half an hour, they came to a tarmac road. Choosing a direction at random, they walked along the road; Joseph carrying the bag. For want of something better to say, Magda asked

"Do you know which bag it is?"

"Fortunately, its the one with our night clothes, your jewel box and, perhaps more important, our bundle of Swiss francs. It is a good job that thug did not take time to search the bags. But he was so pleased with himself at grabbing my lovely Mercedes that he did not care about anything else. I hope it brings him disaster!".

An hour later they were still stumbling along the road, with no sign to show when the forest would end, when they heard a vehicle approaching from behind. Joseph was the first to react as he cried urgently

"Quick, into the bushes"

But they were not quick enough. The patrol car pulled up opposite their hiding place. The sergeant, in charge of the border patrol, held his pistol pointed directly at Joseph. He spoke in German

"Well! well! and where did you come from? Invading our country, are you? Of course, you might be Austrian Jews, in which case we have orders to turn you back or to shoot you if you refuse?"

Magda burst into tears

"We can't go back. Please don't send us back! You have a mother and father, don't you? Would you send *them* back to be shot by the Gestapo?"

The sergeant's face softened as he replaced his gun in its holster

"You look harmless enough, but I can't leave you wandering

about out here. Get in the back of the truck. We'll take you to headquarters in St Gallen and let the chief of police decide what to do with you"

It was a bumpy ride but it was more comfortable than stumbling along on foot; so Joseph and Magda huddled together, fearful of what was to come, but glad to be out of the rain and going somewhere definite.

Paul Gruninger, Chief of Police for the Swiss Canton of St Gallen, sat on the edge of his desk; his thumbs tucked into the leather belt of his uniform. He eyed them grimly as he addressed Joseph and Magda in German.

"So you are the two travellers my patrol found wandering at the border?"

It was a rhetorical question but Joseph nodded dumbly

"And I am told you have no passports or papers to prove your identity!"

"No! They were stolen from us, along with most of our belongings, by the guides who showed us where to cross the border"

"What guides? Do you know their names? Where did you meet them?"

Joseph told him what they knew, which was precious little. The policeman grinned ironically

"Don't you think you were a little foolish to trust someone like that?"

"I do now! But we were desperate and had no choice in the matter"

"Well! Now I have to decide what to do with you. But first I shall take down some details concerning your origins; then I think you should have some food and rest while I give some thought to your situation. I *should* detain you here under lock and key but there is no room in the cells at present. So these two guards will take you to the Inn across the road, where you will stay until I send for you. I warn you not to attempt to leave the hotel because the guards will remain on duty there. So, for the present, I wish you 'Goodnight'. Get some rest and we shall talk again later".

Joseph and Magda were in the inn for three anxious days before they were summoned by Inspector Gruninger. A few nights sleep and good food had done wonders for their appearance but Joseph was still fearful regarding their fate. The police chief dismissed the guards and Joseph's hopes rose as he recognised a kindlier light in the eyes of their interrogator as, with a slight smile on his lips, he addressed Magda

"You told me, madam, that your maiden name was Magda Zeiss and that you lived in Zurich before you were married?"

Magda nodded and the policeman continued

"You will be glad to know we have traced your sister Eloise who is married to Paul Galionne, a respected doctor in Zurich. So we are pleased to welcome you back to your homeland. As for you, Herr Goldschmit, I am informed that this entry permit was found in your pocket when you were searched. No! Do not protest. It allows you to enter and stay in Switzerland for an indefinite period of time. Did you not know you had this permit? No? Ah well! Here it seems to have been all the time and, since it bears an entry stamp dated prior to 19th August, 1938, I am not obliged to send you back to Austria. It is a pity you have both mislaid your passports; but these are difficult times and allowances must be made to avoid chaos. Nevertheless, I am obliged to inform you that, should you come across your passports or obtain replacements from the Austrian Embassy, you are required to submit these to the Swiss Authorities for stamping with your entry visa. In the meantime these documents, with those relating to your wife, will allow you both to stay in Switzerland for an indefinite period"

Joseph almost wept with relief and Magda was in tears as they thanked Gruninger. He smiled and held out his hand.

"Not at all! I do my best to help where I can, but I must impress upon you the need for secrecy concerning your entry to our country. I understand you have plenty of money so I suggest you leave right away and go to the German speaking quarter of Zurich; where you can merge in easily"

He handed a small piece of paper to Magda

"In case you have mislaid it, here is the address of your sister in Zurich. She knows you are in Switzerland and will be expecting you to call on her. But, be careful! There are many officials who sympathise with the Nazis and, although your papers are sound, I would advise you not to mention any knowledge of the present situation in Austria or Germany; even in private conversation with friends"

He rose from the table and held out his hand

"I hope all goes well for you. Goodbye"

Leaving St Gallen the same day Joseph and Magda made their way to Zurich, where they were able to obtain comfortable lodgings in a house, not far from the Main Railway Station, and overlooking the River Limmat.

Their daughter's address in England had been in Joseph's wallet which had been stolen. So Joseph could not write directly to Eve to let her know they had escaped from the Nazi terror and so set her mind at rest. They had a substantial fortune in the bundle of Swiss francs and had no need to make demands on their daughter's bank account. Nevertheless, Joseph visited the bank to introduce himself to the manager. It was then that he learned the bank could arrange for a letter to be delivered to his daughter and her husband. He did not hesitate to write the letter which Ernest now held in his hands.

Ernest put the pages of the letter down on the table. There was, of course, nothing in the letter concerning the fate of Joseph's car, or its occupants, and Ernest was left wondering how Kluger got hold of Magda's locket and chain. But this was, probably, unimportant now; although it still left him with niggling doubts about loose ends. For the time being he would thrust such thoughts to the back of his mind and concentrate on the overwhelming relief he felt at the knowledge that Eve's parents were safe and the threat of Nazi vengeance falling on them for the death of Hans Kluger had been averted. He felt like jumping in the air and rushing home to give the good news to Eve. In fact, he nearly did just that, but, as he started towards the door, he remembered the bank manager wanted to see him. He pressed the bell push and sat down again. After a few minutes the door opened and Mr Templeton came in.

"Good morning, doctor. I trust there was no bad news in your letter"

"On the contrary. The news could not be better and I cannot wait to get home to convey it to my wife. But I understand you want to see me before I go?"

"Yes, doctor. Our Regent Street branch has received a communication through banking channels from the bank in Zurich that sent the letter you have there. I do not wish to pry into your personal affairs; but, as I understand it, an account in the name of Eva Mittelburg is being held at the Zurich bank pending your wife's instructions. Is that so?"

237

"Yes, Mr Templeton, but this is a confidential matter and I trust none of your staff has been so informed?"

"You may rest assured about our security. Not even my chief clerk is aware of the situation and, if you and your wife wish it, such confidentiality shall be maintained. The point of the matter is that there is a substantial sum of money in the Swiss account and the Zurich bank needs further instructions regarding its disposal. It appears that a Mr Joseph Goldschmit, a refugee from Austria who is claiming to be your wife's father, has opened an account at the same bank. He wishes to set up a business in Zurich and has asked for a loan based on the security of Mrs. Middleton's funds. I am told your wife gave instructions to the bank regarding her father and the bank will be happy grant the advance on condition that Mrs Middleton confirms the sample signature they have sent to us and authorises the use of her account as security for the loan"

"I don't think that presents a problem, Mr Templeton. The Zurich fund was set up precisely for the use of my parents-in-law, should they need financial help in Switzerland, and my wife will be delighted to come into Dunchester to give the necessary authorisation. When will it be convenient for her to make an appointment?"

"Let us see. Tomorrow is Friday and our busiest day of the week. But, in view of the confidentiality of this matter your wife should deal solely with myself and as soon as possible. Suppose I keep myself free to see her at eleven tomorrow morning? Discuss it with Mrs Middleton and if that time is inconvenient you can telephone me this afternoon to make another appointment. It might be a good idea if she brings her passport, if she has one, and any other papers that can identify her as both Eve Middleton and Eva Mittelburg. We already have her signature on record as an account holder here; but only as Eve Middleton. I know you are a busy man, Doctor, but it would be preferable if you came with your wife"

"I am afraid that cannot be done. A general practitioner's surgery is, theoretically, open twenty-four hours a day and one of us has to be there at all times to answer the phone in case of an emergency. Perhaps one day someone will invent a telephone system which enables my wife and patients to contact me in my car; but, until then, we have to muddle along as best we can. If there is nothing more, I should like to be on my way. As it is my wife will be putting my lunch in the dustbin"

The bank manager accompanied Ernest to the front door of the building. Ernest shook him by the hand.

"Thank you for your co-operation in this matter, Mr Templeton. You have been most helpful"

"My pleasure, doctor. Should you need to telephone this afternoon I shall be here until six this evening"

Eve had the table laid when Ernest arrived back at the cottage; but she had not eaten her lunch. He had been tempted to telephone her from Dunchester with the good news but, considering her overwrought state of mind, he decided it would be better to wait until he arrived home. He was about to burst out with his good news when Eve interrupted.

"There is an emergency in the surgery. You will have to deal with that first"

As he started for the surgery door Eve grabbed his arm and whispered.

"What did the bank want? Who was the letter from?"

He hesitated, but his professional duty came first.

"It is important. But we cannot discuss it until we are alone"

Betty Twist was in the surgery with eight year old Harry Moon, one of the evacuee children. He had banged his head swinging on the school gate during the dinner break and had a nasty cut on his forehead. Ernest examined the wound and decided it was nothing serious and did not require stitching. Eve was about to put a plaster on the cut when Harry Moon spoke up.

"Can't I 'ave a bandage round me 'ead, Miss? Me friends'll all laugh at a little bit 'o plaster. An' I want that copper wot I live wiv to worry in case I'm bad 'urt"

Eve smiled at the boy "Of course you can, Harry"

She bound him up like a wounded soldier and he, proudly, strode off back to school with an apologetic Betty Swift.

Ernest and Eve returned to the lunch table and Ernest poured two glasses of wine. Eve set out the lunch

"Good job it is only cold boiled egg and ham salad. Now! come on, what is this mysterious news?"

"The letter was from your father, darling"

For a moment tears welled in her eyes

"It is not about Mama. She hasn't been..........?"

Ernest interrupted quickly

"No! No! You must not think that. They are *both* alright and they

239

are safe in Zurich"

Her eyes lit up as she stared at him, unbelievingly,

"But Kluger said..........."

"I know what he *said* but he was lying. I don't know how he got hold of your mother's locket but she had it stolen from her by some woman who was supposed to be helping them to escape. It is all in the letter here. I think the best thing is for you to sit down and read the letter; then we can talk about it and about the other reason the bank manager wanted to see me"

Ignoring her lunch, Eve took a sip at her wine and began to read the letter. Once or twice she put a handkerchief to her eyes prevent a tear from dropping onto the paper but she said nothing until she had finished the last page. Then she looked up at Ernest

"Poor Mama and Papa. What a terrible experience"

Ernest took her hand

"But the main thing is they are not harmed and they are safe"

She smiled. It seemed ages since he had seen her smile; yet it was only a couple of days. Two days they would never forget. She squeezed his hand

"Now tell me about the other thing, darling"

"Well! It seems your father managed to take a large amount of money with him to Switzerland. I don't know why he didn't lose it when he lost the car and their luggage. But there it is. He had this money and he opened an account at the bank that sent the letter. He has enough money to live on but not enough to finance a business venture he has in mind. The bank in Zurich has agreed to finance the venture provided they can hold the money in your account as security for the loan"

"Of course they can. It is really his money anyway"

"I knew you would say that. So I told Mr Templeton, the bank manager, you would go to Dunchester tomorrow to see him. You have to verify the sample signature he has received and sign the necessary authority. And, by the way, you must take some form of identity. Your driving licence should do but you had better take your old Austrian passport too; also the papers regarding our British naturalisation and change of name"

"Ernest, do you think it wise to disclose so much information locally?"

"The bank manager has assured me that this matter will be strictly confidential between himself and us; but take the papers in case they are needed. Produce them only if he asks. Incidentally, do not discuss your business with anyone else at the bank. Just give your English name and ask for Mr John Templeton. If he is not there tell them you will telephone later, then leave the bank without answering any questions and come home".

CHAPTER FOURTEEN

1939

After telling Eve about his visit to the bank, there was one loose end that bothered Ernest Middleton and he must do something about it. The wireless was still installed in the loft and he had to consider the implications if he did not make the scheduled call to Ireland that night. He checked the day and date on the calendar. So much had happened since the death of Kluger that he found it difficult to believe it was still only the 7th of September. Since it was a thursday, the listener in Ireland would be expecting him to transmit at 10 pm; being fifteen minutes earlier than the time of the previous day's transmission. He decided it would be safer to make the call, if only to buy time. But it would be better if he could do so in such a way that no further transmissions would be expected. Now they knew Eve's parents were out of danger his only concern was for the safety of Eve and himself. As ex-aliens he could not expect anything but suspicion from British Intelligence if he contacted them with what he knew. Innocent though he and his wife were of spying for the enemy, there was still the matter of murder for which Eve could be called to account. If he informed the police about Kluger's activities he and Eve would, inevitably, become suspects when the body was found. No! he could not take the chance of going to the authorities; he must deal with the situation himself.

There had been several patients that evening and the surgery had stayed open late. They were having a cup of coffee, after clearing up, when Ernest looked at his watch and turned to an anxious Eve

"It is a quarter to ten. I had better get the set ready for the call"

"Do you mind if I stay down here? That wireless makes me nervous"

"Of course, darling, but I shall need you later to help me with the furniture. I'll call when I want your help. Wish me luck!"

Ernest hefted a small pair of step ladders, which he kept in his garage, up into the loft. Now that he no longer had the wandering power lead Ernest took a torch with him when he climbed up to the loft; and, using the step ladders, he plugged the power lead attached to the wireless set into the light socket. By the light of the torch he tuned in the set. At exactly ten o'clock he switched to 'send'.

"Zeta calling. Zeta calling. Acknowledge"

He switched to 'receive' but heard only mush coming from the earphones. He waited exactly thirty seconds then switched to 'send' and spoke again into the microphone

"Willard One, calling. Over"

He switched back to 'receive'. The Irish voice came through loud and clear

"Where have you been, Willard? Your London controller has been ringing your drop but can get no reply. Over"

"This is not Willard. I used his call sign only to identify the transmitter. We have not seen Willard since yesterday evening and suspect he may have been caught. He told us that we should close down and dismantle this station if he disappeared and wait for further instructions. We are carrying out Willard's orders so do not expect a transmission tomorrow. Do you have any comment. Over?"

"No! You had better get off the air now before you are traced. Do as Willard says. Dismantle the set and wait for Willard to contact you. Good luck. Over and out"

Ernest breathed a sigh of relief as he put down the earphones, switched off the set and sat back in the chair. So it was as easy as that! But there was no time to waste. He carried one chair to the hatchway and called Eve. He handed it down to her, followed by the second chair. He climbed the step ladders and twisted the bayonet plug from the light socket; replacing it with the light bulb; which immediately shed a bright light in the loft space. Now he could see what he was doing he used the step ladders again to pull down the aerial wire. He looked around the loft space; then climbed down the loft ladder and went into the kitchen where Eve was pouring out two cups of coffee.

"Thanks!"

"I expect you can do with that? Did everything go alright?"

"More than alright! The Irishman accepted my story that Kluger has disappeared and we don't know where he is"

"But he is in the cottage"

"Yes. But they think we know nothing about the cottage. The Irishman used the word 'drop'; by which I presume he meant Kluger's cottage. But he did not tell me where it is or ask me to check there. He probably has instructions not to tell us anything.

Anyway, the important thing is the Irishman agreed I should dismantle the set and wait for Kluger to contact me. He obviously thinks Kluger has gone to ground"

"What *are* you going to do about that wireless? Its too heavy for us to manhandle down the ladder by ourselves and we can't leave it up there"

"I shall dismantle it in the loft, after I have finished my coffee, and dispose of any burnable parts in the incinerator; with the broken wood from the table and chairs. But, we can't risk an outdoor fire this late at night, so I will do the incinerating first thing in the morning"

They both donned surgical gloves before Ernest climbed back into the loft. He made sure the set was disconnected from the power, then wiped all its surfaces and knobs with a damp cloth. With the aid of pliers and a screwdriver, he dismantled the set. He broke up the wooden case and tossed the pieces, with the bakelite base, the tuning knobs and the valves into a cardboard box which he handed through the hatch to Eve, who was waiting below. The metal chassis and the remainder of the parts, including the wire, he stowed in the, larger, cardboard box in which the set had been delivered to Kluger; having made sure, first, there was nothing on or in the box that could be traced back to him. He used the aerial wire to tie up this box. It was too heavy to hand down through the hatchway, so with the use of a heavy rope slung over a convenient roof beam, he lowered the box slowly to the hall floor. With Eve's help, he carried the box into the surgery; to be sorted out in the morning. Returning to the loft, Ernest unscrewed the legs of the table and handed them down, one at a time, to Eve. The table top was too heavy for Eve to manage so he lowered it, by using the rope, as he had done with the big cardboard box.

Ernest stood still in the loft, thinking. He had a damp cloth in his hand which he had just used to wipe the loft ladder and the hatchway clean of any fingerprints Kluger might have made. He climbed the step ladders to replace the light bulb with a new one and to wipe the wire and bulb holder. The old bulb he put in his pocket to dispose of later. He climbed down and looked round the loft but could see nothing else that needed to be done.

Immediately after breakfast on Friday, 8th September, Ernest Middleton broke up the chairs and table outside in the yard. He set fire to the timber in the incinerator and, once the fire was well alight, he tossed the smaller cardboard box, with its contents, into the flames. He took the precaution of standing well away from the incinerator to protect himself from flying glass as the valves and the light bulb exploded. The metal wireless chassis was not, in itself, particularly heavy so Ernest cut up the larger cardboard box; making sure he disposed of the Railway markings and delivery instructions. With the material left over he made a rough parcel of the chassis and wire. This he could handle with ease so he carried it out to lock it in the boot of his car.

Eve caught the ten o'clock bus at the stop opposite the surgery on friday morning. It was just about to start off when Muriel Twist, from the garage, came puffing up. Muriel was in her late forties. She was a short, jolly sort of person. The driver waited and greeted her with a cheery

"Come along, missus. Hubby been keeping you in bed?"

"Get along with you. He was up long before you were, I'll be bound"

"I'll bet he was!"

"Now don't you be so cheeky, Jim Smith, or I'll tell your wife about your rude comments. Return to Dunchester, please"

She made her way along the aisle and sat down next to Eve.

"Good morning, Eve. Going shopping?"

"Hello, Muriel. I have to go to the bank, but I will probably do some shopping afterwards".

They chatted away, making small talk, until the bus drew into the curb at the stop in the High Street.

"It has been nice talking to you, Eve. How about meeting me in Lyons tea shop at about twelve? We can have a cup of coffee and catch the one o'clock bus back together"

"OK. I'll try! But don't miss your bus if I can't make it".

The business at the bank did not take Eve long. She not only approved the use of her funds in Switzerland as security for the loan; but also made provision for her father to transfer any amount he liked from such funds into his own account if he so desired. Her business concluded she made a few purchases and went to the library to borrow a book before joining Muriel in the teashop. Muriel greeted her

"I was looking out the window and saw you coming so I have ordered you a coffee and a buttered tea cake. Is that alright?"

Eve thanked Muriel and sat down. Muriel picked up the book Eve had put on the table

"I have read this. It is jolly good. Have you read much of Jane Austin?"

"Oh, Yes! She is one of my favourites"

Muriel changed the subject

"By the way, your visit to the library reminds me of something. Have you ever heard of a Frederick Grimble?". Mentally, Eve almost jumped out of her skin at the sound of the name which she had seen on the driving licence Ernest had found in Kluger's pocket, but, outwardly, she managed to answer casually.

"No! Should I have?"

"Well, No! There is probably no reason why you should. But I thought he might be one of your husband's patients. I don't know him either, really. It is just that he collected a car from my husband a couple of days before the war broke out and I ran into him, by chance, the other day in the library"

Eve tried to keep her voice steady

"But what makes you think he is one of Ernest's patients and what is your interest in him?"

Muriel fumbled in her handbag and brought out the scrap of paper she had picked up from the library floor when she was with her sister, Joan

"Well! It is silly really. I am not interested in him, as such, at all. But when he was in the library he dropped this piece of paper"

"I still don't see the connection"

"But can't you see, Eve? It says Middleton on the paper and I thought.........."

She tailed off lamely; looking at Eve like a puppy dog pleading for forgiveness for being so stupid. Eve picked up the scrap of paper. She read 'Middleton MV 3843'. She put the piece of paper down on the table.

"How do you know its not a place? There is a place called Middleton up near Kings Lynn. In any case this refers to an M V Middleton. My husbands name is E. Middleton; so is mine. If it *is* a person there must be lots of Middletons in the county. If you feel its important why don't you look it up in the telephone directory". Eve picked up the paper again and pointed "And this number doesn't make any sense to me either. Perhaps its a car registration number"

Feeling she was making a big issue of an unimportant trifle Muriel apologised

"I am sorry I mentioned it, Eve. It is of no consequence"

She reached out to retrieve the scrap of paper but Eve, sensing she had upset Muriel with her curt, accusative, manner, softened her tone and retained it.

"Anyway, if it will set your mind at rest, Muriel, I shall take it home to Ernest. Perhaps he can make sense of it"

"Well! I was going to give it to Mr Grimble if I see him again. But I don't think that is likely to happen. So you might as well have it"

Eve dropped the scrap of paper into her handbag

"Come on Muriel. It is nearly time for our bus."

Ernest sat at his desk in the surgery, looking at the scrap of paper Eve had brought home with her. Another loose end, he thought. He picked up the telephone directory and found there were ten Middletons in it; but none of them had the initials MV. Of course, he thought, possibly it is not someone local or the person might not be on the telephone; few people in the countryside indulged in a private line. But it was a strange co-incidence that Kluger should have a piece of paper on him relating to a Middleton other than himself. He suddenly remembered that the Irishman had mentioned a London controller. A thought occurred to him and he picked up the telephone. The operator answered

"Good afternoon, doctor. What number do you want?"

"Er Sorry! I knocked the telephone over. Sorry to trouble you"

"That is alright, doctor"

He hung up. Of course the operator would know his connecting number and recognise his voice. He must make his enquiry through an exchange where he was not known. He went in to Eve who was reading her library book in the sitting room.

"I have an idea about this note and I think it best if I make my enquiries from a telephone where the operator does not know my voice. Will it be alright if I leave you here alone? I am going into Dunchester to dispose of that cardboard box and I'll use a public telephone there. I should be back in an hour or so and there is no longer anything here to frighten you"

"OK, darling. I shall be alright. But try not to be too long"

Ernest parked the car outside the main post office in Dunchester. He asked a clerk for a list of the telephone districts in

London. He was looking for one which had the initials MV. There it was! Maida Vale. He might be wrong but it was worth a try. He could always hang up without saying anything. He left the building and wandered around the streets until he found a public call box. He placed the piece of paper in front of him and lifted the receiver.

"Number please"

"I would like a London number, please. It is Maida Vale 3843"

He waited for the operator to tell him how many coins to insert in the box and, when he heard a female voice answer at the other end, he pressed button A to make contact. He remembered Kluger's call sign and, deciding to risk it, he spoke in German.

"Listen. This is Willard. The operation is blown and I cannot call you from the cottage phone because I think it is tapped. This is a public call box and I do not have a number for you to contact me. I have left the cottage and am on my way out of the district. Do not approach Mittelburg because I am sure he is compromised and being watched. He is no longer of use to us. Have you any further instructions for me?"

There was a long pause, during which time Ernest had to insert some more coins. For a moment Ernest thought he had made a mistake. He was about to hang up when a man's voice, speaking German, came on the line

"Kluger, this is Winkler. Follow the escape plan agreed and get out of the country. Do not call this number again. You are on your own now. Good luck!"

Ernest was elated. He had fooled them into calling off the dogs. What a bit of luck it was that Eve had brought home that tiny scrap of paper. He screwed it up and dropped it down a drain. Now to dispose of the cardboard box. He remembered there was an electrician's shop in one of the side streets so he walked round to look at it. His memory was not at fault; the shop also sold spare parts for amateur wireless enthusiasts. It was a quiet street and an alley ran alongside the shop. There was no-one about so Ernest walked casually up the alley. As he suspected, there was a yard behind the shop where many odd boxes and other items had been left. He quietly retraced his steps and brought the car round, to park a few yards short of the shop entrance. The street was still empty. He put on a pair of surgical gloves, then lifted the box out of the boot and, carrying it down the alley, dumped it in the yard. No-one saw him. The electrician might be surprised to find the box but he was unlikely to object to receiving a few spare parts for nothing. Ernest returned to his car and drove home.

To the visiting town-dweller the countryside might have appeared idyllic but one of the less savoury aspects of rural life in the 1930's, which might not have been apparent to the weekend tripper, was the disposal of sewage. For centuries householders had suffered the disadvantages of outside toilets; to be visited in all weathers with particular discomfort in mid-winter. The weekly accumulation of human waste in such cases would be buried in the garden behind the property. Farm workers often commented that this practice accounted for the size of their marrows and other garden produce. This might well have been so, but the waste also contaminated the drinking water drawn by hand operated pumps from wells in the gardens and, no doubt, contributed to outbreaks of disease in an, otherwise, healthy community.

The introduction of a piped water system to Frensham Down early in the 20th century did a great deal to improve the health of the community. Clean running water supplied from a tap to all but some outlying cottages made life much easier; but, perhaps more important, made it possible for flushing toilets to be installed in houses adjacent to a public soil drainage system. With the latter in mind, the County Water Authority engineers laid sewage pipes along the Scolling Road, in 1929, and connected the toilets of adjacent properties to this system. The soil-pipe network incorporated in the building of the Benley Council Estate, with its modern internal toilet facilities, was also connected to the Scolling Road system and, as new buildings, such as Dr. Middleton's cottage, were constructed along the Scolling Road, these also benefited from an internal flush toilet. But, by 1939, the service had not yet been extended to the other houses, cottages or farms in Frensham Down. No doubt this service would come to the village in due course, when the gravity problem could be solved; but, for the time being, the demands of the war left no funds available to continue the development. Hence all such plans on the drawing board were shelved by the local Authorities 'for the duration'; this latter phrase becoming commonplace to represent an indefinite future as the war progressed.

When they were connected to the general water supply system, the Frensham's, the Hanshott's and others who were rich enough to provide such luxuries for themselves, lost no time in installing internal toilet facilities which would flush into a private cess-pit. The cess-pits, subject to an appropriate increase in the water rate, were pumped out by a motor tanker, as and when such service was requested, and the waste was disposed of by the County Water Authority.

Less fortunate inhabitants, whose properties were not adjacent to the Scolling Road, had continued to rely on outside toilets; but, in 1934, an important change affected the ancient practice for disposal of soil. A new regulation was introduced in the interests of public health. Under this regulation householders, who had no approved cess-pit, were prohibited from disposing of the contents of their toilets in the garden. Instead, they were to leave the collection of the soil to Council workmen. A Dunchester Council tanker would call at each house or cottage once a week, early on Friday morning in the case of Frensham Down, to take away the contents of the outside toilets. This was a noisome time for the villagers who would contrive to be away during the collection or would shut all their windows and try to ignore what was going on. Troublesome boys on the way to school would hold their noses as they ran past the workmen engaged on this odoriferous task and cry out, mockingly, to the public at large "Bring out your dead".

Hilda Benhope lived in an 'end of terrace' cottage at number 23, Black Hut Lane and access to the toilets for the other cottages in the terrace, numbers 25 and 27, was through gates that connected her back garden with the ends of the adjoining back gardens. Thus, she suffered the added disadvantage that the full soil cans for all three domiciles were carried past her kitchen window. In September, 1939, she became increasingly conscious of an unpleasant smell lingering in the atmosphere and, noting that the council collectors were not carrying out cans from her neighbours' toilets, she wondered whether the unpleasant smell was coming from her next door neighbour's toilet. She tackled the foreman at her garden gate, at nine o'clock on the morning of Friday, 29th September, when the sewage disposal tanker was standing in the road outside.

"I'll 'ave to take your word for it, missus, 'cos my sense o' smell 'as dulled since I've bin on this job. Just as well, really, don't y' think? So, I can't smell nothin' unusual. Why don't you check with your neighbours? Although I think they must both be away. Just a minute"

He looked in his grubby record book.

"We checks the toilets each time we comes round but, 'ccordin' to my book, the soil cans for both cottages 'ave stayed empty since our collection on Friday, 8th September. So the smell can't be coming from them toilets". Hilda pondered

"I know Harry Smith and his wife have been away for some time but there *should* be someone next door in number twenty five"

"Are you sure they aint gorn away too, missus?"

"Well! No! I am not *certain*. But I must admit I haven't heard anyone moving about next door or the wireless going. These walls are paper thin and I think I would have heard something. I have never met the man who lives there. He only moved in a short while ago and he keeps very much to himself. Anyway, look over there. I think that is his car. I would have thought he would have taken that if he had gone away"

"Sorry, missus. I don't see as 'ow I can 'elp. If your neighbour's still there 'e aint usin' 'is toilet. That's for sure!".

Hilda returned to her kitchen. The smell was becoming a stench. She must do something. She went next door and rattled the knocker, but there was no answer. Perhaps he was away, after all. She was not going out to work that day so she decided to have a word with her son-in-law about it. Returning to her kitchen, she picked up her hat and bag and left the cottage. Cutting through the alley by the general store, she walked up to the Post Office. Her granddaughter, Sally Hanshott, was delighted to see her.

"Hello, Gran. You look worried. Is there something I can do?"

"I am alright, dear, but there *is* something you can do for me. There is an awful smell in and around my cottage and I wondered whether your Dad could come down to see if he can trace the cause and, hopefully, do something about it?"

Mrs Higgins, who had been working on the accounts, looked up

"Sorry to hear you have a problem, Hilda. Why don't you give your Mum a ring, Sally, and see if Reg can come down?"

Shortly after Hilda returned to her cottage Maddie arrived with Reg. She held her handkerchief to her nose

"However did you manage to sleep here, Mum? What do you think it is, Reg?"

"I am sure I know that smell. I remember it from the last war and, if I am right, we must get in next door. You say you can't get an answer from your new neighbour?"

Hilda shook her head.

"Well, in that case I am going to take a look through the back windows. You two stay here"

It was gloomy in the kitchen and Reg Hanshott could see little when he peered through the window. The stench was stronger at this point so, convinced he was right regarding its source, Reg tried the back door. It was unlocked. When he, gingerly, opened the door the stench was overpowering. So he held a handkerchief to his nose as he stepped into the kitchen. The black shape in the tin bath, from which rose a crowd of flies, hardly resembled a body. Seeing the electric fire in the water he could guess what had happened so he did not touch the body or the bath. He picked up the cloth covering the kitchen table and threw it over the corpse; then, still holding his handkerchief to his nose, Reg went back into the garden and drew in several gasps of fresh air. Maddie was still waiting with her mother by Hilda's cottage door.

"I am afraid your neighbour is dead and from the look of it he has been dead for some time"

"I hardly saw him; but, from the little I *did* see he appeared to be quite young. How did he die?"

"It looks as though he was taking a bath and accidentally electrocuted himself". Hilda clasped her hands to he mouth

"How dreadful! Could I have helped if I had known?"

"I doubt it. It must have been all over very quickly. There is nothing anyone could have done for him"

Maddie put her arm round her mother as she spoke to Reg

"What do we do now, Reg? Shouldn't we call the police? Didn't you say your neighbour is on the 'phone, Mum?"

"Yes. I heard it ringing a few times a couple of weeks ago but no-one seemed to answer it and I have heard nothing since. You don't want to go back in there, Reg, do you?"

"No! But I suppose I shall have to"

Reg Hanshott re-entered the next door kitchen and looked around the cottage until he found the telephone instrument. He picked it up and jiggled the lever several times. The operator answered almost immediately

"Number please?"

"This is Reg Hanshott of Frensham Down. I am calling from

number 25, Black Hut Lane. There has been an accident. Could you put me through to the police cottage in Hanshott Lane?"

"Do you want an ambulance or a doctor?"

"I don't think an ambulance would help at this stage. But, perhaps, you could call Dr Middleton and tell him to come down here. Tell him I have already called constable Bell"

Valerie Bell answered the `phone.

"Valerie. This is Reg Hanshott. Is Richard there?"

Constable Bell came to the telephone immediately

"What is the trouble, Reg?"

"I am at number 25, Black Hut Lane and I have just discovered a dead body. Can you come straight away? I will wait for you outside in the front garden and tell you what little I know when you arrive. The telephone operator has already called Dr Middleton"

"OK, Reg. Stay where you are, but don't touch anything and don't let anyone else into the cottage. They have given me a new BSA motor bike in place of my old pushbike so I should be with you in a few minutes"

Ernest Middleton was having a coffee break when the telephone rang. Eve answered it and almost dropped the instrument when the operator gave her the message from Reg Hanshott. She hesitated for a moment; not knowing what to say. Then, pulling herself together, she said as calmly as she could

"Thank you. The doctor will go down there right away"

When she gave him the message Ernest put his arm round her shoulder

"Come, dear! It is far better they should call me in rather than someone else. Now I can enter the cottage with a perfectly valid reason for being there and I can leave my fingerprints all over the place without exciting interest"

"But you will be careful, won't you. dear?"

"Of course, darling. Don't you worry. It is only natural they should call me and it is, probably, for the best!"

Reg Hanshott had propped a piece of stone from the garden against the front door to keep it wide open, and to let out as much of the obnoxious odour as possible, while he waited by the front gate. In a few minutes he heard the roar of a motor cycle engine and saw the burly figure of Richard Bell, clad in full uniform and with his helmet held fast on his head by its chinstrap, stop outside the gate. Reg walked over to him.

254

"How did you manage to get petrol driven transport, Richard, when the Government has just introduced fuel rationing?"

"It is the way of the world, Reg! The allocation of the machine had been made before the war broke out and no-one thought to cancel it. Funny thing is I get extra coupons because of my job. I expect you do too?"

Reg nodded as the constable removed his helmet and mopped his brow with a large handkerchief before slipping the chinstrap over the brim and replacing the helmet firmly on his head. He looked across the road

"Whose is that car over there?"

"I don't know. But Hilda thinks it belongs to the occupant of this cottage"

"You mean the dead man?"

"Yes!"

Constable Bell heaved his motor cycle up on its stand, took out his notebook and wrote down the date. Looking at his watch, he also made a note of the time. He walked over and, after checking the locked doors, wrote down in his notebook a brief description of the vehicle with its registration number. Returning, he grinned at Reg.

"Police procedure, you know. Can't be too careful. I would look pretty silly if someone came and drove the car away while we are in the cottage. By the way, how did you get in?"

"Hilda Benhope was concerned about the smell which was apparently coming from here. She couldn't get an answer, when she knocked at the front door, so she called me. I tried the back door and found it was unlocked. The body is in the kitchen"

Constable Bell wrinkled his nose

"It certainly niffs a bit. Must have been there for some time"

Constable Bell wrote in his notebook again and Reg stood aside as the policeman pushed past him, entered the kitchen and surveyed the scene. Reg stopped him as he walked towards the tablecloth.

"Be careful, Richard. I think he was electrocuted"

The constable drew his hand back.

"He probably blew the fuse box but I had best make sure the power is disconnected"

The constable followed the wandering electric lead to the wall socket and, covering the plug with his handkerchief, pulled it out; leaving it on the floor. He wrinkled his nose as he lifted the edge of the tablecloth but he did not touch the bath or the body.

"Did *you* throw the cloth over it?"

"Yes! I couldn't bear to look at it"

The constable made no further comments while he was looking around the room making entries in his notebook. The silence was broken by the sharp rattle of the front door knocker. Although they had left the door open Dr Middleton preferred to announce his presence before entering.

"Well constable. What have we here?"

"It looks like a nasty accident, sir"

Doctor Middleton approached the bath and looked down at the corpse

"It certainly looks that way. Do either of you know who the victim is?"

The constable shook his head and turned to Reg who also shook his head but felt some explanation was necessary.

"Hilda tells me he moved in a few days before the outbreak of war but she has never spoken to him and does not know his name"

The doctor took out a small book from his inside jacket pocket and made some notes of his own. He replaced the notebook, took off his jacket and rolled up his sleeves. He opened his bag and took out a surgical mask which he donned.

"Well! I had better have a look at the body. I take it the power is off, constable?"

"Yes, Sir. I pulled out the plug myself before you arrived"

"Just the same, I will check it for myself. I am sure you are thorough constable, but we do not want another accident do we?"

Ernest picked up the wandering lead and followed it with his fingers to where the plug was lying on the floor. He, apparently absently, picked up the plug and rolled up the lead back to the fire; where he disconnected the socket at the other end of the lead from the plug on the power lead attached to the fire. He put the rolled up lead to one side on the floor. Next, he removed the table cloth and, carefully lifting it out of the water, he placed the electric fire on the bath towel that lay on the floor. He reached over to his bag and took out a pair of surgical gloves which he donned before touching the body. After the briefest of examinations, he stood up, peeled off the gloves and dropped these into his bag. He covered the body again with the tablecloth, took out his book again and began making notes.

"I can confirm the death of an unknown male at........" He looked at his watch "....at one-thirty pm on Friday, 29th of September, 1939. But I cannot tell you *when* he died. Judging by the smell and allowing for the warm weather I would say he must have been in the bath for a couple of weeks or more. The cause of death would appear to be electrocution but I cannot say more until a proper medical examination has been carried out".

After making more notes in his book, the doctor put the notebook back in his jacket pocket and went over to the sink and turned on the tap to wash his hands. He dried them on the teacloth that hung by the sink and, rolling down his shirt sleeves, looked enquiringly at the constable.

"This body should be moved as soon as possible, constable. Do you want me to make arrangements for it to be taken to a mortuary?"

"No, thank you, doctor. Although this would appear to be an accident the police have certain procedures that must be carried out in cases of sudden death and I must call my superintendent for instructions. I expect he will be in touch with you later"

Ernest put on his jacket and picked up his bag

"Well! there is nothing more I can do here. So I'll say good day to you both"

When Dr Middleton had gone the constable turned to Reg Hanshott who had followed them to the door.

"Thank you for your help, Reg. There is no point in your hanging around. You can leave this to the police now. I expect Hilda will be wondering what is happening. Why don't you go next door and put her mind at rest? Tell Hilda we will get the body moved as soon as possible but it might be a good idea if she stays with you up at the Farm until the smell goes away. The police will get in touch with Hilda at your place if they need her; but tell her not to worry. It will be only routine questioning. By the way, before you go, where did you say the telephone is?"

Reg took Richard Bell to the telephone and left him standing next to it when he let himself out of the cottage by the front door; closing it behind him. Constable Bell waited until he heard the door close then, using his handkerchief to avoid disturbing probable fingerprints, he picked up the receiver. He asked the operator to put him through to the Dunchester police. When he had finished explaining the position to his superintendent he put the telephone down, returned to the kitchen and turned the key that was in the lock inside the kitchen door. He thought about opening the kitchen window to let in some fresh air but decided he should leave things as they were. He left the stone against the front door to keep it open and, hopefully, let out some of the stench. Then he sat on an old wooden seat under the front window to wait for his colleagues to arrive.

Constable Bell was still sitting there, his helmet on the seat beside him, when a convoy comprising a black police car, a private car and an ambulance pulled up in front of the cottage. Detective Chief Inspector Norris Cross and Detective Sergeant James Dean of Dunchester CID were in plain clothes but looked unmistakably like police officers as they climbed out of the police car. Richard Bell recognised them both as well as the stocky civilian, wearing a smart dark suit with a black Homburg hat and carrying a small black bag, who emerged from the other car. It was the police surgeon, Dr. Belling. The sergeant was also carrying a bag. The constable sprang to attention and, rapidly donning his helmet, saluted his superior officer. He nodded to the Sergeant and acknowledged the police surgeon, but he addressed only the chief inspector.

"Good afternoon, sir"

"Good afternoon, Bell. It is a warm day for a job like this"

"Yes, sir!"

"Stand easy, constable. Your super filled me in with the details you 'phoned in but he says you reckon there is something odd about this one. You had better be right! I was supposed to be taking my wife out this evening and I shall not be pleased if you have brought me out on a wild goose chase. Will I, sergeant?"

The latter remark was addressed to DS Dean who merely raised his eyebrows as he nodded at Richard Bell. The DCI continued.

"OK, constable. Lead the way"

Constable Bell led the others into the kitchen. The DS blanched and the DCI looked grim as he lifted the cloth.

"My God! That is not a pretty sight and the stench!! Has the local doctor seen the corpse?"

"Yes, sir. Dr Middleton lives at the top end of the village green and he was called by Reg Hanshott, the person who found the body"

"Who *is* this Reg Hanshott and what was he doing here?"

"He is a local farmer. His wife's mother lives next door. She asked him to come down to investigate the smell"

"I see! And how long did this doctor say the victim had been dead?"

"He said he could not tell for certain but he estimated it to be at least two weeks"

The police surgeon took over "I had better have quick a look at the victim. Then you can call in the ambulance boys in to take the body away before it becomes a health hazard. I will examine the body properly at the mortuary and let you have my report tomorrow chief inspector"

"Thank you, sir"

The DCI looked round the room.

"Did you put the cloth over the body, constable?"

"No, sir. Reg Hanshott said he covered it up before I arrived. Said he couldn't bear the sight"

"I don't blame him. Has anything been touched since you arrived, constable?"

"I had to pull out the plug on the power lead in case the bath and the water were still lethal and the doctor rolled up the lead and disconnected the plug from the fire for the same reason. The doctor also took the fire out of the bathwater and placed it where it is now"

"So the fire was lying in the bath when you arrived and the electric lead was plugged into the wall socket?"

"Yes, Sir. It seems that was what killed him"

"You are probably right, constable"

"After he had finished his examination the doctor turned on the tap at the kitchen sink to wash his hands and he dried them on the teacloth, there"

"I suppose that could not be helped. But everything else is as it was when you arrived?"

"Yes, sir. I used a handkerchief to pick up the 'phone to call the Dunchester Station; but I believe Reg Hanshott used the same 'phone to call me"

The others went out into the fresh air until the corpse, wrapped in a white sheet, had been taken away in the ambulance. The police surgeon, his task on the spot finished, had also left in his car to follow the ambulance. The DCI stood by the door, watching them go, then turned to Richard Bell

"By the way, constable, what made you think there was something odd about this?"

"Well, sir, it was more intuition than anything else. This man

259

seems to have turned up out of the blue and without warning. Hilda Benhope, his next door neighbour, has seen practically nothing of him since he arrived and she says he doesn't even shop at the local store. Nobody seems to know who he is or what he is doing here"

The DCI looked across the road

"Do you know anything about that car over there, constable?"

"No, Sir. None of the local residents has a car; so I assume it belonged to the dead man. I checked the bonnet when I first arrived and found it to be cold, so the vehicle has not been used today. I also wrote details of the vehicle in my note book"

"Well done, Bell. Now, the sergeant and I are going to have a look around the cottage. Perhaps we shall find something to shed some light on the matter. You stay out here and make sure nobody comes nosing about.......and shoo those boys away!"

The two Graham boys had been passing on their way home from school when they saw the police car and ambulance. Wally Tanner, Freddie Smith and Harry Moon were with them. The gang ran up to the gate to see what was going on and Wally cried excitedly.

"There. What did I tell you. I said the other day there was something fishy about that car"

Richard Bell addressed Harry Moon, who lived at the police bungalow as an evacuee from London,

"What are you doing down here, Harry? This is not on your way home from school. Mrs Bell will be getting your tea. So get off home now; and tell Mrs Bell I shall probably be here for some time yet. The rest of you clear off too. There is nothing for you to see here"

The DCI and sergeant had gone back into the cottage. The chief inspector called Richard Bell back into the kitchen.

"The water in that bath stinks. Help the sergeant to carry the bath outside and empty it in the back garden. The bath probably hangs on a hook on the wall outside. Hang it up but don't wipe it out. I might want to look at it later. Then go back and keep watch outside again"

When the constable had gone out again the DCI asked DS Dean

"Well! What do you think, Jim?"

"It looks straightforward enough to me, Sir. More like stupidity than anything else. It was probably a chilly night and he used the portable fire to keep warm. However, no-one but a fool would stand a portable electric fire on a towel which he had placed on a chair next to the bath. He only had to get soap in his eyes and reach for the towel and that was the end of him"

"I agree. But, since nobody seems to know who he is, we had better search the place. There must be something here to identify him. I expect these cottages are all rented; probably through a Dunchester agent. If we cannot find anything here you can have a word with the people in the other cottages and trace the landlord to see what he knows. And while you are searching keep an eye open for the keys to that car outside. There might be something in there to help us"

The two detectives looked through the clothes in the kitchen but found nothing of interest. They found the cinema ticket stub and electrician's receipt in the raincoat, hanging in the hall, but left them where they were. The contents of the jacket which they found on the bed upstairs were much more revealing. Particularly, the driving licence and the Nazi party card. The DCI looked at them with grim satisfaction.

"It would appear that he used the name of Fred Grimble; but this card is for a Hans Kluger. It is a pity the body was not found earlier. We might have been able to identify it using the photograph on the party card. It could be that there were two people living here and, if the one in the bath was Hans Kluger, we could be looking for a Frederick Grimble as a murder suspect"

Sergeant Dean commented

"Or vice-versa, sir"

"Quite so, Jim. But the clothing around here is not consistent with more than one person living here and there is only one bed. So let us not jump to conclusions. We had better give the place a thorough search"

It did not take them long to find the Luger and shoulder holster on top of the wardrobe and the ammunition in the suitcase. The DCI was an old fashioned British copper who did not want to get involved with enemy agents and espionage. He decided this was getting out of his league and it was time to call in Special Branch

"I think we should hand this over to the specialists, Jim. Let us get back to the station"

They checked to make sure the kitchen door was locked and bolted; then, taking the gun, ammunition and holster with them, they removed the stone and pulled the front door to until the yale lock clicked. The DCI gave the front door key to Richard Bell. Before they left the detectives, using the keys they had found in the jacket, unlocked the car doors and boot. Their search revealed nothing more than a map of Dunchester, which they took with them. The DCI returned to Richard Bell and gave him the car keys to keep with the cottage key.

"Your intuition was right, constable. There *is* more to this than meets the eye. I want this place sealed off until someone from London has been to look at it. Pity the electricity is off. It would be a good idea to put an electric fan in there to clear the air a bit. Never mind! Why not let the big boys suffer too? You have done a good job here today and it will not go unnoticed. But you will have to stay here a bit longer until I can send someone to relieve you. I know you have other things to do in your patch and that you have been here most of the day, but it should not be too long before you are relieved. Good afternoon, constable"

Richard Bell saluted and resumed his seat by the window.

It was seven in the evening and Richard Bell was still sitting on the seat outside the cottage when Sally Hanshott and Jean Stokes came along on their bicycles. They stopped and propped their bikes up against the fence. From the little carrier on her handlebars Sally lifted a basket covered with a cloth

"My Mum rang Mrs Bell to find out if there was any news. Mrs Bell said she could not leave Dicky and Primrose alone but she was worried that you had been out all this time with no food or drink. As I was coming down to see Jean, here, I picked up these things for you on the way"

"That *is* sweet of you, Sally. You are an angel! Hello, Jean. How is that brother of yours getting on in the RAF?"

"He is fine, thank you. He is at a fighter base in Essex..........."
The constable interrupted her

"There is a war on, Jean. I suppose I should not have asked the question. But you certainly must not tell people where a serviceman is stationed and what he is doing. For all you know there could be a German spy close by. From little snippets of information like that the enemy can build up a picture of our air defences across the country. So we must all be careful what we say". He chuckled "As it says on the poster 'Be like Dad - Keep Mum' ".

Richard Bell was glad of the company and he invited the

girls to join him on the seat while he delved into the basket to find a meat pie, a packet of sandwiches, a large piece of fruit cake, a thermos flask of hot tea, a large medicine bottle filled with milk, a small paper bag with sugar in it and a spoon. Richard had not eaten or had a drink since breakfast but he offered to share his repast with the girls. They both declined; claiming they had already eaten and, in any case, they must watch their figures.

Before Richard had finished his meal the two constables arrived in the police car from Dunchester. They eyed the girls' figures appreciatively as Richard handed over the keys to the cottage and car. While the older constable was signing a receipt in Richard's book for the keys, the younger of the two policemen tried to persuade the girls to stay and keep them company. They were flattered but, smiling sweetly and a little coquettishly, they cycled off along the lane to the alley that led to the general store; leaving Richard Bell talking to the his colleagues. Richard said "There is a telephone in the cottage if you need it, but I doubt you will want to stay in there"

"Why not! We don't want to sit out here in the car all night"

"Well! Please yourselves; but there is a horrid stink in the cottage. Personally, I prefer the fresh air out here. Anyway, I'll leave you to it. Good evening"

Richard set off, in the opposite direction to the girls, on his new BSA, with the food basket balanced on the petrol tank in front of him.

The bar-room at The Bowman was practically empty. Len Mundy drained his pint mug and banged it rather more forcefully than was necessary on the table, hoping Reg Hanshott would take the hint; but Reg was engrossed in the Farmer's Weekly and ignored him. Len tried another tack

"Rum ol' do down in Black 'ut Lane, weren't it?"

Reg looked up.

"I suppose it was! But I don't know much about it. The stink of that body was dreadful so I left as soon as the police came. He was a damned fool to take a bath with an electric fire on a chair next to him. Still! Some people never use their commonsense"

"Who was he then; the man you found?"

"I don't know. Never seen him before. Hilda said he only moved in a few weeks ago and she never met him. So she knows nothing about him or where he came from"

Len Mundy twisted his chair round to face Constable Bell, who was standing at the bar in conversation with the landlord, Angus McKuy,

"Did *you* find out who `e was, Richard?"

Richard Bell turned round.

"Who who was, Len?"

"Why, that bloke wot electrocuted 'iself next door to 'ilda`s place"

Richard Bell had been warned by his superintendent not to talk about the incident and to quell any enquiries diplomatically; so his reply was short

"No, Len! Nobody seems to know anything about him. Hilda said he just turned up from nowhere and he never spoke to her"

He turned back to Angus McKuy. Len looked pointedly at Reg Hanshott, who clearly was not going to take the hint to buy a second drink for his foreman. Len shrugged, picked up his empty beer mug and walked over to the bar. At the same time Ernest Middleton came in and crossed the floor to join Richard Bell. Len Mundy ordered another pint and, speaking across the constable, addressed the doctor

"Did you 'ave to go to examine the body, doctor?"

"What body, Len?"

Richard interrupted.

"He is talking about the man who electrocuted himself in Black Hut Lane"

"Oh that! Yes, I was called in but there was nothing I could do for him"

"Who was 'e then?"

"I don't know, Len, and it seems no-one else in the village knew the stranger or what he was doing here"

Ernest felt mean having to lie. After all these were his friends but Kluger was a secret that he and Eve must keep to themselves. So, to avoid further embarrassing questions, he emptied his glass and turned to go

"Excuse me Richard! I only came in for a quick one before lunch. 'Bye Len!"

He nodded to Angus and to Reg as he left the bar.

The police issued no official statement concerning events at the cottage in Frensham Down; so the incident did not come to the attention of the Dunchester Gazette. Kluger's car was taken away by the police for examination; following which it was returned to the garage in Dunchester from which it had been hired. The garage proprietor did not think to tell the police that the hirer had not collected the car directly from them. So the police did not contact James Twist at the Frensham Down garage; otherwise their enquiries might have taken a different turn. It did not occur to either James or his wife, Muriel, that the stranger who had died was the same man who had called at the garage to collect the car. After all, there was no reason why they should connect the two incidents; since the police had not released the name of the victim of the tragedy. Grimble had let James Twist think he was a commercial traveller and that he would not be staying locally. So the tragedy became a 'nine day wonder' and the villagers soon pushed the matter to the back of their minds as they found other things of more immediate concern to gossip about.

For a few days a constable stayed outside the cottage. The windows were left wide open to clear the air. But, once the stench in the cottage had abated, the police locked up number 25, Black Hut Lane and Hilda Benhope returned to her cottage. She was not a gossip and, when the foreman of the sewage cart asked, casually, how she had got rid of the smell, Hilda avoided getting involved in explanations by telling him her son-in-law had dealt with it and offering no further information.

Ernest Middleton and Richard Bell gave evidence at the coroner's inquest, which was held 'in camera', but it was a mere formality. A verdict of 'accidental death' of an unidentified male was recorded. When Ernest told Eve of the verdict she clung to him with sigh of relief.

"Do you really think it is all over, Ernest?"

"It seems no-one suspects what really happened, so I suppose it is"

Ernest did not tell Eve of his fear that the Nazi spy ring might still try to contact him. It did nothing to allay this fear when he found out that he and Eve were, technically, registered as aliens under the new regulations; although they were assured that, as naturalised British citizens providing a domestic medical service, which constituted vital wartime work, the pattern of their lives would not be disturbed. Nonetheless, Ernest felt guilty because he knew a group of German spies was operating in London and he had not reported this knowledge to the authorities. He gave the matter a lot of thought but was unable to come up with a plan which might solve his problem without exposing himself to the attention of British security services.

One day Ernest was in the Woolworth's store in Dunchester high street when he saw something that gave him an idea. It was a child's toy; a printing set comprising a piece of wood with grooves in it for the insertion of, supplied, rubber reversed letters of the alphabet and an inked stamp pad. Ernest bought the toy and a wrapped set of writing paper and envelopes. That evening, after Surgery had closed, he donned a pair of surgical gloves and unwrapped the writing paper and envelopes at the desk in his surgery. He inserted the rubber letters in the grooves in the wooden block to make up a simple message which he stamped onto a plain piece of the writing paper he had bought that afternoon. The message read

TO WHOM NATIONAL SECURITY MAY CONCERN CHECK THE LONDON ADDRESS WITH TELEPHONE NUMBER MAIDA VALE 3843

Satisfied with the message he replaced the rubber letters in the wooden block with an address which he stamped on one of the envelopes. The address was 'The Chief Security Officer. The Police. Scotland Yard. London'. He inserted the message in the envelope. Opening the, previously unopened, book of postage stamps he had purchased in Dunchester he extracted a gummed postage stamp which he held under the tap to moisten before attaching it to the envelope. He moistened the gummed edge of the envelope flap in the same way before sticking it down. Placing the sealed envelope in a paper bag, he thrust it in the inside pocket of his jacket.

The next day Ernest drove into Dunchester and caught a train to Norwich. Mingling with the busy crowds among the market stalls he was able to, unobtrusively, put on a pair of surgical gloves. Thus protecting himself from placing fingerprints on the envelope he withdrew it from the paper bag and dropped it into the nearest post box. He crumpled up the paper bag and dropped it into a waste bin behind a market stall. He had already disposed of the spare

266

writing paper and envelopes with the toy printing set and its container in the incinerator behind his cottage, so there was no evidence left of his connection with the note to Scotland Yard. 'That should tie up all the loose ends' thought Ernest. But it was not until he was standing on the platform waiting for the train to Dunchester that Ernest broke into a cold sweat when it occurred to him there might be some record of his own involvement with Kluger at the London address he had just disclosed to the police. But there was nothing he could do about it now and as time went by, with no approach from either the police or the intelligence services, his concern gradually dwindled away and life for him and Eve at Frensham Down settled down to normality once more.

The End

The Frensham Down Saga continues in BROKEN DOVE

The village of FRENSHAM DOWN has existed for more than 400 years and has grown from a collection of farm cottages to a thriving community.

During the summer of 1921 a chain of events started which was to disturb the tranquillity of village life.

The Years Between is a novel where passion and intrigue lie under the surface of everyday life and problems must be resolved quietly even if the only solution is resort to murder.

This book covers the lives of the inhabitants of the village from June 1921 to September 1939.

The story continues in Broken Dove

ISBN   10 0-9552453-0-3
ISBN   13 978-0-9552453-0-5

Published by R H Brown, 125, The Fairway, Leigh on Sea, Essex, SS9 4QP, England